Sold Into Shackles

David Sage

For information about this title or to order other books and/or electronic
media, contact the publisher:
David Sage
davesageinstory@gmail.com

ISBN: 978-1-7336402-1-3
ISBN for ebook: 978-1-7336402-2-0

Printed in the United States of America

With Thanks

First, to all my readers everywhere, who have been waiting for this book. Thank you for your patience and I hope you enjoy it.

To our grandson Tucker: dude, you are incredible!

To our son Tyler, who suggested that I write a Christian book because it fit with my beliefs, and because there are people looking at Christian fiction for inspiration and guidance. I'm glad I followed your suggestion.

To our daughter Tierney, whose editing skills have contributed to a vastly improved narrative. Your 'word smithing' is awesome and your design creativity is boundless! This book would not have been the same without you.

Finally, to my wife Marcia, who originally suggested I write a story about the Barbary Coast Pirates. The ensuing research stirred my imagination to the fullest. Without your encouragement this tale would never have been created!

I love you all.

David Sage
Story, Wyoming

TABLE OF CONTENTS

Foreword

UNDER COVER OF DARKNESS in the early hours of Monday June 20, 1631, two Barbary Coast Pirate ships slipped into the harbor of Baltimore, Ireland. They were led by a renegade Dutchman and guided by a local fisherman captured the day before. Baltimore was, and still is, a village on the southern tip of Ireland. Primarily focused on tourism today, at that time it was engaged in supplying sardines to Irish and English markets.

Swarming ashore, the pirates captured 108 men, women, and children from the sleeping population. A few villagers managed to escape into the surrounding hills. The prisoners were taken to Algiers and sold as slaves: part of the 1.25 million Europeans enslaved during the 300 year reign of terror of the Barbary Coast Pirates.

Of the 108 people taken in the Baltimore raid, possibly three made it back to Ireland over the next decades. This book is inspired by those events.

The Sack Of Baltimore

1

TWO PIRATE SHIPS GHOSTED into the fog-shrouded harbor just before dawn. Faint starlight revealed the dark shapes of houses on the Irish hillside above and a sudden break in the mist showed squat buildings and a stone wharf 200 yards ahead. The turbaned captain's eyes glittered in triumph: his helmsman, following the whispered instructions of the fisherman beside him, had successfully guided the lead ship through the twisting channel between rock jetties into the seaport. No lights appeared and no warning had been sounded; the sleeping residents were unaware of the horror he was about to unleash on them.

"That's the village," said the fisherman. "I've guided you into the harbor, just as I told you I would. I've kept my part of the bargain. I'll go ashore with your men and be off."

"No, you won't," said the captain. Despite the loose clothes of a North African pirate, he spoke perfect English. "It may be a trap. If the raid is successful, I'll let you go; but not before." His tone brooked no argument.

At the captain's command, boats were lowered and ferried men silently to the dock, oarlocks wrapped in cloth to muffle sound. Before long, well over 100 pirates were gathered on the wharf around their tall commander. At least half wore the blue and gold uniforms of Ottoman Empire soldiers; the rest were clad in a motley variety of clothing and turbans. Although a sword hung at every waist, the men carried short staves with one end wrapped in oil-soaked cloth. This expedition was not to kill the villagers, but to frighten them into submission: the objective was to acquire slaves. Tension was tangible as they awaited their commander's orders.

"Fire the roofs," whispered the captain in Arabic. "Off with you now and let none escape!"

Torches were lit and the barefooted men raced silently into the village like a pack of wolves. Each was well aware that a successful raid meant extra gold for all of them. Within minutes, fingers of fire were twisting into the sky from a dozen buildings and soon the flames lit the night with a hellish blaze.

Halfway up the hill, a small stone house fronted the town's only cobblestone street. Like all the other homes, there was a tidy vegetable garden out back, protected from rabbits by four-foot high stone walls. A chicken coop and a pen for geese completed the property. The dwelling contained a front room for cooking and eating, and two small rooms to the rear for sleeping. In one of the back rooms three siblings slept on a thick bed of straw; in the other their father lay gently snoring.

"What's that?" said Cormac, sitting bolt upright in the dark. He was 16, with flaming red hair and deep blue eyes. Four years of working with his father on their fishing boat had given him a lean, muscular body. He cocked an ear toward the faint shouting outside, which began to get alarmingly louder.

"What's the matter?" said his brother Finn groggily, rising to one elbow on the other side of their sister Bran, cuddled between them. At 14, tall and slender, hair bleached gold by days on the ocean, his body was already beginning to take on muscle like his brother.

"Bran, wake up!" Cormac jumped to his feet. "Something's wrong!" When she didn't respond, he reached under the blankets and pulled the eight-year-old upright.

"Do I have to?" she said, sleepily brushing long black hair back to rub her green eyes. Too young for the boat, she worked in the garden with their mother. She'd been left in charge of the chickens and geese that afternoon when Mother went to deliver a sack of sardines to her sister in the hills. The whole family was looking forward to the basket of blueberries she had promised to bring back.

"Father!" Cormac shouted, running into the next room. Donegan O'Shea was already on his feet, racing for the front door, double-headed axe in hand. When he jerked it open, Cormac saw shadowy figures sprinting through an eerie scene of smoke and flames beginning to envelop the street. In that instant the youth knew the village was under attack by the dreaded Barbary Coast Pirates.

"Get out the back with your brother and sister!" Donegan shouted as he charged bare-chested into the street. A pirate was running past with little Shamus Fitzgerald tucked under one arm, the boy screaming at the top of his lungs. The heavily muscled fisherman swung his axe into the man's neck with all his considerable strength, dropping him to the cobblestones in a heap.

"Run, Shamus, run! Get to the hills!" bellowed the Irishman, yanking the boy to his feet. The child streaked off between two houses.

As Cormac watched, frozen in the doorway, two pirates set upon Donegan. He managed to bury his axe in the chest of one, all the while shouting in his deep voice for his own children to flee, but the other ran a sword entirely through his body. As the fisherman fell to his knees, he unleashed a mighty backhand swing of the axe partially severing one of the pirate's legs. The man screamed in an unearthly voice and crumbled to the street. Donegan staggered to his feet, one hand clutching his wound, the other still gripping the axe.

"Save yourselves!" He glanced at Cormac beseechingly, then turned to face three pirates advancing on him.

The three approached warily, steering clear of the murderous swings he directed at them. But Donegan was weakening, blood pouring from his side. One of the pirates feinted a thrust at the Irishman's chest, but as he blocked it with the axe head another pirate thrust his blade through the fisherman's abdomen. As he fell, mortally wounded, Donegan somehow found strength to throw the axe full into the first man's face, splitting his skull. The bodies of fisherman and pirate hit the street at the same time.

Cormac turned to escape, but it was too late. Two men rushed into the house and seized the three siblings. They were dragged into an inferno of smoke and fire, joining the neighbors being herded toward the dock by strange and terrifying men yelling incomprehensibly and waving swords. Cormac grabbed Bran's hand and told Finn to stay close as the two raiders screamed in his face, pointing toward the harbor. All around them people were stumbling along, wailing and crying. As they left the house, the redhead pressed Bran's face into his side so that she wouldn't see their father's body. An agonized moan beside him indicated Finn hadn't been spared the sight.

In minutes they were on the wharf, mingled with clusters of captives. As he looked about in the eerie light from burning buildings, Cormac realized that very few of their neighbors had escaped. Apart from his father, he had seen no bodies; most of the men were present, surrounded by their wives and children. A short time later, they were herded together and a tall pirate began moving among them. He wore a turban, baggy blouse and pants, and a wide sash around his waist, but the redhead was shocked to see in the growing light that he was European. His black beard and deeply tanned skin matched the appearance of the others, but gray eyes gave him away.

Making his way through the crowd, this man, who Cormac surmised was the leader from the way the pirates bowed slightly as he passed, would occasionally point to one of the villagers. They would immediately be marched to the other side of the wharf. In the end, six people were separated from the group. Two of the men hobbled on wooden legs and another had lost an arm. The remaining three, including two women, were quite elderly and barely able to walk. As the captives watched in horror, flashing swords cut all of them down.

2

FERRIED TO THE WAITING SHIPS in longboats, the prisoners were crammed into dark, smelly storage lockers below deck used for holding extra paint, varnish, rope, wood, sails, or any of the materials that might be needed on a sailing vessel. They huddled together, many sobbing and moaning. The boys managed to keep Bran between them as they and 15 other people were forced into a small paint closet. The space was so crowded that Cormac took Bran onto his lap to shield her from bodies jammed against them on all sides. From the left, Finn gently stroked her head, murmuring assurances in the dark.

Gradually, the girl's sobs slowed and her voice steadied.

"What will become of us?" She asked.

"I don't know, but at least we're together." Cormac held her tightly.

"They didn't catch Mother," Finn added. "She'll be waiting when we get home!"

"What about Papa?"

"I didn't see him in the crowd on the wharf," Cormac said truthfully.

"Maybe he escaped," she said. Neither boy spoke.

There came a lurch as wind caught the sails and the ship moved toward the harbor entrance. Behind it, flames still rising from burning structures were reflected in the dark water, giving a macabre appearance to the erstwhile peaceful village. The whole attack had taken less than 90 minutes.

The first few hours were agonizing as the captives faced the reality of their plight. They knew about the Barbary Coast Pirates, but a raid such as this was unusual. The raiders generally attacked vessels on the high seas, taking whatever merchandise they carried and delivering crew and passengers to slave markets in North Africa. The rare shore attacks were normally focused on looting rich manor houses, but this strike had clearly been to capture people. The emotional shock of the experience was compounded by the fact that many women and children had never been on the open ocean. As the ship cleared the harbor and heeled under a freshening wind, the sound of retching and the smell of vomit invaded the crowded locker.

"Curse those pirates; they could never have found the opening into the harbor in the dark on their own," said Morgan Dougall. "Hackett betrayed us!"

"Aye, I saw him on the dock," Cormac spoke into the dark.

"He was there all right," said Morgan. "After they rounded us up, the leader let him go. He must have guided them in."

"Why?"

"All I know is he wasn't with us when we came off the ocean yesterday afternoon. They must have captured and tortured him until he agreed to show them the way."

"He didn't look tortured to me."

"Nor to me, laddy," there was a sigh in the dark. "He was a sullen sort, though, and had no family. Maybe he did it out of spite."

"Or maybe he did it to save his life," said Finn.

"Aye. If I ever get back …" Dougall's threat hung in the air.

"If any of us get back, there's a debt to be paid," Cormac's voice was flat.

"I've not seen your mother among the captives," said Morgan.

"She's in the hills at our Aunt's farm." The boy gave a little squeeze to his sister's shoulders, hoping that she would take comfort in their mother's safety.

"I saw what Donegan did," Morgan added. "Little Seamus must have escaped because he wasn't at the dock." At the memory of his father's death, Cormac's throat tightened up and tears came to his eyes. He made no reply and the fisherman kindly dropped the conversation.

3

CORMAC WAS DOZING FITFULLY when the locker door was yanked open hours later. A pirate motioned them out and disappeared. Cramped and sore, one by one the villagers eased themselves from the locker and eyed the passageway. No one was present, but bright light spilled down a short ladder-well nearby and soon all were standing on the deck above, squinting in brilliant sunshine. A few clouds showed white in the sky and blue ocean stretched away on all sides. About a mile ahead, the second ship led the way with all sails set to catch the quartering wind.

Pirates lounged about, sitting on hatch covers or standing by the railings talking and staring at the water. In the light of day they appeared rather normal, just like the villagers, apart from their darker skins and clothes. These men seemed far removed from the screaming berserkers surging out of smoke and flames in the village. Most took no notice of the captives, except one who pointed at several large baskets filled with bread, cheese, and fruit. Fearful it might be a trick, the group hesitated to approach the food until the man said something in a strange language and motioned them forward with a broad smile. Noticing other villagers already on the deck busily eating, Cormac decided the man meant no harm.

"Aren't you hungry?" he asked Bran, who was holding tightly to his hand. "I certainly am!"

Feigning cheerfulness, he strode to the baskets and helped himself to a wedge of cheese, a hunk of bread, and two apples. He found a spot on the railing where they could sit and offered food to Bran. At first she shook her head, tear stained face staring at the deck, but when Finn sat down close beside she finally accepted a piece of cheese. Soon all three were busily eating.

"Will you look at that!" said Finn a while later. Across the deck and toward the bow, two pirates were doing sleight-of-hand tricks for 10-year-old Tavish Jones and his cousin Angus McCreed.

"Nothing scares those two," Cormac shook his head. "They've always been as curious as puppies!"

Indeed, now that they were well clear of the Irish coast and Royal Navy patrols, the pirates treated their human cargo quite well. Many of them seemed to genuinely like children and spent hours teaching them to tie knots, build toys out of bits of leather and hemp, or play simple Arab games. Understandably, the men and women were more reserved, but it soon became apparent that their captors considered them valuable cargo and wanted to deliver their captives as well fed and fit as possible. As the long voyage progressed, for those prisoners who were willing, there were lessons in Arabic, North African history, and even cooking. Eventually Bran relaxed and left the company of her brothers to observe the interaction between other children and the crew.

One of the women, Mrs. Doyle, was unusually calm from the very beginning. She had been captured along with her five-year-old twins, Betsy and Blythe: blonde, blue-eyed, and totally fearless, they quickly became favorites of the pirates. The two scampered off after breakfast each morning, leaving their mother seated on a hatch cover talking to a score of the Baltimore women. She seemed so peaceful that Cormac paused near them one morning to listen.

"Don't be afraid," she said, "God will take care of us. He knows our situation and everything that's happened. Remember what the priest was teaching in church the day before the attack?"

> *"He is my refuge and my fortress,*
> *My God in whom I trust.*
> *You will not fear the terror of night,*
> *Nor the arrow that flies by day ...*
> *For He will command His angels concerning you,*
> *To guard you in all your ways ..."*

"That very night the pirates came, but we had been warned <u>not</u> to be afraid of the 'terror by night!'"

"What will happen to us?" cried one of the women.

"I don't know," said Mrs. Doyle, "but I do know we can trust Him."

The O'Shea family had been at the same service that Sunday but their minds had been far away. Cormac was thinking of packing gear for Monday's fishing. Finn was dreaming of riding a racehorse and Bran was trying to figure out how to avoid getting nipped by the geese when she fed them that afternoon after Mom left for the hills. The priest's words had been background noise.

"Where were the angels when they hacked Father down?" Cormac thought to himself as he moved to the far side of the deck.

4

DAYS STRETCHED TO WEEKS before the two ships entered the Mediterranean, having passed through the Straits of Gibraltar in the dead of night to avoid detection by the English garrison. A few days later the vessels drew close to each other and there was a shouted exchange between the grey-eyed captain of Cormac's ship and his first mate aboard the sister ship. Shortly afterward, the second ship veered away southeast, becoming smaller and smaller until she was hull-down on the horizon, only her sails showing. A few minutes later she was lost to sight.

"Where do you suppose they're going?" Cormac asked Morgan Dougall.

"Algiers, I think," said the older man. "I heard two of the men talking and the name came up repeatedly."

"Then, where are we going?" Cormac asked.

"I'm not sure, but it could be Tunis. In my youth I served as a cook's helper on a frigate and we stopped there once. Our heading is right … it's further east than Algiers."

Morgan's guess proved correct as the ship swung to a southeasterly heading some days later. One bright morning it rounded a headland and entered a large bay. An hour of sailing brought them to the narrow opening of a vast harbor. On the hills at the far side, a walled city, gleaming white in the sun, bordered the water's edge. From an enormous gate in the city wall, a great stone wharf stretched far out into the harbor, to which were tied ships of every size and description. Before long, the pirate ship was steered to a spot among other vessels along the wharf.

"I'm scared," Bran's voice quavered as she watched their ship being made fast to the dock.

Once it became apparent they were headed for the city, the sense of security, created by weeks of camaraderie with the pirates on the open sea, vanished. Swords reappeared at the waists of their captors and friendly looks were replaced by frowns and scowls. There was palpable tension among the Baltimore captives lining the railing. Even Mrs. Doyle's face looked grim as she clung to her twins.

"It's all right. Finn and I are right here with you," said Cormac, holding his sister close.

They stared down at a kaleidoscope of color and humanity covering the huge wharf. Under brightly colored awnings, merchants in equally bright robes offered goods to crews coming off the ships. Their business strategy was to out-shout other merchants, resulting in a cacophony of competing voices assaulting the warm air. Compounding the situation were buyers haggling at the top of their lungs, waving arms and contorting their faces in disgust as they tried to negotiate lower prices. Flocks of seagulls swooped and dived overhead, ready to snatch any morsel from food vendors; small boys with long sticks were employed to keep them at bay, adding their cries to the general hubbub. Down into this chaos the prisoners were herded. At the bottom of the gangplank they were stunned to see a portly Englishman in a white suit.

"Mr. Shrewsbury, envoy to Tunis, at your service," he said, hurrying over to them. "I heard there was a ship coming in with prisoners and sent a message to the Crown last week by a vessel headed to England."

The captives crowded around him with cries of joy, overcome to see a friendly face and hoping he would help them. Many asked how soon they could go home.

"I'm not sure, to be precise," explained Shrewsbury, mopping his florid brow with a large gray handkerchief. "Ransom funds are scanty and it takes months for the messages to get back and forth, but I want you to know that England is concerned about its captured citizens."

"Ransom funds are non-existent," said Morgan Dougall to Cormac. "England has a representative in every port, but they're powerless to do anything for the slaves because the Crown gives them no money. Only rich relatives can bargain for the return of loved ones and that's tricky because the slave might never be released, though money is sent."

In a gesture of sympathy, Shrewsbury accompanied the Baltimore citizens as they were driven along the dock toward the city. The pirates guarding them paid no attention to the Englishman, occasionally even bartering with nearby vendors, knowing he was powerless to help the captives. As they moved along the wharf, Cormac observed scantily clad men carrying loads of cargo on and off the ships. They were closely watched by overseers with long coiled whips. He saw one of the men stumble and a whip immediately snake out to lash his legs. The man regained his balance and trudged on with lowered head, blood seeping from angry welts on his calves. Cormac realized the laborers were slaves and was shocked at their haggard appearance. He noticed they were careful not to attract the guards' attention.

Upon reaching the end of the wharf, the prisoners encountered a long line of heavily laden camels walking along the beach, each led by a barefoot man in ragged clothing. Spaced along the line were turbaned overseers, all armed with whips.

"What are they?" Finn's love for animals overcame his terror of what was waiting for the captives in the city.

"Camels," said Morgan Dougall. "I learned about them when I was here before. This is a vast land of sand and rocks, with very little water. A camel can survive for days without water; it's the common beast of burden in the desert. I even rode one for a short distance." Finn stared at the retreating caravan.

"You rode one! It's the strangest animal I've ever seen!" Mercifully lost for a moment in his imagination, the teenager wondered how anyone could manage such a beast.

"Finn, look at that black horse," said Bran, one hand firmly in Cormac's grasp, the other pointing at a nearby animal. It had a bowed neck and delicate head and was ridden by a man in a colorful robe. "It's not like our horses."

"You're right," said her brother, captivated by similar horses moving among the crowds on the beach. They were vastly different from the plow horses and shaggy ponies seen in Baltimore.

"It seems these people like to ride." He pointed at a group of veiled riders on beautiful horses with long manes.

Their conversation was cut short as the prisoners were herded through a large gate in the city wall and onto a narrow street between stone buildings. On both sides, covered stalls displayed bolts of colorful cloth, fish, bread, fruit, vegetables, weapons, and clothing. Each merchant did his or her best to attract customers by proclaiming the excellence of their wares with loud shouts. Customers thronged the stalls, bargaining in equally loud voices. To the ragged prisoners it was a chaotic bedlam of discordant noise.

A twenty-minute walk brought them to a large plaza, bordered on the right side by a gleaming white palace behind which stretched the blue ocean. The three-story structure was made entirely of marble, with wide windows at all levels and golden domes at the four corners topped by minarets flying colorful flags. Enormous sets of double doors opened onto the plaza, each flanked by soldiers. Facing the palace on the left side of the plaza was a massive building also made from marble, but which looked like a two-story fortress. There were no openings at ground level, save a large wooden door bound with iron. The second level contained many spacious windows, all of which were barred with iron grates.

People were hurrying from side streets to join a crowd of more than 100 others gathered before the palace doors. As the prisoners appeared, the entire assembly turned to stare, parting to either side to let them pass. There was much gesturing and loud talk in Arabic, as the citizens sized up the captives' potential for labor.

5

Entering the palace through the huge doorway, the people from Baltimore found themselves in a wide hall 15 feet high, with floor and walls covered in colorful mosaic tiles. A rich blue and gold Persian carpet ran down the middle of the hallway, with potted orange trees set at intervals along the walls. A series of 10-foot high dark mahogany doors along the left wall apparently gave entrance to rooms on the ocean side of the building. The captives were made to line up down the middle of the hall, shoulder to shoulder, facing the doors.

After 30 minutes, one of the mahogany doors swung open and a man strode out close to where Cormac was standing. He was of medium height, with dark skin and a closely trimmed short black beard accenting wide-set brown eyes. Judging from his inquisitive gaze, Cormac guessed that this was a man of intelligence and confidence. His magnificent blue and gold robe and matching turban were complemented by a beautiful golden chain and pendant hanging from his neck. Several men trailed behind as he walked to the head of the line and started making his way past the prisoners, examining each one carefully.

"The Pasha," breathed Morgan, on the other side of Bran. "He has first right to any slave." From time to time the Pasha would stop beside a prisoner and speak softly in Arabic. One of the followers would pull the person's head back and pry open the mouth, grip the muscles in an arm or leg, or poke some part of the body. A soft conversation would ensue before the entourage moved on. Three times people were pulled from the line to be escorted away by a soldier.

When the Pasha reached Bran, standing on Cormac's right, he stopped and had one of the attendants tip her head back and press her eyelids open. Her unusually lovely green eyes elicited a flurry of comments before the Pasha smiled, not unkindly, at the girl and moved on to her brother. Cormac kept his eyes forward, not wanting to do anything that might cause him to be separated from Bran. One of the followers gripped his left bicep and squeezed; the redhead relaxed the muscle as much as he could, instinctively knowing that tensing it might draw attraction to his strength. After a minute, the group moved on and Cormac breathed a sigh of relief.

Nearly an hour passed before the Pasha finished his inspection and returned through the double doors. Four people had been removed from the line: three of the younger men and one middle-aged woman. The rest were turned and marched back through the plaza to an unusually wide street with colorful stalls lining each side. A group of buyers had already assembled along one side of the street and the Baltimore captives were lined up facing them.

A man in white robes and turban started at one end of the line, shouted loudly in Arabic to the crowd and pointed at the first prisoner. He was the auctioneer and hands were raised and bids shouted from the collection of buyers. As he moved along the line sometimes prolonged bidding went back and forth as men vied for a prisoner they thought would make a good slave, but a price was always reached and the unfortunate captive was marched off behind his or her new owner. The auctioneer finally arrived at the three siblings and fixed his eye on Bran, standing between her brothers.

"Take courage and be strong," said Cormac, as she whimpered and pressed close against him and Finn. "I'll find you both one day, no matter where they take you. Do not give up, but wait for me. I will find you."

He put an arm around her, but the auctioneer grabbed her roughly and dragged her to the edge of the crowd. The girl screamed and tried to pull away but the man was too strong, gripping her tightly by the back of the neck while shouting in Arabic to the company. Immediately a flurry of bids were proffered. Cormac, flushed with rage at the treatment of his sister, started to step out of the line, but stopped when he felt a soft touch on his shoulder.

"Careful lad, there's a pirate guard watching you. Don't do anything foolish," said Morgan Dougall softly. The redhead raised his eyes and recognized one of the men from the ship eyeing him from four feet away. It was the pirate who had first offered them food, but his menacing stare was anything but friendly now.

"Cormac, help me!" screamed Bran suddenly.

Cormac saw a small man with a pointed beard and oily face step from the crowd and nearly yank the girl off her feet as he claimed his purchase. Forgetting Dougall's warning in an overwhelming surge of rage, the Irishman surged forward with a guttural roar, only to trip and fall face down on the flagstones. Pirates rushed in, kicking and beating him violently with their fists until he lost consciousness.

6

A BUCKET OF SALT WATER roused Cormac. He groaned and forced his eyes open, his body consumed with pain. Morgan and another man were the only captives remaining. The fisherman helped him to his feet.

"Sorry lad," he said, "I had to trip you or they'd have taken your head off. The one next to us was watching you closely, sword out and ready, when your sister was taken. Fortunately, you're worth gold to them; so when you fell they only beat you."

"What happened to Bran and Finn?" Cormac was barely able to stand, his back and sides wracked with agony from the beating.

"The little man with the pointed beard took the girl away and a tall man in dirty robes claimed your brother." Cormac felt a stab of deep despair. His brave words to Bran now seemed hollow and futile and he'd not even said goodbye to Finn.

It was late afternoon and a handful of buyers remained. Morgan's strong arms and shoulders created a stir and bids were numerous as slavers recognized his potential for hard labor. When he was led away, one of the pirates approached Cormac and, without warning, unleashed a mighty blow to his back with the flat of a sword blade. New pain flamed through his torso and he fell to his knees, gasping. The Irishman would have pitched face forward had not the pirate grabbed his hair and yanked him upright.

In spite of his anguish, Cormac aimed a murderous look at the man, causing remaining buyers to grin but also preventing any bids: they'd seen enough to believe he'd be more trouble than the price was worth. The auctioneer did his best, but the slavers were turning away. He was about to send this last prisoner to the Pasha's bowmen for archery practice when a lone offer was shouted and he immediately accepted it. A tall robed Arab in a red turban, black beard covering his chest, strode forward. He handed some coins to the auctioneer and turned to face Cormac. It was the pirate captain.

"You didn't seem so aggressive during the voyage, boy," he growled in English. "Your little show of anger cost me gold. We'll let the quarry break you … if it doesn't kill you first." He turned and walked away.

Cormac

....

1

A SLAVE HURRIED FORWARD AND motioned for Cormac to follow the captain. As they made their way through crowded streets, the redhead found himself stumbling, lightheaded and dizzy from the beating. The slave grabbed his arm, both for support and to propel him after the rapidly striding captain. A blurry glance revealed the slave to be European, about his age, dressed in a loose white blouse and baggy blue britches. Surprisingly, he wore handsome leather slippers. When the Irishman reeled and almost fainted, he felt a strong arm grasp him around the waist and keep him upright.

Mercifully, they left the raucous markets and ear splitting noise to enter a narrow, twisting street with high walls on either side. In minutes, the only sound was the thudding of the owner's boots on the pavement. A short time later the slave eased his hold on Cormac, steadied him for an instant, and stepped forward to pound on a large wooden door set in the wall. The door swung open and the slave stood aside to let the captain enter. He then guided Cormac into an enormous courtyard surrounded by a two-story house. Swaying on his feet as his attendant turned to close the door, Cormac stared in dazed astonishment at a scene seemingly out of a fairytale: lawns, fruit trees, and colorful flower beds filled the area, giving off fragrant aromas. Water cascaded from fountains into stone channels cut through the lawns, creating a soft pleasant babble. Manicured walkways of white stone, edged occasionally by marble benches, crisscrossed the courtyard. Down one of them his owner strode, disappearing into a wide hallway on the right.

The slave guided Cormac across the courtyard and down another hallway to a door with a large bolt. Drawing the bolt, he gestured for the prisoner to enter. The empty room was small, a ragged layer of straw covering the stone floor.

"I'll get you some food as soon as I can," said the slave in accented English as he began to close the door. Startled from his haze of pain and despair, the Irishman turned to stare into steady brown eyes.

"What's your name? How did you get here?"

"Francois, but there's no time to talk," said the slave as he shut the door. Sitting against a wall in the dark, Cormac wondered about Francois and how he'd come to be part of this household. The thoughts were short lived, however, as a great weariness claimed him and he instantly fell asleep. He never felt the first rat run across his legs. Hours later he woke to the sound of the bolt on the door being pulled open. In the faint light from the hall he saw Francois motioning.

"Come and get this food; if I put it down the rats will have it," said the Frenchman, holding a pitcher of water, a basket filled with bread, a brick of cheese, and an apple. "New slaves are usually starved for a while to enforce obedience, but you'll need every bit of strength to survive where you're going. I talked the cook out of the food by telling her you're a redhead. She's an old one, but still has some crimson among the grey and a soft spot in her heart for any with the same color hair. No time to talk now, I've got to go." Ignoring his throbbing bruises, Cormac moved quickly to the doorway to accept the provisions.

Retreating to the wall, the redhead ravenously ate every scrap of food and guzzled the water. Almost immediately he felt energy surge through his body and with it an inexplicable calm. He'd heard Morgan and the men from Baltimore talk about North African slavery and knew that virtually none of the captives made it home. Yet somehow the despair of losing Bran and Finn at the slave market had diminished, replaced by the strange conviction he'd see them again.

2

FRANCOIS WAS ABLE TO sneak food to Cormac twice more before he came to fetch him the following morning. Hours of sleep did wonders for the aches and bruises from the beating and the redhead was moving almost normally as they walked to a door at the end of the hall. The Frenchman had only minutes to describe his past.

"I was taken from a ship and brought here when I was five; my mother and father were sold at the slave market just as you were," he said. "The old cook raised me and trained me to serve meals. As the years went by, the Master expanded my duties until I became his assistant.

"His name is Suleyman Reis, but he's actually a Dutch sailor who left his country many years ago to join the pirates. In time he became rich, and now commands a fleet of sailing ships and galleys. The ships raid in the Atlantic and the galleys throughout the Mediterranean. Lately, he's been commanding a galley rather than a ship because the trips are shorter and he can be home regularly to handle other affairs. The Baltimore raid was an exception.

"There's no mercy for those he attacks; however, like many of the Arabs, he has great respect for bravery and can be kind to men he favors. He's sending you to the quarries, normally a death sentence, but I heard him grunt in approval when you tried to intervene for your sister in the slave market, so don't give up hope."

Before he could say more, they emerged onto a street behind the residence. A wooden cart with tall wheels was waiting. After shackling Cormac to the floor behind his seat, the driver climbed aboard and clucked to the horse. Francois watched the cart rattle away down the street until it turned a corner and was lost to sight.

"The quarries are certain death if the Master forgets him," he muttered as he returned to the house.

3

For some time the cart clattered its way through almost empty narrow streets, finally emerging onto a main thoroughfare to be assaulted by the raucous market hubbub and profusion of colorful awnings. Busy crowds reduced progress to a crawl, but no one paid the slightest attention to Cormac other than a few small children. The earsplitting din increased as they inched toward an enormous double gate in the city wall. Here a great multitude of people, horsemen, camels, and carts met head-on as they competed to enter or leave Tunis. The driver was forced to stop repeatedly, as the masses swirled around them, before creeping through the gate into a bleak landscape of rocks and sand. Free of the crowds at last, he directed the horse along a faint track leading west toward a distant line of hills. Looking back, Cormac realized the city was fortified with massive stone battlements three stories high. The great wooden gates looked as though they could withstand huge battering rams. He wondered what sort of enemies would cause the Arabs to build such defenses.

Soon they were completely alone, the crunching of the wheels on hard ground and an occasional snort from the horse the only sounds breaking the stillness. Powdery dust raised by the cart's passing filled the air, infiltrating the captive's eyes, nose, and ears. It was brutally hot and Cormac curled on his side, one hand on his head for protection from the sun's searing rays. Every time the cart hit an obstruction he was jolted brutally on the rough boards, aggravating every bruise on his body. Despair settled like a dark cloud. He was haunted by the image of Bran's terrified eyes as she was dragged away, the memory of her scream for help like a dagger in his heart. Despite the strange calm that had come over him the night before, tears filled his eyes and he couldn't help wondering whether he'd ever see his brother or sister again. For a while he tried to think of the ocean, imagining blue swells stretching to the horizon under a fresh breeze, dolphins cavorting in the bow waves of a ship with the green hills of Ireland in the distance, but it was no use—Bran's frightened face returned again and again as he huddled miserably on the rough planks.

It was late afternoon when the cart ground to a stop before a tall iron gate set between steep rock walls in a narrow side-canyon. Although the main canyon had provided some shade as the sun lowered in the west, Cormac was consumed by a raging thirst. The inside of his mouth felt like it was coated with dirt, his throat so constricted he couldn't swallow. All he could think of was water. The driver had frequently drunk from a full water bag on the seat beside him, serving to further torment the captive slave lying behind him.

A dark-faced man in white turban and robes appeared and, after exchanging words with the driver, unlocked the gate. The redhead was unshackled, pulled off the cart, and handed over to the gatekeeper. Stumbling from fatigue and thirst, Cormac was hauled by one arm through the gate. As it was being closed and locked, he dully watched the cart clatter away.

"You look strong enough for the galleys," said the gatekeeper, gazing with black eyes at his new charge. "You must have offended the Reis to be sent to die in the quarry." Cormac just stared. The strange words meant nothing to him.

"Don't understand me, do you?" the man laughed harshly. "Fresh off a ship, no doubt. Oh, you'll learn the language ... if you live long enough." He gestured for Cormac to follow him. They passed some stone houses and emerged from the canyon a few minutes later into a huge pit, 300 yards square, surrounded by high cliffs. Despite his thirst, the Irishman stared in astonishment. At the far end, several large wooden scaffolds rose from the ground. Slaves atop them could be seen swinging long mallets, the faint sound of hammering accompanying their actions. In the shadows of the lowering sun, the floor of the quarry was filled with activity. Men were engaged in dragging great slabs of rock from beneath the scaffolds to nearby piles; others were breaking slabs into smaller blocks. Still others appeared to be shaping and smoothing the stones. Wooden sleds, piled with finished blocks were being dragged to the pit entrance where the rock was neatly stacked.

Cormac guessed there were more than 200 slaves at work, thin and filthy with long unkempt beards, naked save a bit of cloth around their waists. Scattered everywhere were turbaned overseers robed in white, long whips in their hands. Gradually he became aware of an ominous feature: except for the sound of mallets striking chisels and the scraping of the sleds, the scores of slaves were working in utter silence!

4

As he stood there, the redhead's attention was drawn to a group of men working on a block of stone a few yards away. Beside them was a wooden water barrel and a stone bowl. Overcome by agonizing thirst, he stumbled forward with an inarticulate cry and thrust both hands into the barrel. As he was raising the precious liquid to his lips, he was hit from behind with such force that he pitched face forward on the ground, white-hot pain searing his back. Again and again, the whip fell as he writhed and moaned beside the barrel. The overseer was raising his arm for another blow when a soft voice broke the silence.

"Please sir, you can see that he's a very young man; he meant no insult. He just arrived and doesn't know the rules." Speaking broken Arabic, one of the nearby slaves had fallen to his knees in front of the overseer, head bowed, arms raised in the air.

"Tell him!" growled the Arab after a moment.

"You must get on knees and hold out bowl," said the man in halting English. "Keep head down until permission given. Only one bowl.

Move quickly now or no water." Gritting his teeth against unbearable pain, Cormac did as he was told. A long moment passed while the overseer watched him struggle to his knees and stretch the bowl out with shaking hands. Finally he muttered something and turned away.

"Good. Dip full bowl and drink; then stand until told what to do," said the man so softly the redhead could barely hear him. Fortunately, the bowl was big enough to give the redhead five large swallows of life-giving water. After setting it down, it was all he could do to remain upright with bowed head. There was a short conversation between the gatekeeper and the overseer before the latter snapped fingers at the nearby men and pointed to Cormac.

"You are to work with us," said the man still kneeling beside him, his voice barely audible. "Follow me." He rose and, taking Cormac by the elbow, carefully guided the nearly delirious slave to the others. "Take tools and copy. No talking." Cormac took the wooden mallet and chisel held out to him and slumped to his knees beside the man.

The chisel handle was a round piece of wood about 10 inches long. A small piece of sharpened iron was held in a groove at one end, while the other end was flattened from being hammered with a mallet. He tried to observe how the men used the chisel, but his eyes kept blurring and it was all he could do to remain upright. Finally, the man beside him guided Cormac's chisel to a small bump on the block's surface and whispered for him to strike it with the mallet. Four tries later, he weakly connected with the end of the chisel.

"Good!" said the slave. "They see you working. Stop soon for dark." Sure enough, the desert night fell like a blanket over the quarry 15 minutes later. Leaving their tools, two slaves supported Cormac as the men shuffled to a spot at the base of the cliffs near the scaffolds. Here a sort of cave had been cut into the rock. Tall enough to stand in, it was 75 yards long and 40 feet deep, sufficient to shelter all the slaves. In minutes, small fires flared up along the entire length of the cave. Fueled by camel dung collected from caravans hauling blocks to the city, the flames were used for cooking the rancid fish they were given and for warmth against the chill desert nights. The bread accompanying the fish was hard and moldy, but no one cared. Lowered to the ground beside a fire, the redhead passed out. When one of the men kindly rubbed fish oil into the torn flesh on his back, he never stirred.

5

For days, as his back slowly healed, the new slave struggled to copy the actions of the four others on the team. They were working on a rough slab four feet thick and six feet long, creating corners and edges with quick blows from their chisels. Protruding bumps were knocked off and the block gradually acquired a smooth surface. In the beginning, Cormac's efforts were weak and ineffective, but he slowly began to improve. Six days after arriving, the redhead settled to his knees beside the man who had interceded for him at the water barrel. He placed his chisel at the base of a knob an inch high and tapped it with his mallet. The chisel simply slid up and over the knob. In silence the slave grabbed his wrist and showed him the sharp angle needed for the chisel to bite into the rock. Cormac swung his mallet. Nothing happened, although the blade stayed in place. The slave gestured to swing harder. Lifting his mallet, Cormac delivered a mighty blow on end of the chisel. With a sharp "clink" the piece of rock split away, leaving a flat spot on the slab. Cormac grinned in triumph at his cohort and the man nodded in approval before returning to work.

At night, Cormac was plagued with nightmares about Finn and Bran. Sometimes they were being cruelly whipped and beaten and he would awaken with a violent jerk, sweating despite the cold night air. He would stare at the brilliant stars beyond the cave's overhang and pray that his siblings were safe. Gradually, his physical wounds healed and his scarred body grew thin and hard like the other slaves, but the team members kept warning him about the sun.

"Before you cook your fish, run your hands over it and rub the oil on your face, neck, and arms," said Cedric, whom Cormac had identified as English. "The worst problem when you arrive here is the sun."

"Aye," he said, "the sun can be bad on the ocean, too."

"You're a sailor, are you?" said Angus, another Englishman.

"I spent five years on my father's sardine boat."

"I was raised with the nets myself, off the coast near London," Angus said as he turned his fish over the flames with a small stick. "It's been 15 years since I saw the water and I'll not see it again. There's no escape from this godforsaken place! We'll die here like all those that have gone before."

When Cormac told them about the sack of Baltimore and his determination to escape and find Finn and Bran, the men expressed sympathy but no encouragement.

"They captured me twelve years ago, off the coast of Italy," said Giovanni, who'd stopped the overseer's whipping. "All comrades who came to quarry with me are dead. No chance of escape from here."

"I'm a sailor like you," said Armando, white-haired and Portuguese. "I was a young man when they took me from a merchant ship. I was sent to the galleys and tried to escape, so they moved me here as punishment."

Both Englishmen urged him to abandon thoughts of escape and focus on survival. "You're here for the rest of your life lad," Angus said. "All you can do is try to stay clear of the whips." Remembering the agony of his first day, the Irishman knew it was good counsel.

6

CAREFUL TO FOLLOW CEDRIC'S advice on the fish oil, Cormac became almost as brown as the overseers until finally the sun no longer bothered him. His clothing grew worn and tattered until he was left with just a bit of rag around his waist. The only thing that distinguished him from the others was the brilliant red mane of hair spilling over his shoulders.

Before long, he learned to apply his chisel against the stone at just the right angle, but it took months before he could drive it nonstop in a straight line across a slab with a series of sharp raps. Harder still was to make the chisel lines even, giving the surface a smooth, uniformly finished appearance; nevertheless, the idea appealed to him. Thoughts of his impossible situation fled during the day as he focused on conquering the obstinate rock with his crude tools. The whippings he sometimes received for obscure reasons filled him with murderous rage, but failed to diminish his growing obsession with creating perfectly smooth surfaces on the blocks. At night he began honing his chisel blade on a piece of stone, something none of the other slaves bothered to do. At first, it was with the idea of turning the chisel into a weapon, but the sharpening so vastly improved his performance and speed that he put aside such ideas and began to focus on the work.

One day, watching one a finished blocks being towed away, Cormac realized an outsider would consider the rock smooth. He knew it wasn't: there were numerous imperfections still on the surface, preventing strong adhesion to the blocks placed against it in construction. As these thoughts were going through his mind, he became aware of an overseer standing quite close to him. The man's sword was within easy reach, with a quick motion he could ... as his arm started to move toward the sword the silence was broken.

"There's another way."

Startled, Cormac whipped his head around to see who had spoken, but the others were bent over their work and the overseers were all gazing elsewhere. The voice came again, loud and clear.

"Become the best stone dresser in the quarry."

Leaning forward over the new block to hide his confusion, Cormac's mind raced. Who had spoken? He knew the accents of his teammates and it hadn't been one of them. Had he imagined it? No, it had been absolutely clear and, although he'd acquired a rudimentary knowledge of Arabic, the words had been English.

That night he shared the message with his team. All were as mystified because no one had heard anything. Later, sharpening his chisel while the others slept, Cormac pondered the message. It would provide him an objective that might block out the hopelessness of his situation. He decided to give it a try.

A year later, his skill and speed had increased to the point where the other four concentrated on shaping each block, leaving all the finishing work to him. He was able to create almost flawless surfaces in half the time it had taken two men before. As a result, not only did the team easily exceed its daily quota, but it also turned out the highest quality blocks ever produced by the quarry. At first, the foursome was just happy to avoid the whippings that accompanied failure to meet their quota. As time went by, however, their attitude began to change.

It started with Armando. One day he broke the silence rule and begged an overseer not to have a block pulled away because one corner needed more work. The Arab was so astonished by the request that he actually stopped the hauling crew from removing the block, to allow the old sailor to finish the job. When Armando actually signaled thanks, the overseer just shook his head and walked off.

Cedric was about to be whipped for leaving their work site to follow a block to the delivery pile, until the overseer finally understood that he merely wanted to smooth what seemed to be a nearly perfect edge along the length of the rock.

Giovanni actually chiseled on a block as it was being hauled to the stack at the quarry entrance. The Arabs stared, rooted in place, hardly able to believe their eyes.

Inspired by Cormac's dedication to excellence the team, almost without realizing it, had begun to take pride in its work. Mystified guards observed the men using sticks lashed together at right angles to create straight edges and corners cut precisely at 90 degrees. As the four older men concentrated on shaping each block, the redhead was engaged in smoothing the surfaces. The results were beautifully finished pieces of stone. At the end of the day, the five men no longer shuffled off to the cave like all the others; they walked in measured step with straight backs. It wasn't lost on the overseers that such work reflected well on them and the Arabs began to vie for assignment to this team. The slave community itself began to notice and questioned the team about it at night.

"You don't have to do it; the builders in Tunis don't require such quality." The comment was voiced repeatedly.

"It's the Irishman," explained Giovanni. "He's convinced that somehow this will help him get out of the quarry and find his brother and sister! Why, he's even got Ibrahim teaching him Arabic in the dark, so he can make inquiries when he's free!" Ibrahim was a desert raider who was captured during an attack on one of the Reis' caravans several years earlier. Cormac had sought him out months before and the lonely desert fighter had readily agreed to teach him the language.

"He'll never escape," said one of the men. "The only inquiries he'll be able to make are to the blocks themselves!"

"Perhaps," Armando replied. "But he's become so skilled that it inspired the rest of us to match the quality of his work."

"What difference does it make?" said another man with a snort. "It won't cause them to free you!"

"No," said Angus, "but we've realized they may own our bodies, but not our minds. There's nothing wrong with taking pride in our work."

"You don't owe them a thing!"

"You're right," said Cedric. "But we no longer get whipped … and we now have two water barrels at our station." With that statement, the others shut up because there was never enough water at their stations to compensate for the searing heat. One evening, weeks later, Armando approached a slave who had been captured with him years before.

"The slabs coming from your scaffold are more uniform than they used to be. It makes our work much easier."

"You've noticed," said the man with a smile. "We discussed it among ourselves and decided you weren't the only ones capable of good work."

"What are you doing differently?"

"We're sharpening our tools at night for cleaner and deeper cuts in the cliff," explained his friend. "During the day, we're making marks on the rock to size each slab the same. It's not perfect, because the rock doesn't always split evenly, but the results have been good … and the whippings have stopped." There was unmistakable satisfaction in his voice. "There's also an extra water barrel at the bottom of our scaffold."

7

B Y THE TIME CORMAC had been in the quarry for twenty months, the overseers were well aware that a remarkable change had occurred. The rate of production and quality of blocks had dramatically increased. The cave area had been cleaned of trash accumulated over dozens of years. Men no longer staggered about as though carrying an invisible load on their backs, but strode to and from work with firm steps. In response, the Arabs began distributing extra water barrels and most left their whips coiled at their waists. Although the men were thin to the point of emaciation, there had been a perceptible increase in the fish and bread they received: silent acknowledgement from their masters of the praise they were receiving from builders in Tunis. For the first time in the history of the quarry, snatches of song could be heard at night from around the flickering slave fires.

Cormac's team was busily at work one morning creating another nearly perfect block for the builders, when the silence was shattered by an enormous crash and agonized screams. A scaffold at the far end of the quarry had partially collapsed and buckled into the cliff. Three men working on top had been thrown nearly forty feet to the ground; one was dead, his skull split open, the other two shrieking with pain from horribly twisted limbs. Above, the nine remaining slaves could be seen clinging desperately to the crazily tilted framework which threatened to crumple at any moment. The rectangular scaffolds, made of logs lashed together with thick vine ropes, were unsteady at best and constantly subject to failure as the vines weakened with age.

Work came to a stop in the pit as slaves and overseers alike watched, frozen in horror, to see what would happen. As the minutes dragged by and there was no further movement, it seemed the broken structure had stabilized against the cliff. Proceeding tentatively at first, then more rapidly as the logs held steady, seven men scrambled to the ground like oversized monkeys and scuttled to safety. Two slaves remained above, clinging precariously to severely twisted logs, which visibly moved when either shifted his weight.

"Get down! Save yourselves!" shouted one of the men below, breaking the silence rule.

The guards didn't react to the breach, staring in morbid fascination at the men stuck 35 feet above. Suddenly there was a loud crack as a vine rope broke under the strain. For a moment longer, the wooden framework teetered against the cliff, but a series of loud popping noises reverberated through the quarry as the strain broke other lashings. Slaves and overseers alike watched in silence as the scaffold slowly began to collapse, carrying the two men down with it. One let go and was flung down head-first onto a block, perishing instantly; the other disappeared as the scaffold disintegrated in a massive cloud of dust. As the air began to clear, a scream rang out.

"Help me!" It was the second man, astoundingly unhurt, but trapped in a cavity under crisscrossed logs at the edge of the rubble. He could clearly be seen, one leg pinned by a thick piece of wood. A couple of men started to move forward, but an ominous grating noise drew everyone's attention to the cliff. High above, a slab partially separated by the workers was tilted out and threatening to fall on the wreckage. The would-be rescuers retreated.

"Save him!"

The voice rang out from behind Cormac as he and his team stood staring at the destruction on the far side of the quarry. He glanced about, but no one else seemed to have heard it although the tone had been loud and commanding. Without hesitation, the redhead raced across the pit, followed in a minute by the four other men.

"Stay away!" bellowed Armando's friend from high on a nearby scaffold, guessing Cormac's intent as he sped past men frozen in place by the impending disaster. "That block's going to fall!"

Cormac disregarded the warning and diving for the small opening, squirmed his way into the debris. The team stopped at the edge of the rubble and dropped to their knees, peering into the tangle of wood. Reaching the pinned man, Cormac saw with astonishment it was Ibrahim, the desert raider!

"I'm here, old friend," he said as he tried to lift the timber off the man's leg, but it was no use: there was a massive log above pressing down on it. Wriggling around, he was able to lie on his back and get his feet under the upper beam.

"Get out while you can," said the Arab. "This wreckage is going to kill us both!"

"If so, I'll at least die with my language teacher." said the redhead in flawless Arabic, straining with both legs against the log.

The slab above was now emitting continuous cracking noises as it began to pull away from the vertical face. The Irishman pushed with all his strength, streams of sweat running from his face, but nothing happened. Seconds dragged by as outside the pile of rubble the watching men glanced repeatedly at the teetering slab. Cormac's breath was coming in gasps, his legs were quivering with the strain and threatening to give out, when the log moved slightly and Ibrahim was free! The raider scrambled frantically to safety just as the granite block broke away from the cliff and crashed onto the rubble with a thunderous roar.

For a stunned instant, the gathered slaves stood gaping. Then Angus rushed into the billowing cloud of dust, followed by the three other team members. In desperation, they began hurling pieces of broken wood and rock to the side as they dug into the wreckage. A few other slaves started moving toward the pile of debris; then suddenly men were running to it from all over the quarry. The overseers moved out of the way to let them join the rescue effort.

As the slaves attacked the rubble, groups automatically formed to lift the heavier pieces of rock and wood; the scene took on the appearance of ants working furiously, as dozens of silent men joined in the undertaking. Within minutes, Angus and Giovanni were studying the fallen half-ton stone slab leaning against a crushed jumble of timbers. It took eight men to tip the rock upright. Under it, in a small space covered by a heavy log, they found Cormac.

8

CEDRIC AND ARMANDO GENTLY lifted his body from the debris and carried it clear of the wreckage. Armando knelt and placed an ear to the chest; after a long moment, he signaled to the others with a smile that the Irishman was still alive. There was a wide gash running from the outside of his right eye across his forehead to the hairline above his left eye, but his breathing was steady. Running hands gently over the Irishman, the Portuguese again signaled that he hadn't found broken bones. By now at least a hundred men had gathered to watch, including a number of overseers.

All at once the Irishman's body shuddered and his eyelids flew open. For a moment Cormac lay still; then he pushed himself slowly to a sitting position, one hand gingerly touching the wound on his forehead. As he looked around, smiling faces greeted him on all sides; even the Arabs seemed pleased. Ibrahim stepped forward and gently gripped him on the shoulder.

"Thank you, my friend, for saving my life," he said.

Supported on either side by Armando and Cedric, the redhead struggled to his feet and made his way unsteadily back to their work site. The others dispersed to their areas, leaving the scaffolding and hauling crews to clean up. Overseers returned to their stations and quarry work resumed. Save the screams of the trapped man, the warning shout from the other scaffold, and Ibrahim's thanks, the entire rescue and recovery had been performed in silence.

For the rest of the day, the four men took turns working at Cormac's side as he weakly tapped his chisel, supporting him with a firm hand whenever he threatened to pass out. The guards allowed them extra water to soak the rag tied over his wound, but he was close to delirium much of the afternoon. The team took on the surface smoothing, knowing they had to finish the block by the end of the day to meet their quota. Although the work suffered from lack of Cormac's precise chiseling, they finished by dark and carried him to the cave. The four men insisted he eat some bread and roasted fish before succumbing to sleep.

"You need it for strength, lad," coaxed Angus.

"The quarry needs you to recover," said Giovanni simply. "You've restored pride in these men and freed them from the tyranny of their circumstances. Every one of us owes his life to you."

"We all need you to find your brother and sister and give us hope," whispered Cedric, with tears in his eyes. A gentle snore was the only response as the Irishman gave in to exhaustion.

"Did you see that man?" asked Angus, turning to Giovanni a few moments later. The two of them had been kneeling at the edge of the rubble, with a clear view through the debris to the trapped Ibrahim. They had observed the redhead crawl to the pinned slave and lie beside him, trying to raise the huge timber with his legs.

"Yes, I saw him," said the Italian, staring hard at Angus. "I've been thinking about it all day. It's impossible."

"Who did you see? What's impossible?" asked Cedric, looking from one to the other. Long, silent minutes passed before Angus turned to him.

"There was another man under the rubble with them. He wasn't thin and weak like a slave. He had long yellow hair and a powerful body. He was kneeling, with his shoulders and both hands pushing on the log Cormac was trying to lift. He gave a mighty shove and held the log for Ibrahim to scramble out. As the slab broke loose, the man positioned the log over Cormac to prevent him from being crushed. Then dust hid everything."

"But there was no other body in the debris!" Cedric stammered.

"We know," whispered Giovanni, staring into the flames.

They kept the fire going all night, lost in their thoughts. When dawn broke Cormac sat up, asking why the evening fire was still burning. The others gathered around him, immensely relieved to see that he was all right.

"You made it laddie!" Angus grinned, "The only problem is the Arabs might think you've donned a mask!" Indeed, from cheekbones to hairline his skin was purple and black!

9

THE SCAFFOLD WAS REBUILT and life in the quarry returned to normal, with a noticeable change. The slaves began producing such quality material that soon all the builders in Tunis demanded block from this quarry. They sent representatives to compliment the overseers and learn what they had done to enhance the work. Unwilling to credit the slaves, the guards explained that they had realized the thralls needed more food and water; the increased rations had resulted in the improvement. They were more than happy to take credit for what had become a remarkably efficient operation. The builders responded by occasionally sending small gifts of silver to be distributed among the overseers.

Two years after Cormac arrived, the normal routine of the quarry was broken by a procession of robed horsemen appearing on the floor of the pit. At their head was a man in a red turban riding a beautiful gray stallion. All the Arabs bowed.

"Your Excellency," said the head overseer, hurrying forward. "We had no notice you were coming." He bent low to the ground with a flourish. "Welcome to your quarry."

"One of my quarries," corrected Suleyman Reis, "but one that seems to have surpassed the others. I'm told by the builders in Tunis that you're producing the highest quality building material they've ever received."

"It is our pleasure to make these blocks," said the Arab.

"But you do not make the blocks," said the Reis, "the slaves do. How have you managed this?" Seeing that he was not going to impress the Reis with flattery, and fearful of offending him with the water and food explanation, the headman decided to tell the truth.

"It all started with the young man that you sent us two years ago," he said.

"What man?"

"The one over there, working with a chisel, smoothing that block." When the Reis saw long red hair, something stirred in his mind, but the thin muscular body confused him for a moment. Then the morning in the slave market came back with a rush.

"Oh, that man," he said. "He was an insolent dog!"

"With all due respect, sir," the overseer bowed his head. "We've seen no such temperament. He's worked hard since the day he arrived. In fact, he inspired the older men on his team until they surpassed all the other stone dressers with their work." He then went on to describe the scaffold accident. "Since then, your Excellency, the attitude of the entire slave population has changed. They meet all their quotas and the work is uniformly excellent. We rarely use whips now."

The Reis rode slowly through the quarry, the overseer walking beside his horse. Everywhere he looked, the slaves were working steadily and efficiently despite the oppressive heat. What startled him was the complete silence, save for the sound of mallets striking chisels. Arab masters stood with whips tied to their waists: the operation proceeding as smoothly as though there were an invisible foreman directing it.

"Are they always like this?"

"Only since an accident five months ago, when the redhead rescued a slave trapped in the debris of the collapsed scaffold," answered the headman. "Prior to that half the slaves had begun to follow his lead and improve their work, but the others were still lazy. Since then, however, production throughout the quarry has increased dramatically. In the old days, we used the whips constantly to meet our quotas, but it's unnecessary now."

The Reis said nothing, but his eyes kept returning to the redhead. Even from a distance, he could see that Cormac worked quickly and efficiently. Finally, the stallion stopped directly beside the block being dressed by the Irishman. Cormac and the others went on working, but the Reis knew they were well aware of his presence.

"I thought the quarry would break you, boy," he said in English. Cormac made no response and kept striking the chisel.

"Have you nothing to say? I'm addressing you!" The Irishman remained bent to his work. Enraged, the Reis raised his quirt to strike but the quarry master hastily interrupted.

"Sir, they are not allowed to speak during the day. You must order him to answer if that is your wish." The Reis raised eyebrows; he had forgotten the severe conditions imposed on his slaves.

"I order you to speak," he commanded. To his astonishment, Cormac immediately dropped to both knees, lowered his head to his chest, and raised both arms up toward the Reis.

"It is my pleasure to serve the quarry to the best of my ability," he said in perfect Arabic. The Dutchman's eyes widened: he'd expected English.

"I see you've learned to speak the language, as well as to curb your passions. I'm told that you're the best stone dresser in this quarry."

"It's a skill I'm pleased to offer your Excellency," said the Irishman.

"We shall see if there are other skills you can learn."

The Reis turned his horse and lead the group away. At the quarry entrance, the Dutchman stopped and looked back. Cormac was hard at work chiseling. Suleyman Reis turned to the Arab standing beside the stallion.

"I'll send the cart. The redhead is to be returned to the city."

10

Two days later, a guard ordered Cormac to lay down his tools and follow him. A quick hand signal to the team was all he could manage before trailing the man out of the pit to the gate. His companions glanced at each other in astonishment; that night there would be animated discussion throughout the cave about Cormac's fate. Not only had he shown all of them a way to greatly improve their circumstances, but also it seemed he had managed to escape the quarry's death sentence. Was it possible he had been given the chance to take a step toward finding his brother and sister, a dream which they had all rejected as deranged fantasy? They had no way of knowing the outcome, but they would not soon forget the redhead who had made such an impact on their lives with his odd ideas.

At the gate, a two-wheeled cart waited and the slave recognized the same driver who had delivered him to the quarry two years earlier. As the cart pulled away, Cormac looked back and remembered how he'd arrived: terrified, hopeless, in complete despair over losing Finn and Bran, badly bruised, sunburned, agonizingly thirsty … a terrible whipping just minutes away.

What a difference now! He'd survived, gained skills, found leadership through example and spoke perfect Arabic. His body, although thin like any slave, was hard and muscular from months of lifting and turning the big stone blocks. Blue eyes under his great white scar were confident and direct. Thick red hair, falling down his back, was controlled by a bit of blue cloth tied about his head and matched a bushy beard, giving him a wild appearance. This was a man quiet and deferential to his masters, but unbroken by their dominance.

As the cart rattled on for hours under the blazing sun, the Irishman pondered his situation. The visit by the Reis wasn't coincidental because all the slaves knew their work had become valued; however, the Dutchman had clearly singled him out. The man's harsh tone revealed nothing, but clearly his death warrant had been lifted. Whatever lay ahead couldn't be any worse than the quarry.

The trip out of the hills was actually pleasant. For the first time in 24 months he wasn't working and could just sit and stare at the sun-bleached sand and rocks of the hills. An occasional hawk floated overhead on a thermal and once he caught sight of movement near a pile of rocks in the distance, perhaps a jackal or wild sheep. The sun had no effect on him, he was now as brown as any Arab; only his blue eyes and red hair gave him away. Even the driver's water bag failed to taunt him; he simply found a pebble on the floor of the cart and slipped it under his tongue to keep his mouth moist: an old trick Armando had passed on soon after he'd arrived in the pit.

The sun was low in the west when the cart approached the great walls of Tunis. As they drew close Cormac studied the battlements with a practiced eye, spotting seams where the rock should have fitted more tightly and wondering how many buildings inside were made from dressed stone produced by his team. A vast throng of people and animals was gathered before the massive gates, pressing to get in before they were closed. The din of voices and braying of beasts caused the Irishman to cup hands over ears that had experienced near silence for countless months.

The cart was soon in the midst of the raucous crowd, surrounded by masses of people, camels, horsemen, goats, and sheep, highlighted with colors of every description. Cormac was captivated by the overwhelming onslaught to his senses and, forgetting his ears, scrambled to his feet and gripped the top rail of the cart with both hands as he tried to take it all in. All at once a trumpet blast sounded from the ramparts, announcing the closing of the gates in ten minutes. The multitude surged forward; no one wanted to be left outside for the night. Above the din, the slave became aware of a loud commotion at the back of the crowd and turned to see a group of horsemen forcing its way into the masses, led by two soldiers standing upright in their stirrups and waving swords.

"The Pasha's daughter! Clear a path for the Pasha's daughter and her friends," the two bellowed.

Behind them came a closely packed band of twelve veiled riders, clothed from head to foot in black and mounted on beautiful Arabian horses. The animals were prancing with excitement and under tight rein from their riders The crowd parted to let them through and the group swept forward, passing within feet of the watching slave. In another instant the horses were lost to sight among the throngs on the far side of the gate.

In shock, Cormac gripped the rail and stared after them, knuckles white with pressure from his powerful hands. He was certain he'd heard his name cried out by one of the riders!

11

Stunned, the Irishman sank down to the floor of the cart. Could he have imagined it? The noise of the crowd was overwhelming: bleating sheep, whinnying horses, snorting camels, and people yelling at the top of their lungs. No, he'd not been mistaken.

"Cormac, Cormac!" The piercing scream had risen above all the noise.

Who could it have been? The soldiers had identified the riders as the Pasha's daughter and her friends, certainly all Arabs. Furthermore, no one taken from Baltimore knew how to ride; there was only one plow horse in the entire village! As he thought about it, suddenly he was reliving the terrible morning of the raid. He saw his father cut down and lying in a pool of blood. He heard the terrified cries of the villagers and experienced once more the frightened look in Finn and Bran's eyes. He remembered the way Bran held his hand in a death-grip as she whimpered in fear. The voyage was a blur, but the slave auction as clear as though it happened yesterday. Slumped on the cart, he was overwhelmed with grief he thought he'd buried forever.

"Make way, make way, this is the cart of his Excellency Suleyman Reis, Captain of the high seas! Make way! Make way! Do not bring the wrath of the Reis upon yourselves!"

The driver's voice finally intruded on his thoughts and Cormac raised his head to stare about. The cart was passing through the last of the crowd inside the gates and soon entered quieter streets. It was dark when the driver stopped the horse and leaped down to pound on a door set in a high wall. The door opened, spilling light on the rough cobblestones, and a figure appeared holding a lantern.

"Unshackle him," said a vaguely familiar voice. "I'll take him inside." In minutes the redhead was standing in a hallway, staring at Francois. The Frenchman was taller now, dressed in a loose white silk shirt and baggy blue pants. Gold slippers adorned his feet.

"You are thin, but muscled. A desert lion with a red mane," said the Frenchman in awe. "I never thought to see you alive again!"

"One survives the quarry or quickly dies," said Cormac in Arabic. "It also helped that our rations were increased in the past few months."

"Ahhh, you've learned the language," the Frenchman smiled.

"There was a slave, a desert raider, who taught me. He was captured during an attack on one of the Reis' caravans."

"I remember; it was years ago. I'm surprised he lasted this long in the quarry," said Francois. His eyes were drawn to the white slash on the other man's forehead. "How did you get the scar?" When Cormac told him of the collapsed scaffold, his eyes widened.

"We heard about an accident just preceding a dramatic increase in work quality. The builders' growing insistence on blocks from your quarry finally induced the Reis to visit. When he returned, he told me to expect 'the troublesome redhead' back."

"The 'troublesome redhead' learned a lot from older and wiser men," Cormac smiled.

"In the morning, I'm taking you to the wharf. You'll be an oarsman on the Reis' galley. The food will be the same and the work just as hard."

"But, I'll be back on the ocean," said Cormac with a grin, as an image of the sea swept over him.

"I forgot you were a fisherman," said Francois. "The difference with this work is that you can be killed in battle," he added somberly. "Did the Reis say anything about why he was bringing you back?"

"No. Perhaps he thought I could be useful because I speak Arabic."

"That might be part of it. Few Christian slaves bother to learn the language, and it makes their lives so much harder. I picked it up quickly because I was very young when captured and it's helped me reach a privileged position with the Reis. Whatever he has in mind for you, I know the language will help."

"I noticed your clothes," said Cormac. "It's obvious the Reis regards you with more favor now."

"As I've grown older, he's given me increased responsibility," explained Francois. They walked to the holding room.

"The rats are still present, but you look like you could crush the life out of them with either hand! I'll be back."

Although their interaction had been brief, Francois had felt a kinship with the Irishman, and elated that Cormac was still alive, he rushed to the kitchen and filled a basket with a brick of cheese, apples, fresh baked bread, cooked fish, and a large jug of water. Returning to the cell, he lit a small candle and set it on the stone floor.

"This light won't last long, but it will give you enough time to eat. I must go now. The Reis is in residence and needs me."

"The Reis is here?"

"Yes, the galley leaves in a few days and there's a lot to be done." With that, he was gone. Cormac slowly feasted on the food, savoring every bite. Such a meal might never come his way again and he was going to enjoy it to the fullest! He finished just as the candle sputtered out. Lying back on the straw, he spoke into the darkness as the rustling began.

"Nothing left for you, scavengers."

12

WELL BEFORE DAYLIGHT, FRANCOIS appeared with another basket filled with food raided from the kitchen. This time he stayed, squatting in the light of a candle.

"When the cook asks about the missing food, I'll tell her that we had a starving redhead to feed again! Her head is almost entirely white now, but she still has a soft heart for anyone with red hair, and for the Irish in particular. When I explain what a mop you have, she'll be pleased! Actually, I think she's Irish too."

"You tell her that I'll be going home someday," said Cormac through a mouthful of carrots, "walking the green hills again." The Frenchman's eyes widened.

"You're going to escape?"

"I'm not sure; slaves are closely guarded as you know" said Cormac. "But I promised my sister and brother I'd find them and take them home. I believe one day the opportunity will come."

"When we sent you to the quarry, I knew there was a good chance you wouldn't survive." Francois stared into the other's blue eyes. "But here you are. A galley slave is chained in place until he dies. Is another miracle possible?" He left the question hanging as he stepped out and locked the door.

Two hours later, the Frenchman reappeared carrying two sets of shackles. The smaller set he put on Cormac's wrists, drawing them close together. The larger set, connected by a chain long enough to permit walking, were attached to his ankles.

"I'm sorry to do this to you," he said. "Although, it will give us a few more minutes together. The Reis would normally tie you behind his horse when he rides to the ship, but he has an appointment with the Pasha. I'm to take you." He grabbed a short length of chain attached to the wrist shackles. "I have to do this because it's the way we walk slaves from one place to another." Cormac nodded his understanding.

Once they left the quiet residential area, the Irishman reveled in the color and noise of the market streets after years of gray cliffs and silence. His eyes feasted on the variety of colored awnings, rugs, bolts of cloth and merchandise of every sort. Moreover, the voices were no longer unintelligible.

"The most luscious pomegranates in Tunis!"

"Knives so sharp they can split a hair!"

"The Pasha himself has no finer rugs than these!"

"Eggs laid this morning!"

"Silk from China!"

"Fish so fresh they still quiver!"

"Ivory carving unmatched in all of Africa!"

Every merchant tried to drown out all the others through sheer volume. No one paid the slightest attention to the lean figure in shackles with the scarred forehead. They were far too busy to notice another slave being led through the streets.

"It's a bit different than the silence of the quarry," remarked Cormac wryly as they made their way through the shoppers.

"Silence?"

"Total silence, except at night," he said, going on to describe quarry rules.

"I didn't know," said Francois. "In the household we're quiet and respectful, but permitted to speak if the Reis, or a guest, addresses us."

"What about whips?"

"Not necessary. The Reis isn't cruel; in fact, he's quite capable of generosity. But he won't tolerate lack of performance or disrespect. Either means transfer to the galleys or quarries. No one wants that."

The redhead nodded. "You're better off in the household."

13

WHEN THEY REACHED THE long stone wharf, Cormac observed the same beehive of activity he had witnessed upon emerging from the pirate ship so long ago. Between merchant stalls on one side, and ships on the other, the wide jetty was filled with a stream of people and animals traveling in both directions. At the bottom of one gangplank huddled a group of panic-stricken prisoners surrounded by armed men: chattel destined for the slave block.

At the end of the wharf, beyond several twin-masted ships, they came to a craft that rode low in the water, its sides only three or four feet above the surface. She was over 100 feet long when one considered the heavy wooden ram extending from the bow. The boat measured thirty feet wide, with decking at the bow and stern areas connected by a walkway, four-foot wide, extending down the middle of the ship. On either side of the walkway were benches stretching to the gunwales. Cormac counted twenty-eight benches to either side of the walkway, on each bench sat five men.

"There are 280 oarsmen," he said to Francois, keeping his voice low, "about as many as worked at the quarry!" Oars had been pulled across the width of the galley on the wharf side to allow it to be drawn close; the harborside oars were extended out into the water. With a practiced eye, Cormac noted that the ship had two masts and a relatively flat hull.

"Is this the Reis' ship?"

"Only one of his ships. This is his personal raiding galley. He has two others like it and two sailing ships."

"That's a small fleet!"

"It's made him very rich," said Francois as two men approached from the galley.

"So, this is the replacement," one of them said in Arabic, looking Cormac up and down. "He seems a bit young."

"He survived two years at the quarry." The Frenchman spoke respectfully. Both men looked startled and peered closely at the shackled slave.

"I wonder why the Reis brought him here; he must have been a troublemaker to be sent to the quarries," said the first.

"A troublemaker won't last a week in the galley," said the other. "I don't suppose he can tell us what happened."

"Oh yes, sir," said Francois, "he speaks Arabic." For the second time in less than a minute the pirates looked startled.

"Why did you get sent to the quarry?" said the first. Although he understood every word of the exchange, Cormac stood quietly with lowered head, staring at the ground. He gave no response to the question.

"Don't play with me or we'll feed you to the harbor sharks right now; the Reis doesn't tolerate insolence!" When the redhead remained silent, the man grabbed for the sword in his belt.

"Please, sir," interrupted Francois, suddenly remembering his recent conversation with Cormac. "The slaves at the quarry aren't allowed to speak until given permission."

"What?" cried the man staring in disbelief at Cormac. "Answer me. You have my permission to speak!" The slave's sudden movement caused both men to jump back and reach for their weapons. With the habit of years, he dropped to his knees and raised both shackled wrists above his head.

"I tried to stop them from taking my little sister from me at the slave market," he replied in perfect Arabic. There was silence for a moment as the men looked at each other.

"Take the shackles off," one growled at Francois. "We'll find out soon enough whether he learned his lesson in the quarry."

Cormac was freed from the chains and led down a short gangplank onto the stern of the ship. Almost all the oarsmen were slumped over their oars sleeping. A few stared with dull and listless eyes as he was directed to a vacant spot in the middle of four men on the fifth starboard bench from the rear deck. All the slaves exhibited the same look of hopelessness that he had seen at the quarry. As his left leg was being shackled to a ring in the flooring, the Irishman glanced up at the dock. Francois was standing there holding the chains and staring at him; he gave a slight nod before turning to disappear in the crowds.

14

Seated on the bench, Cormac stared at the thick oar handle in front of him. It was chest high and just over two feet away. The wood was smooth and had black marks along the top, stained by the sweat of countless oarsmen. The oar was thirty-five feet long and extended at a shallow angle well out from the side of the ship, its blade just under water.

The other four men, interrupted when the newcomer was brought to the bench, had all resumed sleeping, heads resting against forearms crossed on the oar. Cormac grimly remembered that slaves were never unchained from the benches, and realized there was nothing else for the men to do except sleep when in port.

Oarsmen faced backwards, so Cormac had a good view of the stern area, four benches in front of him. An awning covered most of it. To one side was a pallet with silk coverings; he guessed it was where the Reis slept when they were at sea. A high-backed chair was bolted to the deck a few feet from where the walkway ended. It faced forward, and the new slave surmised the Reis directed the affairs of the ship from it. Directly in front of the chair was a three-legged stool and what looked like a round log. Weapons and other paraphernalia were scattered about the area, showing that some of the pirates accompanied their leader on the rear deck. On the other side of the deck from the Reis' pallet, a man lay sleeping against the gunwale.

Turning around, Cormac looked at the deck up front. Unlike the stern, there was no awning and a few men were lounging in the bright sun, talking. The amount of gear and weapons piled everywhere indicated a large number of pirates were stationed there. Again, there was a railing, not over a foot high, around the deck area. He wondered why it was so low; if the ship rolled, a man could easily fall overboard.

The cry of a gull drew his attention; overhead the greedy birds were wheeling and diving, some swooping in to steal a morsel of food from one of the merchants. Without realizing it, Cormac began to smile. The slight movement of the galley under him, the smell of salt water, gulls in the air: it was so familiar. Under a cloudless sky, sunlight glinted off the harbor water and, far out on the sea, he spotted the sails of two approaching ships. Shutting out sounds from the wharf, his body already moving in rhythm with the gentle rocking of the galley, he spent the rest of the afternoon gazing at the water and remembering fishing trips with his father.

"Don't look to me like you're new to the slave world, lad," said the gray-bearded slave on his bench, seated at the end of the oar handle. Hours had passed and the oarsmen had begun waking up. The older man leaned forward to stare at the rough hands and darkened skin of the new arrival.

"Can we speak?" The Irishman said after a moment. "In the quarries one risks the whip for talking."

"The quarries, eh? 'Out of the frying pan into the fire,' as they say. Aye, we also know the whip, but they don't bother us in port. At sea, silence is the rule. But, from that scar, I'd say you've felt more than the whip!"

"It's from an accident that almost killed me."

"You'd be better off dead," said the man immediately beside him on the right. "No one survives the galleys or the quarries. Why did the Reis bring you here?"

"I don't know, but I grew up on the Irish Sea and this is something like coming home."

"Not much of a home, lad." The thin man to his left was wracked by a long cough before continuing. "There's no shelter from the weather and if the ship goes down we go with it." He rattled his leg chain. "The Reis is a good commander but, should the galley be overwhelmed, he and the rest will save themselves and abandon us. Normally, victors set fire to the galley and let the slaves burn to death with it."

"I'm not much for dying," said the redhead. "I've got promises to keep." All four heads swiveled toward him; even the five oarsmen in front swung about to stare.

"A slave with promises to keep?" The big man directly ahead of him chuckled in a deep voice. "Surely you know, after years in the quarry, there's no hope for any of us."

"I'll not argue it with you," said Cormac, "but I made a pledge and it weighs heavy on me." He told them the story of the raid and his promises to Finn and Bran.

"Somehow, I'll find them! I survived the quarry with God's help and I'll survive the galley, too." The redhead was astonished as the prayerful words left his mouth. He hadn't thought of her for years, but Mrs. Doyle's words suddenly came back with crystal clarity.

"He will command His angels concerning you
To guard you in all your ways …"

Angus and Giovanni had told him about the man they'd seen under the rubble with him and Ibrahim, but he'd thought they were seeing things in their anxiety. Could it be true? Did an angel move the beam to protect him from being crushed? And what about the voice he alone had heard? Was that also an angel, or was it God? He stared out over the water, brooding.

The men turned away, lost in memories of their own families. Most of them had been sailors, captured at sea, and took comfort from the fact their wives and children were safe at home and spared the frightfulness of slavery. None had experienced the horror of watching family members auctioned off. The new slave carried a special anguish they wouldn't ridicule.

Activity in the stern caught Cormac's attention. The slave whom he had seen sleeping on the deck had begun carrying large wooden buckets towards the benches. He handed one to the oarsman closest to the walkway on each side, whereupon the bucket was passed from man to man on the oar, then given to the bench behind. In this manner, six buckets were ultimately progressing through the 140 men seated to either side of the walkway. Two overseers, uncoiled whips trailing behind them, trod the walkway watching the advance of the buckets.

"Food," said the man with the cough. "There's bread, dried fish, and water in the buckets. One fish, one loaf, and a good swig for each man, and heaven help the one that tries to take more because they'll whip him half to death!" The buckets were passed quickly from man to man.

"When it comes to you, hold a dried fish up with your right hand and pass the bucket to me with your left; that way they can see that you only took one. Do the same thing with the bread. The water is different: you can drink from the bucket as much as you want but be careful not to spill any because it will bring the whip."

15

T HE NEXT MORNING, CORMAC was awakened by shouts and
commotion. His body was stiff and sore from sleeping on the
hard bench in an unaccustomed position. Men were carrying supplies
on board, stowing them under the deck areas and walkway. Before
long, Suleyman Reis appeared, riding the beautiful gray stallion the
Irishman had seen at the quarry. He was wearing a white silk shirt and
scarlett pants tucked into high black boots; a purple cloak and turban
completed his outfit. Francois accompanied him, holding the horse's
bridle while his master dismounted.

"The ship is provisioned and ready, Excellency," said a tall pirate,
bowing and extending his arm toward the gangplank.

"Very well, let's be off. We have two days to intercept the prize."
The Reis strode onto the galley and took his place on the high-backed
chair. Men on the dock untied the mooring lines and tossed them
onboard. The slave who had passed out the food sat on the stool in
front of the Reis and, placing the round squat length of wood upright

between his knees, raised his hands in the air over it. Three overseers, whips trailing, stationed themselves along the walkway.

"Pretend to row, but don't put any pressure on the oar," said the man next to Cormac in a whisper so soft that he could barely hear it. "Learn the rhythm first; the four of us can handle the oar until you get the hang of it. If you cause the slightest change in our cadence, we'll all be whipped." Sure enough, one of the overseers was positioned at their oar, watching it closely.

The redhead placed his hands on the handle, copying the others. Every slave on board was staring at the man on the stool. At a word from the Reis, the man suddenly began striking the end of the wood slowly in a repetitive pattern. From the loud booming it created, Cormac realized the wood was actually a drum. Immediately, the four men beside him pulled back on the oar until it reached their chests, pushed the handle down to just above their thighs (causing the blade to rise above the water), extended their arms forward to a point beyond their knees before letting the oar rise to chest level (which dropped the blade into the water) and pulled it back again. This was done slowly, in perfect timing with the drum. All 28 oars on the starboard side did exactly the same, moving as precisely as though they were connected to each other.

After three beats, the drummer abruptly stopped just as all the starboard oars were poised above the water. The three strokes had caused the bow of the ship to pull to the right, away from the wharf and into the harbor. When the left, or port, side was clear of the dock, there was a rumbling noise as its 28 oars were extended to full length and held above the water. Now the drum started beating with a slightly faster rhythm, all 56 oars stroking in unison. As they moved slowly through the harbor, alterations in the drum pattern caused one side or the other to stop rowing, oar blades held clear of the water. This made the bow swing in the direction of the pulling oars and Cormac realized the drummer was actually steering the ship through the action of the oarsmen. There was a man with a small rudder at the back of the ship, but the oars were more effective for turning it. Once, the drum somehow directed the slaves on Cormac's side to push oars forward, while the other side pulled backward, causing the ship to make a sharp turn around a vessel at anchor. In this way, the galley passed smoothly among a number of ships anchored in the harbor and proceeded out to the open sea.

Free of the marina, the drummer picked up the beat. Oars rose and fell smoothly, propelling the ship forward at a surprising rate. Once clear of the coastline, the galley encountered a steady south wind, and the sails were unfurled. The drummer reduced the pace and let the wind do the majority of the work. Yet, even at a slow cadence, the combination of oars and wind caused the galley to move at a speed that astonished Cormac. He had been careful to let the others do the pulling at first, but now he began to get into the rhythm and was gradually able to add his strength to theirs. It was sheer delight to feel the wind on his skin and to experience the distinctive smell of salt water in his nostrils.

16

Two days later, muscles screaming from the unaccustomed work, Cormac got his first taste of piracy. A small sailing vessel was spotted on the horizon at dawn. The galley's sails were immediately hoisted and the drummer began a rapid beat. The merchant ship turned and ran with the wind, but the galley was too fast and overtook her in less than three hours. Fortunately for his passengers, the merchant captain did not try to resist and finally turned into the wind with furled sails. The drummer skillfully guided his ship alongside the other and the pirates swarmed aboard. An hour later, the merchant continued on its way, less eight boxes of gold and two chests of silver, but with its full complement of passengers and crew onboard and alive--the Reis took no slaves this day.

That night, as the galley drifted on a black sea under a brilliant full moon, the pirates laughed and sang about their good fortune. Cormac was curious whether the Reis knew that there would be gold and silver on that particular vessel and whispered his question to the man on the right.

"Of course! He has spies in every port, mate," was the soft answer. "They find out when a rich ship is to sail and send word by a fast sloop to Tunis. Sometimes the information is inaccurate, but not often. Slow cargo ships are often used to move riches, because armed vessels are expensive and sometimes suspect--greedy crews have been known to make off with the valuables. The theory is that pirates often overlook unarmed transports; that's why spies are so important."

"Why didn't he take slaves?"

"Probably because he has another target," replied the man. "If we'd taken slaves, we'd be rowing hard for Tunis right now." Indeed, three days later, they attacked another merchant ship. This one was armed and carrying mercenaries for protection. Too slow to escape the speedy galley, it opened fire with two cannons mounted on the bow, as soon as the pirates drew close. The Reis swung his ship in a wide circle and approached the merchant vessel from the rear, where the galley's narrow width was actually shielded by the bulk of the merchantman, preventing the gunners from bringing their cannons to bear. The slaves rowed furiously to a rapid beat from the drummer, causing the pirate vessel to race through the water. Suddenly the command was given to raise oars and coast.

"Brace yourself," muttered the man to Cormac's left. An instant later, there was a tremendous crash and violent shock as the ram plowed into the stern of the merchantman, bursting open a gaping hole at the waterline. As seawater began to pour into the stricken ship, grappling hooks were thrown over its railing and pirates swarmed up the ropes. The drum was silenced and the redhead twisted around to watch a pitched battle ensue as the mercenaries at the rail tried to prevent attackers from reaching the deck, but there was no stopping the screaming pirates. In short order, the defenders threw down their weapons and surrendered the ship.

Before long, grinning pirates hoisted two large brassbound chests for the Reis to see from below ... his spies had done their work well! The treasure was carefully lowered and stored on the stern deck, then every able-bodied man from the merchant vessel forced over the side and down to the galley: live treasure for the slave market. The wounded were left on the crippled ship, which was set ablaze as the galley pulled free. Screams carried across the water as the vessel was engulfed in flames, stopping only as the sea finally dragged the whole smoking mass down by the stern.

"Be thankful for the Reis' skill," said one of the oarsmen, voice pitched low. "Those mercenaries would have done the same to us if they'd won."

By now, pirates and captives occupied every inch of deck space and the Reis ordered the galley back to Tunis. Upon arrival, four days later, the prisoners were marched off in a scene Cormac remembered all too well. A runner was sent off by the Reis, and Francois soon appeared at dockside with the gray stallion and a horse-drawn cart. The treasure chests were loaded on the cart and Francois followed his master's horse along the wharf and into the city.

17

For the next fourteen months Cormac never left the galley bench. His body quickly grew used to the new work and muscles adapted. Life took on a pattern of voyages lasting up to ten days, often involving intense periods of hard rowing, followed by stretches of total inactivity back at the dock. He soon became skilled at responding instantly, in perfect synchrony with the others, to any command from the drum. As time went on, he compensated more and more with his own strength for the man to his left, who was slowly wasting away with a coughing sickness, to spare him from the deadly whips. When Pierre finally died, Cormac helped his replacement mesh so smoothly with the bench that the overseers found no fault.

One night at sea Alphonse, the rower closest to the walkway, suddenly slumped over and fell down between the benches. Cormac and the others tried to rouse him, but it was no use: he was dead. The next morning the body was unshackled and thrown overboard.

"Give them no cause for the whip," Cormac said, and for the rest of the trip the four flawlessly did the work of five.

The day after they returned to Tunis, a huge black man was led on board to fill the empty seat. He was well over six feet tall, with massive shoulders and arms. An enormous black beard cascaded down over his chest, but his head was bald. As he was being shackled in place, the rest of them could see a web of scars covering his back: he was no stranger to the lash. As he sat quietly, questions were directed at him from nearby slaves in a variety of languages: English, French, Italian, Portuguese, and German. There was no response; he simply sat staring at the oar, hands resting on his lap.

"Are you from the desert?" Cormac said in Arabic, leaning forward to look at the newcomer.

The other men were startled: after all this time they had no idea he spoke the language. The big head slowly turned to stare at the young man. Now 19, Cormac sported a red beard almost as long as that of the newcomer. Already strong when he left the quarry, his body had filled out with rowing and, despite its thinness, showed corded muscles on shoulders, chest, and arms. Piercing blue eyes, under the great white scar, gazed at the black giant.

"I'm from south of the desert," said the big man in a deep voice. "Far from here."

"How were you captured?" The Irishman couldn't imagine such a huge man being taken alive.

"Raiders attacked our village one morning. I fought them to give my wife and children time to escape, but there were too many and they all rushed in and clubbed me unconscious. When I awoke, I was tied by my neck to others and forced to march for many weeks across the desert. I was sent to the salt mines but tried to escape so many times they sent me here." He turned his back slightly to show the network of scars. "The whips couldn't stop me, but they think shackles will." His eyes burned murderously.

"My father was killed trying to protect us," Cormac said, "but they captured me, my brother, and my sister. You're lucky your family escaped."

"I'll never give up trying to get home."

"The whips couldn't control you but the iron will." Cormac gestured at the chains.

"Perhaps."

"We have a common purpose, you and I," explained the redhead. "We both want to be free and find our families. We can't defeat the chains, but I found a way that freed me from a death sentence in the quarry. It's the way of cooperation, not the way of resistance. On this bench, we work together and the whips don't come calling any more. In time, if we are patient, cooperation will be the answer to our prayers, as it has been to me once before." Long moments of silence followed as the newcomer pondered these words.

"Do you really believe that?" He was oddly moved by the other's conviction.

"Yes. I can't explain it, and I don't know how long it'll take, but I've found it's the only way," said Cormac. The black slave stared at his feet, slowly shaking his head. When he finally looked up, the cold defiance in his eyes had been replaced by something else.

"My way hasn't worked," he said. "I'll try your way for a time."

"What'd he say?" Ivan, seated between the two, had been staring from one to the other as their unintelligible conversation progressed.

"He's going to work with us to keep the whips away." There was a sigh of relief from the other three oarsmen; the black man's scars meant rebellion, and rebellion would cause all of them to be beaten.

From that moment, a bond began to grow between the big African, whose name was Dumaka, and the Irishman. Under the redhead's guidance, the new slave quickly learned how to blend his strength with the other four; the great oar timed perfectly with 27 others on the starboard side. Warned about Dumaka's past, the overseers watched closely, but he gave them no opportunity to use their whips.

18

THREE MONTHS LATER, THE galley was returning from a successful raid near Malta, 300 miles northeast of Tunis. They had
plundered four ships; treasure chests and prisoners filled every available
inch of deck space, even taking up the walkway running between the
benches. The final encounter had required many miles of high speed
rowing and, after the merchantman was looted and burned, the Reis
directed that they start toward home under sail. The oars were tipped
out of the water and most of the slaves slumped over the handles in
exhaustion as a strong east wind drove the galley forward.

About mid-day, the few men remaining awake saw great black
clouds rising thousands of feet in the air behind the galley, occasionally
pierced by long flickers of lightning. The wind grew colder and many
of the sleeping oarsmen woke to stare at the approaching storm. The
men on the front deck watched it too, but the speed of the ship under
sail made it seem like they were going to outrun the weather. The Reis,
dozing in his chair, was awakened when the awning over him began

flapping wildly in the wind. He jumped from the chair just as the wind gusted dramatically, ripping the awning completely away and sending it flying across the water.

Suddenly, the horizon all around them was black, with great masses of dark clouds boiling directly overhead and jagged bursts of lightning arcing in every direction. Deafening claps of thunder grew closer, until it seemed the sound itself would damage the boat. Great swells began to rise, towering many feet above the galley. The Reis bellowed for the sails to be furled, but there were too many bodies crowding the walkway and before anyone could act, a tremendous blast of wind hit the taut sails. With an ear splitting crack, both masts were snapped in half. The wreckage fell across the starboard benches and onto the water, crushing several oarsmen and creating a drag that slewed the ship sideways, threatening to capsize it in the gale. Pirates leaped among the benches, slashing shrouds with their swords, joining the slaves to heave the masts overboard. Without having to be told, oarsmen on both sides coordinated their efforts and managed to swing the bow downwind again.

By now the swells were huge, rising 20 feet in the air, white spray spewing off their crests. The galley was driven down the slopes of each, to bury its nose into the back of the wave in front. Shudders ran the length of the ship as the bow sluggishly lifted through tons of water, only to crest the wave and shoot down the other side into the next watery wall. The Reis, along with every seaman on board, knew that they needed to turn the vessel and head into the wind or risk being swamped. He shouted to the drummer and took to his chair, gripping its arms tightly.

The drummer knew the ship couldn't pivot quickly enough in a trough, so he waited until they were approaching the crest of a swell before frantically pounding the signal for one side to pull oars and the other side to push. This maneuver normally caused the ship to spin rapidly; however, the Reis hadn't comprehended the number of slaves killed and injured when the masts fell on the benches. The surviving oarsmen couldn't generate enough power to spin the galley as quickly as usual and it responded sluggishly. In fact, the turn was so slow that the drummer knew they weren't going to make it. Without waiting for the Reis' command, he reversed the signal and the port bank of oars, pulling desperately, barely managed to straighten the ship as it plunged down the back of the wave.

Rain was driving in sheets across the sea, making the oars slippery and obscuring vision. As the bow disappeared under water, every able-bodied slave began to pull on the oars with all their strength. Fear was the only command they needed when everyone saw the monstrous wave rising 50 feet in the air behind them, white foam pouring down its side.

"Pull for your lives!" Cormac screamed, but his words were lost in the gale. Far above, the top of the wave began to curl and he knew it was going to break on them.

"Dumaka, hold the oar steady, don't let go!" the redhead roared, leaning forward to stare at him. The black man nodded his understanding: the oar slamming around in the wave could easily kill them. The giant slid down between the benches, wrapping a huge left arm around the handle and locking his right hand on the bolted bench. All four slaves copied him and literally held on to the oar for their lives as the wave thundered down.

The force of the water was incredible. A great roaring filled Cormac's head and his body was pummeled so violently by the surging turbulence that it threatened to tear him from the oar. With all the considerable power of his arms he held on, wondering whether this was the end. It might well have been, but Dumaka's great strength prevented the oar from breaking loose and smashing the other men around in the fury of that raging maelstrom.

Down, down the galley was driven into the sea by the monster wave and, amid the mad violence of buffeting, roaring, and bubbles, Cormac knew the keel couldn't take the pressure. He felt the galley begin to bend in the middle and knew it was a matter of seconds before it would split apart and drag them down to a watery grave.

"I'm so sorry," he thought, addressing his siblings. "I truly believed I'd rescue you and we'd all go home." But in that very instant he felt the ship shudder and start to straighten. It was as though the hull was being lifted from beneath, rising against the tons of water pressing down on it. For what seemed like an eternity he and the others hung on, lungs near bursting, as the galley sluggishly rose under them. Suddenly they were above water, gasping for air and trying to clear their eyes, around them a scene of total devastation.

The front and rear decks had been swept completely clear of pirates, captives, and gear. Except for the slaves, all of whom were chained to the ship, only Suleyman Reis, who had somehow managed to wedge himself under his bolted chair, was left on board. Oars were skewed in all directions, some broken; others with long handles pointed straight up, held in place only by the oarlocks, their blades deep in the water; still others strewn loosely across the ship. Dead and wounded slaves littered the benches; it looked like at least a third had perished.

Cormac realized they were still in great peril. The galley was wallowing sideways in a trough between waves, although the swells were calmer and more spread-out once the great wave passed. It seemed as though the giant wave had somehow robbed the sea of energy. Nevertheless, the wind was still howling and the ship needed to be turned into it or risk being swamped. Shouting at Dumaka to keep their oar steady, Cormac scrambled on top of the bench, leg chain stretched to the limit.

"Pull! Follow our lead," he bellowed through cupped hands. "We have to turn the ship!" Dazed faces turned toward him, but the wind whipped his words away. "Pass the word!" he yelled directly into the ear of a survivor on the bench in front. He turned to shout the instructions to those immediately behind.

"Right!" roared a big slave, apparently unhurt. The words were passed from bench to bench toward the bow and a few oars were pulled back into position, raised to follow the lead. The Irishman spun and waved his arms frantically at the slaves across the walkway, making a pushing motion, his great mane of red hair streaming in the wind. Several men, scattered throughout the wreckage, signaled their understanding and began readying their oars.

"Now!" The redhead dropped to the bench and grabbed the oar. The five of them leaned forward, dropped the blade into the water and pulled. The men behind matched the stroke and, after a brief pause, the men opposite began to push their blades forward.

The galley slowly swiveled, under the opposing action of the oars, until the bow pointed into the wind. A ragged cheer rose from the benches and Cormac, jumping to his feet again, gestured for a slow rhythm to hold the ship steady. For the next two hours, the survivors on each side managed to pull with just enough power to keep the galley slowly climbing the oncoming swells and sliding straight down their backsides. The Reis finally regained consciousness and squirmed from under his chair to see Cormac keeping the ragged slaves rowing into the wind. He staggered to the edge of the stern and grabbed the handle of the small rudder to help steer, allowing the exhausted oarsmen to ease their desperate rowing.

The storm ended in late afternoon, and darkness found the galley adrift on a calm sea. Except for the moans of the wounded, all was quiet as bone-weary slaves slept over their oars and the Reis sprawled comatose on the rear deck.

"We should have died," said Cormac to Dumaka before they gave in to exhaustion. "I felt the ship start to bend in two. The keel was going to split."

"Yes, I felt it too, but then a giant force seemed to push us up and we rose to the surface. How can this be?"

Cormac shook his head, but Mrs. Doyle's words were echoing in his head as he nodded off.

19

"WAKE UP!" CAME THE command in Arabic. Cormac raised his head. A few stars still twinkled overhead, but rays of light on the eastern horizon announced the sun's approach. Standing above him on the walkway was the Reis, a long curved sword in his right hand.

"Excellency?" Cormac rubbed one eye with his fist.

"The drummer is gone. Can you manage the beat?"

"Yes, your Excellency." The redhead came wide-awake, focused on the gray eyes staring at him.

"There is no drum."

"I understand, Excellency."

"I will be behind you, holding the rudder. If there's trouble, I'll kill you." He raised the sword slightly.

"There'll be no trouble. The men will stay at their oars. You have my word, Excellency." There was a pause while the exiled Dutchman studied his slave.

"Unshackle yourself and throw the key back to me before you move." Suleyman tossed him an iron key. By now, the other men on the bench were awake and watching. Moving slowly, Cormac did exactly as he was told, remaining seated until the Reis ordered him up. The pirate commander backed along the walkway and beckoned him to follow, sword pointed at the Irishman's face.

"Remember, it's MY way," Cormac had whispered as he slid past Dumaka. The big black man nodded slightly.

From the elevated walkway, the redhead could see the full extent of the galley's damage. It was worse than he'd thought: only the group on his bench had survived intact, undoubtedly because of Dumaka's great strength in controlling the heavy oar. All the other benches had lost men to death or injury; some of them had been completely wiped out. It was a miracle the survivors had managed to handle enough oars to swing the ship into the wind. Upon reaching the stern deck, he bowed to the Reis.

"Your Excellency, we cannot make headway like this," he said calmly. "With your permission, I would like to reorganize the survivors into rowing crews." The Reis nodded. He was well aware it took five men to effectively handle one oar.

"Yes, but one man at a time." Cognizant that he was vastly out-numbered by the slaves, the Reis was going to take no chances. "Throw the dead overboard and fill the empty seats on the benches with able bodies. I'll hold the key after you free each uninjured slave. When he's re-shackled, you'll get the key to free another. One misstep and I'll kill both of you, and the rest of us will die together."

"Excellency, with your permission I will arrange the surviving oarsmen in such a way that we will have even strength along the length of the ship," Cormac replied. He knew the galley would move faster through the water if oars were stroking along its whole length, rather than concentrated in one area.

"As you wish," growled the Dutchman, instantly grasping the wisdom of the request.

Under this process, it took most of the day to make the galley ready for travel. Working alone, Cormac discarded broken oars, debris, and dead bodies into the ocean. Then he reorganized the entire configuration

SOLD INTO SHACKLES

of the vessel: injured men were relocated to empty benches between those holding slaves able to row. Many of the latter were badly bruised, he suspected that some had cracked ribs, but all of them volunteered for the oars, knowing it was the only way to survive.

In the end, he had nine five-man benches and one four-man on the portside, plus eight five-man benches and two four-man to starboard. Dumaka and the three men from Cormac's oar were relocated to the first bench on the right, directly in front of the Reis' chair and the drummer position.

Before starting, the Irishman searched the crawl-space below decks for food and water. He found one barrel of fish and two kegs of water that hadn't burst open; the rest were fouled with seawater. The fish he passed to the oarsmen. The water he shared first with the wounded, many of whom were feverish. The rowers needed no reminder to ration the remaining water; they were all too aware of the distance to Tunis.

"We're ready, your Excellency," announced the redhead late that afternoon.

"Very well," said the Dutchman, moving to the rudder. "Proceed." Observing the weakened condition of the slaves, and seeing how positively they responded to Cormac, the Reis wisely refrained from ordering a rate of speed. The redhead knew the seriousness of their situation; let him be the judge of how hard the men could row. If it wasn't fast enough, the Dutchman could always order an increase.

Cormac stepped onto the walkway and stretched his arms out at shoulder height. In unison, all oar blades were lifted from the water and swung in the direction of the bow. When he slowly lowered his arms, the blades were lowered and pulled through the water in one motion, to be raised again and swung toward the bow as he lifted his arms back to shoulder height. Earlier, he had explained this new way of signaling to every bench.

"The first strokes will be the hardest," he had said, "because we've only half the normal oars. Once underway I'll maintain a slow rhythm to extend our strength as long as possible. Watch my arms; they'll be your drum."

As he'd predicted, the start was sluggish, but the hull finally began sliding smoothly through the ocean and he settled the oarsmen into a slow but steady pace, then squatted on the walkway beside Dumaka.

82

"Keep this stroke until they need rest," he said in Arabic, before giving the same instructions in English to the Brit at the end of the oar on the other side of the walkway. Both men voiced their understanding, their benches rowing in perfect symmetry, matched by the oarsmen behind them.

The men rowed for four hours; it was well after dark when Cormac asked permission to let them rest. The Reis agreed. Having observed the redhead moving constantly up and down the walkway encouraging the rowers, many of whom were suffering from the battering of the great wave, he knew the Irishman had a good sense of how much they could endure. Getting home would depend on rationing what remaining strength they had.

When the order was given to stop, every slave collapsed over the oars and instantly fell asleep. After shackling Cormac to the drummer's ring, the Dutchman lay down on the deck and began to snore.

20

AT DAWN THE REDHEAD roused the men, but had no food left to offer them and the last of the water quickly disappeared. The slaves were used to scanty rations; however, thirst began to take a toll when the day turned brutally hot. As the hours dragged on the rowing became ragged, slowing the ship to a crawl. No matter how Cormac encouraged them, moving constantly up and down the walkway, even jumping down to lend his strength to the four-man benches, the blazing sun and lack of water sapped the men's remaining energy. By noon, the galley was barely moving.

"Excellency," Cormac's voice was hoarse as he approached the Reis at the rudder. "I think we should rest five benches at a time for the men to regain strength." Having taken no water for himself since the accident, he could barely get the words out.

"It will slow the ship." The Reis' voice was just as hoarse.

"Yes, but if we don't let them rest I fear we will lose all headway." The Dutchman stared at the slave. He knew their survival was in the hands of the Irishman.

"All right." His voice a croak, The Reis turned to scan the vast blue sky for any hint of clouds. Nothing but deep blue met his bloodshot eyes.

With a supreme effort of will power, Cormac forced himself to walk steadily down the walkway, despite his lightheaded condition, to address the oarsmen.

"On my signal, the first five rows will cease rowing and ship their oars. The remaining benches will continue to row for an hour and we'll alternate for the rest of the day."

The tactic worked to keep the galley inching forward. Cormac moved up and down the walkway encouraging the men, but the heat and thirst took a terrible toll. Finally, unable to stand, the redhead had to crawl, his voice little more than a croak. Somehow the men responded, but their blades moved through the water with less and less power. Only Dumaka seemed unaffected. When the redhead began to collapse after each trip along the benches, a great black arm reached out and held him upright until consciousness returned.

The sun was still high when the Irishman weakly waved an arm to halt the rowing. It was hardly necessary because only a handful of men were still pulling, the rest crumpled over their oars. No one noticed the Reis lying on the stern deck in delirium. The afternoon hours passed with just the great head and shoulders of the African remaining upright, one hand resting lightly on the arm of the prostrate redhead sprawled on the walkway beside him. At last the black head tipped forward, eyes closed. As darkness fell, the galley drifted on a gentle swell, occupied by an unconscious crew of doomed men.

21

"Hurry, hurry, there's not much time," a deep voice forced its way through Cormac's stupor, prying him awake. "You've got to wake up; you're the only one who can save us!" The voice was urgent. Slowly he struggled to consciousness.

"Dumaka?" He tried to speak, but wound up coughing and spluttering as water poured into his open mouth. He tried to shut his mouth but it was being held open by strong fingers and all he could do was swallow as fast as possible. Jerking upright, he came fully awake to see a black head streaming with water grinning at him.

"It's raining! Get the barrels from under the walkway and let them fill. This won't last long!" Heavy sheets of rain were falling on the ship: it was a cloudburst. Many of the slaves were awake, holding heads back, hands cupped around their mouths to take in the life-giving liquid. Cormac stumbled to hatches in the rear deck, frantically feeling for the water barrels he had disgustedly emptied and thrown back because of brackish water. Setting them upright, he hurried to the storage areas under the walkway and below the front deck, pulling out any container he could find. Soon, there were 20 large upright barrels open to the heavens. Almost as though it had been waiting for him, the rain suddenly increased in violence until Cormac felt he was standing under a mighty waterfall, barely able to see three feet in front of himself! The water hit the deck so fast the scuppers couldn't keep up and he stood ankle deep, drinking out of his cupped hands as though from a bottomless mug. Then, as abruptly as it had started, it was over. A full moon and brilliant stars appeared in a sky that moments before had been totally dark. Cormac checked the barrels and found them nearly full. There was easily enough water to get them home.

"Release us," a voice shouted, pointing to the motionless figure of the Reis lying on the rear deck. Others echoed the cry, holding up their chains.

"If he's dead, I will release everyone," said the Irishman from the walkway. "But if he's alive, I cannot. I gave my word." He stared at Dumaka and the black man nodded in understanding.

The men went silent as he walked to the body of the Reis. Lifting him by the shoulders, Cormac poured a bit of water from a bucket down the man's throat. There was no reaction; the water dribbled out the sides of his mouth. On the third try, the Dutchman's throat convulsed and he started choking and gasping, eyes opening wide in bewilderment before focusing on the shadowed face in front of him.

"There was a rainstorm, Excellency," said Cormac. "I've collected enough water to last us for at least three days." He grabbed the bucket and held it steady until his owner had quenched his thirst. The pirate captain leaned back against the rudder and stared at his slave for many minutes.

"You've done well," he said at last. "See to it the oars begin at daybreak."

Three days later, the galley limped into the harbor at Tunis.

22

WHEN FRANCOIS APPEARED WITH the stallion, the Reis strode past Cormac, now shackled to the stern gunwale.

"You're the drummer now," he said, as he reached the gangplank.

"Yes, Excellency." The redhead bowed his head in acknowledgement. Francois stayed and supervised a crew removing all the wounded men. At Cormac's request, he also arranged for the surviving oarsmen to be re-chained to the first five benches on either side, facing the drummer. Dumaka and the three men from their original bench retained their spot in the first starboard row. Over the next few weeks, replacement slaves were brought to fill the empty rows behind the storm's survivors, until there was a full complement of 280 oarsmen. Cormac's successor on the first bench was a wiry Scotsman named Patrick, captured from a mail packet by another galley.

A new crew of pirates began to appear, stowing their weapons and gear on the forward deck, while the slaves, as was usual when in port, languished on the benches sleeping much of the time. Their routine, however, involved one remarkable change. It began the day after they returned, when Francois showed up with a small wagon. Numerous large baskets were unloaded and carried to the rear deck, where Francois and Cormac started them circulating among the men. The astonished slaves found broiled fish, freshly baked bread, and great wheels of goat cheese! Never had such food been supplied to a galley, and the pirates watched with wide eyes. Even Dumaka, whose appetite was prodigious, ate his fill.

"I told you that he was a hard man, but not unfair," said Francois, as they watched the extraordinary event. "He knows you could have thrown him overboard when he was unconscious, freed the slaves, and fled. But you kept your word and rallied the men to row the galley home." The Frenchman stared at his friend with something bordering on awe. "He's ordered me to continue to supply the ship with food like this, so long as there is one slave aboard who survived the storm."

Cormac was silent for several minutes. Never in his years of bondage had he heard of such action by an owner and his mind filled with the implications. If the oarsmen were well fed ... He finally walked to the drummer's position and shared the news with those who'd survived the ordeal. The dumbfounded men stared at him in amazement, stunned by their good fortune. Kneeling on the planks, he addressed them in a low voice.

"My way," he said. Heads nodded. "Pass the word to the newcomers that this crew has a privileged position and no one is to do anything to cause us to lose it." More nods.

"Yes brother, it's to be your way," rumbled Dumaka.

New oarsmen were quickly counseled about the unusual attitude of their drummer and adapted to the survivors' approach, aided by the proof of a steady and nutritious diet. When sea trials were begun to hone drum commands and rowing synchrony, the replacement pirates realized these slaves were different from any they'd ever seen. Mistakes were quickly corrected and, sooner than the overseers believed possible, rowers were flawlessly executing maneuvers signaled by the redhead's drum.

When the Reis resumed raiding, he experienced remarkable success. Strengthened by their new diet, the oarsmen rowed with such power that merchant ships were run down faster than ever before. He became the talk of Tunis as his plunder and captives doubled that of any other captain. He bought two more sailing ships to prey on Atlantic Ocean treasure vessels, but his personal preference continued to be the galley and he expanded its operations far out into the Mediterranean. Little did he imagine that his predations would result in a secret pact among Mediterranean merchants to bring him down and stop their losses.

23

ONTHS LATER, AS THE rays of the rising sun turned the ocean to gold one morning, the galley left the harbor and headed northeast. Although sails had been hoisted to catch a freshening breeze, the Reis ordered Cormac to maintain a strong beat and the craft flew over the water under the combination of wind and oars. Spies had arrived two days before to report a large treasure under transport from Rhodes to Spain, aboard an ordinary cattle ship. Unfortunately, the spy's sloop had sprung a leak and had been delayed for two weeks in Alexandria for repairs. By now, the cattle ship had already set out and the galley needed all possible speed to intercept it. Two mornings later, the lookout spotted sails on the eastern horizon. Rising from his chair, the Reis lifted a long spyglass and studied the distant ship.

"I think that could be the one," he said. "Two masts, blunt bow and stern, and wide amidships. Just the sort for carrying cattle." He barked an order for the pirates to make preparations and directed Cormac to pick up the beat. The slaves leaned into their work and the galley surged ahead. In two hours, they had closed to within a mile of the ungainly vessel plodding slowly along.

"It looks pretty ordinary," said the Reis to himself as he stood behind his chair. When the galley had closed to within 500 yards, he ordered Cormac to slow the beat. The two ships were almost on a head-on course and men appeared at the bow of the cattle ship frantically waving their arms to warn the galley of a collision. From months of experience, the redhead hardly needed commands from the Reis. A quick drum beat caused every oar to be raised. Then came a short combination of beats that directed all the starboard slaves to push one stroke forward. This maneuver swung the galley so its bow and ram extended at a 30-degree angle toward the hull of the oncoming vessel. There followed a swift beat, which sent oars flashing at full speed.

The attack was executed perfectly. With a tremendous crash, the ram entered the hull of the sailing ship just behind the bow, splintering wood in every direction. Cormac's precision was such that oars were lifted out of the water at the instant of impact, allowing the galley to strike with full momentum and no drag. For a moment both ships were motionless, attached at the bows by the ram. Then the forward motion of the sailing vessel caused the galley to slew around, so the hulls of the two craft swung parallel to each other as the ram acted like a pivot. The slaves were trained for this occurrence and those on the starboard (right) side pulled oars across the galley to avoid smashing them against the side of the sailing ship as the two vessels began to swing together.

Intent on executing the collision, Cormac didn't see dozens of armed men suddenly appear along the railing of the cattle ship. With the bows of each ship held close together by the ram, it was easy for men to leap down onto the forward deck and attack the pirates. The latter, expecting no resistance from a cattle ship, and preparing to throw grappling hooks, were caught totally by surprise!

"It's a trap," screamed the Reis' second-in-command, as he and the men up front engaged in a desperate struggle for their lives. The snare had been sprung: the livestock vessel was actually filled with Turkish mercenaries who had been promised great riches for the head of Suleyman Reis.

24

Fortunately, the overzealous mercenaries had jumped onto the bow before the galley's stern had swung close enough for men to reach it from the cattle ship. Assaulting front and rear decks simultaneously would have spelled the end for the outmanned pirates. Instantly recognizing the danger, Cormac bellowed at the starboard slaves to extend oars and push the galley away from livestock vessel; if the hulls got to within 10 feet of each other, the mercenaries crowded along the rail above could easily jump onto the galley and overwhelm it.

Simultaneously, he drummed a beat for the port oars to pull at full power, further aiding the stern to swing away from the cattle boat. The combined actions produced enough of a gap to create a momentary hesitation among the mercenaries about attempting the jump. Then it was too late: the redhead's commands had pivoted the rear of the galley well out of reach. Screaming with rage, the frustrated boarders dashed forward and threw themselves down into the seething mass on the galley's bow deck.

The pirates up front were badly outnumbered and the Reis led a charge up the walkway with the dozen fighters who sailed with him on the rear deck, their yells mingling with roars and curses of the combatants. The forward deck became so packed with fighters that no more mercenaries could leap down. There was so much blood covering the planking that fighters on both sides stood a good chance of losing their footing and being trampled to death by the antagonists.

Watching the desperate battle, Cormac knew the pirates couldn't hold out for long and began signaling reverse to separate the ships. When the galley didn't move, he realized the ram must somehow be wedged, locking the vessels together. He switched the cadence to alternate pushing and pulling between the two banks of oars, swinging the galley from side to side. Seeing his strategy, more mercenaries leapt down onto the bow, heedless of the danger, swords swinging. He knew the pirates couldn't last much longer. At that moment, he saw a mercenary's blade strike deep into the Reis' left shoulder, dropping him under the tangle of surging legs.

"Do not let him die! Unchain Dumaka."

As it had been the quarry, voice was loud and clear, despite the battle tumult. Instantly, he knew what to do. He was unshackled while drumming, so he sprang from the stool and dashed to the rudder. Grabbing two eight-foot lengths of chain used to secure the ship at dock, he rushed to the first bench and handed one to the big black man. In a flash, he snatched the iron shackle key from its hook under the Reis' chair and unlocked Dumaka and Patrick.

"Get the drum and keep up the beat; we've got to pull the ram free," he instructed the Scotsman. Patrick nodded and jumped for the stern deck.

"Follow me! Use the chain!" he shouted to Dumaka, grabbing the other chain and leaping onto the walkway. The big man needed no urging and, quick as a cat, followed the redhead. As they reached the fighting, a grinning mercenary was kneeling beside the Reis, holding him by the throat and enjoying a moment of triumph as his dagger started its descent toward the Dutchman's stomach. Without breaking stride, Cormac swung his chain into the side of the man's head, splitting his skull and toppling him like a rag doll. Dropping to his knees beside the stricken commander, the redhead saw the gray eyes closing.

"Hang on, Excellency!" He thundered. "We need you!" The eyes opened and stared at him. "Good, don't give up!" The Irishman pressed close to the Reis and willed him to stay conscious.

"Protect us," he yelled to the black man, handing him the second chain. The command wasn't necessary. Dumaka had already planted his huge bulk above them and he began to swing the lethal chains as if they were buggy whips. The mercenaries tried to close, but four went down so quickly, limbs and heads crushed by the swirling iron, that the others quickly backed away. All at once, the huge man let out a savage shout and with one hand hurled the body of the man Cormac had killed over the heads of the battling men and into the ocean.

For an instant, there was shocked silence as pirate and mercenary alike turned to stare at the source of that fearsome sound; then the inspired pirates began to fight like madmen, shrieking war cries at the top of their lungs. Dumaka advanced a step or two with his spinning chains and drove the terrified mercenaries backwards into pirate swords. The men waiting at the railing above had no stomach for jumping down to face the giant whose vicious chains snaked out to cripple and kill; they concentrated, instead, on exhorting their comrades to kill him. But their comrades left a wide circle around the black man wherever he moved. Many, trying to dodge the chains, died from pirate blades they never saw coming. Adding to their fear, Dumaka kept throwing dead bodies into the ocean, where frenzied sharks were now churning the water red.

"Defend the bow. I'm taking the Reis to the stern," shouted Cormac to his compatriot, as he lifted the limp body of the leader in his arms.

"Follow Dumaka's lead and kill all boarders," he bellowed to the oarsmen as he hurried down the walkway.

Mercenaries had begun leaping onto the starboard rowing benches, hoping to launch an attack on Dumaka from behind. The slaves, however, spurred on by the Irishman's instructions, assaulted them ferociously. These were not the emaciated and weak oarsmen of a normal galley; they were strong and robust from their new diet. They quickly stripped weapons from the boarders and turned on them with no mercy, heaving the bodies, sometimes still alive, overboard to the sharks. But, spurred by thoughts of reward, the attackers kept coming and the front half of the galley became a scene of pandemonium as mercenaries engaged with both pirates and slaves to overcome the vessel. Battle cries from a dozen different cultures rose above the screams of the dying, as shackled oarsmen gave vent to years of anger and resentment and unleashed it on the mercenaries.

Cormac laid the unconscious Reis on his pallet and quickly bound the shoulder wound with strips of linen; the commander's face was pale, his breathing ragged and his clothing soaked with blood. When he was done, the redhead spun around to assess the battle. Patrick was continuing to pound the drum, but so many slaves were fighting that oars were idle and the galley wasn't moving.

Thanks to Dumaka, the remaining pirates were beginning to gain an edge at the bow, but two mercenaries had made it past the oarsmen and, hacking with their swords at arms thrust from the benches to grab them, were advancing rapidly along the walkway toward the unsuspecting black man from behind. A step or two more would bring them within striking range. The Irishman screamed a warning, but the uproar was too great. Leaping to his feet, he sped down the walkway and hurled himself at the men, just as their weapons were descending toward the giant's back. The impact knocked both into the benches and the waiting hands of the slaves. In seconds, each was run through with his own blade and tossed into the bloody sea. Hearing the doomed men behind him scream, Dumaka whirled about.

"Watch out!" Cormac yelled in horror, as a mercenary ran forward and aimed a killing thrust at the exposed black body. But the man hurried his attack and the sword glanced off the ribcage and pierced Dumaka in the side. With a snarl of pain and rage, the black slave spun and grabbed the man's sword arm, snapping it like a stick. Seizing him by the neck with one huge hand, he lifted the man off the deck and head-butted him so hard the mercenary's eyes rolled up into the back of his head and he went completely limp. Flinging the body off the ship, Dumaka dropped one of his chains and pulled the sword from his side, using it and the other chain to kill two other men rushing at him.

It was too much for the rest of the mercenaries: they began to give way, many attempting to scramble up to the deck of the merchant ship, only to be cut down by pirates, or slip and fall to the sharks.

25

THE FIGHT HAD TURNED, but it wasn't over: men on the ship were struggling to jam the barrel of a cannon through the railing at the galley. One shot at such close range would open a hole in the light craft from which it could never recover. Cormac sprinted back to Patrick and grabbed the drum, desperately pounding a signal designed to swing the galley around to its original angle of attack; perhaps he could free the ram by backing it out from the same angle it had entered the hull. One glance at the cannon and every slave understood the danger; they grabbed oars and the great blades bit deep into the water to the time of the drum. Ever so slowly the stern began to swing.

From the merchant ship, the mercenary captain realized what the drummer was doing and roared at the remnants of his men on the galley to kill the redhead. But blocking the walkway was Dumaka, a demon armed with whirling death that no one dared face.

Suddenly, smoke belched from the railing and a cannon ball whizzed over Cormac's head to erupt in the ocean thirty yards beyond.

In their agitation at the prospect of losing the prize, the mercenaries had fired too soon and over-shot the target. The cannon was pulled back and they frantically started to reload. By now, the galley had reached its original angle of attack and Cormac ordered full reverse. For a moment nothing happened as the men pushed on the oars for their lives. A normal crew might not have had enough strength, but this was no normal crew. Then, with a booming "crack!" the ram began to emerge from the hull of the cattle ship.

Once again the cannon barrel was thrust again through the railing and Cormac could see four men straining to lift the end of the carriage up, in order to tilt the weapon steeply down at the galley. With his hands still pounding the drum, he watched the black hole at the end of the barrel drop lower and lower until it pointed straight at him. As though in slow motion, he saw the gunner raise a hand holding the glowing taper. In a second, it would touch the fuse and send them all to a horrible death.

Something flashed through the air; the cannon belched flame and the Cormac involuntarily ducked, closing his eyes. Instead of the shuddering crash he expected, there was a splash and he felt drops of water hit his face. He opened his eyes to find he was still drumming and the galley was rapidly pulling away! Staring at the cattle ship, he saw the cannon still poking through the railing, but askew, with its barrel pointed straight up. No mercenaries were visible near the cannon.

Once safely out of cannon range, Cormac signaled a halt. On the bow, the pirates and Dumaka had dispatched the last of the attackers and were heaving the bodies overboard. Cormac busied himself distributing clothing from the rear deck to slaves, wounded in the fighting, who needed bandages. He then broke out food and water for the entire crew. When he finally went forward, he observed the surviving pirates staring in awe at Dumaka and talking quietly among themselves.

"We were caught by surprise. They would have killed us all, except for him," said one whose leg was bandaged from hip to ankle.

"I never saw anything like that in my life!" said another, a bloody cloth wrapped around his right arm. "I knew we were dead when they lined the cannon up for the second shot because it was aimed directly down at us."

"What are you talking about," asked Cormac, as he approached.

"Didn't you see it?" The wounded pirate stared at him incredulously.

"No, I saw the carriage being lifted by four men to depress the barrel; in fact, I was looking straight down the bore!"

"Well, your friend here realized what they were doing. He swung one of those big chains around his head until it was actually whistling, and then flung it like a bola! It hit the gunner and the others full in the face as the taper touched the fuse. They fell, as if struck by lightning, and dropped the carriage just as the cannon fired. The movement was enough to cause the ball to hit the water beside the galley. It was so close, I think it shattered the shaft of an oar!" The quaver in the pirate's voice, and a tremor in his hands, revealed just how close it had been.

"You saved us, old friend," Cormac said, turning to Dumaka. "And now we have to make all speed to get the Reis back to Tunis. He's been badly wounded." Without a word the big man followed the redhead and took his seat on the first bench.

The merchant ship was listing badly, and no one was visible on deck. Almost certainly all remaining personnel were occupied with preventing it from sinking. Finally the vessel stabilized and swung slowly eastward under sail.

On a sudden impulse, the redhead used his drum to send the galley flying after the stricken ship. Matching speed along its starboard side, he waited until the rails were lined with the surviving mercenaries, who were clearly expecting another ramming. Giving the command to raise oars, Cormac let the galley cruise silently beside the other craft.

"If you make it to port," he shouted, first in Arabic and then in English, red hair streaming in the breeze, "tell your employers that Suleyman Reis is not to be toyed with!" To his astonishment, the slaves joined their voices to the pirates' in a rousing cheer!

26

TWO DAYS LATER, THE galley docked at the great stone wharf in Tunis. After resuming his place on the bench, Dumaka had remained unshackled and Patrick had assumed the position of drummer, freeing Cormac to tend to the Reis. Unable to staunch the bleeding, the Irishman had heated a knife over the commander's cooking brazier and cauterized the wound in his neck with the flat side of the red-hot blade. The Dutchman remained unconscious for many hours as they sped toward home. When he finally woke, Cormac gave him water and small portions of food, but he was delirious most of the time. A runner was immediately sent for Francois and the Reis was carried home on a litter. A week later, the slaves discovered, to their delight, that dates and roasted camel meat had been added to the daily fare.

"I've been ordered to spare no expense for food," explained Francois, when he first appeared with the extra provisions. "The pirates who survived called on the Reis as soon as he was able to have visitors. They described how you and your friend saved the galley. He immediately told me to make sure the oarsmen have a diet as complete as that of the pirates."

As they discussed it among themselves on the benches, even the most negative slave admitted that Cormac's philosophy had caused an impossible change in their circumstances. They were still thralls, but bodies and muscles had filled out until they began to resemble their former selves. No longer did they collapse over the oars in exhaustion when the rowing stopped but they engaged in animated discussions with each other about how this raid or that might have been conducted differently. Those with naval backgrounds were keenly interested in the tactics the Reis used against his targets. All agreed that the least benefit of the provisions would be to extend their lives.

Remarkably, there was also a dramatic change in the pirates who had lived through the battle. From time to time, a gift would mysteriously appear on the walkway. Once, it was a huge bolt of cloth, enough for every slave to replace the tattered rags that served as clothing. Next, it was large pots of salve for blistered hands. One morning, enormous baskets of grapes had materialized between the benches. It was apparent the pirates understood and appreciated they would all have perished in the trap but for the intervention of the slaves.

Sixty days passed before the Dutchman reappeared on his magnificent stallion. Clad in a brilliant green turban, long-sleeved white silk shirt, and red pants tucked into high black boots, he strode down the walkway to the stern deck. His left arm was pressed at an awkward position against his hip, but the gray eyes above the black beard were as commanding as ever. At a glance he took in the robust physiques of the slaves, their uncommonly erect posture on the benches, and the blue cloth hiding each one's nakedness. If one had looked closely, he might have seen a glint of approval in the Reis' gaze. He beckoned to Cormac.

"I understand you saved my life," he said in English.

"I had to do something, or the mercenaries would have overrun the ship. But the big man," the redhead nodded at Dumaka, "saved both of us. He stood over me while I was gathering you up and kept them at bay."

"But my men said you used a chain to kill the one that was going to put his knife through my stomach," the Reis' tone softened a bit.

"The chain makes a good weapon," said Cormac. "I couldn't let him kill you. It would have been the end for all of us if our captain died. The situation was so desperate that all the oarsmen fought the mercenaries who jumped onto the benches."

"So I've heard."

"Dumaka made the difference. With one arm he threw men overboard; his roars terrified the Turks and inspired your pirates." There was a hint of a grin in the drummer's eyes. "He also demolished the crew bringing a cannon to bear on us."

"I've also heard about that," said the Dutchman, his voice now quiet. "They also told me he took his usual place at the oar without complaint when it was over."

"Yes, although he's no longer shackled," said the Irishman, seeing the Reis' eyes widen in astonishment. The captain was silent for a moment.

"My men said you stopped me from bleeding to death," the statement was made with a hint of wonderment. "You could have let me die and taken over the galley with your big friend and the other slaves once you were clear of the cattle ship."

"We follow a code. When you unshackled me after the storm, I gave you my word there'd be no trouble, and my word is good. Since then, you've treated us well and one kindness deserves another." He paused, and then added with a grin, "Nevertheless, the fact remains that if I hadn't released Dumaka to help rescue you, the mercenaries would have overrun the ship and killed us all!"

The Dutchman nodded in agreement, at a loss for words. The conduct of this slave was unlike that of anyone he'd ever owned. The redhead had now saved his life twice. Even the pirates under his command didn't display this kind of loyalty. Minutes went by as he formulated what had been on his mind for days. When he finally spoke, it was with firm conviction.

"I want you to captain the galley, under my command. My left arm is useless now, so you'll fight at my side during battles. For the next two years, I'll set aside 5 percent of all the riches and treasure we capture for you. At the end of the time, if you survive, I'll turn over your share to you and you'll be a free man. Thereafter, I want you to consider becoming one of my lieutenants, entitled to your own galley and 25 percent of all you take." The Irishman stared into the gray eyes, overwhelmed by the implications of this astounding statement.

"I accept," he finally replied. "But, there's one condition: Dumaka remains unshackled, free to fight when we go into battle."

"Done," answered Suleyman Reis without hesitation.

Finn

....

1

WHEN FINN WAS DRAGGED to face the buyers, he tried to hold on to Cormac's last words, promising that someday they'd be reunited, but his eyes betrayed the terror gripping him. Never had he been separated from his family, and during the voyage he had clung to the hope that the three of them would be sold together. The awful reality that he might never see his brother or sister again, let alone the fear of what might happen to him, had him in a state of near shock as he faced the crowd of men. Dozens of hard eyes stared at him, appraising his worth for work. He was hardly aware of a few men who came forward to examine him, pinching his arms and legs, sometimes yanking his head back by the hair to stare into his mouth.

Most of the buyers were looking for men whom they could use for hard labor. A youth was of little interest except as a house slave and, from the ensuing silence, it seemed no one was looking to add to his household. Minutes dragged by while the auctioneer extolled the virtues of the slender lad, but no bids were shouted. Just as it seemed the pirates might have to take Finn and donate him to the Pasha's soldiers as a live archery target, a tall, thin man in a stained robe and dirty turban raised his hand and tendered an extremely low price. Glad for any offer, the auctioneer quickly accepted.

"He'll never survive the desert," muttered one of the Arabs, as the thin man motioned to a slave and Finn was led away. Following his new owner through the narrow streets, a dazed Finn was oblivious to the kaleidoscope of color from vivid awnings, vendors' booths, and the dazzling robes of the shoppers. The cacophony of commerce, conducted at full volume by dozens of voices, was lost in his numbing grief at being separated from Cormac and Bran. When they passed through great gates and left the city, only the firm grip of the slave on his arm kept the boy from being knocked down and trampled by the jostling crowd.

Once outside, the tall man turned left and walked beside the towering ramparts for many minutes, until they finally rounded a corner and approached dozens of low, circular tents pitched on the east side of the city. Clusters of men in leg irons sat near each dwelling; robed and turbaned Arabs stood nearby with coiled whips. Finn was momentarily distracted by the sight of a great herd of animals at the edge of the encampment. He remembered the words of Morgan Dougall at the wharf. "Camels," he'd called them. He was startled to see that most of these strange humped creatures were resting, knees bent beneath them in the sand.

The Irishman was pushed roughly toward a group of slaves and shoved to the ground. The man who'd accompanied him from the market attached leg irons, connected by three feet of chain, to him before disappearing into a nearby tent to procure a filthy robe, which he unceremoniously threw at the new arrival. Most of the slaves seemed to be sleeping in spite of the heat: heads slumped on their chests or bent against upraised knees. A few stared at the ground in abject resignation. Finn realized these slaves, despite their brown skins, were almost all Europeans. They all wore full-length, filthy white robes similar to the one he'd been given.

"Better get that robe on, lad, you'll need it for the sun," whispered the man beside him, forearms resting on crossed knees, his matted and bushy beard showing streaks of gray through the grime. "Welcome to the world of camels. It's better than the quarries or the galleys, but not much."

"You speak English?" said the youth, as he struggled with the garment, wrinkling his nose against its smell.

"Speak softly, boy, and keep your head down." He gave a slight nod toward a small Arab standing nearby. "The guards don't allow much conversation. Aye, I'm from Scotland," he said, "but most captives here are from other countries and speak different languages. Not that it makes any difference, the whips all talk the same."

"What do you do?"

"We accompany caravans across the desert, loading, unloading, and caring for the camels," said the Englishman. "Those of us who survive, that is," he added grimly.

"How can you walk with these leg irons?"

"Oh, they're just to keep us from escaping while we're in Tunis. They're removed as soon as the camels are loaded and the caravan starts. There's no escape in the desert, just death if you run away: either from an Arab sword or thirst, whichever gets you first."

"What are camels like?" said Finn, staring at the big animals.

"Quite easy to handle, actually," the man said. "They make some noises that sound menacing, but they're normally gentle and often like to be stroked. Some of them even seem to like people and will follow right behind as we walk."

"How much can they carry?"

"They're very strong and can bear heavier loads, but for the long distances we travel, each carries about 21 stone."*

"How do you feed them in the desert?"

"They're amazing animals," said the Englishman. "They can go for many days without food or water; in fact, they carry water for us when there's more than one day's travel between oases."

"Oases?"

"Places in the desert where there's water." The man smiled slightly at Finn's ignorance. "Such spots have grass and trees, sometimes a small lake. We usually stop for the night and let the camels eat and drink as much as they want." The Irish boy stared out of the corner of his eye at

---

*A stone equals about 14 lbs. A load would total 294 lbs.

the nearest camels. He'd always liked animals and the discussion served to distract him from the trauma of being alone and separated from his siblings. He wondered what it would be like to handle these strange beasts with swooping necks and long legs. He would soon find out.

2

FINN LEARNED THAT THE man beside him, Thaddeus, had been captured from a fishing sloop in the North Sea. He had children at home, including a son about Finn's age, whom he had last seen three years ago. He'd set out with his men to fish one morning when a pirate ship had materialized out of the fog and captured all of them. Upon reaching Tunis, his men were sold one by one, and Thaddeus had never seen any of them again. The same caravan operator who purchased Finn had bought him. Thaddeus had survived the desert primarily because of a great love for animals: the camels became four-footed friends he cared for and cherished.

When dark fell, Finn was introduced to the cold of the desert night. Thaddeus urged him to lie among the men, all of whom pressed close together for warmth; however, the smell of unwashed bodies was so strong the teenager resisted. He huddled miserably, arms wrapped around his legs and shivered uncontrollably, until he gave up and crept among the sleeping men, savoring the warmth, but holding his nose against the odor.

It seemed he had hardly shut his eyes when he was awakened by shouts and the impact of a hard, moldy piece of bread hitting him. The rest of the slaves were already sitting up, chewing on the bread thrown at them by the overseers. A bucket of water was passed around and Thaddeus told him to drink deeply because it was all they would get until afternoon. As the sky grew orange in the east, the slaves were marched along the great stone battlements to the city gate. Finn noticed other groups falling in with his, and by the time they reached the gate there must have been nearly 300 thin, ragged men shuffling along in leg chains.

When the huge doors swung open, a flood of large carts, piled high with boxes and bales, emerged from the city. The slaves began to off-load them and carry the goods on their shoulders to the camel encampment. If anyone stumbled, or even paused for a moment, Finn would see whips immediately lash out, tearing flesh wherever they struck. Around noon, as he was struggling to balance a heavy bale of cloth, he stumbled and almost fell. White-hot pain seared his legs as a whip struck three times, accompanied by a warning shout from a nearby overseer.

"Don't fall," murmured Thaddeus from behind. "They'll lay you open good and proper with the whips and expect you to carry on as before. If you can't, you'll be dragged to the garbage dump and left for the dogs." Finn gritted his teeth, tears running from his eyes, and moved forward.

The pain shocked him out of the dreamlike state he had fallen into carrying load after load to the growing mountain of material near the camels. The Englishman had managed to stay close all morning, often seeing that the boy got a smaller load than the other men and encouraging him with soft words of praise and approval. He knew the key to Finn's survival was making it through the first week. It was the first seven days that killed many men: unaccustomed to the searing heat and heavy labor, they simply gave up and collapsed. Whether this happened in Tunis, or out on the caravan trail, dogs and hyenas soon put them out of their misery.

The sun was like a blast furnace; Finn couldn't understand how it could be so cold at night and so unbearably hot during the day. The hours passed and in the afternoon, when parched throat and aching muscles were robbing him of the will to go on, another bucket of water was passed. He thought nothing had ever tasted so good, and energy poured back into his body.

"Pace yourself," said Thaddeus during the short water break. "They won't force you to go fast; just keep a steady stride and you'll make it through the rest of the day. There's another bucket of water, along with fish, in the evening. You're doing well; I've known many men who never made it through the first day."

Refreshed by the water and buoyed by the words, Finn managed to keep going. He slowed his steps slightly, though not enough to draw the wrath of the overseers, and found a rhythm that he was able to sustain as the hours went by. Once again he fell into a trance-like state, but part of his mind remained alert to the threat of the whips and kept him from stumbling. He endured the passing hours in a sort of semi-conscious numbness. At last the day ended, and he slumped to the ground in exhaustion among his group of slaves. A bucket of water was passed, along with loaves of moldy black bread and small fish.

"Rub your hands on that fish before you eat it," said his friend. "Then wipe the fish oil on those leg wounds; it'll help." Finn observed the men, all at the edge of starvation, eating the whole fish: heads, bones, and tails. He was so hungry he followed suit without another thought. When they arranged themselves for sleep, he pressed in between Thaddeus and another slave and was asleep before he had a chance to feel the cold.

3

At first light, they began to pack the camels. Each animal kneeled while pads were put on its back, followed by a load of goods. As he worked alongside Thaddeus, Finn realized that literally hundreds of camels in the camp were being packed. When he asked his new friend about it, he was told the caravans often used 1,000 camels, although it wasn't uncommon for large parties to have several thousand of the animals. Throughout the day, Arabs mounted on camels appeared at the encampment. Thaddeus explained they were mercenaries hired to protect the caravan.

"There are raiders in the desert who would like to steal the goods we carry," he said. "The hired mercenaries are given a percentage of the profits if the caravan is safely delivered."

"Wouldn't the mercenaries be tempted to rob the caravan themselves?"

"Perhaps, except they would be hunted down and killed by the Pasha's soldiers," answered the Englishman. "Over the course of time, protecting these caravans is lucrative. The work is easy because raiders rarely attack, due to the sheer size of the expeditions, and the pay is high."

"Where are we going?"

"Probably south to the salt mines at Bilma. Our goods will be traded there for slaves and gold coming from Timbuktu or Gao, to the west. Those caravans will trade some of our merchandise for salt, a commodity badly needed in the west. Occasionally, we go southwest directly to Timbuktu and trade for gold. That route, though shorter, has few oases and little water. The animals get water before the slaves," he added ominously.

By mid-day the camels were loaded and the slaves returned to their sleeping sites. After the water bucket had been passed, the slaves' leg irons were unlocked and the men were escorted by heavily armed mercenaries back to the line of kneeling camels. Thaddeus had explained that each man would be responsible for five or six animals. Directed to his charges, Finn found himself beside a large camel.

"It's a female, called a 'naga,' the Scotsman said softly from behind him.

The animal turned her head towards him and uttered what sounded almost like a growl. Finn reached out a hand tentatively and rubbed her on the neck, ready to jerk back if she tried to bite. To his surprise, the large eyes closed and she actually leaned her neck against him! He continued stroking and talking softly to her until the order came down the line; the handlers shouted and all the animals rose to their feet. Fortunately, Finn's experienced naga, hearing Thaddeus' loud command, stood up as well. As the procession began to move, he was astonished to see how far it stretched in front of him.

"There must be hundreds of camels in the line," he said to himself.

Within a short time, the caravan left the walls of Tunis behind and was engulfed in the vast Sahara Desert. The trail, comprised of hard, sandy soil, wound between hills of soft sand. Overseers riding horses were scattered along the line, coiled whips in hand, and mercenaries on camels traveled the ridgelines to either side.

Finn found that the loaded camels moved along at what was for him a brisk walk. As the afternoon hours passed and the heat took its toll, he found himself clutching the hair on the naga's neck for balance and to keep from falling. Fortunately, working on his father's boat had toughened his feet, but they still began to blister on the baking dirt underfoot. Just when it seemed he could go no further, the sun sank below the western horizon and a stop was called.

Although the animals didn't need to be fed or watered until the caravan reached an oasis, they did need to be unloaded for the night before food and water was issued to the slaves. Moving almost in a trance, Finn began unloading the heavy bundles from the naga and stacking them beside her. By the time he got to the third camel in his charge, he was semi-conscious; only his fear of the whips kept him on his feet. Suddenly a shape materialized beside him in the dusk, and the cargo from the rest of his camels was soon unloaded. Thaddeus, having maneuvered himself into the line directly behind Finn, had quickly unloaded his own animals and come to help.

"Hang on, lad," he said in a whisper, "food and water are coming."

Sure enough, as soon as the camels were free of their loads, a slave with water and bread buckets made his way down the line. Finn sat on the ground leaning against the side of the female camel, arms around his legs, so exhausted he could hardly raise his head. When the food arrived, he was given a hunk of black bread, but it was the water that revived him. Allowed to drink long and deeply, he felt new life surging through his body and, when the slave moved on, he attacked the bread savagely. All too soon it was gone, but he felt as though he had been pulled back from death's door. Following the Englishman's advice, he pulled a camel pad over him, stretched out along the naga's warm body, and was instantly asleep. It seemed a minute later when he was awakened by a hand gently shaking his shoulder.

"Time for work. We'll load the camels together. They need to be ready at daybreak or we face the whip and go without food," said Thaddeus.

It was dark, with millions of stars shining brightly overhead, but across the eastern horizon stretched a thin band of orange. Finn groaned as he stood up, legs so stiff he wasn't sure he could remain standing, but the threat of punishment was so unnerving he forced himself to move. In the beginning, each step elicited a moan as his sore muscles rebelled and the naga swung her head to look at him as though wondering what was wrong. Within a few minutes, his body started to warm and he was able to help Thaddeus load the animals. Well before dawn, the camels were ready to go. Buckets of bread and water were passed down the line, providing energy for the slaves.

At length, a great orb of brilliance began to rise in the east, magnified by dust to 20 times its normal size. All along the caravan, overseers shouted for the handlers to command their charges to rise and gradually the great procession got underway like an enormous brown snake weaving its way through the hills. The air was still cool, but the climbing sun promised intense heat before long. Many of the slaves had somehow managed to acquire pieces of cloth to cover their heads and shoulders against the blazing heat. At the Englishman's suggestion, Finn tore a piece off the hem of his filthy garment and fashioned a sort of cap for his head that extended forward enough to shield his eyes from the sun's rays.

4

As Thaddeus predicted, the first week nearly killed Finn. Miles of walking left his feet so blistered and swollen he hobbled along like a cripple, leaving bloody tracks on the dirt. Although his calf muscles warmed and stretched as each morning progressed, he suffered excruciating cramps at night from dehydration. Any skin left uncovered by the robe was burned, despite his tan gained on the fishing boat. At the end of the day, he was so weak he couldn't have unloaded his five camels without Thaddeus' help, and he would have fallen victim to the whips. During the day, the only thing that sustained him was the comforting presence of the lead camel. He stumbled along beside the head of the old naga, talking to her as though she were human.

"Cormac's going to come. You'll see," he would say, the words almost unintelligible.

"Can't give up. Mother will need help with the fishing," he said when his his numb legs threatened to stop working.

"You should see Ireland. Green hills and lots of water. You'd like it," he said with the fingers of one hand locked on to her neck for balance and support because he feared he'd faint.

"No need to worry about water in Ireland. We've lots of rain."

"Cormac will help get you there. He can do anything."

No matter how bad the pain, heat or thirst, Finn clung to the singular thought that he couldn't give up. His brother would expect him to be ready when he appeared. So he talked on and on to the camel through the hours of broiling heat. By reassuring her, he kept hope alive for himself. The large beast seemed to respond, often growling in her peculiar fashion, as though she understood his plight. Close to delirium at times, he never let go of her neck, using the camel to stay upright and keep walking. At night, he would lie beside her under his pad in exhausted sleep, warmed by the heat of the great body, dreaming of fishing nets and water sparkling in the sun.

The end came during the fifth day out of Tunis. The blazing sun was nearly overhead when Finn, to the alarm of Thaddeus, began to take short stumbling steps in a sort of shuffling run, his body starting to lean forward. The Scotsman knew it was the beginning of a collapse, which would end with the lad lying unconscious on the ground, unable to be revived. The older man groaned as he watched in anguish for the inevitable to happen.

Finn, clutching desperately to the naga's neck, felt blackness begin to settle over his mind. He tried to focus on the green hills of home, the blue ocean, anything to keep from giving in to the dark, but it was no use and he started to slip away. He had a momentary flash of regret that he wouldn't see Bran or Cormac again, and his fingers began to lose their hold on the camel.

Suddenly a cup was thrust against his burning lips and cool water filled his mouth. He swallowed and the descending blackness was arrested, then began to dissipate as he gulped mouthful after mouthful of the precious fluid. Like a bolt of energy, strength flowed into his body and he stopped stumbling and began walking normally. His eyes flew open, and he saw a man walking beside him in a clean white robe, supporting him with one hand under the elbow and holding the cup to his lips with the other. Kind brown eyes smiled at him as Finn drank and drank until he could hold no more. When he finally pulled his head back from the cup, the man had vanished!

Finn looked wildly about, one hand again firmly holding the neck of the camel. The caravan plodded on as before, a faint cloud of dust rising from the packed dirt. Mercenaries on their camels were outlined on the hilltops, and mounted overseers patrolled the great line of beasts. No one paid him any attention. He looked back at Thaddeus, and was amazed to see a shocked look on the man's face. He gave the Scotsman a small wave, but Thaddeus just stared at him. Turning his attention to the naga, Finn gave her an affectionate pat.

"Well, old girl," he said, "I suddenly feel strong enough to walk all night."

Thaddeus was dumbfounded. He had been watching his young friend begin the familiar, shuffling stagger that spelled collapse into fatal unconsciousness. All at once, the lad tipped his head back, straightened his body and began walking normally. He'd maintained this curious position for several minutes before lowering his head and glancing about, giving Thaddeus a smile and a small wave. Now, he was walking beside his camel with the firm stride of an experienced caravan slave.

That night, long after everyone was asleep, the two of them sat leaning against a kneeling camel and Finn softly described what had happened. The Scotsman listened in silence.

"That's impossible," he said in awe. "I was watching the whole time and there was no one walking beside you."

5

As the days went by, and his newfound strength remained, Finn slowly began to take notice of the rest of his charges: two males, or 'Jamals,' and two younger females, one of them with a 'Warh,' or youngster, accompanying her. Both of the males were indifferent to him in the beginning. They would allow themselves to be loaded or unloaded without difficulty, but showed no reaction to his presence. The females were different. The one with the warh was decidedly friendly and clearly enjoyed being stroked or patted. Before long the warh was bumping Finn with its head when he stood with the naga. Finally he had to keep one hand available for it, while stroking the young mother with the other hand!

The other female had a mind of her own. Although not unruly, she exhibited more independence than the others, wandering out of line on the march and kneeling or rising before the verbal command was issued. She had a habit of partially rising before her load was secured and dumping all the parcels out on the ground. Sinking back to her knees, she would stare at the handler innocently.

"Did I do something wrong?" she seemed to be asking. Fortunately, Thaddeus kept a close eye on her because the animal's misbehavior, if allowed unchecked, could bring the wrath of the overseers on the Irishman.

Gradually, Finn's body adapted to caravan travel. Calluses formed on his blistered feet until he was impervious to the pebbles and heat of the baked earth. His legs strengthened until they no longer shook after hours of walking. He didn't need support from the naga, although one hand usually rested on her neck companionably, and he never stopped talking to her. While the Englishman continued to help load and unload Finn's camels, the work went more quickly as the youth gained strength. Under the robe, his thin body took a lean muscularity despite the meager diet. By the end of the second week, Thaddeus knew the boy had more than turned a corner after his miraculous revival.

"I'm as proud of you as if you were my own son," he said one night as they watered their camels at an oasis. "You've had to become a man all too soon."

"I've got to be ready for my brother," the boy said. "Why else would that man have come with the water? Some day Cormac will rescue Bran and me and maybe you too. We'll all get to see Scotland and Ireland again."

"I hope you're right," said the man.

Although he was unable to explain how Finn had received water that terrible day, Thaddeus couldn't deny the boy's astounding recovery from what he knew would be certain death. The future of caravan slaves was hopeless; nevertheless, something miraculous had happened to Finn. The Scot felt a tiny flicker of optimism. Was it possible they could escape?

"I'm right," Finn said with conviction. "Cormac's good for his word."

With a sigh, Thaddeus glanced up at the millions of lights in the sky overhead. At home his children were sleeping under those same stars. He hoped they were looking after their mother.

6

As the caravan approached Bilma, the trail meandered over large sand hills. The camels, with their broad two-toed feet, managed the soft terrain far better than the handlers, who slipped and slid on the unpredictable surface. Finn found that his practice of walking with a hand on the neck of the naga provided an unforeseen benefit. With fingers locked into her shaggy hair, he was both stabilized and pulled along on the steep climbs. On the steep descents, the handhold prevented him from falling and tumbling among the animals in front of him.

For the final two days of the journey, there were no oases and the water bags ran dry after the first day. The second day was a brutal ordeal for the slaves until they stumbled into the little trading community, located under a great rock escarpment. There was a good-sized lake, surrounded by grass and palm trees. After watering their animals, the slaves were permitted to drink their fill. Haggard with exhaustion, Finn sat beside Thaddeus in their group, waiting for bread. He noticed hundreds of other camels in the oasis and dozens of men dressed in blue robes and dark turbans, a flap of cloth covering their faces except for the eyes.

"Who are they?" he asked, his throat still tight from 24 hours without water. Minutes passed while the older man collected himself. The last day had been hard on both of them.

"They're Tuaregs." Thaddeus' voice was hoarse also, despite the water they'd just drunk. "A fierce people that live in the desert wilderness; known and feared as raiders, they control the caravan route from here to Agadez, Gao, and Timbuktu in the west. Our goods will be traded to them for gold, and probably slaves, which they've brought from those towns."

"Why do they cover their faces? I thought only women did that."

"I've heard the men wear veils for protection from djinns," said Thaddeus. "Apparently, they don't remove them except to eat, even when alone in the presence of their families. The women are reported not to wear veils."

"What are djinns?" Finn asked.

"Evil spirits, which the Tuareg believe are present everywhere."

"They look dangerous," the boy said, as a group of blue-clad men strode past, robes swirling. Although covered from head to foot, their posture was erect and somehow bold.

"They are dangerous and fearless," said the Scotsman. "The Arabs from Tunis are scared of them, although they won't admit it. That's why our caravan is so heavily guarded. Most of the time there's a truce, because both sides have goods to trade, but given the chance, the Tuareg would just as soon take our merchandise without having to give anything in return!"

"So, they'll take all our goods to the west?"

"Perhaps not all of it, because caravans also go east from here to Egypt. Bilma produces salt, which the people to the west desire, so the Tuareg caravans usually bring slaves from the west and return with salt and anything else they can sell in those markets; however, the Egyptians often bring horses to Bilma and the Tuareg prize good horses. Our goods may be used for a variety of purposes, depending on who negotiates the best deal with our owner."

"What will we take back?" Familiar with the sardine business at home, the youth was intrigued by desert commerce.

"That can be positive, if there is such a thing in this miserable existence," said his friend. "Sometimes we take back slaves, so the camels are used to carry bread and water. The owner wants to deliver the slaves to Tunis in good condition, because they'll bring a higher price, so he buys plenty of provisions. If we're careful, there's an extra swallow or two of water and food for us when the overseers aren't watching."

"Something to look forward to," the boy said, remembering his terrible thirst the last 36 hours.

For two days, Finn labored with Thaddeus and the other men to deliver to three other caravans the nearly 150 tons of material they'd brought from Tunis. Two of the caravans belonged to blue-clad Tuaregs; the third to people the Scotsman identified as Egyptians. A few loads were brought back to their encampment in return, but only a fraction of what they delivered.

On the third day, a long line of black people, roped together at the neck, was led to the Tunis caravan and made to sit beside the camel herd. Finn estimated there were at least 400 adults, not counting children. They were scantily clad and portrayed the same dejected and hopeless attitude as his own slave group. He and the others were put to work filling great skin bags with water and large baskets with bread, all of which were loaded onto the camels. The next morning they set out for Tunis, with a long column of black slaves walking beside the camels. Since the camel handlers were separated from each other by their animals there was no opportunity for talking and, save the occasional shout and crack of an Arab whip, the entire procession moved in an eerie silence across the sands.

By now, Finn had completely befriended all the camels in his charge. The males stretched their heads toward him as he approached and protested loudly if he didn't stroke them on the neck before passing. The warh followed him around like a dog and only sought its mother to nurse. The unruly female kneeled or stood at a soft word from him and kept her place in line at all times.

"The lad has a way with animals," Thaddeus said softly to another Englishman one day while they filled skins at an oasis.

"I swear, the old naga seems to understand his running conversation with her, although he keeps it too low for the overseers to hear," said the other man.

"Camels may be his salvation. His dream of a brother coming to rescue him is a fantasy that'll only drive him mad," said Thaddeus, who had long since extinguished the spark of hope he'd once felt.

7

IN THE MONTHS THAT followed, as the Tunis operator plied his caravan back and forth to Bilma, word spread among the slaves that the slender youth with long blonde hair had a special gift. No matter what camels he was given, whether young and rebellious or old and stubborn, all soon responded to his soft commands. During the long treks, he would invariably walk beside his lead animal, hand resting lightly on its neck, speaking softly as though to a person. As with the old naga on the first trip, strange noises would come from the beast, as though it was talking back to him.

At times, other slaves had their hands full trying to control difficult animals and fell prey to the vicious whips of the overseers. The Arabs earned bonuses for the prompt and safe delivery of the caravan; any disruption to the daily routine that could cause delay brought instant retribution on the offending slave. If the beatings rendered that man incapable of continuing, his work fell to the others in the line around him. Consequently, there was an unspoken agreement among the

200 slaves to help one another on the brutal desert crossings. When a camel threw its load, even as the handler was being beaten, nearby slaves quickly repacked and calmed the animal. If they acted fast enough, sometimes the overseers would stop the beating in order to get the caravan under way and the victim would escape with only minor injuries. Occasionally, an animal became so unruly that its handler was actually beaten to death before it could be reloaded.

When the caravan returned to Tunis after Finn's third trip, the handlers began to employ a subtle strategy with problem animals. It started when Finn went to take one of his camels for water on the second morning in camp. When he returned, one of the animals in his string had been replaced by a nervous young naga. She jumped up, threw her head from side to side, and threatened to spit as he approached. Spitting and biting represented aggression, so he stopped 15 feet away and began talking in a soft voice. His four other camels remained kneeling; their heads turned toward the sound of the familiar voice. Within 20 minutes Finn was gently stroking the new female and later, when the other animals rose to follow him to the watering trough, she ambled calmly along with his hand on her neck!

Twice more before the caravan left, an unruly camel was mysteriously switched with one of Finn's well-trained animals. How the exchange was accomplished, without the guards' knowledge, was a mystery. Most of the overseers slept in tents at night, secure in the knowledge that leg irons, and the penalty of death, were sufficient to keep the slaves from escaping, but there were guards posted around the perimeter of the herd. Leg chains made a distinct clatter and getting a camel to rise and walk soundlessly was no easy task.

In time, switches began to occur en route. This was a much more dangerous proposition, even though there were no leg irons, because the guards slept in the open along the line and mercenaries were always posted against a night attack. It was almost as though the perpetrators were invisible. Within a day, at most, Finn had gentled the new arrival and the overseers were no wiser.

The Arabs did observe, however, that the Irishman's animals were always calm and obedient on the trail. Even older slaves, who had survived caravan work for years, had trouble at times with their camels.

The youth's habit of walking with his hand on his lead animal's neck didn't go unnoticed either. Although the Arabs thought he was slightly daft, they acknowledged there was never a problem with Finn's animals.

One of the slavers, Abbud, had a particular penchant for cruelty. The fourth son of an upper-class family in Tunis, he had disgraced himself through an addiction to gambling, at which he lost great sums of money, and had been forced to seek employment outside his family's interests. Humiliated at having to take work as a caravan overseer, he vented his rage on the slaves. Heaven help the handler whose animal strayed out of line, threw a load, or held up the caravan in some slight way. Out would come Abbud's whip and, if the slave didn't react quickly enough to the lash, the handle was used to beat him to the ground. When other slaves jumped in to help, it only gave Abbud more time to punish the offender.

By the time the fourth round-trip ended, two years after Finn was purchased, the camel switching conspiracy among the slaves had become so successful that virtually every animal in the caravan was docile and obedient. The result was such a smooth trip that the owner complimented the overseers and gave them a bonus. All the Arabs were pleased except Abbud. He was angry because the slaves had given him virtually no excuse to mistreat them.

A smallish man with glittering black eyes, Abbud had a thin moustache shaped down either side of his mouth to the chin. When he confronted a victim, he would run two fingers down the sides of the mustache and smile slightly as he shook out his whip. Back in camp at Tunis, Finn observed him standing nearby one day, staring fixedly in the Irishman's direction and fingering his mustache. Abruptly, a big smile lit up the overseer's face and he ducked into a nearby tent.

8

ONE MORNING A FEW days later, loud squealing and snorting awakened the slaves. Four Arabs approached, leading an enraged male camel. Each man held a long rope tied to its neck and kept a good distance from the animal's head and legs. The beast, almost eight feet at the hump, was jumping and bucking in resistance, digging its feet into the sand and wildly struggling in the opposite direction. It took all their strength for the men to drag the angry creature close to the tents and attach their ropes to four long stakes driven deep into the ground. One of them approached the group of slaves containing Finn and Thaddeus. It was Abbud.

"He's yours," the sweating Arab said, pointing to Finn with a nasty grin. "Be sure he's ready to load when the time comes." He and the other three men disappeared into a nearby tent, cackling to each other.

"They're setting you up lad," said Thaddeus. "That is a renegade camel and they want some amusement, at your expense."

"I know," said the youth, staring at the animal struggling against the ropes.

"What'll you do?"

"Talk to it," Finn rose to his feet.

"Don't go near it!" cried an English sailor just brought in from the slave market. "That thing's going to kill ya!"

"Na, watch the boy," said the Scotsman, "he's got a way with them."

By now, the entire group of slaves was wide awake, watching Finn shuffle in chains toward the frantic camel that was pulling and bucking against the ropes. When he reached the stakes, the Irishman sat down and began to murmur in a low voice. For a long while, nothing changed: the animal continued to snort and lurch about in a frenzy. But gradually, to the astonishment of the shackled men, the great beast ceased straining and finally stood, watching and apparently listening to the figure on the ground before it. An hour later, the camel actually took a step toward Finn!

Rising to his feet, the slave held out his hands and slowly walked forward, speaking steadily in a low voice. At his movement, the animal lifted its head and stepped back against the tethers. Finn immediately stopped and sat down, not more than 10 feet away, uttering a soft stream of words. Another hour went by as the men, oblivious to the afternoon heat, watched the youth with the long blonde hair talk to the camel. All at once it took another step forward, head lowered.

"It's not possible," said the new slave.

"I told you." Thaddeus said, "He's got a way with them." When the Arabs emerged from the tent an hour later, the great jamal had moved to within five feet of Finn.

"Hah," said Abbud, "he may have calmed that one for now, but wait until time comes to pack it!" The others laughed.

"Boy," he said with a menacing grin, "that animal had better be loaded on time …" He thrust the coiled whip in Finn's direction as they strode away.

Finn rejoined the group briefly to get his bread and water before resuming his place in front of the animal. As dark fell, the others saw the big head thrust to within a foot of the sitting figure. When Thaddeus awoke at the glimmer of dawn, he poked the shoulder of the new slave.

"Take a look at that," he said. The camel was kneeling, head completely free of the ropes, with Finn sitting against its side fast asleep!

"I wouldn't have believed it if I hadn't seen it with my own eyes!" said the man. As orange crept across the eastern sky, Finn stood and began to rub his hands along the back and sides of the huge jamal, talking to it in a soft voice. The big head turned to stare back at him as he moved from one side to the other, and the men could hear noises rumbling in its throat. The process went on unabated until the order came for the slaves to march to the city gates and begin transferring tons of goods to the encampment. At the end of every trip, the boy briefly stroked the jamal's neck. Hours later, when all the material had been moved, Thaddeus asked Finn if he would need help loading the camel in the morning.

"No, but I may need your arms for loading the other four, because it will be slow with this one for a while," said the youth.

Next morning, the four Arabs gathered to watch the renegade camel being loaded while entertaining thoughts of how they would make the quiet boy pay for delaying the caravan. Finn moved slowly around the kneeling animal, sorting bundles and talking constantly. When he began lifting pads onto the great back the beast shifted its body a bit, head always turned toward the boy, but otherwise didn't move. As gently as he could, Finn began loading the bundles and baggage, keeping a constant murmur of words and occasionally stepping forward to stroke the animal's neck.

Thaddeus and another slave, surreptitiously packing the boy's other beasts, kept an eye on the proceedings, quietly amused at the growing scowls on the overseers' faces. At last, the entire caravan was loaded and orders came to raise the animals to their feet. The four men began to smile with anticipation, certain the renegade would stampede, shed its load, and give them the excuse they were looking for.

Finn stepped in front of the crouching animal and stared at it, murmuring softly. He reached out both hands and held them on either side of the camel's head, exerting a slight upward pressure while uttering the command to rise. For a moment nothing happened; then the jamal rose to its feet, tail twitching and legs slightly bent as though it was going to explode into action. But the youth kept the great head steady in front of him and spoke soothingly. The animal's tail gradually ceased its restless swirling and, with straightened legs, it stood quietly. Stepping around to the side, with one hand resting lightly on the renegade's neck, Finn moved it into the long caravan line and marched off at the head of his other charges.

9

FROM THAT TIME ON, no one but Finn could handle the massive jamal. If anyone approached when the youth wasn't present, it became extremely aggressive, lashing out with its feet, spitting, and threatening to bite whatever part of the human was within reach. The overseers seemed to enrage the beast far more than the slaves and soon they learned to give it a wide berth when the boy was attending to his other camels. With Finn, it kneeled quietly to be loaded or unloaded and calmly followed him to water when they were at an oasis. At night, the youth could be found stretched along the large beast's side under a packing pad, sleeping soundly.

Finn's victory, however, came with a price. The four overseers, and Abbud in particular, made a point of singling out the Irishman in retaliation for besting them with the rogue. After the camels were loaded some mornings, one of them would loosen the pack ties on one of his other camels. As the caravan started to move off, the load would spill to the ground and the Arabs would rush up to curse and whip him for the delay. With blood dripping from his robe, Finn was made to reload the animal without help from another slave. Thaddeus and the others could only watch in silence, hoping the youth wouldn't be beaten senseless and left behind.

"If I give up, they'll kill you," Finn would say to the big camel when they finally got under way. "They'll lance you for meat and I'll be left for the jackals." A growling noise would issue from the animal's chest.

"If that happens, I won't be around to help Cormac with the fishing boat." Another rumbling from the camel.

"Did I ever tell you what those green hills look like above the Baltimore harbor in the morning sun?" On they would go, their peculiar conversation extending through the day until the dark came crashing down and it was time to unload. Pressed against the camel at night Finn's wounds were soothed by its warmth.

They were halfway to Bilma when the attack came. At dawn, shouting and a few musket shots signaled that raiders had engaged the outlying guards around the oasis where the caravan had stopped for the night. The slaves had finished packing their animals, but the camels were still kneeling -- which probably saved the column. Had they been spread out, or even standing, the Tuaregs might have succeeded in stampeding the beasts. As it was, when the blue-clad figures on slender, fleet camels rushed into the camp, the kneeling camels with their loads became protection for both slaves and overseers to hide behind. Even in the midst of the danger and confusion, the Tuareg camels captivated Finn. They were fast and agile, completely unlike the pack-camels.

"Did you see that?" he shouted to Thaddeus, as a sword-wielding raider flew past.

"Get down," roared the Scotsman, crouched behind a kneeling camel nearby. "They'll lance slaves as well as Arabs!"

"I've never seen anything like it!" yelled the boy, still standing beside the great jamal. "They're as fast as a horse!"

"Never mind about that! We're all in great danger! Watch out behind you!" Thaddeus suddenly screamed. Finn spun around.

Through the pandemonium of the attack, a familiar figure in white robes and turban was running at him with a raised scimitar. Abbud had decided to use the raid to rid himself of the slave who'd humiliated him in Tunis. The Tuaregs had no more affinity for European slaves than the Arabs, so the boy's death could be blamed on them. The overseer was smiling as he lifted his sword and raced at the unsuspecting victim. To his surprise, the boy suddenly swung to face him and ducked under the stroke aimed at his neck. The momentum of the swing spun Abbud in a half circle and, when he straightened, he saw the slave had dodged to the far side of the jamal.

Snarling in rage, the overseer raced after the defenseless youth, only to feel excruciating pain as the great jamal clamped teeth on his left thigh when he brushed past its head! With an agonized shriek, Abbud tore himself away and staggered off clutching his leg, thoughts of revenge dispelled by the pain of the wound. He lifted his robe to stare at the large purple bite mark oozing blood. The sight seemed to infuriate him and, dropping the robe, he turned back and started limping toward Finn with a murderous look in his eyes. He had barely taken two steps, when a blue-clad rider on a swift camel appeared out of the dust cloud behind him. In one smooth motion, the Tuareg leaned forward and ran his lance through Abbud's back and out his chest. With a quick jerk, the raider freed the blade and disappeared back into the dust. The overseer slowly crumpled to the ground, a startled look on his face and a great red stain spreading across his white robe.

It didn't take long for the mercenary force to rally and drive the raiders back into the hills. No slaves had been lost, but several defenders and three overseers, including Abbud, were dead. In the aftermath, the caravan was three days late getting into Bilma and the traders waiting for it had already disposed of their goods to other caravans leaving for Egypt. Incensed at his loses, the Tunis operator made it clear he would tolerate no interruptions to the smooth functioning of his caravan. Fearful of his wrath, the overseers ceased harassing Finn and actually encouraged the slaves to bring recalcitrant camels to him for taming!

10

O N THE FIFTH TRIP, Finn encountered the giant man. The caravan
was in Bilma and had acquired a large group of black slaves for
the return trip to Tunis. As the Irishman and Thaddeus loaded their
camels with huge water bags, the slaves were driven toward them in a
long dark line. In their midst strode a massive figure, towering above
the others. His head was erect, dark eyes staring straight forward as
though he were marching at the head of an army. Although roped at
the neck to the persons in front and behind, the fear he commanded
among the slavers was reflected by manacles on each of his wrists, connected by a short length of chain, restricting the use of his great arms.

Finn was no longer a youth: he now stood 5'10," with a thin body
that belied considerable strength. A cap of faded blue cloth, knotted at
the back, covered his head and gave some control to the mass of blonde
hair stretching halfway down his back. A short yellow beard covered
his face, highlighting gold flecks in the wide-set brown eyes. His face
was deeply tanned and there was a slight hook to a nose broken in an

early beating; he would have been considered striking were it not for his gaunt cheeks.

As the caravan got underway, Finn was pleased to see the large black man not far behind his string of camels. The slave fascinated him because he bore himself as though free: his countenance conveyed disdain for those who owned him. Newly healed scars on his shoulders and neck showed that he had not been captured easily. During his years in the desert, the young man had seen hundreds of slaves delivered to Tunis, all radiating dejection and hopelessness. This man was different, and Finn felt inexplicably drawn to him. Somehow he had to make contact.

The opportunity presented itself during water distribution. At dusk, when the caravan stopped, the roped slaves collapsed on the ground where they stood. After the camels were unloaded, the handlers were required to pass out bread and water among the captives before settling down themselves. The process was repeated at dawn, before the camels were packed. In both cases it was dark, or nearly so, when the distribution was made. It was an easy matter for Finn to trade places with the handler behind him in order to deliver water to the big man.

"How did they capture you?" said Finn the first night, as he held out the big water bag. The man drank long and deeply before handing it back, but made no answer.

Finn moved to the next person, wondering why there had been no response; perhaps the man felt he was above other slaves. It wasn't until he was leaning against the jamal that the Irishman realized he had spoken in English! Like all the handlers, he'd learned Arabic to avoid misunderstanding the shouted commands of the overseers, but rarely spoke it himself because most of the handlers were European. The next morning, when he repeated the question in Arabic, a deep voice answered before the man drank.

"I fought to let my wife and children escape, but in the end there were too many of them."

"I'll come again." It was all Finn had time to say as he stepped down the line. Throughout the march that day, whenever the blonde handler glanced back he saw the eyes of the big man fixed on him.

From that time on, there was a one or two-sentence breathed conversation between the two each night and morning until the caravan reached Tunis many weeks later. Finn was entranced by whispered descriptions of vast plains filled with herds of wild animals. He learned about cattle grazing, guarded by men with spears standing on one leg with the foot of the other pressed against their knee. In his imagination he saw clusters of huts with great thorn fences around them to keep lions out during the night. He marveled at the account of yellow and brown creatures with necks so long they could eat from the tops of trees. And through all these descriptions ran the big man's unwavering commitment to regain his freedom and return to the life he'd had before.

"But how?" Finn would counter. "I've been a slave almost three years and there's no escape. If we run into the desert, we'll die of thirst. In Tunis we're chained and under a death sentence if we try to leave the encampment. They give us barely enough food to survive; men give up and die on these trips!"

"I'll never give up!" came the answer. "Somehow, I'll have my freedom!" There was a conviction in the harsh whisper that defied reality. And so, a spark of hope was rekindled in Finn. With the passing of the years, he had come to realize that Cormac's words in the slave market were born from the desperation of the moment. He remembered snatches of conversation overheard from the Baltimore men captured with them: none had heard of escape from North African slavery. Focusing on his beloved camels had insulated him from the overwhelming despair so common to slaves. Even Thaddeus had lapsed into lethargy during the past few months.

At night, lying beside the rogue jamal, he began to visualize again the scenes he had often described to the naga during their marches. He saw waves crashing against the rocky shore beyond the harbor and rock houses with sod roofs on the green hillside above the docks. He visualized the vegetable garden behind their little house, with its stone fence and creaky gate. He remembered Bran screaming for help because the geese were nipping her. Memories flooded back and he smiled in the darkness, imagining what it would be like to see his brother and sister. He had almost given up, but the black man's relentless focus on freedom gave him hope again.

The morning after they arrived in Tunis, there was only time for a whispered farewell before the slaves were led away toward the city gates. Head held proudly as ever, the manacled giant walked away without a backward glance.

11

I T HAPPENED A YEAR later.

The caravan was two days from Bilma, winding its way through the sand hills, when the sky suddenly darkened and a monstrous storm descended without warning. Sandstorms were not unusual, but the practiced eyes of the Arabs usually spotted the cloud build-up several hours in advance and overseers would direct the slaves to bring the enormous herd of camels together in a great mass for protection. But this time the storm blew in so fast the beasts were still strung out in a long line; there was only time to get them down on their knees as howling wind and blinding sand struck. Arabs and slaves alike huddled against camels to escape the force of the wind.

After getting his animals down, Finn crawled on hands and knees to the jamal and crouched beside it, pressing his face into its side for protection from the scouring sand that felt like needles piercing any exposed flesh. He could feel the animal's body buffeted by blasts of wind and he began to think about taking the pack off to relieve it of some wind resistance. Having loaded and unloaded camels hundreds of times, he was intimately familiar with the lashings and could loosen them with his eyes closed, but he was fearful of the load blowing away in the storm. If it were lost, there was a good chance the enraged overseers would kill him to protect themselves from the owner.

A hurricane-strength gust of wind, which actually caused the jamal to sway sideways against him, finally decided the Irishman. He pulled the blue cap down over his eyes for protection and rose to his knees, reaching for the straps holding the camel's load. Using them as anchors, he got to his feet, buffeted by shocks of wind that threatened to tear him away from the animal. He had barely loosened one of the knots, when the bale of cloth under it was ripped away by a burst of wind and flew off. Once the load was loosened, other parcels began work free in the wind and disappear into the whiteout like specks of foam in a storm at sea. In less than two minutes the entire load had been lost, although the lashings, still tied together, whipped about in the air like frenzied snakes.

Stunned by the abrupt disappearance of the load, Finn sank back down along the camel. He was doomed. If not beaten to death, he would be left behind, so severely whipped that the jackals and vultures would make short work of him.

He felt a hand on his arm. He raised the cloth cap to his forehead and cupped both hands around his eyes. Squinting against the blizzard of sand, he saw a man in a white robe squatting beside him. Oddly, his robe wasn't blowing in the gale and his brown eyes were wide open, despite the blinding sand. With a start, Finn recognized him as the same man who'd brought him the cup of water when he was close to death.

"Take the camel and escape." The words were spoken quietly, but he could hear them as clearly as if they were sitting in a quiet room, rather than in the middle of a deafening sirocco. Further, there was no mistaking it as anything but a command. The brown eyes bored into his. "Now," the voice said firmly; then the man was gone.

It was insane to go into the desert in this storm, but he didn't hesitate. He had no idea of where to go, nor how far he could get before the storm abated. If it wasn't far enough, the mercenaries would surely hunt him down and kill him, or he would simply die of thirst.

But there had been no mistaking the command, and the words of the big slave came to him.

"I'll have my freedom."

While these thoughts were racing through his mind, a heavy blow from above drove him to the ground. He wondered whether the jamal had actually been blown over on top of him but discovered it was one of the large water bags that had been lashed to the camel. The bag had been nearly emptied the night before, but if rationed there was enough water left to sustain a single person for several days. Clutching the animal's hair for stability, he rose again and untied all the lashings except one. This he fastened with a loose knot around the jamal's neck. The others he released to the fury of the wind.

Thaddeus. He had to get the Scotsman. Crawling back along the line of camels, he counted five. The next one would be Thaddeus' lead naga, a wise old beast that had been with the older man for the last two trips. There was no use calling, so he scrambled back to her and felt the handler's two legs. Wisely, Thaddeus had stretched out to keep the lowest profile to the wind; he probably had his face pressed into the naga's soft stomach hair. Finn pulled sharply on one leg, but there was no response. Maybe the man had passed out. He crawled forward and thumped the Scotsman's back, but as he did his hand brushed something hard and he forced his eyes open. In the gloom of swirling sand he saw a large, wooden box lying on the slave's shoulders and head. It must have blown off the camel's load onto Thaddeus.

"No!" Finn screamed, as he rose to his knees and tried to lift the box from Thaddeus. It had taken both of them to lift it onto the naga; it was the only thing she'd been carrying this trip. Straining against the wind, he finally managed to tip the box to one side and dropped to his knees beside the Scotsman. Rolling him gently over, the Irishman cradled Thaddeus, feeling blood running onto his arms from the great head wound.

"Thaddeus, wake up! We've got to escape in the storm," he yelled, bending close to the man's face. "Wake up! We must go!" his voice trailed off into a sob. The Scotsman's eyes fluttered open and he peered at Finn, mouth moving. The young man bent down so his ear was against Thaddeus' mouth.

"You go, lad. I'm done for; knew I should have lashed that box tighter this morning ..." The voice trailed off and the eyes started to close, only to fly open and fix Finn with a penetrating stare. "Find your brother and sister and take them home to the green hills of Ireland. Someday, sail to Lochinver and tell my family I thought of them every day ..." he said clearly. His eyes closed and he went limp as life left his body.

"I will," promised the Irishman, tears streaming down his face.

Finn lowered Thaddeus' head gently to the sand and started back to the jamal. There was no telling how long the storm would last and he felt the urgent need to escape. Reaching the big camel, he lashed himself and the water bag to the rope around its neck. Bending close to the large head, he put his face right against its ear and gave the command to rise. Nothing happened. The jamal, hunkered down in the storm, had no intention of getting to its feet. Finn tried again, speaking all kinds of soothing words into the animal's ear against the howling wind. Nothing.

"It's time to go. We'll both be free. Don't you want to see the wild desert again?" the handler yelled above the tumult. "I want to see those green hills I've told you about. I want to see the ocean again. If we stay here, we'll both die: they'll kill me for losing the load and you for food. It's time to go!"

Finn thought he felt a vibration in the jamal's neck as though it had rumbled in response to his voice, but he couldn't be sure. He shouted the command in its ear again, against the deafening sound of the wind. For a moment nothing happened. Then, just as he was about to give up, there was movement and the great beast was on its feet, braced against the wind!

Secured to the animal by the lashing, and clutching its neck with one hand, the Irishman somehow guided it off the caravan trail and began traversing a great dune to the west. In such conditions, a camel would normally have resisted and gone to its knees, but miraculously the great jamal kept plodding forward, half dragging Finn into the brunt of the wind, which instantly obliterated their tracks. On and on they went, the Irishman's cap tied across his eyes like a blindfold to protect them from the driving sand, free arm bent across his face for more protection. Finn willed himself to keep moving forward; one hand locked onto the jamal's neck. If he fell, he knew his weight on the lashing would cause the camel to stop and settle. Distance was his only defense against searching mercenaries once the storm was over.

Hours later, at the bottom of a great hill where the wind was slightly blocked, Finn could go no further. He pulled on the lashing and shouted a command that came out as a croak from sand-battered lips. The jamal seemed to understand and sank to its knees. He collapsed beside it, face jammed into its side, oblivious to the roaring wind. Sometime later, he woke to complete silence. Overhead, millions of stars glittered and a sliver moon shone low on the horizon. The storm was over. Sleep overtook him again.

12

Conditioned by years of routine, the Irishman woke as a thin band of orange appeared on the eastern horizon. Almost unconsciously, he was on his feet and loosening the water skin. To his consternation, it was lighter than he remembered and a stain across the bottom confirmed his fear: somehow a leak had sprung and nearly all the precious fluid was gone! There were no more than a few swallows. He allowed himself a small sip and reattached the container to his back, tying the bottom off to prevent more leakage.

Going to the great camel, he spent many minutes talking to it about their escape and its perseverance during the storm. Rumbling noises emerged from its throat as though it understood every word and was answering him. Finally, he hoisted himself onto its back and gave the order to rise. The jamal obediently gained its feet and turned to look back at its passenger. Never, in all the months they had worked together, had the animal carried a human. The handler had always walked beside it.

"It's all right," said Finn. "You're a lot stronger than I and I need to conserve strength because I have practically no water."

He gave a gentle nudge with his knees and lightly flipped the free end of the lashing on the jamal's head to start it forward. They headed northwest: away from Bilma to the south and the caravan route to the east. The Irishman knew their chances of survival in the vast wasteland were miniscule, but dying as a free man was infinitely preferable to being whipped to death as a slave. In spite of the bleak terrain stretching to the horizon on every side, he was filled with exhilaration. Regardless of what happened, he had taken charge of his destiny and freed himself from slavery.

But had he really been responsible for the escape Finn wondered, as the hours went by. Without the stranger's appearance, he would have simply remained beside his camel until the storm ended. He thought of the huge black slave striding away to the gates of Tunis like a conquering general about to enter the city. That man would have used the storm to escape without being told. The Irishman realized he had almost succumbed to the numbing hopelessness so common to caravan slaves. Even with the inspiration of the giant, it had taken intervention by the strange man in white to direct him to leave the caravan. He was free now, but he must guard against the tyranny of despair as he faced the impossible odds of the desert. As long as there was life in his body, he had to persevere.

Used to scant rations, and relieved of the necessity to walk, the Irishman made the best use of his scant water over the next few days. He allowed himself only the smallest sip at dawn and dark, but at length, the precious fluid was gone and he was reduced to chewing on the bag for any moisture trapped in the leather. His body began to weaken rapidly when the water ran out.

By the eighth day, he was semi-conscious and no longer guiding the jamal; an unrelenting grip on its hair was all that kept him from pitching off. Only when the camel stopped of its own accord at dark and settled to the ground, did Finn allow himself to fall beside it. The next morning, it was all he could do to drag himself onto the beast before lapsing again into a stupor. The jamal rose and went forward as though it knew its master couldn't utter the command. It fared better than Finn, because it had drunk its fill at the last oasis, but before long it, too, would need food and water.

During the morning of the 11th day, the sky suddenly darkened and there was an intense cloudburst for 10 minutes. The pouring rain roused Finn from delirium and he raised his face to the sky, mouth wide open. The downpour was so heavy that both he and the camel actually got several swallows of the lifesaving liquid. He even managed to hold out the shredded water bag to let it become soaked. The effect of the water was dramatic: his head cleared and energy surged through his body. From the position of the sun, he realized that the camel was still moving to the northwest, but very slowly now. The jamal was close to the end of its reserves. Endless hills of sand stretched in every direction without a glimpse of green.

Three days later, Finn had chewed every ounce of moisture from the remaining scrap of the water bag. Both he and the camel were suffering intensely from dehydration. The animal was beginning to stumble; its rider knew the end was near for both of them.

13

A S SHADOWS LENGTHENED, THE jamal finally sank to its knees in a swale between two dunes and Finn toppled onto the sand. He staggered up and crawled to the great head. "You've done a good job to get this far, old friend," he mumbled "and you've been my best companion and protector. Remember how you bit Abbud when he was trying to kill me?" There was a faint rumble from the beast's throat and the man tried to chuckle, but all that came out was rasping breath. "At least they can't kill either of us now." He tried to laugh at the irony of the situation, but his throat was too dry.

The jamal's head slowly sank to the ground and Finn collapsed on his back beside him, staring with bloodshot eyes at the stars emerging in the deepening black above. He wondered if Cormac and Bran were still alive. He thought about his mother and whispered an apology for making her have to go on without him. He pictured the green hills above Baltimore, imagining the sun reflecting off small waves in the harbor. He was about to close his eyes when movement some yards away caught his attention. Fearing hyenas, he weakly raised himself to one elbow and stared down the swale between the dunes. At first he saw nothing but, determined to fight to the end against wild animals, he forced himself to his feet and peered into the growing dark. There it was again: something moved in the shadows.

He staggered a few steps forward and focused on the spot. Suddenly, he saw a man standing a few yards away. Something about him seemed familiar, but it was the large hawk perched on his outstretched arm that caught Finn's attention. He had seen falconers flying their birds outside the walls of Tunis: they always wore a gauntlet to protect their flesh from the razor sharp talons of their birds, but there was no heavy leather glove, or gauntlet, on the man's outstretched forearm. As Finn stared, the man gestured with his free hand to follow him and started walking slowly down the swale.

As a seasoned veteran of desert travel, Finn was well aware of mirages. Many times, he and the other slaves had seen the tempting spectacle of palm trees and water just ahead, knowing full well the next oasis was many miles away. He knew the image of a falconer could somehow be transmitted from a far-off camp, although he had never seen a mirage in the evening. As he stood, swaying with dizziness, the image of the black slave striding toward the walls of Tunis flashed through his mind. He determined that while there was life in his body he could not give up: somehow he knew he had to follow the man.

Like a drunk, Finn shambled along the swale behind the falconer, who was growing dimmer by the minute. With great effort he focused on the man's white robe as night fell and only brilliant starlight kept him faintly in view. Suddenly, there was motion as the hawk rose on beating wings high into the air and, barely visible, began to soar around them in a wide circle.

"Follow the hawk." The words carried clearly across the yards separating them. Then the man turned and extended his arm, pointing at the bottom of the sand hill to their right.

"Water," he said, and vanished.

It took Finn a few more minutes to reach the spot where he thought the man had been standing when he last saw him. Ahead, nothing but sand and rock greeted him; it must have been a mirage after all. Bitterly disappointed, he stood for a moment gathering strength to return to the camel. Without warning, a huge figure loomed at him out of the dark! Throwing up his arms, Finn staggered backward, only to realize it was the jamal. The great beast brushed by him at a shuffling trot, veered to the right behind the end of the sand hill and disappeared as though swallowed by the earth.

Finn staggered after him and came to the edge of a wide ravine that had been hidden from sight. At the bottom, water gushed from the ground to form a pool, glittering in the starlight, nearly five feet across. The jamal was already on its knees, slurping up great mouthfuls of the lifesaving liquid; in seconds, Finn was on his stomach beside him doing the same. After a long time they slept, the great camel a few feet from the water and Finn pressed close against its warm body.

The next day was spent resting and drinking. Finn bathed in the pool, scouring years of accumulated grime from his skin and feeling almost as refreshed as if he'd had a meal. He tried to repair the shredded water bag, but he had chewed off so much of it in his desperate search for liquid that he could only fashion a container good for a few swallows. The water from the spring would sustain the camel for quite a while, but the handler knew they both needed food. At dawn the following morning, both man and beast drank deeply from the pool and set out. As the jamal crossed the first hill, the Irishman turned his head for a last glimpse of the pool. Nothing but rocky soil met his gaze.

14

THE ENORMOUS RED ORB of the sun had just cleared the horizon when Finn first spotted the hawk. High above the desert, it was effortlessly riding the thermals about a quarter of a mile to the west. Memory of the falconer's words came flooding back and he nudged the camel away from the north westerly heading and toward the bird. For the next four days, the hawk appeared in the sky from morning to evening, circling on the wind, always at the same distance and always to the west.

In spite of Finn's careful rationing, at the end of the second day from the pool his water was gone. He used the trick of sucking on pebbles to stem his thirst, but by the fourth evening he was again suffering terribly from dehydration and lack of food. Normally, the jamal would stop on its own as the sun fell below the horizon, but on this day it didn't. Finn's command to kneel, spoken barely above a whisper, had no effect: on went the jamal through the night, as a sliver moon rose in the midst of a million stars. The Irishman had tied the strap around the camel's neck to one wrist. If he fell off, he wasn't going to be left behind: the jamal was his only hope. Hours dragged on, the rider barely conscious, his fingers locked in the animal's hair.

Just before dawn, the camel stopped so abruptly that Finn's grip was broken and he pitched forward through the air, landing with a great splash in three feet of water! Spluttering and gasping, he got to his knees and pushed his entire face into the water, swallowing as fast as he was able. The jamal beside him, muzzle buried in the water, was doing the very same thing. Later, the Irishman had no memory of untying the strap from his wrist or dragging himself out of the water to collapse on the bank.

15

A BLOW TO THE RIBS jolted Finn to consciousness. The eastern horizon was aflame with orange, and he instinctively raised an arm to protect his head from the handle of a slaver's whip: oversleeping had severe consequences. Then memory rushed back as he saw the lake a few feet away. It was several acres in size, surrounded by a large area of grass and palm trees. On the opposite shore there was a cluster of low-spread tents, and on his side grazed a herd of camels.

Another blow brought his eyes to bear on a figure in blue standing over him. Dark eyes stared menacingly from a face hidden by a band of cloth attached to a black turban. One hand held a lance, the butt of which had struck Finn, the other hand gripped a shining sword. Careful to make no sudden move, Finn slowly rose to face the Tuareg. Swaying on unsteady feet, he was a pitiful sight: an emaciated body clad in the remains of filthy, tattered robe. Although his skin was almost as dark as an Arab, brown eyes and the disheveled blond hair streaming down his back clearly identified him as a foreigner. There was a long moment of silence as the man studied him.

"How did you find us?" said a deep voice in Arabic.

"I didn't," said Finn. "My camel must have scented the water and brought me here."

"Where did you come from?"

"The caravan route. A storm hit just before we reached Bilma, and I escaped."

"Bilma," the man's eyes widened. "That's many, many days travel from here."

"We should have died," acknowledged the slave, "but for one cloudburst and a small pool of water four days ago."

"There's no water between here and the caravans," said the other flatly. Finn had no answer.

"You're a slave." It was a statement not a question.

"Yes. I'm a camel handler."

"Good. We need a slave to take care of the herd." Finn suddenly staggered and fell to his knees. He tried to rise, but his legs had finally given out and he could only sit and stare abjectly up at the man.

"When did you last eat?" The voice was slightly softer. The Tuareg have high regard for bravery; it was apparent the emaciated figure before him had survived a great ordeal in his bid for freedom.

"The day before I left the caravan."

Finn felt himself fading. The water he had drunk the night before had refreshed him enormously but his body was now in desperate need of nourishment.

"I'll send food."

The man turned on his heel and strode away. He knew the fair-haired slave was no threat to the camp and that there was a good chance he'd die before they could revive him. Reaching the tents, he called out instructions and within minutes, two women were hurrying around the lake with food. When they reached Finn, he had toppled to one side, unconscious. The iron willpower, which had kept him alive for days, was gone. The women gasped at his skeletal appearance and were barely able to rouse him. One had to prop him up while the other fed him a few spoonfuls of millet porridge, followed by several bits of camel cheese. When he passed out again, they dragged him into the shade of the nearby palm trees, covered him with a light robe and left a skin of water at his side.

When the women returned that evening, the skin was empty and he woke to their touch, although he still needed to be held up to eat. After feeding him more porridge and cheese, the women covered his body with a warm robe, left another skin of water and returned to the tents. They were careful to give a wide berth to the enormous camel nearby, which made menacing sounds while they tended Finn.

Under the care of the two women, the Irishman slowly began to recover. Within 48 hours, he was able to walk, though he never strayed far from the water's edge. They often found him dozing against his kneeling camel or plopped in the lake, pouring handfuls of water over his head and shoulders. They smiled to see him take a mouthful of water, slosh it around and spit it out in a long stream back into the lake. It was clear that the proximity and abundance of water was a magnet he couldn't resist.

On the fourth morning he wandered among the camels, touching and speaking to each one. The boys charged with watching the animals had already discovered the temper of the great jamal. They knew it was not to be toyed with; however, they watched the stranger spend many minutes with it each day, stroking its neck and talking in an odd language. After Finn walked through the herd, the boys reported to the camp that every Tuareg camel responded to the blonde stranger in the same way: rumbling in response to his quiet voice and often leaning into him for more attention.

One day soon thereafter, the blue-clad warrior approached Finn as he was leading some camels to water. Without being told, the slave had automatically fallen into the role of caretaker. The night before, he had positioned the jamal at the edge of the herd and slept beside it in his customary place, covered with the robe the women had given him. Any disturbance among the animals would have wakened him instantly.

"I will no longer send the women. You may come to the outside of my tent for meals," said the Tuareg. "Otherwise, you are to stay on this side of the oasis and tend the camels. You will have them saddled and ready whenever we need them and care for them when we return." Finn nodded his understanding and bowed.

"One more thing." The words were slow and deliberate. "We are not like those stupid mercenaries from Tunis: we're children of the desert. If you try to escape, we'll track you down, cut out your eyes and leave you to die."

As the man strode away, the Irishman knew this was no idle threat: the Tuareg leader would do exactly as he'd described if the slave fled. However, that night as he stared at the millions of twinkling stars above, Finn realized his situation had drastically changed. A caravan slave lived totally at the whim of the overseers; he could be been beaten and left for dead at any time. The desert leader, on the contrary, had made it clear the decision to live or die now rested completely with Finn.

16

A s the days turned into weeks and weeks into months, the pattern of Finn's life assumed a pleasant routine. During the day he looked after the camels, making sure they were watered, tending to bites from the occasional fracas or other mishap, and gentling the sometimes-rambunctious warhs. At night he would sleep alongside his own beast, confident the jamal would stir at any sign of danger.

Although the herd contained a few pack animals, it was mostly comprised of the more slender riding camels. The Irishman knew these animals could run at great speed for short distances* and could sustain a rapid pace** for more than an hour. The Tuareg used them for traveling, hunting the fleet desert antelope, and for raids on the distant trade routes. From time to time, a party of men would be gone for many days on such an attack, usually returning with captured camels carrying plunder, an event warranting a happy celebration among the tents.

*Up to 40 mph.
**25 mph.

Finn estimated that the camp numbered about 70 men, women, and children. In short order, the latter began paying daily visits to the stranger with the long blonde hair and friendly eyes. He would sit with them and tell stories about far-away places. Later, they would stand in a little cluster, watching the camels crowd around him, rumbling and bumping to gain his attention as he talked in a strange language. At night, in the tents, the children would swear to their families that Finn and the camels were conversing!

The Irishman never tired of the lake. Fed by underground springs, it was cool and refreshing in the blistering heat. After the camels had been watered, he loved to wade out and sit chest-deep, reveling in the feel of the moisture against his skin. The kids would crowd the bank, calling for him to come out and tell them a story. When he finally waded back, they would watch warily, until they saw him reach down to direct the first great splash of water at them, then run shrieking and laughing out of range!

In the morning and evening, he took meals on a small carpet outside the entrance to the leader's tent. Gradually, his body filled out from a nutritious diet of cheese, dates, millet, and yogurt. Gone were the emaciated features: his bleached hair and hawk-like face, with its slightly hooked nose, gave him a striking appearance. As he approached the tent for supper late one afternoon, he was surprised to find the Tuareg leader sitting outside on a large carpet.

"Sit down; we'll eat together," he said, gesturing for Finn to join him. One of the women who had originally cared for the slave began to bring out food. As they ate, his owner questioned Finn about the camel herd: Were any beasts ailing, and what was he doing about it; how were the new warhs growing; and were any nagas ready to deliver young?

"The children say you talk to the animals and they answer you," said the older man after these details had been discussed.

"When I talk to the camels I speak English, which the children don't understand," Finn said with a smile. "I started doing it years ago on the caravans before I learned Arabic. As you know, the animals sometimes rumble when they're stroked."

"Yes, but they also say the animals crowd around when you approach."

"They do," said Finn simply. He paused. "I can't explain it but they seem to know I mean no harm and that I won't mistreat them."

The warrior sat silently for a few minutes. The children had reported his new slave's remarkable affinity for the camels and it had given him an idea, but he wanted to wait a while before acting.

From that day forward, the leader joined Finn for at least one meal a day. Their talk began to focus on specific young camels the slave was gentling and what he felt their potential might be. It was during these conversations that Finn started to become aware of movement inside the tent while they talked. At first he thought it was his imagination or a trick of the breeze, but he soon realized it never happened when he ate alone. He knew that the brazier on which the food was prepared was located far back from the tent entrance, so cooking couldn't be causing the disturbance. The woman serving them slipped in and out of the tent with a slight rustle, but the subtle sounds went on long after she was gone. The man sitting beside him appeared to take no notice until one day, several months after the slave had arrived, the distinct sound of muffled laughter came from just inside the dwelling.

"Silence!" barked the warrior, turning to stare at the tent. Utter quiet followed. He turned back to the food, shaking his head.

"It's my children," he said. "They want to hear what we're talking about."

Finn thought that strange, because the children watched him work with camels every day. They observed everything he was describing to the other man, so why did these particular kids need to hear him tell about it?

"What about the one with the white spot on her cheek, when will she be ready to carry a rider?" said the leader, staring with interest at his slave. He was finally ready to put the children's reports to the test.

"About a month," said the Irishman. "I think she's going to be fast, perhaps one of your best runners."

"But her disposition seems unruly; none of the men can get close to her. Usually we resort to force with such an animal."

"Ah," Finn smiled. "No need for that. It's only because she doesn't understand the joy of running with a rider! After another month of gaining strength, she'll surprise you."

"I hope you're right," said the Tuareg as he rose to leave, but his tone reflected his doubt. A month later, the slave led the naga with the white spot to the front of the leader's tent. Slender and long legged, with a light brown coat, she was gentle under his hand. When the blue-robed figure emerged from the tent and approached, however, she threw up her head and spun away, running off for a few yards. Finn, having dropped the lead rope when she bolted, made no move to go after the alarmed animal.

"I thought you said she'd be ready," said the Tuareg.

"She is, but since you've not given me permission to ride, I haven't been able to show her what we want." By now, a group of men and children had gathered to watch the proceedings.

"You know how to train these animals in addition to taming them?" the black eyes above the veil widened in surprise.

"I've been working with camels every day for years," the slave said calmly.

"But this isn't a pack camel. She's bred to ride and run!"

"It makes no difference," said Finn. "I just need to show her what to do and how much she's going to enjoy it." There was a long silence as the leader stared at the Irishman, torn between disbelief and recognition of the man's special abilities.

"I'll give you one chance," he said at last. "Fail, and you'll never see the back of a camel again!" The slave nodded and turned toward the naga.

Everyone could hear him talking in a strange language as he approached her, and the children poked each other to affirm what they had been telling the adults all along. A number of women had joined the others, and a small crowd watched silently as the bearded stranger picked up the lead rope and slowly walked to the animal. Reaching out, he gently held her head in both hands and looked straight at her, murmuring softly. After a moment, the watchers heard him laugh and give the command to kneel. When the camel was settled he moved to its side, hands continuously stroking her, and with one smooth motion slid onto her back. The naga turned her head to look back, as though wondering what he was doing there. Another word and she stood.

What happened next brought a murmur of astonishment from the assembled people. Although the lead rope remained loose in the slave's hand, and there was no apparent signal, the camel suddenly whirled and sped off across the oasis at top speed! And could she run! The startled warriors exchanged looks, shaking their heads in amazement; they had never seen an untrained camel perform like this. Faint crinkles at the leader's eyes betrayed the beginning of a smile under the veil. After two hundred yards, the animal spun and raced back, stopping just in front of the headman. Finn gave the command to kneel and slid off, handing over the lead after rubbing the camel's head and speaking a few words to it.

"She'll behave now," he said.

Sure enough, when the Tuareg was aboard she got to her feet at his command and turned in response to pressure from the lead. A nudge of his feet sent her running toward the edge of the oasis with breathtaking speed. Upon his return, the leader slid to the ground and handed the lead to his slave. The children's stories about the man were true.

"You have my permission to ride the camels at any time." Despite the gruff tone the Tuareg adopted for the benefit of the gathered men, his eyes gleamed with pleasure.

17

As Finn turned to lead the naga back to the herd, his eyes caught movement at the back of the gathered observers. Three figures were hurrying toward the tents, each clad in a black robe, faces hidden by veils. They walked close together, heads almost touching, as though in serious discussion. They disappeared among the dwellings, but the Irishman thought it odd they had left so quickly.

Later, when the slave approached the tent for the evening meal, he found his owner waiting. Among the dishes was a bowl with strips of roasted antelope covered in a delicious, spicy sauce, the first such food Finn had ever been offered. For a while, the silence was only broken by the sound of chewing, as the two men attacked the food. Finally, licking his fingers and replacing his veil, the Tuareg turned to the younger man.

"Where did you learn such skill with the camels?"

"I worked with them day and night on the caravans."

"I know," said the other, "but all the caravan slaves do the same. You're different."

"I've always loved animals," Finn said. "Even the geese at home. They would bite my little sister, and she would scream for me to save her, for they never attacked me."

"She was lucky to have you." For the first time in their acquaintance, the warrior chuckled, leaning back on one elbow in a relaxed posture.

"She's not so lucky now," said the slave grimly.

"Also sold as a slave." It was a statement, not a question.

"Yes, and my older brother as well. In fact, most of our village was brought to Tunis and sold on the auction block one by one."

"Where do you come from?" inquired the leader.

"A beautiful island, as green as green can be, surrounded by the sea. It's called Ireland."

"Ah, I've heard of it."

"You've heard of Ireland?" Finn stared in surprise.

"I spent some time at the Pasha's court in my youth, and learned about other countries," said the warrior. "Before an indiscretion required me to take leave quickly."

"An indiscretion?"

"One of his daughters and I wanted to marry. When he refused, I was obliged to steal her and flee."

"You stole her?" Finn gaped in astonishment.

"Yes, but at a cost." the voice became harsh and the Tuareg raised himself to a sitting position. "His men caught us outside the city and one of my brothers was killed while covering our escape. A cousin was captured and tortured to death in an attempt to discover the location of our camp. They didn't break him, but for several years the Pasha's men never stopped trying to find us. At times they came close, but our desert comrades always brought word and we were able to move away."

"You must have little regard for the Pasha," said the slave.

"None. But he's dead and my brother-in-law now occupies the throne." The curt tone indicated the end of discussion on that topic.

"There was an old naga that probably saved my life on the first caravan," said the Irishman, returning to the safer subject of animals. He recounted desperately clinging to the camel for support during the first days, when falling could have cost his life, and described mumbling to her about home and family.

"Her rumblings were like responses to my ramblings," he said with a laugh, "and kept me talking rather than giving up. With the help of another slave, I managed to survive the work of those first weeks but I never stopped talking to the camels. The animals seem to respond to English."

"It's more than the sound. They sense something in you that they don't feel with other people," said his owner. "I've only seen it once. When I was a youth, there was an old man in our camp who had the same gift. The camels crowded around like children whenever he got near them. My father had ridden with him in battle and told me he never guided his mount: the camel instinctively knew what to do. Father said the man would be charging an enemy, lance poised for the kill, when the camel would suddenly change direction to avoid an attacker coming from the blind side." After a moment's reflection, he added dryly, "That warrior lived to a ripe old age."

18

BACK WITH THE HERD, Finn wondered what it must have been like for the young couple to live on the run, never sure if the Pasha's men had slipped past their desert brethren and were about to attack. She must have been very special for the Tuareg to defy the odds and spirit her away. The slave was certain neither of the two women who served meals was the wife, because their demeanor reflected the role of servants or slaves. He knew practically nothing about the mother and children inside the walls of the tent. One day, he decided to try and learn more.

Returning from a short training ride on a young warh, he found the usual gathering of children waiting. They never seemed to tire of hearing him talk to the animals and when there was time, still loved to sit around him on the ground to hear stories of his native land. Occasionally, one of the young girls would be carrying a baby, so Finn would oblige the wee one's curiosity by getting close and letting him or her finger his yellow beard.

Today, he shooed the warh away and settled to the ground, surrounded by his young audience. Once again he described the actions of a whale in the ocean, huge body emerging from the depths to blow a cloud of spume before diving again, great flukes lifted high in the air. As always, every eye was riveted on him, as the children tried to imagine a scene totally alien to their environment. When he finished, he stared at them.

"Your leader must be a great warrior," he said with a smile.

"Jugurtha is the greatest fighter in all the desert," piped up a boy about six. "No one dares challenge him, especially the men from Tunis! He'd cut their heads off like this!" The boy swung one arm around his head with a violent motion.

"Ohhh," Finn drew back his head, eyes wide. "His wife and family are very safe with such a man. She must be beautiful."

"The most beautiful woman in the desert," said one of the little girls simply.

"No doubt his sons are as brave as he," said the slave.

This brought a gale of laughter from the cluster of children.

"He has no sons," shrilled another boy, as though Finn had lost his mind. "He has three daughters!"

19

From that time forward, a subtle game began during meals outside Jugurtha's tent. When eating alone, Finn squatted or sat by the bowls of food as before, with his back to the tent. But now he was listening intently for any sound from inside. At first there seemed to be nothing but, after a few days, he became aware of an intermittent rustle, so soft it was almost undetectable. By tilting his head slightly to the left, as though studying the food in front of him, he was just able to see the entrance to the tent from the corner of his eye. One day he caught a slight movement of the flap covering the entry. He realized the kids were at it again: watching him eat.

When Jugurtha was present, the noise of their conversation caused the spies to become slightly bolder. By sitting to the right of the leader and positioning himself at a slight angle, Finn could actually see the doorway; it was easy to glance up innocently when one of the serving women ducked out to bring food. One evening he was certain he glimpsed a figure standing just inside as the servant brushed through the opening.

As the days went by, the slave concluded that the leader's young daughters were spying on him at almost every meal. He had noticed that no girls older than seven were permitted to visit him at the herd, although there were several boys much older than that who often helped with the camels. He decided the Tuaregs didn't want female children above a certain age to associate with a slave; therefore, the girls hiding in the tent must be at least eight. They weren't allowed to be in his presence, but they could get very close when he was eating!

The game went on. Finn began to adopt an attitude of complete indifference to his surroundings when he ate alone. He started talking to himself in English, humming or singing what Irish songs he could remember, even smacking his lips loudly as he ate and commenting in Arabic about the excellence of the food, as though he had a companion. He showed no interest in the tent, gazed off at the lake and prolonged every meal as long as he could.

The strategy worked. Bit by bit the unseen watchers grew braver. One day when the slave tipped his head back in a feigned laugh over an incident with a warh, which he had described out loud to himself, he saw the covering was being held open at least three inches. So successful was his ruse, the child never realized he'd caught sight of the opening!

Eating with the leader, the Irishman began to be amused because he realized that Jugurtha knew what was going on. So long as the children were quiet and discreet, their father tolerated the slight sounds, thinking that his slave didn't hear them or, if he did, paid them no attention. Finn did nothing to dispel this notion, engaging in protracted conversations about various camels with which he was working. The young girls became so brave he could actually catch snatches of whispering from time to time.

At last it was time to spring his trap. The slave waited for an evening when the Tuareg men were away on a hunt. Arriving at the tent, he began his usual talking and antics while he ate. The sun was low in the west, turning the lake to gold in front of him. No sooner had he sat down than little sounds from inside revealed the girls had crept to the doorway. He lingered over the food, describing in Arabic to himself a hilarious incident between a naga and the old jamal, which had allegedly occurred that afternoon. His performance was a tour de force, and he clearly heard giggling from inside the doorway as the cover was pushed out almost a foot. With no warning, Finn spun around and stared straight into the opening.

"I see you," he announced with a big grin. In the light of the lowering sun, he saw three shocked faces, stacked one above the other, unveiled but framed in black head cloths. An instant later the cover was pulled shut, accompanied by muffled shrieks of laughter. The slave sat for a minute, dumbfounded. These were no children. The daughters of the Tuareg leader were beautiful young women!

20

"THE TWO YOUNG JAMALS you have been working with per-formed well on the hunt. In fact, they outran a small band of antelope and we were able to bring down three quite easily," Jugurtha said as he settled beside Finn the morning after he returned.

"I'm glad they pleased you; they should be even faster when they gain more strength."

"I understand you gave my children quite a start." The words were spoken quietly but the Irishman thought he detected a touch of amusement, and the father's choice of words indicated he had not been told just how much Finn had seen.

"I'd become aware the children were curious about me," he said, deliberately using the Tuareg's term for his daughters, "so I decided to give them a full view of my face. Thinking themselves undetected, I believe it was quite a surprise!"

"That it was," said the other with a soft laugh. "I think they've learned their lesson!" From that time on the activities at the tent door ceased, but a few weeks later Finn began to notice a subtle change in the village when he showed up for meals. Previously, at those times there was little or no activity among the tents because people were usually inside. Now, no matter when he appeared, there was almost always a small cluster of veiled women in black robes standing under a group of palm trees beside Jugurtha's tent. They seemed to be in deep conversation, but he felt their eyes discreetly watching him.

21

A YEAR AFTER ARRIVING AT the oasis, Finn was directed to accompany a hunting party on a long trip to distant mountains where game abounded. Extra animals were needed to carry back meat and to serve as supplementary mounts for the hunters. The slave's skillful management of the additional camels allowed the hunters to have fresh mounts to continue after antelope when their camels became winded. The strategy was so successful that Finn became a regular addition to hunting parties. On one such trip six months later, his life was changed forever.

It happened in a remote mountain valley. Leaving the camp early that morning, Jugurtha was accompanied by his slave on a young naga, leading a speedy jamal as an extra mount. Following a narrow canyon, they emerged into a hitherto undiscovered basin containing a small herd of ibex. Giving chase, the Tuareg chief quickly brought down two of the animals with his bow before the rest scampered up the rocky slopes. One of the ibex was not dead and Jugurtha leaped from his camel to dispatch it with his lance. The deed accomplished, he dropped the weapon and bent over the carcass to disembowel it with his knife.

Finn had watched the chase from a distance and was pleased with the performance of his owner's mount. He approached to within 50 yards of Jugurtha when a mounted camel appeared at his side. Thinking it was one of the other hunters he glanced over, eager to explain how well their leader's mount had performed. To his astonishment, it was not a Tuareg hunter but a rider in a white robe aboard a beautiful cream-colored naga. He recognized at once the man who had held the cup of water to his lips that terrible day his first week in the desert, and who had counseled him to leave the caravan during the sandstorm. The thought flashed through his head that this may also have been the man with the hawk on his arm who led Finn and the jamal to water. The man pointed urgently at a jumble of boulders across the little valley from Jugurtha.

"Danger," he said.

Finn's eyes snapped in that direction but there was nothing except brown dirt and rock in the sunlight. When he glanced back, the rider was gone.

The camels had continued walking forward quietly, but suddenly a sense of peril filled the Irishman so strongly that he felt the hair on his arms and neck rise. He frantically scanned the hillsides to either side, but nothing was amiss. He started his mount forward at a trot, staring again at the collection of boulders the man had gestured to. All at once, a slight movement caught his eye. Finn focused intently on the area.

Suddenly, as though it materialized from thin air, a large tawny animal appeared, crouched low to the ground, staring at the man eviscerating the sheep just yards away. It blended so well with the rocks that Finn would never have seen it without the movement it made as it crept slightly forward. Whispered visits with the black slave resurfaced and he knew this was a lion. The tip of its long tail was twitching side to side and the memory of barn cats hunting sparrows at home flooded his mind: the animal was about to charge!

Dropping the jamal's lead rope, he put the naga into a dead run and screamed a warning. At the shout, Jugurtha straightened and looked behind him. His movement caused the lion to charge. There was no time for the Tuareg to grab his lance; the cat was only 30 yards away and coming so fast that it would be on him almost instantly. The warrior was no coward; he crouched with knife outstretched, determined to inflict as much damage as possible on the lion before he was overcome. The lion's yellow eyes were fixed on the man's face as it raced across the dirt. With a deafening roar it launched itself at Jugurtha, fearsome claws extended.

There was a blur of motion to the right and the hurtling body of Finn's camel appeared, smashing into the lion in mid-air just three feet from him. In a kaleidoscope of images and dust, the two animals went down. The lion rolled over and over and the naga somersaulted across the ground, throwing its rider into a patch of brush.

In a flash, the carnivore was on its feet, snarling ferociously. It leapt toward the camel, but the animal had regained its feet and was dashing away. The big cat then turned its attention to the slave flailing in the brush trying to free himself. It crouched, tail lashing, ready to spring, but a blue-clad figure suddenly appeared in front of it uttering a war cry that drew the cat's attention and caused it to charge.

Finn had given Jugurtha just enough time to snatch up his lance and get in front of the lion. With incredible speed, the cat took two steps and leapt at the Tuareg. Jugurtha, crouched before it, braced the butt of his lance against the ground. Committed to its trajectory, the cat impaled itself on the deadly weapon. The wound was fatal but the lion wasn't finished. It snapped the shaft of the lance with a swipe of a paw and turned toward the warrior with a vicious snarl, slashing at him with its claws. The man wasn't finished either: jumping back, he snatched the shining sword from his belt. As the animal crouched to leap, Jugurtha stepped forward and delivered a terrific blow to its neck with the razor-sharp blade. The cat staggered, wobbled, and fell, eyes slowly glazing over.

Finn stumbled out of the bushes to find Jugurtha leaning on his sword and breathing heavily, the dead lion at his feet.

"What happened?"

"Your intervention with the naga gave me time to recover my lance, and the lance gave me time to free the sword," said the Tuareg, gesturing at the broken shaft lodged in the cat's throat. "It was close."

"I didn't think we'd get there in time," said the Irishman, "but the naga is one of the fastest in your herd."

"Without your training, she wouldn't have been fast enough, nor would she have dared run at a lion," said the owner simply.

The naga was standing nearby, her body still quivering from the effects of the violent confrontation. Talking softly while he checked her for injury, Finn told her how proud he was of what she had done. His voice calmed her almost immediately and, having suffered no ill effects from the collision, she began to push against him for more attention. For the rest of the hunt, the Tuareg leader seemed lost in thought much of the time.

22

THE NIGHT AFTER THE hunting party returned to the oasis Jugurtha, carrying a sizeable bundle, joined Finn for the evening meal. The younger man's eyes widened at the variety of food brought out from the tent. There were several dishes of meat with differing sauces, bowls of figs, yogurt, cheese, and millet porridge—the most fare they had ever been served at one time. The two men ate leisurely, discussing the camels' performance on the trip. At length, the Tuareg adjusted his position to sit facing the slave. His face was covered again now that the eating was over.

"Many months ago you took a great chance in leaving that caravan." he said. "If they had caught you, whipping, torture, and death were in store."

"Yes."

"Your determination and that of your great jamal, brought you across the desert in conditions that would have killed most men. Indeed, when I found you that morning I didn't think you'd survive."

The slave stared at him, but made no reply.

"Our camels are better trained and faster than ever before."

"All they needed was for someone to reach out to them," said Finn.

"Perhaps. It wasn't only the *beasts* you befriended. Our children love you."

"Ahhh, the stories," smiled the handler.

"In part, but you treat them like little people and they want to be near you."

"The babies like my beard." It was all he could think of to say.

"You risked your life to save me," said Jugurtha. The statement hung in the air.

"You would have done the same for me," said the slave at last.

"I'm not so sure, but I *am* sure the lion would have had me but for you running it down. It was very close, closer than I thought at the time," he said. Once again the younger man remained silent.

"My daughters are dear to my heart," said Jugurtha. "But if I had a son, I'd want him to be like you. For saving my life, I would adopt you into my family, but it's impossible because you're not of the desert. However, I can repay the debt by giving you a new life. I declare you a free man, welcome in my tent, and invited to wear the robes and turban of a Tuareg warrior."

The wrinkling of his eyes revealed a broad smile behind the veil, as Jugurtha unwrapped the bundle and handed a blue robe and black turban to the shocked ex-slave.

23

Finn was astonished at how Jugurtha's people responded to his being freed. It seemed the leader had spoken without embellishment. The men had been secretly awed at his skill with the camels, reveling at the speed and agility of the animals after he had worked with them. The women had viewed him as a gift to their children, having been won over by reports of his gentle good humor. When word spread about what their leader had done, the now blue-clad Irishman received invitations to visit every tent.

Sitting on thick carpets, surrounded by children, he would regale the adults with tales of fishing, whales, and Ireland. Many of them, of course, knew about the harbor in Tunis but had only a vague notion of vast oceans and other lands. Whales and large fish were a source of amazement to them and the idea of a land covered with green grass and trees almost unimaginable. Only the unmarried girls were separated from these gatherings, listening from behind curtains strung across the inside of each dwelling.

The pattern was the same inside Jugurtha's tent, although it was more spacious than the others. Near the center, a sturdy pole raised the covering to almost six feet, from which it gradually sloped, propped at intervals by shorter poles, to the ground. The back extended further than the sides and was screened off to provide living quarters for the women. Finely woven Persian rugs covered the ground, making the footing plush and comfortable.

Finn now ate meals with the Tuareg couple inside their tent, beside a small brass stove. He slept on a bed of soft blankets just inside the entrance. The village children had been accurate: Jugurtha's wife Kella was beautiful. Unveiled, as were all the married women, she possessed sparkling white teeth and almond-shaped eyes set in a perfect oval face. She had a radiant smile and tender kindness, causing the new warrior to appreciate why Jugurtha had taken such risks to win her.

When Finn was in the tent, the three daughters remained on the women's side of the screen. Outside, however, it was a different matter. Now accepted as a warrior and having shaved the beard marking him a slave, the strikingly handsome Irishman began to encounter a group of eight or nine young women whenever he moved about the tents. Because they were unmarried, all of them wore black robes and were veiled after the fashion of the men. Thus disguised they were quite bold, often walking with him through the trees, or standing in a semi-circle around him to ask about his past. They wanted to hear of his capture by the pirates, his escape from the caravan, the lion attack, or any other matter they could think of. Usually, there was an older woman nearby pretending to be busy with some task, but actually watching to see that the young women were behaving properly. Only when Finn headed for the camels did the group turn back.

"Our friend has a cluster of admirers," said Jugurtha one night as he plucked a piece of cheese from the bowl in front of him.

"I know," said his wife softly.

"Do you mean the women who follow me around?" Finn broke in. "I have no idea who they are, but they ask a lot of questions."

"The better to know you, I'm sure," said the leader in a serious tone, but with the wrinkles of a grin around his eyes.

"Why would they want to know about me? I'm just a slave."

"An ex-slave," corrected the older man quickly. "A man who risked his life to save mine and who now wears the robes of a warrior."

"But surely they know my past," said the Irishman.

"Do not misunderstand the gift of freedom," said Jugurtha sharply. "For us your past is gone. You are now a member of my band and of my tent, just as though you were my son. Regardless of the color of your skin or hair, you *are* Tuareg!"

"I meant no disrespect," Finn said. "I just don't understand why the young women are so curious about me."

"No doubt, they have their reasons," said the leader obliquely. "Now, what experience do you have with the lance and sword?"

"None," said the herder simply.

"I thought as much. Tomorrow we begin your training. We'll start on foot and move to the backs of camels once you've mastered the skills. Usually mounted fighting is the most difficult to learn, but in your case I think the reverse will be true."

24

From that time on, Finn spent the first three hours of each day learning to fight with a sword. In the beginning, he and Jugurtha used sturdy three-foot sticks and practiced among the palm trees across the lake. Their only observers were the camels, who perhaps wondered what their beloved master was doing leaping around and frequently falling over his own feet. The Tuareg leader had been schooled in the use of weapons starting as a child and moved with bewildering speed and precision. He seemed to vanish whenever the Irishman lunged at him, only to appear at Finn's side with the point of the stick touching his throat.

"Feet flat, don't take steps! Slide, blade close to your body; chest forward, posture straight," the instructions came in a bewildering array. The former slave struggled to remember them as he tried to counter the other's movement.

"Use the sidestep. Don't spin, sword vertical for defense, elbows in and slightly bent," the running commentary issued from Jugurtha as he swirled around the helpless student, tapping or poking him lightly with the stick to show where a sword would have struck. In the evenings, sitting beside the glowing brazier, he would coach Finn on the mental aspects of a fight.

"Be relaxed; you will be able to react more quickly than if you're fearful and tense. Assess the physical situation around you. Where is the sun, can you use it to blind the adversary. Are there animals or structures nearby that you can back him against and press the attack? Position yourself so that one lunge can bring you in for a killing thrust. Above all, remain calm. Most fights are short because, in the initial excitement, one swordsman usually acts rashly and exposes himself to a fatal blow. Should a fight be extended, a calm demeanor will have an unsettling effect on your enemy."

Listening, with his eyes fixed on those of the older man, Finn knew this counsel came from personal experience. He understood the Tuareg was sharing every bit of wisdom he possessed to give his freed slave an edge in battle. Overwhelmed by what the man had done for him, the Irishman determined he would become the warrior-son Jugurtha never had.

As he gradually learned the feints and moves, and his own tempo increased, the former slave began to anticipate the Tuareg's motion and found the other's tactics less intimidating. Jugurtha was a wonderful teacher and never stopped encouraging him, though sometimes Finn felt the skills were beyond his abilities. Finally there came a day, after four months, when the student slipped past the master's guard with lightning speed and tapped him on the chest with his stick.

"Hah!" growled Jugurtha, "the novice insults his teacher!" Above the veil, however, his eyes glowed with pride.

"No," said the student, "the novice emulates the teacher!"

They both laughed and strolled towards the tents, turbaned heads bent together and hands waving as they discussed the series of moves leading up to Finn's success. Intent on the conversation, neither noticed a black-clad figure hidden in the nearby trees. From that day forward, the ex-slave progressed rapidly until he was almost as proficient as his mentor in attack and defense. The Tuareg could still penetrate his student's guard, but increasingly found he had to use the utmost skill to do so. If he got the slightest bit careless, the blond would have a stick at his throat. No father could have been prouder of a son than the desert leader was of his protégé.

The daily practice continued, but they now used two old, dull swords Jugurtha had produced. The ring of steel against steel sounded across the lake, sometimes drawing a group of men to observe the training. Although the desert fighters knew their leader had been working with Finn for months, they were astounded at the skill and quickness of the former slave, often shouting encouragement as the two dodged and parried among the trees.

As Jugurtha had foreseen, the blond was a natural when they began to fight on camelback. It didn't seem to matter which animal he was riding: the camel responded to Finn as though it could read his thoughts. When they practiced charging straight at one another, the student's mount would swerve slightly as the two animals met, keeping Finn just out of reach of Jugurtha's weapon, then swing in so quickly that the Tuareg would feel a slight tap on his back as they passed. In close quarters, the Irishman never overtly guided his camel, but it was always positioned just beyond the thrust of the leader's blade. No matter what he did, Jugurtha could not move his mount away fast enough to avoid the touch of Finn's blade, signaling the end of the fight. One evening, as they leaned back against pillows after the evening meal, Jugurtha produced a bundle.

"It's time for you to move on to the real thing," he said, unwrapping a leather scabbard and handing it to Finn.

"Where did you get this?" The younger man asked, as he withdrew a gleaming blade from the scabbard. The sword had a beautiful leather-wrapped handle and silver crosspiece.

"One of the princes in Tunis objected to my courting the Pasha's daughter. I took it from him after silencing his objections."

"It's beautiful," said the Irishman, gently feeling the razor sharp edges on both sides of the blade.

"I put it away for my son," the leader said simply.

25

JUGURTHA HAD SUSPENDED RAIDS while teaching Finn to fight, but was now ready to get back into action. Spies in Tunis regularly reported the movement of traders to desert people visiting the city and this information was rapidly networked among the remote oases. In short order, Jugurtha and other Tuareg bands became aware of any caravan worth attacking. His practice was to avoid both the ones heavily protected by mercenaries and the ones transporting a preponderance of slaves. Occasionally, however, one of the pack trains would carry silk, precious gems, or even gold. Although guarded, these caravans were generally small and relied on speed to reach the safety of Bilma unscathed. They were ideal targets, and Jugurtha normally assembled a combined group of warriors from two or three oases for the attack. Streaming off the hillsides on their fleet camels, the raiders usually put the mercenaries to flight after a sharp encounter, which left the plunder for easy taking.

As the weeks went by with no news of a rich caravan, Finn continued honing his sword skills, sometimes with Jugurtha or one of the other warriors, often alone in the grove of palm trees. Parrying with another swordsman required intense concentration, because the Tuaregs worked hard to prevent the beginner from scoring any "touches." A touch with the tip of the sword indicated that one had penetrated the other's defense and could have delivered a crippling blow in a real fight. Jugurtha had been a good teacher, however, and the other men found Finn a formidable foe.

The mornings when he was alone, dodging around tree trunks, parrying and thrusting at the air, were more relaxed. There was time to stop and think about a maneuver, reflect on his defensive posture, or analyze the blade angle of a particular stroke. It was during one of those days, as he focused on his footwork, that an odd sensation crept into his consciousness: he was being watched! He stood quietly, sword in one hand, and studied the oasis. To the east, the sun's crescent was just beginning to show. Nearby, the camel herd rested peacefully and, except for the songs of a few awakening birds, all was quiet. A glance across the lake revealed no one moving around the tents. The growing light showed nothing unusual; nevertheless, he couldn't shake the feeling of being observed.

He told himself he was imagining things; no one ventured from the tents in the gray light of dawn unless leaving for a hunt, and the presence of enemies would have alarmed the herd. The practice area was a third of the way around the lake. Behind him, the ground opened out into a large grassy area with a few scattered trees, where the camel herd was kept. In front of him, the grove of palm trees continued around the edge of the lake almost to the cluster of tents 150 yards away. Occasional tall patches of reeds extended from the bank for several yards into the water, but he would have seen anyone wading out to hide in them. The Irishman finally resumed practice, convinced he had been mistaken.

For the next few mornings Jugurtha, or one of the other men, joined him and the vigorous action was so consuming he forgot all about the experience. But a week later, practicing alone, he again sensed an observer. Once more, Finn studied his surroundings closely, even walking through the grove to the tents and back, but could detect nothing unusual. That evening, he deliberately turned down Jugurtha's offer to spar the next morning. He wanted to be alone. Sure enough, no sooner had he arrived at the practice area than he felt he was being watched. Finn decided it was time to expose the spy.

That night, after a long discussion with Jugurtha about three young camels he was training, Finn went to bed as usual. He waited until the tent was dark and perfectly quiet before silently rising and slipping outside. At the edge of the camp, he sat down with his back to a tree, the lake behind him. Light from the brilliant night sky filtered through the branches and gave the ground a luminescent glow. Wrapped in his blue robe, the Irishman was just another shadow in the oasis.

Sitting there, Finn's thoughts wandered back to the morning of the raid on Baltimore. Once again, he vividly saw the crumpled body of his father on the cobblestones, axe just beyond his outstretched hand. The cries of terrified villagers being hustled to the dock echoed in his ears. He remembered being forced into the paint locker of the pirate ship, and the whimpering of the children as the door was slammed shut. As though it were yesterday, he relived the experience of seeing Bran torn from his brother's side and dragged to the slave platform. Then it was his turn, Cormac lying unconscious on the pavement from the pirates' beating. He had not known then that his brother's promise of rescue was impossible. One never escaped the slavers and their merciless whips. Except for the visits of the mysterious stranger, he would have died in the first week of the caravans, or during his flight across the desert.

He wondered what had become of Bran. Smiling in the dark, he remembered her outraged face and screams for help when geese nipped her during feeding time at home. He had always positioned himself close by to rescue her if necessary. After going to sea with his father and brother, he'd reminded Mother each day to keep an eye on the little girl when she was with the big birds. Bran had been sold separately and forced to face slavery alone, with no one to protect her. He sighed; by his reckoning that was six years ago. If she'd survived, his sister would now be 14.

Where was Cormac? In his years with the caravans, Finn had sought word of the redhead from city slaves he encountered at the gates in Tunis, but to no avail. Had his brother died under the whips or suffered some other horrible fate? The ex-slave realized that he would never know.

He pictured his mother returning from her sister's farm with a basket of fruit, to find the village empty and burned--her husband lying dead on the street. Had she gone to live with her sister? Had the fishing village fallen into ruin when most of its citizens disappeared, weeds and brush claiming the once tidy dock and street? Surely some people had escaped to the hills. Perhaps they had brought life back to the little harbor town.

Lost in thought, Finn realized with a start that gray was brushing the eastern horizon: the night had fled. As he glanced up, his eyes caught a slight movement at the edge of the tents. There was just enough light for him to see a shadow slip through the trees out of the camp toward the practice area. He watched its progress through the grove until it abruptly vanished!

26

THE IRISHMAN FOCUSED ON the area where he had last seen the shape. It had stopped beside a palm and simply disappeared. Fixing the location firmly in his mind, he eased slowly around to the far side of the tree he'd been resting against and stood up. Backing away slowly, he kept his tree between himself and the spot he had marked until he reached the edge of the camp. From there it was a simple matter to duck behind tents and sneak back into his bed. He dozed until it was light enough to emerge with his sword at his usual practice time.

The blonde usually left his turban in the tent and strode along the lake, waving the weapon from side to side to warm his arm, long yellow hair falling well below his shoulders. This morning, as he approached the palm he had noted in the dark, he made some overhead sweeps with the blade as though an opponent were attacking from his right. In fact, he was studying the tree, now 30 yards away.

As he passed it, he abruptly spun left, pretending he was being accosted from the other direction. The maneuver hid the broad grin indicating he'd discovered the secret. Swinging the sword furiously, he ran forward a few steps to create separation and convince the observer he had seen nothing. Finn, pleased at having solved the mystery, couldn't help voicing a few shouts, disguising his elation by acting as though he were in the midst of a fierce battle!

The answer was so simple: there were actually three palm trees rising from the ground close together. They had grown in such a way as to form a tight semi-circle facing his practice area, but open at the back. The trunks were so close that only a thin crack separated one from the other. From the practice area, the trunks appeared as a single tree; however, a person standing behind them could peek through the spaces without being seen. Finn chortled. His instincts had been correct after all: someone was spying on him!

At the end of his practice routine, Finn always returned to join Jugurtha for breakfast in the tent. This morning, as he reached the tent he pretended to start through the doorway, but suddenly paused and bent over, as though he had dropped something. A quick glance back into the grove revealed a figure hurrying through the trees toward camp. That evening, Finn again turned down Jugurtha's offer to spar, claiming he needed another day to practice footwork.

"I thought your footwork was excellent last week," said the Tuareg.

"Possibly, but there's a new wrinkle I want explore." said Finn. "You might get to see it one of these days for yourself," he added mysteriously.

When soft snoring indicated everyone was sleeping, the Irishman stole out of the tent in black turban and robes. A few minutes later, he was comfortably seated against a tree 60 feet behind the triple palms, his dark clothing blending perfectly with the shadows. He went to sleep immediately, secure in the knowledge that years of routine would wake him before dawn.

Finn's eyes opened. Without moving, he glanced to the east where another day was beginning to shoulder black sky off the rim of the earth. The noise which had woken him came again: a soft swish of robe on grass. Staring through the dim light, he saw a silhouette approach the the three palm trees, step into the semi-circle of trunks and blend perfectly with the wood. The former slave waited patiently until he judged it was about the time he normally emerged from the tent. Pulling a fold of black cloth from the turban he wore across his face, he rose silently and approached the trees on bare feet.

"Do you always spy on people in the morning?" he said from 12 inches behind the cloaked head.

There was a gasp and the person swung violently around in the small confines, bumping one shoulder against a tree. Finn, a hand on each of the outer trunks, blocked any escape. Above a veil, large eyes wide with shock stared up at him. All was still for a moment. Then, to his amazement, the corners of the eyes wrinkled in what was surely a grin and there came what sounded like a giggle.

"My father taught you well, Amnay. You move like a shadow," said a soft voice.

"Amnay?" Dumbfounded at the realization that this was one of Jugurtha's daughters, he could only repeat the name.

"Yes, 'Rider.' That's what we call you. No one can ride or train camels like you." The eyes were no longer startled, and the girl made no move to flee.

"Who might 'we' be?" Finn said to cover his confusion.

"Those of us who aren't allowed to be present in the tents with you," she said. "Those who must be robed and veiled when encountering you in public because they have not received a marriage proposal."

"Those who follow me around asking questions," Finn said.

"How else can we get to know the favored warrior of the great Jugurtha?" Her words came softly.

"But surely you've listened to me talking with your parents since I've been coming into the tent. Besides," he said, "you and your sisters spied on me for months when I was a slave!"

"Yes, but that was done secretly, until you tricked us. Once you became a free man, we had no interest in overhearing conversations. We needed to meet you personally."

"What's your name?"

"Tiziri."

"Ahhh ... 'Moonlight,' a fitting name for one who sneaks out to hide and watch," he said.

"My father says you learn more quickly than any student he's ever taught," she said abruptly, changing the subject. "He tells us your skills are extraordinary for one who started so late."

"I suppose you've taken it upon yourself to report my progress when he's away?"

"Oh no," her eyes opened wide. "He doesn't know I've been out here!"

"Why do you come then?" He raised his eyebrows.

"You remind me of my father," she said, after the slightest pause. "I see you holding your chin when you think, just like he does."

"Do you and your sisters take turns at the lookout?"

"No. My older sister, Tamenzut, is betrothed to a warrior from another oasis. Tinitran, the youngest, has eyes for Gwasila of our band."

"Gwasila is an excellent rider, one of Jugurtha's best." Finn said.

"I must go now," Tiziri said.

"Not before I see your face," said the Irishman, dropping the black cloth from his own features.

"It's not allowed," she said unconvincingly.

"People will soon be stirring ... you'll be late," he grinned.

Without hesitation, almost eagerly, she slid the covering off her head and pulled the veil away. Finn's heart pounded. Smiling up at him was a stunning young woman! Shining black hair framed an oval face with wide-set, black eyes. Under her perfectly proportioned nose, slightly parted lips revealed striking white teeth. For an instant the two stared at each other, the heavily tanned blonde a head taller than the desert girl. Then she was gone, ducking under his arm and hurrying away, head covered and veil in place.

27

THE NEXT MORNING, FINN was positioned behind the lookout well before dawn, fearful the girl wouldn't return. Just as the first gray was appearing, however, there came the sound of cloth brushing grass and a shadow slid into the protective tree trunks. He wasted no time approaching and was surprised to see the veiled Tiziri facing him from within the tight enclosure.

"I wasn't sure you'd come," he said.

"I knew you'd be waiting."

"What would your family think?"

"My mother and father know nothing; it's forbidden to meet a man alone. My sisters are aware I've been coming to watch you. When I told them you'd found me out, they encouraged me to return."

"They encouraged you?" said the startled Irishman. His head was uncovered today and the long blond hair stirred in a gentle breeze.

"Yes." The word hung in the air, followed by a moment of silence as they stared at one another.

"How old are you?" He finally managed, to cover the powerful emotions stirring his heart.

"I'm 17," she said. "How old are you?"

"Well, I think I'm about 20," he said, relieved to be on a safer subject. "I was 14 when we were taken and at least six years have passed, although it's hard to keep track of time as a slave."

"What was it like to be captured?"

"I was terrified," he said. He described the shock of the raid, the voyage, and the auction. "When they dragged me away from the market, I was completely alone for the first time in my life."

"I must go," Tiziri said, with a start, realizing it was full daylight. "It's late."

"Not before I see your face again," he said firmly, hands locked on the tree trunks to bar the way. As though she had been waiting for the request, the girl shook her head free of its wrap, lowered the veil, and smiled up at him. Finn caught his breath; she was even more beautiful than he remembered! With a quick move, she ducked under his arm and headed for the tents, her lovely smile etched in his memory.

From then on, the two met every morning in the dim predawn. He described his life growing up in the fishing village and the years on the caravan routes. Just like the younger children, she never tired of hearing about the ocean and asked countless questions. She told of growing up in the desert, herding goats and learning to ride camels, explaining that she alone of the three daughters wanted to ride. This pleased her father and, as a child, she'd often accompanied him on trips to other oases. When she became eligible for marriage, her mother put a stop to riding on the grounds that it was unseemly for a young woman.

"I don't agree," the Irishman said. "Riding should be encouraged for everyone!"

"Women can own camels, but riding is usually left to the men."

"But didn't you love it when you were allowed to ride?"

"Ohhh yes! It's exhilarating!"

Complications now arose whenever the veiled young women approached Finn, because Tiziri always positioned herself directly in front of him. He wanted to do nothing but stare into those eyes; however, the others kept him so busy with questions he was forced to look at them instead. Little did he know it was a game, and all the girls were highly amused about keeping him distracted.

One evening a few weeks later, Jugurtha, his wife Kella, and Finn were gathered for supper in the tent. Porridge was cooking on the brazier, and a couple of slave women were bringing figs, yogurt, and cheese from the rear section of the tent. Finn and Jugurtha were deep in discussion about a particularly swift young jamal, which had an unfortunate penchant for biting people. The Irishman was making a point about the camel's disposition, when a bowl of figs was held out to him by one of the women. He grasped the container to pass it on, still focused on the older man, but she didn't release it. When he glanced up, she let go and he almost dropped the bowl in his lap. It was Tiziri, grinning behind her veil! Fearful of Jugurtha noticing her, Finn snapped his fingers to hold the Tuareg's attention.

"The jamal isn't going to be a problem," he said more loudly than he had intended. "Why, in no time, I can have him so calm that even Tiziri could ride him." There was dead silence, and one of the black clad servants fled to the curtain at the back of the tent.

"Tiziri?" The leader raised his eyebrows.

"Uh, yes," stammered Finn. "That's one of your children, isn't it?"

"So it is, but how did you know her name?"

"I picked it up somewhere," said the ex-slave, thinking hard, "perhaps from one of the children."

"That crowd probably has a lot to say about everything," said Jugurtha, reaching for the fig bowl.

"One never knows about children," ventured Kella, dropping her eyes before Finn could see her amusement.

28

"ARE YOU TRYING TO get me turned back into a slave! What were you doing last night?" Finn said the next morning. "I couldn't sleep, worrying what your father would do if he found out we'd been meeting here."

Tiziri had long since removed the veil when they talked and he could see her white teeth gleaming as she smiled in the dark.

"It's time you asked his permission to visit me."

"Are you crazy?"

"Shhhh, you'll wake the whole camp," she giggled. "Mother says it's time."

The blond stared at her, speechless.

"My sisters know, my friends know, and now my mother knows. How else do you think I was able to sneak in with the figs? But you almost gave it away by using my name!"

"I was doing everything I could to keep him from looking at you, and it just slipped out," he said. "Fortunately, I remembered he called you 'children,' and he relaxed when he heard the word."

"Mother was prepared to intervene, but when you disarmed him, she kept silent."

"Not quite," he said, describing Kella's comment. "I thought I caught something in her voice, but she wouldn't look at me."

"She was quite amused by the whole thing," said Tiziri, "although, at first, she almost didn't let me do it. My sisters helped convince her. Underneath all his seriousness, Father has a great sense of humor. We thought we could convince him, if necessary, that it was a prank to get you back for fooling us at the doorway. He doesn't need to know about anything else."

"Tell me about the rules for visiting you."

"Well, if a man wishes to court a woman," she said, staring at the ground and clearly blushing, "he must ask her father's permission to visit her."

With that, she ran toward the camp. As Finn watched her go, it dawned on him that he wanted to court her more than anything he had ever wanted in his life. Smiling at the mysterious ways of women, he made his way to the practice area, but his mind was spinning so fast he forgot all about practicing and sat at the edge of the lake, staring into the water. Late that afternoon, he and Jugurtha were exercising two swift camels in the sand hills nearby, where Finn liked to put mounts through their paces. The sun was nearly down as they finished and started for the oasis.

"Did you see the speed with which he came off that last ridge?" asked the Tuareg, delighted with the young jamal he was riding. "He was almost running when he hit the hard ground at the bottom, and then he really took off!"

"He's fast," said the younger man, "but what I really like is the way he responded to your reining."

Both men were sitting just behind their camels' humps, having discarded the heavy wooden saddles for small cloth ones. When the camels ran, the men would lean back and stretch their legs forward.

The result was a surprisingly comfortable ride, although it gave them an ungainly appearance.

"Thank you, Amnay," said the leader, using the name for the first time. "But the mounts you ride need no reins and few words: they seem to know exactly what you want them to do."

Finn, startled at hearing the name he thought only the daughters used, took a moment to compose himself.

"Sir, may I ask a question?" he said rather formally.

"Yes?" Jugurtha's voice was gruff, but if one could have seen his mouth behind the veil, it was smiling.

"I would like permission to visit your daughter." The words spilled out more rapidly than Finn had intended.

"I'm sorry," said the leader, "Tamenzut is pledged to a warrior from another oasis and Tinitran is being courted by Gwasila."

"I meant Tiziri," said the blond hesitantly.

"Tiziri?" Jugurtha turned to stare at Finn as the camels ambled along. "How do you know her?"

"Well, I believe she's part of the group always questioning me," the Irishman stammered. "You know, I've mentioned them before. It's so hard to tell one from the other when they're all dressed alike and veiled, but one with beautiful eyes always stands in front of me. I think it must be she."

The leader, who knew more than he let on, let the silence drag out for several moments as they approached the edge of the oasis. The sun, sinking behind the distant hills, threw long shadows across the oasis' greenery and the eastern horizon was already beginning to darken. Finally, he decided he had tortured the young man long enough.

"I suppose," he said, "we could let her join us from time to time for the evening meal. Veiled of course, until we decide otherwise," he added in a growl, to disguise how pleased he was with this development. Was it possible the Irishman might become a part of his family yet? Neither spoke for a few minutes.

"I'm not sure I'd agree, but in time the two of you might be able to take short walks by the lake with Kella as chaperone." Jugurtha tried to sound grumpy, but in fact, he was enjoying this immensely. "After the camel training is over for the day, of course," he said.

"Of course." Finn said emphatically.

"It all depends on how Tiziri reacts." Jugurtha couldn't resist one last jab.

"I understand." The Irishman was so excited he thought his pounding heart could surely be heard.

"Now," said the Tuareg, "what's the plan for these animals tomorrow?"

29

THE FOLLOWING EVENING WHEN Finn ducked into the tent for the evening meal, three figures were sitting beside the brazier. Jugurtha, in his usual place on the far side of the cooker, faced the doorway. Kella was to his right and beside her sat a veiled Tiziri. The camel trainer tossed his black tagelmust on the bed and sat to the leader's left, eyes fixed on the girl. She gave him a quick look, laughter dancing in her gaze, before dropping her head to stare demurely at the colorful patterns of the rug beneath her.

"How's the sick wahr?" Jugurtha's question broke the silence, forcing the younger man to turn toward him to answer.

"Better," said Finn. "I think there may be something wrong with his mother's milk, so I tried him on some goat milk with a little millet mixed in. He seemed to like it."

"Millet? I never would have thought of that," the leader said.

"It's a trick I learned in Tunis from an old slave," said Finn.

The two men went on talking about the camel herd, as the servants passed bowls of yogurt, cheese, and roasted meat. For the next 20 minutes the leader plied Amnay with nonstop questions about the animals, trying to keep him from looking at Tiziri. Then, without warning, he abruptly changed the topic.

"My daughter, have you nothing to say to Amnay?" he said innocently.

"Oh, hello," she said, without raising her eyes. Finn, free from having to make eye contact with Jugurtha, thought he detected a faint shaking of her shoulders under the black cloth.

"That veil does no justice to the face I saw the day I caught you and your sisters spying on me," he said.

There was a slight gasp and the girl's hand flew to her mouth as she raised her head to stare at him with a shocked look. So far as she knew, her father had never been told their faces had actually been seen by the slave. This time, it was the Irishman's turn to grin. Kella suddenly found a reason to turn away, a visible trembling in her shoulders. Jugurtha's eyebrows were raised as he stared at his daughter, but the faintest twitch in the corner of his mouth, now uncovered for eating, disclosed he was not totally naïve about what had transpired.

"Some people take advantage of other people's children," Tiziri said, recovering quickly. She looked boldly at him across the brazier.

"I'm so thankful it wasn't children peeking at me that day," Finn said with a wide smile.

"Ohhhh," was all she could get out, but she maintained her gaze and the warmth in her eyes caused a rapid beating of his heart. For a moment it was quiet, as they looked at one another, oblivious to their surroundings. Jugurtha's cough broke the silence.

"We should leave before dawn, to try the speed of that young jamal against the speed of the gazelle herd that wandered into the area," he said. His face was serious, hiding the pleasure he felt at the obvious attraction between his daughter and the man he considered an adopted son.

"Of course," said Finn, tearing his gaze from the girl. "Bring your lance; I think he's got enough speed that you won't need a bow."

"Then you'd better have a bow Amnay," said the older man. "I never doubt you on the matter of camels, but to get close enough to lance a gazelle stretches my imagination!" With that, supper was over.

Later, Finn lay on his back, hands behind his head, and stared into the dark. Never as a caravan slave had he imagined anything like this. In the two years since escaping, he had become a free man, been accepted into the household of a desert leader, and was now courting the most beautiful woman he had ever seen. It was a miracle.

In the back of the tent, the three sisters huddled together for a long time whispering and giggling. Tamenzut and Tinitran had been behind the screening blankets for the whole meal, peeking out whenever possible. Knowing their father's sense of humor, they had watched with amusement his forcing Finn to keep talking about camels and avoid looking at their sister. When the two were finally allowed to interact, the girls almost burst out laughing over Amnay's revelation of how clearly he had seen them all through the doorway. They teased Tiziri about Jugurtha having to break the silence as she and Finn stared at one another, lost in love.

In their quarters, Kella and Jugurtha made ready for bed.

"It seems the young man is smitten with our daughter," he said quietly.

"No more than she is with him," said Kella. "From the first time the girls began peeking out the door, she was taken with him. When you freed him, she was overjoyed. I'm glad you didn't forbid her to sneak out and watch him practice, because she would have gone anyway."

"I never would have known had I not left early that morning, intending to test Amnay's reactions with an unexpected attack, and glimpsed her hurrying back to the tent." He chuckled as they slid under the blankets. "You were right then, as you are now. Short of tying her up, we couldn't have stopped her … and even then, I'm not so sure!"

30

Two days later, a messenger arrived from Tunis with the news that the Pasha himself was sending a caravan to Bilma for slaves. Jugurtha listened intently as the visitor revealed that the Pasha was including a number of horses he hoped to sell to an Egyptian buyer at Ghadames.

"It makes sense," the Tuareg said. "The Egyptians favor our horses for racing." He stared at the other man, who had obviously not come all this way to talk about horses.

"The Pasha's daughter and several friends are going to be riding the horses," said the messenger. "They and the chaperones will have extra protection from a strong contingent of mounted soldiers."

"The Pasha is my wife's brother. I'm not interested in kidnapping."

"Of course not," exclaimed the envoy. "But the soldiers are not there just to protect the girls. A large shipment of gold will be concealed among the usual trade goods. It appears the Pasha is not only a seller of horses, but also a buyer of Egyptian ivory."

"I am interested in gold, however," said Jugurtha, eyes glittering above the veil.

Bran

....

1

Filled with terror, as she was dragged away by a grinning little fat man, Bran screamed for Cormac. She saw her brother break from the line, only to trip and fall on the flagstones. Pirates immediately surrounded him, kicking and beating his body. With a sudden burst of strength she pulled away from the fat man, but before she could take a step, her arms were firmly gripped by a tall black slave behind her.

"Don't try to escape, little lassie; these men would as soon slit your throat as speak to you."

She looked up at him with shock: the words were spoken in English! He took her hand and marched off behind their owner, to the accompaniment of laughs and comments in Arabic about her future from the watching crowd. When they were free of the square, Bran craned her neck to see his face.

"Who are you?" she said.

"Henry Blackstone, gunner in His Majesty's navy," he said without looking down. The hubbub of street vendors nearly drowned out the words.

"What're you doing here?"

"Shhh, missy. Don't raise your voice. Slaves are supposed to be quiet unless spoken to. My ship went down in a great storm five years ago and only a few survived. We managed to hang on to wreckage for some days, before a pirate ship came by and picked us up. We were all sold in that market square, same as you. I was lucky ... my owner, who purchased you, is the buyer for the Pasha's harem. All I have to do is follow him around the city and bring back the women. The other sailors went to the galleys or mines, from which death is the only escape."

"What's a harem?"

"It's where ..." Henry looked at her young, innocent face, and paused to collect his thoughts before continuing in a low voice. "It's where all the Pasha's wives live. You'll see. It has lots of gardens and fountains."

"Is that where you're taking me?" Bran glanced at the fat man ahead.

"Yes, they'll most likely put you to work cleaning for a while." He was careful not to look at her.

"Will you come with me?" she said innocently.

"No," said Henry, the trace of a smile flickering across his face. "No men are allowed in the harem. It's a place for women only."

"Stop talking!" The fat man turned and glared at them. He spoke Arabic, but his expression left no doubt about what he had said.

Bran dropped her eyes and felt a reassuring squeeze on her hand. After they'd walked through crowded streets for 10 minutes, the distinct smell of the ocean filled the air, and they approached the palace where the Pasha had inspected the Baltimore captives. Henry bent down as though to brush something from his foot and whispered.

"You've already been in the palace and seen its beauty, but beneath it is a dungeon and torture chambers, from which no one returns. It's the same with the harem: it's beautiful inside but there's no escape. At least you'll be able to smell the ocean." He flashed her a quick smile.

"What will I do?" The girl was terrified at the prospect of losing this new friend.

"What we all do," the whispered words rushed out, as the sailor saw his owner start to turn. "Survive. Do what you're told and don't resist. It's better to stay alive than be thrown into the dungeon or, worse, turned over to the soldiers."

"I'm sorry, master," he said in Arabic, "a stone in my foot."

"Stop dawdling," said the Arab. "I've got to check an incoming caravan for the Pasha."

"Yes, master."

Upon reaching the plaza, the fat man headed for the one door in the great marble building to their left. He spoke to one of the guards outside, who slid back a small piece of wood covering a barred opening in the door and exchanged words with someone inside. After a moment, the door swung open and a huge black man stepped out. He was a full head taller than the guards, dressed in a loose white tunic and pants, and gripped a shining sword in his right hand. At a nod from his owner, Henry thrust the girl forward.

"Good luck lassie," he whispered, stepping back.

The big man grabbed her by the shoulder and pushed her through the door with his left hand, never turning his eyes away from the men in front of him. In one fluid motion he stepped back, slammed the door shut, and rammed home two massive bolts.

2

Bran stared in amazement at the scene inside the walls, fear forgotten for the moment. The center of the enormous, rectangular building was occupied by a vast garden. It was 300 feet long and almost 100 feet wide, and filled with flowerbeds and manicured lawns. Fruit trees and bushes were everywhere, with numerous birds and butterflies flitting among them. Colorful marble walkways with patterns of pale yellow, pink, and blue meandered across the lawns. Flowing water burbled through tile channels set in the grass, filling the air with a pleasing murmur.

The walls surrounding the garden were gleaming white and two stories high, filled with doors and windows. A walkway extended completely around the second level, from which broad staircases descended to the gardens at each of the four corners. At ground level, a broad marble walk edged the entire garden perimeter. A number of women in beautiful robes were sitting on benches under the trees. Other women leisurely strolled the paths in pairs, their conversations muted by the gurgling water. After the cramped conditions of the ship, the tumult of the city, and the raucous auction, this place felt like paradise to the Irish girl. For one soothing moment she forgot the reality of her situation.

The spell was broken as the huge man took her by the shoulder, though not unkindly, and guided her briskly down the walk on the left side of the garden. As they approached the far end, Bran noticed that there were only a few doors here and no windows; it seemed that this part of the building had a different purpose. The guard opened one of the doors and stepped in with her, shouting something in Arabic before releasing her shoulder and returning to the outside.

3

As the door closed, fear returned to Bran with a rush. Facing her was a cavernous room, lit by a set of heavily barred windows on the far wall. As her eyes adjusted to the dim light, Bran saw that the chamber was filled with tables at which women were arranging food on platters. The smell of roasting meat and baking bread filled the air with tantalizing aromas, reminding her that she hadn't eaten for hours. She saw that most of the women were old, some stooped, all of them dressed in rags. Among the tables, smaller figures scurried with baskets and trays, taking finished platters away and bringing others to be prepared. She realized the latter were girls, also dressed in rags, about her own age. What unnerved her, however, was the total silence accompanying this beehive of activity.

"It's like watching ghosts at work," she thought to herself, wondering in a split second of panic whether they could actually be ghosts!

While she was staring, two women dressed in black robes strode across the room toward her. Although they were smiling, she noticed women and girls moving well out of the way before they passed. Bran stared at the floor, too frightened to move, as they approached. One put a finger under her chin and tipped her head back, forcing her to look at them. What she saw terrified her. Cold, cruel eyes glared at her above the rigid smiles they'd fixed to their lips. A sob caught in Bran's throat.

"Don't be afraid, little one," said one woman, lifting the girl's chin. She spoke in English, but her rasping voice sounded like one of the ravens that nested in the rocky hills above Baltimore. "We're here to help you."

With a lightning move, she grabbed the Irish girl's hair and yanked her backward so hard her feet gave way and she started to fall, a scream bursting from her mouth. The woman didn't let her fall but instead pulled her up by the hair until only the tips of her toes touched the ground.

"That is, of course, unless you misbehave." The words were spoken in what was supposed to be a sweet tone but rather sounded like a dog growling.

"Be careful," said the other woman in Arabic. "He said not to mark her, and that includes pulling her hair out."

"Don't worry, we won't mark her physically," replied the first, lowering the girl so she stood on both feet. "We'll break her on the inside, like all the others." "Come along, dearie," she said, switching to English. "We need to get you cleaned up."

With that she swung the girl around by the hair and dragged her backward across the room, Bran's feet desperately scrabbling to maintain balance. They passed through a door into a long hallway. Not one person in the kitchen raised a head to watch her go. Abruptly, the overseer opened a door and violently pushed Bran into a dark room. Stumbling into blackness from the vicious thrust, the Irish girl screamed again as her feet touched nothingness and she fell. The scream was transmitted clearly back to the kitchen through the open door.

As she fell into blackness, Bran had an instant to wonder whether she was going to die. Then she splashed into cold, greasy, water and went under. Flailing desperately with her arms, she managed to get her face above the surface, gasping for air, just as her feet touched bottom. She stood up, chest deep in the water, sobbing and scraping her hair out of her eyes. It was pitch-black. All she could do was hold her arms in front of her and walk forward until she reached the pool's edge. She shuddered as strange, smelly objects bumped against her. After what seemed an eternity, she discovered the side of the pool and dragged herself onto a narrow ledge, to huddle in cold misery.

Later, Bran would learn that she had been thrown into the refuse pool: a stone pit into which all the kitchen garbage was thrown. Water flowed into it from one of the garden channels and, every few days, an overseer would open a sluice gate and empty the whole mess through an underground sewer to the ocean. Each slave coming to the kitchen was thrown into the pool and left for hours in the darkness. Few attempted any resistance thereafter, although sometimes a stubborn slave refused to be cowed. She would be taken by the two overseers to another room off the same hallway. Tormented screams would go on for hours and she would never be seen again.

The Irish girl, eyes tightly shut, hugged her knees to her chest and sobbed uncontrollably. She was overcome with fear and exhaustion.

"Don't be afraid," said a soft voice.

The new slave's eyes flew open. She stared in disbelief at the little girl standing before her in a blue dress, holding out a bouquet of flowers. She was about five years old, with blond curly hair, pretty blue eyes, and bare feet. They were standing in the sun on a grassy hill; below, the harbor of Baltimore shimmered under a slight breeze. A fishing boat was making its way home past the barrier rocks. The thatched roofs of the village showed yellow and brown against the blue of the ocean. The air smelled fresh and clean as it does after a spring shower, the grass under her feet was soft, and the sunshine was warm. A bird sang cheerfully from a nearby bush.

"Where am I?" asked Bran in wonder.

"That's your home down there," said the girl with a big smile.

"I know ... but how ... who are you?"

"I'm a friend. I brought you flowers."

She held out the bouquet. In the very center was a white gardenia, its delightful fragrance wafting up and filling the air. As Bran reached to take the flowers, there was a great crash as the door to the garbage room was thrown open, and a dark figure blotted out the scene. One of the overseers was standing in the entrance.

"Resting are ya? Well, I'm so sorry to disturb your majesty, but there's work to be done!" The last words were uttered in a roar, as the woman pointed her hand in the direction of the kitchen. "Get moving!"

Bran got to her feet made her way around the pool, but when she started past the overseer into the passageway, she was grabbed by the shoulder and shoved forward so hard she sprawled full length on the floor. Before she could get to her feet, a hard kick in the rear sent her tumbling down the hall. Somehow she knew that more would follow, so she quickly pushed herself up and ran toward the kitchen. Hardly had she reached the big room when a hand from behind grabbed her by the hair and lifted her to the tips of her toes.

"There's a bucket and brush by your feet, dearie," said the woman with the gravelly voice. "Mop this room before supper or go without! You've got 20 minutes."

She'd been given an impossible task: the enormous room could never be mopped in 20 minutes. Nevertheless, when the woman released the cruel pressure on her hair, she dropped to her knees, grabbed the wooden brush, and began energetically swabbing the floor. To her complete surprise, Bran found herself quietly humming! Her terror had disappeared, replaced with an overwhelming sense of peace. All she could think about was the little girl with the bouquet. It had been so real. Suddenly, the unmistakable scent of gardenias filled her nose. Startled, the Irish girl stared about the room, but there were no flowers to be seen!

4

BRAN WAS BUSILY SCRUBBING under her second table when the first scrap of food appeared. When she approached the table, she had raised her eyes to the two women working there, to let them know she was coming. Neither glanced at her as she moved under the table, but each moved to the side so she could clean where they'd been standing. Glancing out from underneath, she saw the black robe, which had been hovering close by, move away toward the center of the room. Apparently the overseer was satisfied the new slave could work.

The tops of the big tables were made of planks set side-by-side in an uneven fashion. No sooner had the overseer moved away than a sliver of apple fell through the planks to the floor. At first, Bran thought the woman above had been sloppy, but when another sliver fell after it, she realized what they were doing: passing food to her! The pieces were thin, but it didn't matter. She was ravenously hungry. Keeping her right hand vigorously swabbing, she reached out the left and snatched up the two bits of fruit. They tasted delicious!

The black skirt showed up when Bran cleaned under the third table, but moved toward the baking ovens as the girl crawled under the fourth. This time, three wafer-thin bits of cheese fluttered down. At the fifth table, it was tiny pieces of grapes. At the sixth, a slice of bread was somehow flipped under the edge of the table to land in front of her. And so it went. Whenever the overseer stepped away, little bits of food materialized from above: slivers of olives, oranges, pomegranates, bananas, even bits of meat. Each piece was tiny, but the total amounted to a mouthful or two as she made her way along the floor. She had scrubbed about a third of the big room when a bell sounded and all the women and children assembled in a line near the ovens.

"So sorry dearie," said one of the overseers, coming to where Bran worked. "You didn't finish, so there's no supper for you. And no sleep either, until this room is finished," she roared.

The slaves' meal was apparently eaten standing, because Bran's surreptitious glances showed no movement in the line for many minutes. Finally, the women and girls filed away down the hall, and she was left alone. In the dim light from smoky torches, it took her another hour to finish. One of the black-robed women constantly harangued her to go faster, frequently kicking her flat on her face for no reason. When she finished, the woman grabbed her by the hair, dragged her down the hall and pushed her violently through a dark doorway.

Fully expecting to plunge into another pool, Bran found herself stumbling over bodies! Suddenly, a hand gripped her arm and drew her gently to the floor. A pair of arms wrapped around her, and she felt the warmth of one of the slave women.

"No sound lassie, they slip in here to listen," breathed a voice in her ear. A piece of bread somehow found its way into her hand. "Take your time and chew quietly. If you're caught they'll throw you into the pool again."

She pulled the girl close and slipped a bit of cloth over her face to muffle the sound of eating. Bran complied, savoring the taste of each bite.

"Now sleep," said the woman. In an instant the girl was dead to the world, dreaming of children and flowers.

"Up," yelled a deep voice, shattering the silence.

Before she was fully awake, Bran was lifted to her feet and guided about in the dark until she felt a hand on her shoulder. Someone raised her arm so her hand rested on the shoulder of a person in front of her. Pushed from behind, she started to walk, realizing she was part of a line filing out of the room. When they reached the kitchen, she saw she was following a girl almost exactly her size; a quick glance behind revealed the girl following her to be of the same height. Later, she would learn that the line was organized from smallest to tallest. Anyone out of place was beaten and thrown into the pool for a day. Somehow, in total darkness, the slaves had positioned her in exactly the right spot for her size! A cup of soup and a piece of moldy bread were consumed standing in line, and then the thralls were released to work.

5

B RAN QUICKLY ADAPTED TO the routine of the kitchen. In support
of her astounding and continued sense of peace in the face of the
overseers' abuse, she was mindful of Henry's advice to always submit
and not resist. It was better to stay alive, he'd said, than to be thrown
into the dungeons or turned over to the soldiers. She now suspected
that would never happen: she wouldn't leave the kitchen alive if she
resisted the overseers. The sadistic eyes of the two women gave them
away, even before the other slaves warned her at night in the dark. She
remembered what the pirates had done to the people they'd judged
unfit on the wharf at Baltimore. Henry's counsel was wise, but the
spark of a dream began to grow in her. Survive she must, not only to
live … but to escape!

Before sleep, warmed by the bodies around her and remembering
the mysterious little girl, Bran visualized scenes from her life in Ireland.
She visualized the millions of rippling lights as the wind stirred the
harbor on a warm summer afternoon. She pictured the big gray goose

in the pen advancing on her, neck stretched out to nip, while she backed up, swinging the feed bucket and shrieking for help. She recalled tripping and falling one day, two of the big birds on her in a flash, only to be saved by Finn vaulting over the stone enclosure and driving them away. She thought of cold winter days, sleet beating against the house and whitecaps in the harbor, when the family shared bread and cheese beside the warm peat fire on the hearth. The memory of feeling safe between her two big brothers under warm blankets brought a catch to her throat ... some day she'd be with them again!

For many weeks she did nothing but scrub the huge kitchen floor all day, taking her place in line for meals at the incongruous sound of the little bell. The harem housed more than 200 people, not counting slaves; it took endless work to feed them. As quickly as the food was prepared, young girls carried it on platters to the garden door, for outside slaves to distribute around the building.

Bran learned that special consideration was given to the household of the Pasha's First Wife. She was the most powerful woman in the harem and lived with her two children in magnificent quarters on the second floor; she was also the one person feared by the kitchen overseers. Heaven help the slave who made the slightest mistake in food sent to the First Wife. A severe beating, followed by two days in the garbage pool, was the minimum consequence. A weevil in the bread, or a worm in the fruit, had caused some kitchen slaves to simply disappear.

Labor was divided by age in the harem. The majority of girls, coming into the harem aged six to eight, were generally unaccustomed to working; they were placed in the hands of the kitchen supervisors to learn obedience and work habits. Many didn't survive the ordeal. Those who did moved on to the outside garden crews, comprised of slave women assisted by girls nine and ten. Although housed elsewhere, and under different overseers, the outside crews also took their meals in the kitchen.

Certain pretty girls, aged 11 and 12, were chosen for a different role. They were turned over to supervisors charged with caring for the Pasha's many other wives. Gradually, they were taught to attend the needs of these women. In the beginning, this might involve fetching things, serving food, or drying the women after bathing. Later, it could evolve into becoming a companion to one or more of the wives. These young trainees were permitted to bathe at night and to dress in colorful robes. They were even allowed to speak if invited and, since all the lesser wives were captured slaves themselves, English, French, and Italian were commonly heard about the gardens. As girls "graduated" from garden work to tending the wives, the Pasha often sold the older, well-trained assistants to friends or business acquaintances.

The pirates also captured many full grown women. They were divided according to age and skill. Cooks were sent to the kitchen, farm wives found themselves on the garden or cleaning crews, and younger women began an apprenticeship to become one of the Pasha's wives. The entire community of the harem existed to serve the Pasha one way or another.

The two kitchen overseers were products of this system. Sisters who had grown up in the desert, they were captured as young women by the Pasha's father and sent to the harem for training. Both were ambitious and dreamed of acquiring the gifts and privileges of a First Wife. But the old Pasha already had a First Wife and a son, both of whom he adored. The sisters tried to spread lies about the First Wife, but she learned of the conspiracy and reported it to her husband. He wanted to have them killed immediately. She convinced him to use a more lingering punishment. When the two were brought into his presence, an enormous soldier was standing there, axe in hand. Convinced they were going to die, the women groveled on the floor, begging for their lives.

Appearing undecided, the Pasha turned to the First Wife. By design, she wondered aloud whether they should be spared, to run the kitchen. The sisters clamored for the assignment, wailing they would do anything if he would spare them. After some minutes, the Pasha seemed to change his mind and agree. He promised to skin them alive and throw them out on the desert for the hyenas, if either of them stepped out of line. It was a sentence of life imprisonment in the dark, smoky kitchen, and it was continued by the Pasha's son when the father died.

Now, well into middle age, the sisters had become embittered over their fate and hated all slaves coming under their control. Since the new First Wife didn't watch them as closely as her mother-in-law had, they'd contrived methods to rid themselves of older slaves who irritated them; however, they rarely attempted it with children. Every girl was a future candidate to become one of the Pasha's wives. The harem guards were charged with insuring the children weren't physically marred in any way and routinely checked the kitchen workers. The two women were limited to kicking, hair pulling, and the refuse pool to break the spirits of the younger slaves.

Bran proved resilient, however, and it wasn't long before she adapted to the behavior of the others. She worked hard, kept silent, and moved just out of reach when either of the black-robed women was close. She never gave the overseers cause to discipline her, but for a while they routinely threw her into the garbage pool before supper and left her there overnight. It did no good, because as soon as the door was closed, the smell of gardenias filled the room and the little girl appeared to walk with her on the hills of Ireland. After every night in the pool, Bran had more energy than anyone in the kitchen! Before long, the sisters simply gave up trying to break her.

6

THE ONLY TIME THE kitchen slaves dared talk was at night. These whispered conversations were vital to comforting one another and teaching newcomers how to survive the persecution. Unfortunately, after they extinguished the torches in the kitchen, the sisters were fond of creeping silently down the pitch-black hall to catch their slaves breaking the silence rule. The penalty was no food or water for 36 hours, a devastating sentence to women and children already on a minimum diet. The slaves had designed a simple warning system to combat the spying: a thin thread stretched low across the doorway. One of the older women held the string every night until the rest of them went to sleep; if it moved, she would sneeze, or cough, to warn the others.

Not long after Bran arrived, the overseers figured out they were being detected and kept clear of the doorway, but close enough to hear the whispering. This resulted in a series of punishments which left the slaves completely cowed. It was Bran who came up with a simple solution that changed the whole situation. She remembered her brothers and father rising well before dawn to prepare fishing gear, so she decided that the slaves should adopt the same strategy. It wasn't easy, but she trained herself to wake early and rouse the others for conversation, while the sisters were still snoring in the hall. When the snoring stopped, all whispering stopped. The tactic was so successful that the attitude of the kitchen slaves improved dramatically.

Bolstered by this success, Bran turned her mind to the virtual starvation diet they were subjected to. She remembered the swarms of mozzies (mosquitoes) and midges appearing in Baltimore during late summer. Any family that gathered outside during this time burned damp peat to create smoke, offensive to both insects and humans.

The Irish girl convinced the bakers to deliberately throw a bit of water on the coals every so often, causing the ovens to emit a dense cloud of smoke without seriously damaging the bread. Terrified of the consequences of delivering burned bread to the harem, the sisters would rush over to see what was the matter. Pointing to the firewood and shrugging their shoulders, the bakers would make a great show of fanning the smoke away. When the bread was seen to be unburned, the overseers were so relieved they usually forgot to be angry. During this distraction, however, there was a flurry of activity in the room. Pieces of food from every table were slipped into secret pockets sewn in the rag clothing and platters instantly rearranged to disguise the theft. The next morning, while the sisters snored, the slaves feasted.

Bolstered by these successes, Bran developed a daring and irrepressible spirit, which inspired everyone around her. Remembering the isolation and fear during her early days in the kitchen, she contrived a strategy to help newcomers with the overwhelming task of cleaning the floor before they could eat. It took timing and courage, but when both overseers were facing some contrived distraction, a few serving girls would suddenly disappear under the tables to give a hand with scrubbing the floor. When the overseers reappeared, a signal from the women working above would cause the helpers to smoothly re-emerge into the general bustle. The consequences of being discovered were severe, but the girls, inspired by the chance to outwit the cruel sisters, became so clever they were never caught.

One morning, ten months after she entered the harem, Bran woke to the faint smell of gardenias. During early morning conversations, she asked if anyone else had scented the flowers, but no one had. Later that day, standing in line for breakfast, she was jerked to her toes by a vicious yank on her hair. The unexpected pain brought tears to her eyes, but she had long since learned to keep her face set, eyes on the floor, no matter what happened.

"We hate to lose you, dearie," said a familiar voice. "But they need help in the gardens. Now get out!"

A violent kick sent her sprawling, but with practiced ease she quickly gained her feet and fled before the woman could kick her again.

By then, Bran had become a delivery girl, hurrying from table to table to collect food platters for the older girls outside. The kitchen door was the only place the two slave groups interacted and the contrast between the rags of the kitchen girls and the robes of the serving girls was appalling. The outside girls, most of whom had started in the kitchen, could only look with pity on the youngsters scurrying up to hand over their heavy loads. It was to this same door that Bran fled, to be met by an old woman in a black robe with the hood pulled over her head. Glittering eyes peered at the Irish girl and a scrawny, claw-like hand grabbed her arm.

"You filthy little wretch," said a voice like a squeaky door, "we can't have you seen like this in the gardens."

The woman dragged Bran along the marble walk outside the kitchen. It was early morning, and no one stirred in the vast gardens. For the first time since the day she had arrived, the girl saw the sky. Dawn was sending a flood of orange to attack the diminishing purple in the west; she thought she had never seen anything so beautiful. The smell of salt water from the nearby ocean mingled with the fragrance of flowers and grass. Water, murmuring in the tile channels, filled her ears like music. It was like waking up after months and months of a bad dream!

The woman abruptly turned and opened a door, pulling Bran after her. Used to the drab and dreary confines of the kitchen, the girl was startled to see a room with brightly colored tile walls and floor. In the middle of it was a small, tiled pool about the same size as the refuse pool near the kitchen. This water was clear, however, continuously fed by a stone-lined channel from the gardens running under the outside wall. A similar channel drained overflow water away, under the far wall.

"Take those rags off," said the old crone. "Clean yourself and wash that disgusting hair." She pointed to a block of soap at the edge of the water.

Bran lost no time discarding what was left of her clothes and jumping into the pool. Never had anything felt so good! She scrubbed and scrubbed, until her skin tingled and her black hair began to shine with a luster not seen since she was captured. The woman gave her enough time to get thoroughly clean before ordering her out and handing her a simple gray shift that reached her knees.

"Ahh, you're a pretty one out from under the dirt," said the woman, noting the girl's fair skin, black hair, and green eyes. "The Pasha won't sell you. If you survive, you'll be added to his harem."

She hustled Bran back outside to join a line of women and girls, dressed similarly, who were standing outside the kitchen. The familiar silence overhung them and the Irish girl took her place at the back of the line. She was unable to resist quick glances at the gardens and flowers. It seemed as if she had come back to life after being buried in the smoky gloom of the kitchen. As they filed in for the meal, she knew the kitchen crew was stealing looks at her, but she kept her eyes on the floor and ate her meal. Little did she know the astonishment shared among the kitchen slaves the next morning at the beauty of their erstwhile ragged companion!

7

THE GARDEN WORK WAS hard, despite the benefits of being outside and having the opportunity to bathe. Crews of girls and women went to work at dawn cleaning and tending the enormous building. Walks, stairs, and walls were scrubbed daily. When the wives arose mid-morning to breakfast in the gardens, their innumerable rooms were cleaned, beds made, and their discarded clothing removed to be washed by hand. In the afternoon the slaves were on hands and knees, clipping grass to a one-inch height with small scissors, trimming dead flowers, and scouring every water channel. If the building and grounds didn't pass inspection by the overseers at dusk, supper was forfeit.

This monumental effort taxed the slaves to the limit. Elderly women frequently collapsed on the job and were taken away ... never to be seen again. Others simply sickened and died. Until children were moved up from the kitchen, or new slaves bought by the Pasha's agent, these losses meant the others had to pick up the load. The result was a mind-numbing succession of days, during which everyone was stretched to the limit to meet the workload. During such times, the slave women and girls lived in a state of near exhaustion, collapsing at night with no energy for whispered conversation.

Into this atmosphere, Bran emerged like a butterfly from the cocoon of the kitchen. The first thing she did was to show the others how to wake early for conversation instead of talking at night. Her inner peace, plus her unshakable conviction that good things were going to happen, caused her to radiate a joy that her new companions found hard to resist. First it was other girls, eager for encouragement, who began finding their way across the crowded sleeping room to where she lay. She couldn't help sharing with them her dream of somehow being reunited with her brothers. Slowly, even the most cynical older women began to respond.

"How can any of us escape this place? There's only one door and it's guarded day and night, inside and out." The question was voiced time after time.

"I don't know, but I can't stop thinking about it," she would say. "Until then, we just have to help one another."

Rallied by her spirit, the girls and women found new energy for their work. Since the overseers operated on a system of checking results, rather that minute-by-minute surveillance, they didn't notice the slaves teaming up to clean rooms in half the time it took a single person. They didn't know Bran had suggested a competition for which team could clean the most rooms in a day, or who could cut the most grass, clip flower beds, or scrub the longest stretch of water channel in an afternoon. All supervisors knew was that the work was being satisfactorily accomplished each day before the evening meal, which greatly pleased the First Wife. Little did they know of the ceremony in the sleeping room, where extra pieces of food, stolen from the kitchen through Bran's old allies, were awarded to the winners!

Then, it was the dolls. When she was little, Bran's mother had taught her how to make small dolls from grass, twisted and bundled together to form torso, arms, legs, and the rough shape of a head. The child would add green leaves and flowers to create the semblance of clothing. She had played with them for hours. At one time, she had three "families" of four dolls each, complete with little stick houses containing pebbles for furniture. This "village" was her play area at home for a long time, until chickens, searching for bugs, tore it apart one day while she was at the dock.

In the harem, she noticed that pieces of straw broke off brooms and brushes during cleaning and she began to accumulate a pile of them in the sleeping room. Using bits of thread pulled from her shift, Bran started to make little dolls from the straw. In the beginning, working in the dark caused her to create lopsided figures with outrageously uneven arms and legs, but gradually her skill improved, until she was turning out amazingly uniform little figures about 5 inches high. She showed her fellow workers how to dress them with petals, leaves, and vines trimmed from the flowerbeds.

Within five months, Bran had supplied each garden slave with a doll. Everyone, including the old women, vied with one another to "dress" their dolls in the best flower finery. Cleverly hidden inside the owner's shift, the dolls would be brought out for comparison when no overseer was looking. Once again, food awards for best "finery" were made in the sleeping room just before dawn, much to the delight of the entire group.

8

THE FIRST WIFE'S TWO young daughters lived with her on the second floor. The girls were frequent visitors to the Pasha's court, sometimes accompanying him on short sailing trips, or excursions into the countryside; however, their ordinary routine was in the harem. During the day, they ventured down to the gardens to pick flowers, play on the grass, or wade in the channels.

Kelebek, five years old, was quiet and shy. Pinar, nine, was adventuresome and boisterous, always pushing the limits of obedience. A favorite with her father, and bored to tears by the humdrum life in the harem, she had pestered him until he finally had a bow and arrows made for her. The bow was sized for her stature and strength, the arrows wisely tipped with blunt points. Most afternoons found her alone at the far end of the gardens, shooting at a man-sized, straw target built for her. It was a bit odd, because none of the women in the huge building had the slightest interest in archery; nevertheless, she persisted, determined to master the craft.

Almost exactly the same size as Bran, Pinar had similar long black hair although her skin was light brown and her eyes were black. The slave girl had noticed her on the very first day she worked outside the kitchen and covertly watched her activities as the months went by.

One night Bran suddenly woke from a vivid dream. In it, she had seen herself standing beside the Pasha's daughter, shooting arrows at goblets on a window ledge. As she thought about it, an idea was born. A week later, a straw doll, colorfully decorated with red and purple flower blossoms, mysteriously appeared on Pinar's bed. At the end of its arms were twigs unmistakably representing a bow and arrow. It caught her eye the instant she entered the room that night, followed by the old woman who took care of Kelebek.

"The cleaners deliberately made a mess on your bed," said the slave, reaching for the doll. "I'll have them all flogged in the morning!"

"No!" Pinar said in a loud voice, thinking quickly. "I made that for Kelebek! Leave it alone!"

"If you wish," said the other, backing away. She was used to the girl's often strange behavior. "But she likes her cloth dolls from Italy. I'm not sure what she'll think of this."

"Well, maybe you're right," said Pinar. "I'll put it away for another time."

After the slave left, the girl sat on the bed for a long while studying the doll. She noted its clever design and colorful adornments. Finally, she carefully put it away in a chest and stood staring thoughtfully at the ocean from her window.

The next morning, Pinar stopped on the upper walkway, where Bran was on her knees, scrubbing tile. She stared for long moments at the Irish girl, but the slave gave no indication of noticing her.

"I know it was you," Pinar said softly in Arabic. "The wives don't notice it, but I've seen the slaves showing their little dolls when they thought no one was looking. You're the only one who doesn't do it. I've seen you gather straw at the garbage pile when I practice with the bow. You must be the one who makes them." There was a long silence as Bran continued swirling the heavy brush round and round, trying to decide whether to answer. Talking out of turn could bring harsh treatment.

"You may speak," said the Arab girl, suddenly understanding the slave's reluctance.

" It's a present for you. I've watched you practice," Bran said in Arabic, so softly no one but Pinar could hear. "None of the wives appreciate your skill as I do. I would like to learn the bow."

"Why? Females don't fight."

"One skilled in the use of the bow could be useful in protecting the Pasha's daughter."

Pinar was so flummoxed all she could do was walk away. Descending to the gardens, she strode to the far end deep in thought, and began to practice on the straw target. As one shaft after another left her hand, a broad grin suddenly split her face and she let out a delighted laugh.

9

"I'M OLD ENOUGH TO have my own slave!"

Pinar's eyes flashed and she stamped her foot, glaring at her mother. In the privacy of the First Wife's apartment, the two had been arguing for many moments over the girl's sudden request for a personal slave.

"You've just turned ten. You're two, if not three, years away from needing a personal slave," her mother said.

"Father said I can begin riding lessons and I'll need someone to ride with."

"There are plenty of soldiers to go along with you."

"Motherrr," Pinar dragged out the word. "You know he would never let me go alone with men, even if they were his soldiers!"

"True," her mother said reluctantly, "but there are plenty of girls from the fine families of Tunis you can ride with."

"Not if I want to go on the spur of the moment! It always takes a series of messengers going back and forth for days to arrange anything. And besides, most of them are more interested in shopping than riding."

"All right, all right," said the exasperated woman, worn down by her daughter's persistence and wanting to plan her own shopping trip for that afternoon. "We'll let your father decide. I'll send a messenger to the palace to request an audience for us."

"Oh, you don't need to, Mother. I'm supposed to be there in a few hours to accompany him on the galley. I'll ask him then."

"Very well." The First wife was secretly relieved. If she requested an audience, the Pasha would insist they conduct it aboard the galley, and the ocean always made her sick.

"Be sure he sends his answer directly to me. I'm not sure about the trustworthiness of my own daughter to report messages accurately," she said, with a twinkle in her eye.

The First Wife dearly loved her daughter, but Pinar's rebelliousness tested her patience. First, it was the outrageous request for a bow and arrows, which most girls had no interest in. Then, it was her insistence on a practice area in the harem gardens, not to mention her unfathomable commitment to shooting every day. Lately, it had been the endless pleas to learn to ride a horse. Now, she was asking for her own slave! The First Wife shook her head, thankful that easygoing and compliant Kelebek never caused a fuss.

That afternoon, sitting on a chair beside her father on the open deck at the galley's stern, Pinar's long black hair fluttered around her face as a strong breeze drove the sleek craft through the water with dazzling speed. In front of her the great oars rose and fell in perfect unison as 280 slaves worked to the beat of the drummer sitting on a stool a few feet from the Pasha. Father and daughter loved these afternoon trips away from daily routines and surrounded by the vast expanse of blue. In his youth, the Pasha had commanded such a craft in numerous sea battles; now his captains did the fighting, but he thrilled to feel the movement of a galley under him. Pinar knew this was the perfect time to approach him.

"Father, would you object to my having a personal slave?" she asked.

"Aren't you a bit young?" he said, staring at the horizon and fingering an old scar, running from beneath the left ear to his chin, earned during the attempt to prevent his sister from being kidnapped by a rogue desert warrior. His mind was elsewhere, however, remembering his first battle at sea.

"Not really," she said. "I need someone to fetch things for me, hold arrows when I practice and accompany me when I learn to ride."

"Won't one of your mother's slaves do?"

"No, they're all so old and slow. Besides, she has them busy with things the whole day! I need someone my own age, who can grow up with me and learn my every need."

In spite of his reverie, the Pasha was amused. He knew his wife's slaves were all young women and to hear them called "old and slow" was something he would pass on to her. They would have a good laugh at the child's perspective. His mind drifted again as the drummer's beat roused in him the memory of the excitement, and fear, just before his galley rammed its target.

"Father?"

"Well, I suppose so," he said, turning to stare at the earnest young face beside him. Although he had no son as an heir, the girl's interests definitely mirrored those of a boy, and it pleased him. "After all, one's personal slave should compliment her. Is there such a person in the harem?"

"Yes, I've found the perfect one." The girl's eyes were bright.

"Then it's done. I'll confirm my approval with your mother. Now, how much would you have to allow for this wind, if we were about to ram an enemy ship and you were aiming an arrow at someone on it?"

10

THE NEXT MORNING BRAN was summoned from the breakfast line, where she was pondering the wonderful scent of gardenias that once more had awakened her. Standing outside the kitchen was a female slave, perhaps 20 years old, wearing a pale blue robe of fine linen. Her perfectly proportioned face was framed with curly blond hair, and long lashes highlighted brilliant blue eyes. Bran recognized her as one of the First Wife's attendants.

"You're to come with me," the woman said, speaking English in a soft voice. "You are lucky enough to have been chosen as a personal attendant to the Pasha's daughter, but we need to make you a bit more presentable." She whispered, "You're going to find this work much more pleasant than that of the kitchen and gardens." The Irish girl followed, heart thumping excitedly, hardly daring to believe what was happening.

They walked around the gardens and entered a door almost directly beneath the First Wife's apartment. Inside was a vast room, nearly half of which was taken up by a large pool, 3 feet deep, with emerald green sides and bottom. Tile in brilliant mosaics of blue, red, yellow, and white covered the floor—accented by colorful benches scattered about. Numerous doors were set in the far walls.

"At this hour, everyone is still sleeping," explained her guide. "During the day wives bathe in the water and are rubbed down with lotions in the side rooms. Slave attendants bathe here in the evening and early morning." She escorted Bran to one of the rooms and handed her a block of soap.

"Go and bathe. Don't leave one spot of dirt on your body and be sure your hair is thoroughly washed. I'm going to find you a robe."

Shedding her shift, Bran walked to the pool and tested the water with her toes. To her complete astonishment, it was warm! Slipping in, she thought she had never felt anything so wonderful and sank to her knees to allow the water to reach her neck. She was a good swimmer and turned on her back to float, black hair swirling around her head. Long minutes passed, as she luxuriated in the experience. A soft laugh roused her.

"That's the same thing I did, when I was brought here after weeks on a pirate ship! But we don't have much time, so get on with the washing."

"What's your name? How did you get captured?" asked Bran, as she went to work with the soap.

"My name is Abigail. I was taken from an English ship," said the girl, sitting down on a bench beside the pool. "For some reason, the First Wife picked me to wait on her soon after I arrived at the harem. She said it was because of my blue eyes. She calls me 'Abraj.'"

"Oh, 'beautiful eyes.' My name's Bran, but I've not been given an Arab name so far."

"No, workers are generally nameless until old enough to become attendants or wives. We mustn't be heard speaking English," said Abigail, switching to Arabic. "It could cost us our privileged positions as members of the First Wife's household."

"All right. I don't want to go back to the crews!" said Bran in Arabic. She was quietly grateful for all the early morning conversations in the kitchen and garden slave quarters, where she had learned the language.

The Irish girl busied herself with the soap, watching the bubbles float toward the far end of the pool. Evidently there was an inlet and outlet to the bath, causing a slight current to carry the soap away and keep the water fresh. When she was clean, she was handed a soft towel and led back to the room. While Bran rubbed a fragrant lotion into her skin, the older girl brushed her hair and tied it with a ribbon. The long ponytail reached her waist. A beautiful lavender robe with short sleeves was slipped over her head, and the older slave stepped back to examine her charge.

"You're very pretty," she said, "almost a twin to Pinar except for white skin and green eyes. If you serve her well, you'll be protected for the rest of your life."

They hurried out of the bath chamber and up to the First Wife's apartment. After a soft knock, Abraj pushed open one of the ornate twin doors and they passed into the residence.

Facing them was an enormous room with soft white walls and a ceiling almost 10 feet high. Ornate couches and settees were scattered about on beautiful Persian rugs. Low tables of rich mahogany accented the furniture and where the tile floor was exposed, its faint orange hue gave the room a warm and pleasing feeling. What immediately drew Bran's attention, however, was the vast expanse of ocean visible through huge windows in the opposing wall. Light reflecting off the gentle waves reminded her of the harbor at Baltimore, and she couldn't tear her eyes away.

"You must be a child of the ocean." The voice was direct but not unkind.

A striking woman with jet-black hair and wide-set dark eyes reclined on one of the couches, a small cup in one hand and the remains of breakfast on the table beside her. Her skin was rich brown, and sparkling white teeth flashed when she spoke.

"Yes, Mistress, my father was a fisherman, and I grew up by the sea." Bran, having been coached by Abigail, bowed her head and spoke softly in Arabic.

"I have no idea how that background will fit with Pinar's passion for bow and horse, but she insisted that she wants you, specifically, for her personal slave."

"Yes, Mistress."

"Abraj, please fetch my daughters." The First Wife gestured toward a door at the side of the room. When Abigail left, Bran continued to stand quietly with her eyes on the floor. The First Wife studied her.

"Come over here, child," she said. Bran walked to the couch.

"Look at me," the woman said. When the girl looked at her, the First Wife's eyes widened in surprise. "Green eyes and white skin. You're very pretty. It's a good thing Kadar didn't spot you," she added obliquely. The silence was broken by the arrival of her children.

"She's here," said Pinar excitedly, running across the room to stand in front of Bran. "Stand back to back with me," she ordered, whirling around. "See, Mother, we're exactly the same size!"

"That you are," said the First Wife. 'But for her skin and eyes, the slave mirrors her mistress."

"Her name is Hibah," said the girl. "Because she's your gift to me."

"'Gift' is a good name," said her mother. "Without your father's persuasion, however, there would have been no gift." But she smiled at her daughter's happiness.

"Are you going to beat her?" Kelebek stared solemnly at her sister.

"Not unless she disobeys me," said Pinar. "But she wouldn't dare because she's mine now and protected from having to work like the other slaves. If she dared to disobey, I would beat her and she would be turned over to Kadar and the archers."

11

A WHOLE NEW LIFE NOW opened to Bran. She spent every waking moment with her mistress, attending to her slightest whim. Rising at daybreak, she would lay out fresh clothes, visit the kitchen for a tray of breakfast food and wait for the girl to wake. Although Kelebek slept in the next room, and was generally cared for by the old woman, Bran frequently brought something special for her from the kitchen, helped her dress and brushed her hair if she woke before her older sister.

During the day, she stayed a step behind Pinar wherever she went, ready to run an errand, fetch something, or procure food when she got hungry. When the Arab girl bathed, Bran had a huge towel and fragrant lotions ready when she stepped from the water, and brushed her long black hair until it shown. At night, after her mistress fell asleep, the Irish girl would slip down to the pool to bathe herself, often chatting quietly with Abigail, if she was bathing at the same time, before stretching out on a mat at the foot of Pinar's bed.

There were unimagined privileges with this new existence. No longer was the slave hungry, dirty, and exhausted at the end of the day. She had more than enough to eat, beautiful robes to wear, and the luxury of daily baths. The work was physically easy. Gradually, lotions softened hands made rough by months of scrubbing floors. But the most astounding aspect of her role was that the harem no longer confined her: wherever Pinar went, Bran accompanied her. Sometimes it was an afternoon on the galley with the Pasha, or it might be a shopping excursion to the markets with the First Wife.

In the beginning, the Pasha's daughter wanted Bran with her so everyone would know she had her own personal slave. Before long, however, the situation subtly changed. The slave, schooled by Abigail, soon made herself so useful Pinar couldn't imagine not having her close at hand. Ultimately, it was archery and horses that started a gradual transformation neither of them could have imagined. It began with the shooting sessions in the garden. For a while, Bran's role was to hand arrows to Pinar and retrieve them from the target. But the day came when the Arab girl handed her the bow.

"You said you wanted to learn," she said. "If you're going to protect me, we might as well get started."

"When I suggested it, I had no idea that guards go with you whenever you leave the harem," said Bran.

"The eunuchs from the harem, who accompany us to the palace, would give their lives for me, but they cannot leave this area." said Pinar. "Sometimes I'm not so sure about the soldiers who go with us to the markets. My mother says intrigue swirls around the court, and she worries that a soldier or two could be paid off to look the other way during a kidnapping. My father would pay a great sum to get a family member back unharmed. Most of the men are completely loyal to him, but I've caught one or two looking at me in a peculiar way."

"Is one of them Kadar?" asked the slave.

"How do you know that name?" Pinar gave her an astonished look.

"That first day your mother said I was lucky he hadn't seen me. Then, you said you would send me to him and the archers if I misbehaved," Bran replied.

"Kadar is a beast. He's in charge of the dungeons, and it's whispered he is responsible for doing terrible things, particularly to women. Just before anyone under his control dies, he sends them to the archers for live practice. I've seen him glance at me …" Pinar's voice trailed off and she shuddered.

"Why would a soldier dare to be disloyal to the Pasha and assist in a kidnapping?" Bran said, returning to the subject of protection.

"It's not surprising in a world where everyone is motivated by riches. Think about your own situation: the seclusion of your village on the Irish coast was no protection against a slave raid to increase the riches of Suleyman Reis. Here in Tunis the desire for gold is strong enough to tempt kidnapping one of the Pasha's family members."

"You know about my village?" The slave's eyes went wide.

"Of course. The raid was such a success that everyone in Tunis knew about it. I heard my mother describing it to some of her friends."

Pinar gestured at the great edifice around them. "That's one of the reasons we're all confined to the harem. It's quite safe with its thick walls and my father's troops stationed across the square. Outside these walls, it's a different matter. If you're carrying a bow and arrows, the men will think it totally childish and ignore you. Let them. I'll make up some excuse. But there could be a time when you provide valuable protection for my sister or me. Now, let's see you handle the bow."

The first few arrows flew everywhere except into the target, and before long both girls were giggling.

"You won't be much good at protecting me with that performance," said Pinar. "Let me show you a few things I've learned through practice."

She proved to be a good teacher and before the session was over Bran had managed to put two arrows into the straw figure. The fact that both were in its feet did nothing to curb her excitement.

12

THE GIRLS PRACTICED FOR two hours every day, and Bran discovered a natural skill with the weapon; by the end of two months, she was handling the bow almost as well as her mistress. Abigail and others warned Bran not to outshoot Pinar, fearing the Arab girl would become jealous, but exactly the opposite took place. Rather than becoming a competition, the practices evolved into skills development, with each girl encouraging the other to greater accuracy. It soon became apparent the single bow was limiting them, so Pinar had the armourer make a bow and arrows for her slave. Then the two set to work and built another target, so they could both shoot at the same time.

Although soldiers weren't allowed in the harem, it turned out that the huge black eunuch Bako, one of the guards at the harem entrance, was an accomplished archer. Pinar frequently sought him out for advice and, before long, contrived to have him attend their practices. Under his guidance, the girls were soon putting arrow after arrow into three-inch, red circles from 15 yards. As the eunuch increased the distance, the armourer twice had to build stronger bows for them!

At the end of six months, they were putting almost every arrow into two-inch circles from 30 yards. During this time, the girls were in full view at the rear of the gardens, but not one of the harem wives paid the slightest attention to what they considered a silly pastime. Bako, sworn to secrecy, never revealed the girls' impressive progress.

Bran began carrying a bow across her back and a small quiver of arrows at her waist every time they left the harem. As Pinar had predicted, the palace soldiers thought it highly amusing (though not daring to laugh openly) to see the young slave so equipped. Little did they know that the arrowheads were not the blunt target models they imagined, but were forged for battle: pointed and razor-sharp. Even the Pasha questioned his daughter about her slave carrying what seemed to be a child's toy.

"It's nothing, Father," Pinar said innocently. "Hibah likes watching me practice and asked if she could carry the bow and arrows to let everyone know I could shoot. I agreed, because it does no harm if she wants to look foolish."

Bako started teaching them rapid fire. They learned to hold three extra arrows in the same hand that gripped the bow. The arrows would be notched and fired, one after the other, with the bowstring hand. It was awkward and difficult to execute. But, as the weeks passed under Bako's expert guidance, the girls' initial clumsiness disappeared. Three months later, their hands were a blur as they loosed three arrows, in lightening quick succession, at the targets with deadly precision.

"I would include both of you with the archers of any army, despite your age," the big eunuch said one day. By then, he had been working with them daily for almost a year. "You don't have the strength of a man, but your accuracy more than compensates."

The girls beamed at each other. Although Bran never forgot her role as slave, when practicing the two were as exuberant as sisters.

"How are your riding skills now?" said Bako. He'd been escorting them intermittently to the stables for almost as long as he'd been teaching them archery.

"The Stable Master has told my father that we are good riders," said Pinar. "The Pasha has given permission for us to go outside the city with some of my friends to ride in the desert."

"Be careful," said Bako.

"Don't worry, Father will send some horsemen to guard us. But, just to be sure, we'll both have bow and arrows under our cloaks."

13

THE RIDING HAD BEGUN shortly after Bran became Pinar's slave. Near the palace, a long narrow building housed the best of the horses owned by the Pasha; dozens more were tended in herds beyond the city walls. When soldiers had escorted Pinar and Bran to the stables the first time, an old man in the blue robe, veil and turban of a Tuareg met them. Friendly eyes, set in a wrinkled face the color of dark chocolate, appraised the two girls, almost identical but for skin and eye color.

"So, you want to learn to ride." The voice was soft.

"Yes, Stable Master, life in the harem is boring," said Pinar.

"I suppose it is," said the old man with a chuckle. "Particularly when the beach and sea are close. Just beyond that gate." He pointed to a large open gate in the massive wall, through which they could see white sand gleaming in the sun.

"Can we take horses out there?" Pinar's voice was tight with excitement.

"In time, in time, child." The old man laughed. "First, you must learn to ride!"

Following him into the stone building, the girls discovered it had a central passageway with enclosed stalls to either side, each with a latched door four-feet high. A scattering of men moved about, loading used straw bedding onto carts to be taken away. Almost without exception, down the whole length of the barn, sleek heads stuck out over the top of each door. There appeared to be at least 50 horses on each side! Pinar and Bran stopped, speechless in wonder. Several of the nearby animals nickered softly and bobbed their heads as the Stable Master moved forward. He addressed them in a conversational voice.

"Hello, my beauty," he said to a gray horse with a shock of hair falling between alertly pointed ears. "Did you have a good breakfast this morning? Are you ready for a run on the sand later?" He rubbed the horse's cheek before moving on to a black animal in the next stall, head turned expectantly toward him.

The girls followed silently as he made his way down the passage, greeting each horse as though it were an old friend. The beautifully shaped heads and bowed necks stretched toward him as he approached. Clearly, he knew them all and treated each animal with obvious affection. Finally, he stopped at a door over which peered a pure white head. The horse uttered a low whinny as he touched it.

"I think we'll start you on her, Mistress," he said, giving the animal a pat on the neck. "She's only four, but has a gentle disposition and loves to run. Step forward and let her smell your hand."

Pinar walked up and held out a hand, watching the animal's nostrils flare as it took in her scent. When the head moved slightly away, she reached out and tentatively rubbed its nose.

"Good," said the old man. "I think the two of you will get along well. Now, are you ready to start?"

"What about my slave? She needs a horse too," said Pinar, gesturing at Bran standing a few steps behind.

"Your slave's going to ride also?" The dark eyes widened as he stared at the Irish girl.

"Of course! She accompanies me wherever I go and whatever I do," said the Arab girl firmly, her eyes fixed on the white horse.

"Well then …" A smile wrinkled his face as the old Tuareg turned toward Bran. "Have you ever been around horses, child?"

"On the farm of my mother's sister at home," she said, "but they were huge and used for plowing. Nothing like these." Bran kept her eyes lowered and spoke in a low voice as befitted a slave. The Stable Master stared at her for a long moment.

"I have just the animal for you," he said finally, turning to retrace his steps. "It's the gray I first spoke to. Stay and get to know your horse, Mistress," he said to Pinar. "I'm going to get a horse for your slave."

The Arab girl nodded, totally engaged with the white filly now trying to rub its head against her. As the two walked back up the barn, the blue-robed man lowered his voice so that only Bran could hear.

"I too was a slave once," he said, "taken as a young boy from the desert by the Pasha's father. He put me to work in the stable and later to train horses. After many years, he freed me because of my success with his animals."

"Why do you stay?" asked the girl.

"My village was small, and I was the only one who survived. The horses became my life; I could never leave them. Besides, I taught the Pasha's son to ride and, although he now spends more time at sea than on horseback, he treats me as well as his father did."

"My Mistress wants me to become her guardian, but I think she also likes the idea of a companion. Her sister's five years younger, and there's no one in the harem her own age except slaves."

"Guardian? Surely her father's men can do that job," said the Stable Master with a questioning look.

"All I know is, when I suggested that someone skilled with a bow might be useful to the Pasha's daughter, she convinced her father to let me become her personal slave."

"You're skilled with the bow?"

"Not yet, but she loves to shoot and we're learning together," said Hibah. The old man shook his head.

"It's a rare thing you've done. No one escapes the harem! Ahh, here we are," he said, as they reached the stall with the gray horse. The animal stretched out its head as they approached.

"She's also four and gentle," the trainer said. "But she's a bit faster than the white filly and it may come in handy for you. Hold your hand to her nose so she can get your scent."

Within minutes, the girl was stroking the horse's neck and speaking to it in a soft voice the way the Stable Master did. Ears forward, the gray stared at the Irish girl with large eyes and pushed its head against her.

"You'll make a good pair," said the old Tuareg. "When she runs, you'll feel like you're riding the wind!"

14

RIDING LESSONS HAD BEGUN that afternoon in a large paddock attached to one end of the stable. The Stable Master started the girls riding bareback, walking their horses around the edge of the enclosure. He explained they would feel the animal's motion directly, and learn how to move with it more quickly than if he started them in a saddle. They learned to press their legs against the animal for stability and to change its direction by leaning their bodies and using the reins at the same time. Leaning forward was a signal that they wanted to go faster.

"I didn't want it to end," said Pinar as they were escorted back to the harem.

"I felt the same way, Mistress," said her slave, a step to the side and behind the other. "It felt so awkward in the beginning, but my horse seemed to understand I'm just learning."

"The Stable Master said the animals would immediately know we were novices by the way we sat on them. They're so gentle: it's almost like they were taking care of us. We'll go back every day from now on."

And so they did. The days flew by, taken up with archery and riding. At first all the exercise was exhausting and both girls were fast asleep soon after dark, but they were up early the next morning, eager to get going. Now Kelebek was the second to rise, stumbling out of her room to find her older sister and slave long gone from their quarters.

"You should see your daughter," said the Stable Master to the Pasha three months after the lessons began. "She and that slave of hers are as comfortable on their horses as people of the desert. All they want to do is ride!" The leader had come over to the stable to find out what was keeping his daughter from the galley these days. "They remind me of you as a boy."

The Pasha clapped the old man on the shoulder and stared at him.

"I'd nearly forgotten those days, Stable Master: the thrill of running a horse on the sand, chasing antelope in the hills, and racing against horses from all over North Africa! It was your gift to me. Now you're passing it on to my daughter." He paused. "Tell me, how does her slave respond to all this?"

"They're like twins, except for the color of their eyes and skin. On foot, Hibah is quiet and respectful, as befits a slave. On horseback, it's different. Sometimes I hear them laughing together like sisters, as they run their animals side by side."

"Interesting," said the Pasha. "The European girl has been well trained. In my presence, she attends my daughter with the utmost skill and attention. But she carries that silly bow and quiver of arrows when they are on the streets. The eunuchs and my soldiers are well armed, so there's no need to pretend she can protect my child. I wonder what Pinar is thinking?"

"I don't know," said the old man. "The bow and quiver are left inside the stable when they ride in the paddock. They've progressed so well I'm about to let them go on the beach with an armed escort, and I'm curious whether Hibah will take her little weapon." They both chuckled. It was inconceivable to them that the undersized bow was more than a toy.

The old Tuareg began to suspect he was wrong when the girls got ready for their first beach ride the following day. After warming up in the paddock, Hibah slipped off her horse and ran into the stable, returning with her bow and arrows. The trainer's eyes narrowed as he boosted her back on the gray filly. The quiver was at her side, but she held two arrows parallel to the shaft of the bow in the hand holding the weapon. This was the style of a warrior going into battle, not something a girl with a toy would do. But where had a slave learned it? Then he noticed the arrowheads: fashioned from sharpened steel, they definitely were not toys. He raised a startled glance to the girl's face, now veiled for going out in public, but her eyes were innocently fixed on Pinar.

The escort was comprised of six men, all trained by the old Tuareg and handpicked by him for this assignment. Each was an expert swordsman and devoted to the Pasha. Proud of their skills and knowing Bran's peculiar habit of carrying a bow, they pointedly ignored her. The Stable Master stepped to the captain's horse and put a hand on its neck, staring into the rider's eyes.

"Guard them carefully."

"The Pasha's daughter is in safe hands," said the leader in a low voice, as the group started toward the gate "Each man would sell his life to save her. But the next time you might tell the slave to leave her playthings at home."

"That's not for me to do," said the old man, adding to himself as they left, "besides, they're anything but 'playthings.'" When the riders returned 90 minutes later, the girls' eyes were bright with excitement above the veils.

"Stable Master," said Pinar, sliding off the white filly. "Our horses are so fast! The captain had to slow us down because the soldiers couldn't keep up!"

"I told you the fillies were fast the very first day I introduced you to them," said the Tuareg. "How about the gray, Hibah: did she keep up?" He turned to Bran, whose arrows were now all in the quiver, bow across her back.

"She managed to stay just beside the white,"said the slave.

He nodded, marveling at the girl's insight. The gray was a good deal faster than the white, but it wouldn't do for a slave to outperform her mistress. That should be reserved for a time when speed might be of critical importance.

15

Nearly two years after Bran had entered the harem, she was accompanying Pinar and her mother on a shopping trip to the street markets when they encountered one of Pinar's friends and her wealthy mother. Although the two girls didn't get to see one another often, Bran's mistress knew that the other girl loved to ride and asked how her lessons were going.

"I ride every day, but it's so boring! There aren't any places within the city where my instructor and I can let the horses run. Mother won't let him take me outside the walls because she's scared of kidnappers." The girl rolled her eyes in exasperation. "My 12th birthday is coming up and I've begged her to let me take you and some friends on a short ride to the oasis just outside the city, but she refuses to allow it."

"It's not 'just' outside the city. It's five miles away!" said her mother. "All of them could be captured and held for ransom, including Pinar!"

"All you have to do is hire some mercenaries to protect us," the daughter said.

"I don't trust any mercenary," the mother said emphatically.

"You're very wise," said the First Wife.

Pinar glanced back at Bran. For months, they had been able to ride outside the city, but it was always on the same stretch of beach. A ride in the desert would be a wonderful change.

"Perhaps I could request an escort from Father," she said, " just like the one that goes with Hibah and me on our rides."

"He'd have to send a lot of soldiers," her mother said, doubtfully. "We'd want to be satisfied about safety for all of you."

"Let me try," begged Pinar. "There's no harm in asking."

"All right," the First Wife said, "but now we really have to get on with the shopping."

They parted ways with Pinar's friend and her mother, but the two girls were so excited about the idea that neither was any help to the First Wife for the rest of the afternoon. The very next day, Pinar approached the Stable Master as soon as the girls arrived for their ride.

"Will you tell Father we're ready to ride in the desert?"

His questioning look and raised eyebrows prompted a full explanation of the meeting with her friend in the market, the words tumbling out as she hastened to explain the situation.

"So you see, my father won't let us go if he thinks we're still beginners."

"What about the escort? It will have to be much bigger for that large a group," said the Tuareg.

"If Father thinks we're ready, I can convince him to provide the proper escort," Pinar said confidently.

The old man turned toward the captain, waiting nearby with his mounted soldiers. He already knew the answer, but felt that the occasion warranted a formal endorsement.

"What say you? Can they handle their horses in the desert?"

"You've trained them well, Stable Master," said the soldier. "They are both excellent riders."

"I'll speak to the Pasha," the Tuareg said gravely, despite the twinkle in his eye. "But you'll have to convince him to let you go."

"I will," said Pinar, with the wise look of one twice her age. And so she did … although it took several afternoon trips on the galley.

16

THE DAY FOR THE oasis trip finally arrived. Pinar and Bran arrived at the stable accompanied by Bako. Both were dressed in black burkas covering them from head to foot. A narrow opening between the top of the nose and forehead allowed them to see. But for Hibah's eye color, the girls could have been twins.

Their horses were waiting, coats gleaming, long tails just brushing the ground and manes cascading down their necks. Each was sporting a bridle and reins inlaid with small pieces of silver, equipment which the old Tuareg had provided specially for the occasion. Tiny leather saddles rested on colorful pads protecting the horses' withers and backs.

"They look beautiful!" said Pinar, as the white turned its head toward her and nickered a greeting.

"I had them brushed and rubbed with soft towels," said the Stable Master, handing her the reins. He bent, cupping his hands to boost her into the saddle. "We want them to stand out among the horses of the other girls."

"They certainly will," said Bran as he helped her aboard the gray.

"No bow today?" whispered the old man.

"It's under the burka," she said in a low voice. "No need to alarm the other girls."

Presently, a clatter of hooves announced the appearance of 20 mounted soldiers, each armed with lance, bow, and sword. At their head was the captain who accompanied the girls each afternoon.

"We'll go through the beach portal," he said, "and around the city walls to the West Gate."

"Guard them well," said the Stable Master, eyes never leaving the girls until they disappeared from sight beyond the gate.

Upon reaching the corner of the city wall, the troop turned to the right, away from the beach. Beside them, the massive rampart reached 30 feet in the air; looking impregnable. In the distance, the wall made a right turn to the north. This was new territory for the girls, accustomed to riding only on the beach, and they were fascinated when the troop encountered an enormous herd of camels. The great tan animals seemed to be everywhere, standing or kneeling on the rocky soil, men moving among them.

"What are all those camels doing there?" Pinar said to the captain.

"It's the caravan herd, Mistress," said the soldier. "Normally there aren't so many, but two large caravans came in from Bilma day before yesterday. Ahead, you can see slaves bringing goods from the West Gate for the return trip."

Indeed, they came upon two endless lines of men. In one line, each man carried, on shoulders or head, a load which was delivered to the enormous pile at the edge of the herd. In the other line the slaves trudged back toward the gate for another load. Overseers with long whips patrolled the lines. Every so often, one of the leather cords would snake out and strike a man's legs with an audible crack. The slave would stagger momentarily and then pick up his pace.

"Look at that," said Pinar suddenly. "Do you suppose the animal's gone mad?" She pointed ahead.

A huge camel was being pulled by four Arabs toward the pile of goods. Snorting and bucking, it alternated between charging the closest man on the ropes, its mouth opened to bite, and digging in its great feet to stop being pulled. The men were laughing and shouting as they took turns hauling on the ropes and scampering away from the charges of the enraged beast. Progress was slow as the four men had to exert all their strength to keep the animal moving. The overseers monitoring the line of slaves stopped to watch the commotion, calling out suggestions and slapping their thighs as they guffawed in amusement.

"It's a rogue," said the captain. "They're probably dragging it off to be killed for supper. It'll feed a lot of these men."

17

T he West Gate was comprised of two enormous wooden doors reinforced with iron, 12 feet high, which opened inward on great hinges. The opening in the wall was nearly 40 feet wide and usually crowded with people and animals entering or leaving the city. Both inside and out, the normal gaggle of vendors shouted wares at the top of their voices. Horses, camels, donkeys, and travelers all contributed to the uproar as they jostled and pushed one another coming and going.

Moving Pinar and Bran a safe distance away, the captain sent a few men to the gate to find the rest of the girls. It wasn't necessary because the riders, assembled just inside, spotted them and eased their way out with the crowds. There were ten: all dressed in black, each excited about escaping the confines of the city. Within minutes the laughing and chattering little group was on its way, surrounded by the mounted escort.

The girls all knew Pinar had a personal slave and paid no attention to Bran. They soon found, however, that the gray filly could not be dislodged from the left hip of Pinar's horse. No matter how hard they tried, the Irish girl would not allow her horse's shoulder to be moved away from the other animal. Nothing was said, but the others finally accepted the fact that the slave would not be separated from her mistress.

As the city disappeared behind them, Bran experienced a sense of elation unlike anything she'd felt in years: she was free! All feelings of humiliation and abuse dropped away, and she imagined that she could just ride off through the sand hills and find her way to Ireland. She knew, of course, that this was impossible: she was still a slave. But the memory of the mysterious encounter with the little girl in the stinking garbage pool had never left her. She was convinced that one day she'd truly be free. Thoughts of Cormac and Finn filled her mind. Had they survived? If so, what were they doing right now? How could she ever find them, if either were still alive.

When they reached the oasis, the riders found a large, white canvas stretched between trees beside a beautiful pond. The ground beneath the canvas was covered with soft Persian rugs. Servants, sent out at dawn with loaded camels, were waiting to take the horses and offer refreshments as the girls lounged about on the rugs. Bran discretely intercepted any items headed toward Pinar and served her personally. Her quiet manner and unwavering attention to her mistress created such an impression on the 10 young women that every one of them put their homes into an uproar that evening by demanding personal slaves!

The soldiers had withdrawn about 100 yards from the oasis and stood beside their horses, keeping a close eye on the surrounding hills. The afternoon was quiet, however, and they watched the young women wading in the pond, their laughter coming faintly across the sandy ground. Just as the captain was getting ready to ride over and announce that it was almost time to depart, he saw the girls mounting their horses.

"Who told them it was time to leave?" He thought to himself as he started toward them. The hostess and Pinar intercepted him halfway.

"We are having a race," said the Pasha's daughter.

"What?" he said, startled by the statement. Young women didn't race horses: it was left to boys and men.

"Yes. Three times around the oasis; we'll stay inside the perimeter of your men. We want to see who has the fastest horse."

"It's almost time to leave," he argued. "We need to be back before they close the city gates for the night. Once shut, they're not opened for anyone."

"We know, but this won't take much time. Please?" Pinar knew the Pasha would hold the captain accountable for their safety and, since she had no authority over him, she put on her most winning tone of voice.

"You must be quick," he said after a moment of indecision. "We'll have to push the animals to make it back in time."

"Oh, thank you!" said the girls, turning their horses and racing back toward the others.

The captain watched, intrigued by the idea. All the men were passionate about horse racing and to see some girls attempt it would be a novel experience. But as he feared, it took more time than anticipated. A starting line had to be set and some general rules established. Last but not least, the horses had to be brought under control. Gentle though they were, the animals felt the girls' excitement and pranced about bumping into each other and facing every which way but the starting line. It finally took all the servants plus Bran, whom Pinar had ordered not to race, to get everyone lined up enough for a start.

Once underway, the riders amazed the watching soldiers. Black burkas streaming, each girl thrust her hands forward and crouched low over her horse's neck, urging the animal on. Three times they circled the little oasis in a tight pack, and at the finish line the white head of Pinar's filly extended just in front of the others. In spite of themselves, a roar of approval burst from the mouths of the soldiers! Notwithstanding that the riders were female, such a finish was in the tradition of all great desert races.

The captain was now worried about reaching Tunis in time and immediately started the group moving, walking at first to let the horses cool off. When he judged the animals ready, he began easing the horses along at an easy canter, frequently casting an eye to the west at the lowering sun. Although they covered ground rapidly in this manner, they arrived at the West Gate just as the trumpet blew to announce the closing. The gateway was packed with people and their animals, all yelling and shouting as they fought to get into the city before dark.

"No time to reach the ocean gate, we'll enter here with the others," called the captain to Pinar above the din of the crowd, directing a couple of men forward to clear a path. She nodded and kept her place among the girls.

Suddenly, there was an opening in the throng and the riders urged the horses forward. Concentrating on keeping the gray bedside Pinar's horse, Bran was suddenly startled by a strong waft of gardenias. She raised her eyes to see where it was coming from just as they passed a cart with big wheels, drawn by an old horse. A chained man was standing in back, gripping the side rail and gazing at the crowd. Her shocked gaze took in a thin, but strongly muscled body topped with a great mass of flaming red hair. Striking blue eyes stared at her from beneath a vivid white scar across an otherwise darkly tanned forehead.

"Cormac!" she screamed through the veil. An instant later, the cart was lost to view as the riders swept into the city ...

18

Soon after they started to ride, Pinar made a dramatic change in lifestyle. Previously, she had bathed in the morning, the customary time for harem wives and children. Bran was always stationed on a nearby bench with a large towel, ready to assist the Arab girl the instant she moved to the pool steps. As their archery skills increased, Pinar began having her slave sit at the edge of the pool, so they could talk about their practices. Speaking in low voices to prevent others from hearing, they would share the highs and lows: arrows that surprised them by flying true, or others that baffled them by shooting off in directions completely contrary to where they aimed!

In the beginning, Hibah had been hesitant about these conversations, only speaking when asked a direct question and quietly affirming her mistress' statements. But Pinar was too enthusiastic about their activity to let that go on.

"You may speak freely," she said one day. "I know you love the bow as much as I do, and it's too much fun not to talk about. Around the family you have to be quiet, but down here we can converse openly." With that encouragement, the two were soon whispering and giggling like best friends during the bath sessions.

When they began to ride, the added experience was so thrilling they frequently forgot to whisper and drew looks from the other women in the pool. Anxious her mother might learn of her growing friendship with the slave, Pinar changed her way of life. Nighttime hours at the pool were for the slaves who attended the wives; however, almost all were busy in the early evening, so the pool was unoccupied for a few hours. Slipping out of the apartment after supper, Pinar and her slave would now bathe together, free from other eyes and ears. Like two fish, one brown, the other white, they would paddle around talking about the events of the day, their long black hair swirling in the water. Sometimes, shrieks of laughter would echo off the walls as they remembered something particularly hilarious. Not entirely fooled by this tactic, Pinar's mother would often send Abigail down to check on the girls, but she actually became an accomplice. She would listen with gleaming eyes and longing heart to their stories, and return to tell the First Wife that the girls were tired from their daily exertions and retiring early. In public, the relationship between mistress and slave remained the same … save the flash of a knowing look flitting between them from time to time.

Pinar was especially animated on the night after the oasis trip.

"Did you see how the white stretched her nose at the end of the race?" she exclaimed as they floated about the pool. "I've never been so excited about anything in my life as I was when I was hurtling around the oasis in the middle of the pack! It was the most amazing experience! If only you could have joined us, your gray filly would have inspired White Lightning to run even faster! What's the matter?"

She stood up, water dripping off her face, and stared at her slave, who hadn't said a word since they returned to the harem.

"I was so thrilled for you during the race. I couldn't wait to talk about it when we got home, but something happened at the gate that shocked me so much that I forgot about everything."

"What happened?"

"I saw one of my brothers! He was chained to a cart we passed as we were entering the gate. I screamed at him, but I don't think he heard me above the noise."

"Are you sure it was one of your brothers?" To the Arab girl, all the slaves seemed to take on an impersonal similarity that made it hard to distinguish one from another.

"Oh yes, he has bright red hair and blue eyes! You could never mistake him for anyone else! But his skin is now as brown as yours, and he's much bigger and stronger than I remember, with a huge white scar across his forehead. And now he's gone again," she wailed.

Pinar was thoughtful. "If he was brown, and going into the city, it means he's been working outdoors somewhere away from the city, perhaps the caravans or the quarries. You say he's bigger; how long since you last saw him?"

"More than two years." Bran's eyes welled up with tears. "But his arms," she fought to collect herself, "his arms and chest were so muscled! He never looked like that when he worked on the fishing boat!"

"He must have been in the quarries," said Pinar. "They work with the heavy rock that's used to make our buildings." She suddenly smiled, "They say no slave leaves the quarries alive. Something must have happened for him to be going back into the city. It's a reminder for you not to give up hope that your brothers are alive."

All at once, Bran remembered the scent of gardenias just before she had spotted Cormac. What did it mean? Was it a sign? She put a hand to her mouth in excitement, but the Arab girl seemed to take no notice and kept talking.

"Maybe we can find him and bring him to the palace!" she said excitedly. "Father can make inquiries around Tunis. Surely, someone in the city will know the whereabouts of a slave who looks like that!"

"Do you really think so?"

"Of course. I'll ask him tomorrow on our way to the stables!"

Not anxious to get involved in the matter of someone else's property, but wanting to humor his daughter, the Pasha did make some inquiries over the next few weeks. The reports were negative. No one had seen a red-haired slave with blue eyes and a great white scar. Cormac seemed to have vanished.

19

As the weeks stretched into months with no news of Cormac, Bran was comforted by the thought that at least he was alive. Some day, some way, she would find him. In the meantime, there was more archery and riding to learn. Bako had introduced a new dimension to their work with the bows. One day he walked to the target wall, stood to the side and tossed a straw ball across the line of fire.

"What? You can not expect us to hit something like that!" said Pinar, even though he had shortened their range to 10 yards. The large black man just smiled.

"I thought you wanted to become expert archers," he said.

"Yes, but you never said anything about moving targets!"

"But you never said anything about riding when you started asking me about archery, Mistress," said Bako in his deep voice.

"Riding. What does that have to do with it?"

"Suppose the escort was attacked and the two of you had to flee to the hills. You became lost … and hungry. How would you eat?"

"We could shoot something," Bran said, anticipating the man's next thought.

"Yes. There are quail and antelope in the hills. The problem is wild things rarely remain still like your straw targets. They move, sometimes very fast, and you would have to hit them to survive."

The girls were silent, digesting this information. Then they looked at each other and smiled.

"Then we'd better learn to hit a moving target," said Pinar.

It seemed impossible at first, but the eunuch taught them how to swing the bow in line with the flight of the ball and shoot just in front of it, so the arrow would intersect its path. Gradually, the girls began to catch on. Their extraordinary accuracy at a stationary target was such that, once they learned to move the bow smoothly, it was only a matter of knowing how far in front of the ball to aim. The further away they were, the more they had to "lead," or shoot ahead of the flying bundle of straw. As the months passed, Bako had to throw harder and harder, often arching the balls high in the air to vary the pattern. Finally, the day came when hardly a ball hit the ground without an arrow piercing it.

Reward for all the practice came nearly a year after the oasis trip. The First Wife had learned of a silk merchant, recently returned from China, who had an exquisite selection of cloth with Oriental patterns. Wanting matching robes for Kelebek, Pinar, and herself, she arranged a trip to the merchant's shop one afternoon. The Pasha provided the normal complement of four bodyguards to accompany them. As usual, Bran walked immediately behind her mistress.

The shop was located on an unusually wide street, normally very busy, but on this day strangely unoccupied save for two men haggling with a rug merchant outside his establishment. As the family passed them, the supposed buyers suddenly drew swords and hacked down two of the soldiers. The other two soldiers ran across the street and disappeared into an alley. The swordsmen waved their bloody weapons at the shocked family to prevent them from fleeing, then vanished into the rug shop as the sound of running horses filled the street.

The First Wife and her daughters were frozen in place, staring at the bodies of the fallen soldiers, when four horsemen rounded a corner down the street and raced toward them, heads and faces hidden by turbans and veils. Acting with precision, three of them bent low and snatched up a family member as their horses passed at full speed. It was a beautifully executed maneuver and the animals thundered away without breaking stride, the fourth rider covering their escape. Intent on the capture, none of them paid the slightest attention to the smallish figure kneeling just behind where the family had been standing. They should have.

The first indication that all was not well occurred when the kidnapper carrying Pinar dropped her from the horse and slumped over, falling to the ground with an arrow through his neck. An instant later, the rider carrying Kelebek released the girl, threw up his hands and uttered an unearthly shriek as the head of an arrow emerged from his chest. The lead rider twisted around to see what was happening just as a shaft penetrated his heart and lodged against his rib cage. Freed from his grip, the First Wife tumbled to the ground, and he fell from the horse.

The fourth rider reined in and turned to see who was attacking them. Facing him, 40 yards away, was a girl, veil down and burka thrown back revealing the white skin of a heathen. There was no one else in the street. Snarling with rage, unable to believe that she could be the source of the assault, he wheeled around, put spurs to his horse and charged with his scimitar raised to take off her head. He paid no attention to the bow she held and was utterly astonished at the arrow which seemed to materialize from nowhere, penetrating his chest and protruding out of his back. His last conscious thought was that girls weren't supposed to know how to handle bows and arrows.

When the attack began, Bran had dropped to one knee and swept the specially designed burka off her shoulder, exposing the quiver at her side and the fully strung bow tied to her back with thin thread. It was a design Bako had worked out to allow instant access to the weapon. As she had practiced a thousand times, she ripped the bow loose and grabbed four arrows from the quiver. The first was in the air while the riders were still adjusting to their struggling captives. No sooner had she launched the final arrow than she was racing toward Pinar, sprawled on the cobblestones.

"Are you alright?" asked the Irish girl, gently rolling her over.

"My shoulder hurts and I bumped my head. When the man dropped me, I knew you must have shot him."

"Yes, Bako trained us well: no one escaped."

"You saved my life. You are the sister of my heart," said Pinar softly, staring into the green eyes above her. Bran blushed under the now replaced veil.

"Let's see about your mother and Kelebek," she said. The younger girl was sitting on the ground crying, but didn't seem to be hurt. Picking her up and soothing her with soft words, Hibah moved to the First Wife. She also was sitting, a nasty bruise on her forehead.

"What happened? Why did they drop us?"

"The life went out of them," said Bran lamely, gesturing at the bodies on the street. "They couldn't hold onto you anymore." The woman looked at her with complete bewilderment.

"I don't understand."

"She killed them." Her oldest daughter approached and pointed at Bran. "Hibah killed them all, before they could take us away."

"How could she do that?" The First Wife was totally confused. "Women don't fight. She's not even a woman, she's only 12!"

"Almost 13, Mother," said Pinar. "It has nothing to do with fighting. Hibah and I are archers. We've been practicing every day for almost three years under the guidance of Bako, the eunuch. He's a great archer!"

The woman looked from Pinar to Bran.

"You did this? I thought the two of you were just playing out at the end of the gardens."

She stared wide-eyed at her daughter. "Can you kill enemies also?"

"If I had to," said the girl. "Hibah has been my protector for a long time now. Our skills are equal, but she carries the weapon because the men think it's childish and laugh behind our backs. You must keep this quiet, Mother. We don't want the soldiers to know what we can do."

The First Wife could only shake her head.

"And I thought you were amusing yourself with infantile games!"

20

THE PASHA WAS FURIOUS about the attack on his family and ordered his agents to find the two soldiers who had disappeared into the rug shop. No sign of them turned up, and the agents correctly surmised they'd fled to Europe. The First Wife promised to keep the girls' secret, but it was no use. Reports of the incident, spread by the merchants, raced like wildfire through Tunis, and soon Pinar and Bran were summoned to the palace. Bako accompanied them.

"What's this I hear about my daughter and her slave," said the Pasha to Bako. He was sitting behind a desk and surrounded by advisors.

"The Mistress began shooting on her own out of boredom, Excellency. You yourself directed the armorer to make her first bow and arrows," said the giant.

"But I thought they were toys."

"Initially the arrows were blunt." Bako explained. "When she acquired Hibah, the Mistress had another bow made and they practiced together. After a while she sought me out for advice and then asked me to train them, because she wanted her slave to be armed. At that point they started using arrows tipped with steel. "

"How long has this been going on?"

"Almost three years, Excellency."

"Three years!" the Pasha's eyes widened. "If the reports are to be believed, they have become quite capable."

"You would be pleased to number them among your bowmen."

At this statement, some of the advisors snickered.

"Show me," said Pinar's father.

"Right here?" asked Bako.

"Right here."

Suspecting something like this might happen, Bako had suggested that Pinar and Bran bring their weapons. Both flipped their burkas back and retrieved their bows. The watching men were astonished; although witnesses had described the kidnapping attempt, no one could explain where the weapon had come from.

"As you can see, Excellency, they are holding target arrows, quite different from what Hibah was carrying that day," Bako said. The Pasha nodded.

"With your permission, Sire," said the eunuch, picking a wine glass with a slender stem from a nearby table. "Would it be possible to have eight of these?"

Pinar's father waved a hand to a nearby slave who collected seven more glasses. Across the room were enormous windows facing the ocean. Pushing two of them completely open, the huge man set one glass on the windowsill of each. He returned to the two girls and moved them as far away from the windows as possible.

"The range here is about 40 feet, Excellency," said Bako. "Your daughter and her slave customarily loose their arrows at 90 feet."

He bent down and whispered to the girls who were holding the bows unbent, an arrow notched and pointing at the floor. Stepping away, he paused for an instant.

"Shoot," he said in his deep voice.

As one, the girls raised bows and fired the arrows in a single motion. There were tinkles of glass.

The watchers stared, open-mouthed. The thin stem of each glass was shattered just above the base. There was stunned silence as Bako went to the windows and placed three glasses on each. When he returned, those familiar with battle were startled to see the girls each holding three arrows in the hand grasping the bow, after the fashion of a fighting man. Again, he whispered something to them before turning to the Pasha.

"As you know, Sire, rapid fire is important in war. It is also important when one's owners are being kidnapped. Shoot," he said without warning.

Hands a blur, Pinar and Bran notched and loosed their arrows so rapidly the whine of the shafts and the crash of the glass was almost one sound. This time, all six glasses had been cleanly knocked out of the windows! A great buzz of conversation erupted in the room as the advisors turned toward one another in amazement. When it was quiet, the Pasha leaned forward.

"Well done! Bako, I see that I need not worry about the safety of my daughter or her slave. Were they boys, I would be well served to have them among my soldiers."

"With your permission, Sire, that's not all."

"There's more?" the Pasha raised his eyebrows. "Show me!"

This time, the eunuch chose several small bowls from the tables. Standing to the side of the two windows, he tossed them through the air across the openings. The girls took turns, shattering one after another in mid-air. In the astonished silence that followed, Pinar spoke.

"You weren't supposed to know this, Father! It was to be a secret until the appropriate time. Those stupid kidnappers ruined everything!" Her eyes flashed.

"I don't think it could have been revealed it at a better time!" said her father, and the room erupted in shouts of approval.

21

"I WAS FOOLISH TO DISMISS the slave's bow as a 'plaything,'" said the captain, as Pinar and Bran approached him and the Stable Master the next afternoon. "Hibah's shots during the kidnap attempt might have been considered luck until the demonstration Bako had them put on yesterday for the Pasha." Word of the girls' skill had flashed throughout the palace before nightfall.

"I suspected something the first time I saw her arrows," said the old Tuareg. "The heads were definitely not for target practice."

"Some of my men need to practice their shooting, if they are to keep pace with those girls" said the soldier. "Those present said the demonstration was extraordinary."

"Their aim appears to be worthy of desert fighters, but the Pasha still needs you and your men to protect them," said the trainer. His voice was calm, but his eyes were shining: he was as proud of the girls as if they were his own daughters. "They've requested you teach them to shoot from horseback."

"What?"

"Apparently the big eunuch told the Pasha they are ready." The Tuareg nodded at Bako walking behind the girls. "It's up to you to train them!"

"They already shoot better than many of my men."

"Perhaps that'll motivate your men to improve," said the old man as Pinar approached.

"So, Stable Master," she said, "our secret is out."

"Yes, Mistress. A wonderful secret it is. If I'd had two sisters like you, your grandfather's attack on my village might have failed!" The compliment brought a blush to the girls' faces which he pretended not to notice. "Your father sent word that you wish to pursue your skills from the back of a horse."

"Yes, if the captain will teach us." She looked up at the soldier.

"I will," he said. "Although I'm surprised. I've seen your love of horses, but I had no idea you were so interested in archery."

"It started because the harem is so boring. All the women do is eat, bathe, and sit around talking. At first, the bow was a diversion. With Bako's encouragement, however, it became a matter of seeking mastery."

"Now *that* I understand," said the soldier with a smile. "I'll get the escort."

During the afternoon, the captain and his men got a lesson on just how good the teenage girls were with the bow. Three targets were set up on the beach, ten yards apart. Pinar and Bran were told to walk their horses past them at a distance of 30 feet and fire an arrow at each. With one arrow notched and three held in the bow hand, both Pinar and Bran put four arrows in each bulls-eye before their horses had walked past. At distances of 60 and 90 feet, the result was the same. Bako, squatting on a nearby dune, smiled. Apparently the captain hadn't quite believed the reports from the day before!

Shooting from a trot was a different matter because of the bouncing movement. Both girls knew how to "post," or move up and down in time with the horses' steps, and the captain showed them how to release the arrow at the upward point of the post, when the body was still for a split second. Their rapid-fire training helped them adjust timing and by the end of the day they were putting arrows into the targets with unerring accuracy.

"It's a pleasure working with them," said the captain later, after the girls and Bako had left the paddock. "They listen carefully to everything I say and master it quickly … unlike some of my men."

"I remember one young soldier from years ago," the Stable Master said. "He was too hard-headed to follow my instructions." He paused. "Because of that, it took you twice as long as necessary to become an accomplished horseman!" They both laughed.

In the weeks that followed, the lessons progressed to a point where the two girls were burying arrows in a six-inch target from running horses at a distance of 50 feet. Although the practices were under the auspices of the captain, Bako was a quiet observer in the background. As they walked back to the harem, he would counsel Pinar and Bran on the finer points of technique he felt they needed. The day came when the captain created a competition between members of the escort and his young charges. The girls held their own admirably against men who had been riding and shooting for decades.

Inevitably, the demand for more difficult targets arose and the Pasha was prevailed upon to let the captain take the girls hunting in the hills near Tunis. The escort was increased for the hunts, although both the captain and the old Tuareg assured Pinar's father that the two were as proficient as any of the men. Despite these assurances, the Pasha would take no chances and the number of soldiers was doubled.

At first it was the speedy desert sheep providing the challenge, but in time the Pasha's daughter and her slave grew to love hunting rabbits from horseback. The target was much smaller and the animals' dodging and turning tested both aim and riding skills. In the beginning, the competition between girls and hares was a draw, with the rocky ground causing a significant number of badly chipped, or broken, arrowheads sent to the armourer for repair. But, much to the armourer's great relief, it wasn't long before the girls gained the upper hand.

22

Some months later, when Pinar was nearly 15, she learned from the captain that her father was planning to send a personal caravan to Bilma. This was unusual because he normally bought slaves and goods from the regular caravan operators. This time, however, he had negotiated a large contract with the Sultan of Turkey for slaves and wanted to eliminate the middlemen.

Seeking a new adventure, Pinar frequented the palace to plead with the Pasha for permission to take horses and ride with the caravan to Bilma. Day after day he refused, citing the dangers involved with desert travel: heat, sandstorms, trouble with animals, and raiders. Her arguments about their archery and riding skills were of no avail until one day he fixed her with a thoughtful look.

"Do you think you could talk a few of your friends into going with you and riding some of our horses?"

"Of course," she said, startled by his abrupt turnaround.

"I've learned that an Egyptian prince is sending buyers to Ghadames to look for race horses. It's on the caravan route, only 10 days travel from Tunis so you won't have to go all the way to Bilma. You can demonstrate the animals to the buyers and bring back the ones they don't want."

It took less than two days for Pinar to assemble eight friends for the trip.

Shackles Broken

1

When he learned about the secret shipment of gold to be hidden in the Pasha's caravan, Jugurtha sent riders to Tuareg camps across the desert. He knew it would take a large force to overcome the ruler's soldiers because, unlike mercenaries, their lives were forfeit if they failed to protect the merchandise. To be successful, Jugurtha felt he needed to assemble at least 100 fighters. Lured by the prospect of riches, a steady stream of men began to show up at the oasis in the days that followed. As preparations went ahead, Finn focused on choosing three young, fast, camels for each of the 16 warriors from Jugurtha's village.

Each evening, the men assembled in Jugurtha's tent to discuss plans for the mission. Information from Tunis indicated the caravan would leave in three weeks. Jugurtha decided to attack early in the morning at an oasis one day's travel from Ghadames. It was a standard overnight site, containing a large lake and many trees; normally occupied by several caravans at once. He hoped the soldiers would be lulled into a false sense of security by the presence of other caravans. Having no intention of kidnapping the young women who were escorting the Pasha's horses, or involving them in the battle, he counted on the escort taking them ahead of the caravan before dawn to escape the dust and heat of the day, thus sparing them from the attack. In this thinking he was entirely correct.

During these meetings, no women were present. Occupied though he was with details, Finn was desperate to see Tiziri, but she seemed to have vanished. In addition, the usual group of veiled young women was nowhere to be seen when he ventured back and forth to the camel herd. In fact, the whole camp had taken on an overtone of tension: children were kept close to the tents and few women moved about.

One night, the Irishman suddenly came wide-awake, every instinct alert. In the pitch black he could feel a presence above him. He was groping for his sword when soft lips touched his ear.

"Meet me at the tree before dawn," a voice breathed, and the presence was gone.

A wide grin split Finn's face. Reaching for the sword had cost him the opportunity to reach for his beloved Tiziri! She had probably anticipated this and made her escape before he figured things out. No matter, he would see her in just a few hours.

The stars were still brilliant overhead when two shadows met at the palm lookout.

"Where have you been?" whispered Finn.

"We've all been busy preparing food, bandages, and supplies for your raid," said Tiziri. "You'll be gone for many days, with little time to provide for yourselves."

"Then I guess we'll have to come back as quickly as possible."

"Of course."

"For our wedding …" he added. There was absolute silence for a moment.

"You've asked my father?" she gasped.

"No, but I will this morning! If he doesn't give his consent, I'll flee with you across the desert!"

"He will. He and my mother have been waiting for you to ask!" Another moment of silence passed as the stunned blond tried to comprehend what she'd said.

"How do you know?"

"We've heard them whispering at night; there are few secrets in a tent." She giggled.

In a rush of emotion, Finn reached out and pulled her to him, bending his head toward her face. Her lips brushed his, and then she was gone, ducking under his arm and running across the damp grass.

"Don't forget to ask him." Her voice trailed softly behind her.

2

PINAR AND BRAN WERE in a high state of excitement as they floated in the pool and chatted with Abigail two nights before departure. For days they had been going through clothes and paraphernalia to pack, but in the end it simply came down to several burkas each: some white for the brutal heat of the desert and some black for their public appearance in Ghadames.

"It will be strange not to have a bath and clean clothes every day during the trip," said the Arab girl. "I've never spent a night outside the harem."

"I will enjoy a daily bath for you both when you are gone," laughed Abigail. "But I envy your ability to leave the harem!"

Bran smiled at Abigail.

"I remember camping on the beach with my father and brothers when we'd sailed up the coast. It's fun sleeping out in the open; you're going to love it, Pinar. Besides, we'll be in a tent."

"Oh, I wouldn't miss it for anything! The other girls are a little nervous but just as excited! Even the chaperones are looking forward to getting out of the city!"

The families had chosen four women to go as chaperones for the girls. All were experienced riding instructors from schools in Tunis, and two had actually crossed the desert with a caravan.

"I wonder what caused my father to change his mind about our going," said Pinar as Bran helped her get ready for bed. "He was firmly opposed for weeks."

"Perhaps it's the horses he's sending: he wants riders more gentle than soldiers," said the slave.

The next morning, Bako presented the girls handsome bow cases made of soft leather. Each could hold two unstrung bows and had a flap over the open end for dust protection.

"They're beautiful!" said Pinar as she and Bran examined the cases. "And there's an extra bow inside!"

"The desert can be hard on weapons," said the big man. "I also made you oversized quivers to hang from the front of your saddles." He handed each a hard leather container holding 15 new arrows; a flip of the soft leather top exposed the fletched ends.

"You know how to string your bow on horseback," he said. "There should be enough arrows for any circumstance. Try to stay on your horses if possible, but if you have to go to ground, don't forget the quiver. It will slip right off the saddle." Both girls stared at him.

"Are you saying we'll have trouble?" asked Bran.

"No," said the black man. "The Pasha's sending plenty of soldiers for your protection, but the desert can be dangerous." His eyes bored into Bran's. "Be alert, Hibah. Take care of your Mistress."

3

"WHAT DID YOU SAY?" Jugurtha was sitting in front of the tent sharpening his sword. He continued focusing on the blade to hide the joy in his eyes, but he knew exactly what his adopted son had said.

"I would like to marry Tiziri," repeated the Irishman squatting before him.

"What do you offer as a wedding present?" The circular motion of the stone slowly stopped, and the Tuareg raised his eyes to stare steadily at Finn.

"Nothing," the Irishman rocked back on his heels in confusion. "I have nothing."

"Nothing? It's customary to present the parents of the bride with a gift." The older man was enjoying the moment immensely.

There was silence while Finn contemplated this problem. Everything he possessed, including his freedom, had come from the Tuareg leader. When he and the huge jamal had stumbled into the oasis, all he had was a rag at his waist. The memory flooded back, and suddenly he grinned and leaned forward toward Jugurtha.

"The jamal!" he said. "I offer the big jamal. It is everything and the only thing I possess in the world!"

"What?" Now it was the Tuareg's turn to rock backward in consternation. "No one can control that animal! He's a menace to everyone in my camp!"

"Ahhh, that's why you need a son-in-law who can take care of your gift," said Finn triumphantly. Peals of laughter from the tent indicated the conversation had not been private.

"Quiet!" roared the Tuareg. "Can't a man have peace in this household?"

The two men sat facing each other for several minutes before Jugurtha's shoulders began to shake. "You're a worthy negotiator." He laughed. "We accept the jamal as bride-price for Tiziri, but you're responsible for the old rascal!"

Finn nodded, unable to speak for the joy inside him. There was no such restraint in the tent, however, and cries of excitement rang out. This time, the head of the household did nothing to quiet them.

"Many riders are already here and we will depart soon," he said, turning serious. "We've no time for a wedding before the raid. When we return, Kella will have made all the preparations and we'll celebrate your marriage."

When Jugurtha's force assembled a week later, it numbered 95 men. The herd accompanying them totaled well over 250 camels. On the morning of the raider's departure, Tiziri and one of her friends were standing by his kneeling camel as Finn approached. Until they were married, the girl was required to be in the presence of a chaperone when they were together in public. Tamenzut and Tinitran each had chaperones so they could say goodbye to their betrothed, even though Gwasila hadn't formally approached Jugurtha.

"So, my love, will you be making the preparations while I'm gone?" Finn said softly. The beautiful eyes above the black veil filled with tears.

"Yes, my beloved, be sure you return safely to me." With a muffled sob she turned and hurried toward the tent.

4

WHEN THE GIRLS AND chaperones arrived at the paddock, the Stable Master had 14 horses saddled and waiting; the soldiers would herd an additional 15 animals. The captain and 40 mounted men were already present, resplendent in scarlet fezzes, gold tunics, and blue riding breeches tucked into knee-high black boots. All wore white cloaks for desert travel and were armed with swords and lances; bows and arrows were strung across their backs. There were nods of approval at the bow cases and quivers carried by Pinar and Bran, for the two had earned deep respect among the proud fighters during the months of hunting in the hills. Bran was the last to mount and, as the Stable Master held cupped hands to give her a lift, he whispered a warning.

"Be careful, Hibah. I had a dream last night about danger in the desert."

"What was the dream?" She paused slightly before lifting her leg over the gray's back.

"A young jamal standing on a hill of sand, staring into the distance."

"A camel?" asked Bran.

"Yes, a camel. Desert raiders often use camels." The old man's worried eyes stared up at her. Swinging into the saddle, she bent down as though to adjust a strap.

"Bako is concerned also. You can rest assured: I'll protect my Mistress."

She straightened and nodded to the captain that she was ready. As he watched the group ride off through the beach gate, the Stable Master shook his head. Taking horses to Ghadames under heavy guard shouldn't be a cause for worry. The people of the desert normally traded for horses, they didn't risk lives to steal them. Yet the dream had been so vivid it had awakened him in the dark ...

When they reached the caravan area outside the city walls, Bran's eyes widened in surprise. There were many thousands of the animals scattered across the low ground to the south. She was used to seeing hundreds of camels as they ventured out on hunting expeditions, but this vast multitude was beyond anything they'd previously encountered. As they made their way around the edge of the herd, she saw slaves loading many of the kneeling beasts. Apparently, several caravans were getting ready to leave. On the far side of the grounds, a long line of loaded camels was visible, already moving south.

"That's your father's caravan," said the captain to Pinar, riding beside him. "They started just after dawn and it'll be another hour before the last animal is in line."

"The head of the line must be far in the distance," she said.

"Yes, but we'll catch them easily," he said, breaking into a slow canter. "I want to be at the front so you and the girls won't have dust blowing into your faces."

5

IN LESS THAN 18 months, Suleyman Reis had doubled his wealth, primarily from the successful raids of his personal galley. His redheaded captain proved to have such a grasp of seamanship and fighting that no prize vessel escaped them. Further, he had proved to be a shrewd businessman, convincing the Reis to pay twice the normal rate for profitable tips from his network of spies. Consequently, the most lucrative targets were exclusively reported to the tall Dutchman with the damaged arm; his generosity extended to all spies, not just his own.

In addition, Cormac continued raiding through the winter months. Most galleys were pulled out for repairs during the winter and the slaves set to other work. The Irishman, who was now being called MacLir Reis (meaning Son of the Sea), realized that ships with treasure could be on the sea at any time of the year and kept the oarsmen well fed and clothed for colder weather. The swift ship, its commander flanked by the warrior with flaming hair, was recognized everywhere.

But it was the giant black slave, rising from the rowing bench with seven-foot chains in each hand, who struck fear into the most hardened mercenaries aboard the targeted ships. His exploits in battle were legendary and few were willing to risk facing the deadly links of iron whipping through the air like great scythes. As a result, most captains simply conceded their precious cargo and were allowed to sail away unharmed. It was another tactic Cormac employed: no passengers or crew were taken if there was no resistance. However, in the event of a fight, all aboard were subject to the slave markets. When Suleyman Reis observed the ease with which this unusual strategy yielded rewards, he recognized the wisdom of freeing Dumaka. The voluntary return of the big man to his seat on the bench always amazed the captain.

In port, Cormac usually joined the Reis at his home for meals, but he always returned to sleep on the galley. After prodigious quantities of food were delivered to the oarsmen each morning, he and Francois would wander along the wharf examining merchandise and discussing the latest news. It was on one such day that the Frenchman told him about a large caravan the Pasha was organizing.

"I thought the caravan operators offered him the chance to buy anything they brought to Tunis," said the redhead absently, as they stood staring at a display of weapons. He was eyeing a beautiful English sword with a green emerald set at the base of its handle.

"They do, but apparently he's looking for a large group of slaves to sell in Constantinople without a middleman. Besides, his daughter and some friends are going along on horseback as far as Ghadames."

"What's Ghadames?" Cormac had picked up the sword and was testing its edge with his thumb.

"A town about 10 days travel to the south."

"Isn't that risky? I've heard about desert raiders attacking caravans."

"Perhaps, but the Pasha is sending a substantial group of soldiers to protect them. Apparently the girls are going to show off some horses to an Egyptian buyer."

"A sword like that could inflict a lot of damage," said the distracted Irishman as they moved on.

6

FINN WAS CROUCHED BESIDE Jugurtha just behind the crest of a rocky hill. The sun setting behind them filled the sky with orange and cast long shadows across the rough terrain. A mile away they could see the green of the oasis; a stream of what looked like ants was approaching from the north. A large tent was already set up by the lake.

"That's for the Pasha's daughter and her friends," said the Tuareg. "The scouts confirm that they ride at the head of the caravan to avoid dust."

"So they'll be the first off in the morning," said the ex-slave.

"Yes, they'll reach Ghadames tomorrow, so I'm sure the group will get under way early to spare the horses from the afternoon heat. We'll let them get a good head-start, then attack from the east. The escort, if they hear the attack, will hurry the girls on to Ghadames for safety rather than return to defend the caravan. With the number of men we have, the remaining soldiers and mercenaries shouldn't be much of a problem."

The two carefully backed away from the ridgeline and strode to the waiting fighters below. At a command from Jugurtha, the raiders began a wide swing to the north, keeping to desert valleys safe from prying eyes.

7

"How do you feel?" asked Bran, noting Pinar's glassy eyes and flushed face. The moment they had arrived at the oasis, the Pasha's daughter had disappeared inside the tent.

"Hot," said her mistress. "I need a drink."

The day had been very warm and their robes only partially successful against the burning sun. Bran ran to get a big cup of water from the barrel just outside. When she returned, Pinar was sitting listlessly on her bedding, oblivious to the chatter of the girls around her. After emptying the cup, she rolled over on the blankets and shut her eyes.

So far, the trip had been a great success. Riding at the head of the caravan, all the girls had reveled in the adventure of being out in the vast expanse of sand and rocks, far from the city. The caravan route included an oasis each night between Tunis and Ghadames, so they were comfortably housed in the big tent floored with thick rugs. Every girl rode a different animal daily to keep the horses fresh. As they approached Ghadames, talk had turned to how they were going to demonstrate the horses to the Egyptians. Some favored running the animals past the buyers; others, who had been on the day-trip two years before, thought a short race was the answer. The debate was suspended now because Pinar was sick. As Bran bathed the girl's forehead with cool compresses, she recalled her mistress suddenly becoming feverish about a year before. It hadn't lasted long, but left her weak and tired for several days.

"I think she'll be fine in the morning," said the slave to the anxious group gathered about the sleeping girl. "It's happened before and she recovered quickly."

The evening passed uneventfully and before dawn the girls were stirring, getting ready to join the soldiers outside waiting with their horses. Bran, who had been awake much of the night tending her mistress, felt Pinar's forehead. It was cool … the fever had broken.

"Time to get up," said the slave softly. The Pasha's daughter made an attempt to sit and fell back.

"Ohh, Hibah," she said. "I'm so tired. Another hour and I'll be ready to go."

Her eyes closed and she went back to sleep. Bran hurried outside. A red band stretched across the eastern horizon and in the dim light she saw camels being loaded. A line of soldiers stood in front of the tent holding 14 horses by their bridles. The captain and the rest of the men, already mounted, were gathered to one side.

"The Pasha's daughter took sick last night," said Bran when she reached the captain. "The fever broke, but she's too exhausted to ride just now. The others are ready; if you could leave some men and our horses, we'll catch up to you in an hour."

The captain hesitated. The caravan was about to get under way; the greatest safety for the girls and chaperones was to be far in front, surrounded by his men and separated from the valuable trade goods. He briefly considered a litter for the girl but decided it was too cumbersome. Best to give the girl more rest so she could ride and catch up.

"I'll stay with ten men and your horses," he said. "Your Mistress will have to be ready to ride in an hour."

"She will be," said Bran with confidence she didn't feel.

8

"ARE YOU SURE I'VE got the fastest jamal?" asked Jugurtha as he and Finn squatted beside their animals waiting for dawn.

"I'm sure," said the Irishman, although he knew his young naga was faster. He had no intention of letting his future father-in-law get too far in front of him and become surrounded by the enemy. He comforted himself with the fact that his statement was accurate: there was no male camel in the herd faster than the one ridden by the Tuareg leader. The female Finn rode was a different matter.

"We'll come out of the sun with 50 men," Jugurtha had explained. "The caravan will have just started and a majority of the pack animals will still be assembled at the oasis. When the Pasha's men are engaged with us, we'll hit them from the rear with the rest of the riders. That should give them cause for concern," he'd smiled grimly. "If there are other caravans, once they see the focus of our attack they will get out of the way. Stay close to me."

"Don't worry, I will," Finn had said, prompting the older man's question about the speed of the jamal.

As the crescent of red began to emerge above the horizon line, the leader told his men to look to their weapons and mount their camels. When the great orb cleared the ground, they swept into the oasis.

9

BRAN AND THE CHAPERONE who'd stayed behind had just gotten
Pinar to her feet when a loud yell sounded outside, followed
immediately by shouts and screams. The tent flap was flung aside and
the captain rushed in.

"The caravan's under attack, we have to leave now!" he said in a
surprisingly calm voice. The Pasha's daughter snapped wide-awake.

"Where's my horse?" She jumped up, took a step forward and
would have fallen but for the hand of her slave.

"Outside, Mistress," said Bran. "We have to hurry."

Supported on either side by the chaperone and Hibah, Pinar was
rushed out of the tent, into a scene of mass confusion. Dust filled the
air. Their horses, held by three soldiers, were bucking and rearing,
frightened by the noise and pandemonium of the attack. Fighting camels
were racing through the camp, their riders dealing carnage with lance
and sword. Caravan camels were adding to the havoc as they ran this

way and that, shedding their loads: the slave handlers had abandoned the animals to save themselves.

The mercenaries, many already mounted on horses and camels for the day's travel, had been taken completely by surprise. Including slave overseers, the defenders outnumbered the raiders nearly two to one and could easily have withstood the onslaught if they'd been organized. As it was, leaders had rallied them after Jugurtha's initial charge, and they were just starting to counter-attack when his western band struck from behind. It was too much. The battle disintegrated into a multitude of smaller actions as the terrified mercenaries tried to escape.

Outside the tent, the screams of the wounded and dying were greatly magnified. As the girls watched in horror, camel riders streaking by lanced three of the captain's mounted men. In another instant, Tuaregs on camels materialized from the billowing dust to attack the remaining soldiers. The Pasha's men fought bravely, but their plunging, terrified horses put them at a disadvantage and they were quickly cut down. The raiders then turned toward the three soldiers still desperately clinging to the women's mounts.

"Hold those horses!" shouted the captain, still on foot. "We need them for the women!" He raced forward to pull an attacking warrior off his camel, running him through with his sword before the man hit the ground. Turning toward the tent he started to shout something at Bran but he was struck in the head with the butt of a lance and crumpled.

"Take her inside the tent," Bran screamed at the chaperone. She knew there was no chance of mounting the frantic horses. Even as she spoke, the man holding Pinar's horse dropped, a lance through his back. The chaperone's horse was nowhere to be seen.

The Irish girl raced to the soldier trying to control her animal. It was the gray filly. Grabbing the bridle, she pulled the horse's head close and spoke to it. At the sound of her voice the animal quieted just long enough for her to reach back and pull her quiver off the saddle.

"Now run!" she yelled, releasing the bridle and slapping the filly's neck. The gray spun and raced away in the dust. The soldier pulled his sword and pushed Bran toward the tent as two raiders on foot rushed him. He managed to disable one with a thrust to the shoulder but, as he spun toward the other, his ankle twisted and he fell heavily.

Bran looked at the fallen soldier, but he was gone. In his place was the little blond girl she had seen in the past. They were standing on the familiar hill below which blue ocean stretched away to the horizon.

"Don't kill them," said the girl clearly, holding out a large white lily in her hand.

Suddenly the image was gone and she was seeing the soldier writhing on the ground, holding his ankle. The remaining Tuareg smiled behind his veil as he stepped forward to deliver a killing blow with his sword. All at once he felt searing pain and the sword fell from his useless hand. In astonishment, he saw an arrow sticking through his forearm! His shocked look took in a small veiled female in a white burka standing 20 feet away, holding a bow at full draw with an arrow aimed at his face. Incredibly, the bow hand clutched three more shafts—the mark of a skilled archer. Knowing she couldn't miss at that distance, the Tuareg held out his left hand, palm forward, and slowly started backing away.

"That girl can put an arrow through your eye at four times the distance," yelled the soldier, hunched over his ankle. "I wouldn't tempt her."

The warrior, staring into those steady green eyes, had no desire to challenge the statement. His wisdom was confirmed two minutes later. Two riders on swift camels were passing the tent as the captain staggered to his feet and stared around dazedly. Catching sight of him, the men swerved their running animals and bore down on the soldier, one to each side, vying to be the first to strike. It was not to be. As the fighter with the lance leaned over and thrust out his deadly blade, an arrow struck his shoulder with such force that he was spun off the camel and fell almost under its feet. The second rider was swinging his sword in a great arc at the captain's neck when the weapon fell harmlessly to the ground as an arrow passed through his upper arm. Both shafts had been released in less than three seconds.

"Told you so," muttered the soldier as he staggered to his feet and limped toward the befuddled captain.

10

"You told me I had the fastest camel," said Jugurtha as he and Finn rode among the raiders, now rounding up slaves to break open the loads. Several times during the battle, the leader had outrun his men, only to have Finn suddenly appear and join him in engaging the enemy.

"I told you that you had the fastest jamal," said the Irishman innocently. "I said nothing about nagas."

The older man was silent for a moment. His future son-in-law had proved to be an excellent fighter, showing moves in the battle that few could match, save Jugurtha himself. By keeping the fastest animal for himself, the ex-slave had demonstrated loyalty that warmed the Tuareg's heart. Tiziri was a lucky woman. As he was pondering these things, one of his men rode up.

"You need to come and see this."

"What?" asked the leader.

But the man had already turned back toward the far side of the oasis. Jugurtha and Finn looked at each other with raised eyebrows and followed. A semicircle of camel riders awaited them, all facing a tent pitched near the lake and all maintaining a distance of 60 yards from the tent. On the ground in front of the camels three raiders sat, arrows still protruding from their arms. Outside the tent lay the bodies of several soldiers. At the tent's entrance sat two soldiers, arms on their knees. A smallish figure in a white burka stood just in front of them, a bow at half draw, extra shafts held in the bow hand.

"What's this all about?" asked Finn as they approached.

One of the wounded Tuaregs rose and walked to the leader, cradling his bloody right arm, careful not to brush the arrow sticking through it.

"She could have killed me," he said. "Instead she put an arrow through my sword arm as I was swinging the blade! In an instant, she had another aimed directly at my face. One of those soldiers sitting by the tent shouted that if I made a move in her direction, she'd put it through my skull: I could see it in her eyes. He said I'd better not tempt her because she could put an arrow through my eyeball at 30 yards. When two of our mounted men charged the other soldier, she put a shaft into each of them so fast I couldn't see her hands move. I told the rest of the men, if they valued their lives, not to get any closer until you showed up."

"It's a girl?" Jugurtha stared.

"That's what the Pasha's man called her," said the warrior. "I won't soon forget the look in those green eyes."

"Arab girls don't have green eyes," said the Tuareg. "They don't shoot bows either. I wonder who she is? The Pasha's daughter and some of her friends were supposed to be taking a few horses to Ghadames. We expected them to be gone before we attacked."

"Well, there are at least two others in the tent. I heard the one with the bow yell at them to get inside when the horses ran off."

Finn suddenly snapped his head toward the tent.

"What did you say about the archer?" He addressed the warrior.

"She's very good with a bow."

"No, what did you say about her eyes?"

"The look in her green eyes was very cold."

Finn ordered his camel to kneel and swung off.

"What are you doing?" asked Jugurtha.

"It's impossible, but I once knew a girl with green eyes."

He handed all his weapons to the Tuareg leader. Throwing back his head covering and veil, he shook loose his blond hair and strode toward the tent. There was dead silence among the watching men.

As he approached, Finn saw that the two soldiers were unarmed. One was watching him closely, but the other appeared to be confused and disoriented. There was no mistaking the intentions of the third person: the bow was pulled to full draw, its arrow aimed directly at his face. He came to a stop 15 feet away. The bow never wavered.

"I knew a girl with green eyes," he said in English, as the unmistakable scent of gardenias filled the dry desert air between them, startling him into silence. "Her name was Bran," he finally managed. Behind the veil there was an audible gasp.

"Finn?"

For another second the two stared at each other, then bow and arrows were dropped and Bran raced headlong into his arms.

11

THAT NIGHT, MANY MILES from the oasis, fires twinkled along a stream in a narrow desert valley. Kneeling camels, dimly visible in the flickering lights, were everywhere and dark shapes encircled each fire.

"So you learned to shoot in the harem?" asked Jugurtha, sitting by a small blaze. He sliced a piece of cheese from a big block and passed the rest to Finn at his right. The two girls and their chaperone were part of a group of trusted fighters gathered around the flames.

"My Mistress was bored and started shooting on her own," said Bran, sitting close beside her brother, his arm around her waist. She and Pinar had not left his side the whole day.

"She began teaching me, but soon both of us were learning from the archer Bako."

"Inside the harem?" The Tuareg's eyebrows lifted.

"Oh yes, he's one of the eunuchs guarding us, but he was a great warrior in his youth. We practice every day. He taught us to hit moving targets and how to shoot rapidly."

"So I've heard." There was a hint of a smile around the leader's eyes. "Your Mistress is skilled as well?" Jugurtha had been careful not to reveal that Pinar was in fact his niece, still confounded by the idea himself.

"Just as skilled," Bran said. "If she hadn't been so sick this morning, many more of your men would have fallen."

She reached out and put one hand on Pinar's shoulder.

"We chase and shoot rabbits from our running horses. Not one of the soldiers guarding us can equal her!" The slave's pride in her owner was obvious. "The very horses we're riding now are the fastest in the Pasha's herd!" After the battle several horses had been found grazing on the perimeter of the oasis, including the white and gray fillies.

Jugurtha, true to his word, had not wanted to bring Pinar or the chaperone away from the oasis. His men had found 18 sizeable sacks of gold among the trade goods, which were the sole objects of their raid. But, despite the presence of the captain and his remaining soldier, Bran wouldn't hear of leaving Pinar among the remaining slaves and mercenaries.

"The rest of his men will return from Ghadames, as soon as the other girls are safe, and rescue her." Jugurtha had argued.

"The captain's improving but he's still not right in the head. He'd have no chance of protecting women from that rabble. They have failed to protect the Pasha's caravan, they are desperate men with nothing to lose." Bran had gestured at 85 men sitting on the ground a few yards away. "Nor could my Mistress hold them off forever, even with unlimited arrows."

He knew she was right, and he knew Finn would never leave his newly found sister, so he'd capitulated. He'd have to find a way to return his niece to the Pasha before a major campaign was launched against him. Right now, however, he wanted to learn more about the slave who had held some of his most hardened men at bay.

"And you, daughter of the Pasha." Jugurtha stared at Pinar. "What say you about your slave?" He was amazed at the similarities in the two girls: but for the eyes and skin color they could have been sisters.

"She is the sister of my heart," said Pinar simply. "She saved my life in the market; she's been my companion and servant every moment of every day since she was given to me."

"Saved your life?" asked Jugurtha.

"Some of my father's soldiers committed treachery allowing four men on horses to race into the marketplace and grab me, my little sister, and our mother during a shopping trip. Hibah killed all of them with her bow before they could escape."

It was quiet for many minutes, as the seated fighters gazed at Bran with undisguised respect. This was a relative worthy of their leader's adopted son!

12

THE GALLEY COMMANDED BY MacLir Reis slid into place at the Tunis wharf, front deck piled with booty collected from a rich merchant vessel out of Venice. The pirates were in high spirits because not one man had been injured. The Venetian captain, upon seeing the figure with flaming red hair commanding the approaching ship, had simply come about and waited for them to board. Cormac's well-known policy of freedom for those who didn't resist normally resulted in easy pickings for his men, and this raid was no exception. In fact, the spy in Venice could look forward to an excellent bonus because the loot included a small chest filled with diamonds.

As soon as the ship docked, Cormac sent a runner for Francois, and shortly thereafter the young Frenchman was standing on the dock with the Arabian stallion for Suleyman Reis, and a wagon with food for the slaves. While Francois escorted the Reis home, Cormac took charge of distributing food to the oarsmen. As usual following a raid, the slaves were ravenous and the great bricks of goat cheese, enormous loaves of fresh bread, and baskets of fruit were rapidly consumed.

"There's not a finer group of galley oarsmen in North Africa," Cormac said to Dumaka as he surveyed the muscular men on the benches. His powerful, deeply tanned body mirrored theirs: sculpted chest and shoulders giving way to arms corded with muscle. He stood 5′9″ and struck an impressive figure, clean-shaven and with an indigo headband controlling his hair. The piercing blue eyes, normally friendly, could turn hard as ice in the presence of danger.

"Your way has been the right way," said the huge black man, "although we're all still slaves."

"Patience, my big friend," said Cormac, munching on a hunk of cheese. "We've made the Reis very rich. Who knows what's to come? The slaves routinely die on other galleys, but look around you. Our men are healthy and strong; not one would give up his seat to work on another ship, or anywhere in Tunis for that matter."

"It's because you saved the Reis' life."

"No, it's because we saved the Reis' life," said Cormac smiling. "We did the right thing."

"I need to keep hearing it," said Dumaka with a rumbling chuckle. "It's so easy to forget in our circumstances … and yet, I've not been so well fed since before I was captured!"

Satisfied that his men were taken care of, MacLir Reis paid the pirates and carried the chest of diamonds to the waiting wagon. As he took his seat beside the driver, he couldn't help remembering the trip to the quarry when he had wondered how long he'd live.

"I've counted the diamonds," said Suleyman Reis during the evening meal. "Your share, added to what you've earned already, will give you enough money to buy your own ship when the two years is over. Or, perhaps we should go into partnership and buy two ships; we could split the profits evenly."

"Or perhaps some other arrangement which doesn't separate us," said Cormac. "You need someone on your left in battle."

"That arm is useless," agreed the Reis. "Having you beside me has been invaluable, and your new strategies have cut down resistance. We take fewer slaves, but our overall profitability has increased. Whatever we decide; however, we'll stick to the sea. It seems to be better business than the caravans!"

"What do you mean? I thought the caravan business was highly lucrative."

"I've just heard a rumor that the Pasha's caravan was attacked by desert raiders near Ghadames. Not only did they seize a large quantity of gold, but they also carried off his daughter!"

13

THE WEDDING WAS HELD before the raiders from distant oases dispersed to their homes; consequently, there were nearly 150 people gathered at Jugurtha's tent as Finn slowly approached with the great jamal. The Tuareg leader and his wife were seated cross-legged on a large gold rug in front of the opening from which their daughters had spied on the erstwhile slave. Jugurtha was completely clad and veiled in blue; Kella, to his left, wore a black robe, but her head and face were uncovered. The three daughters were dressed like their mother, with Tiziri sitting at Jugurtha's right, Tamenzut and Tinitran to Kella's left.

Bran and Pinar were beside the bride and the rest of the crowd sat on rugs in a semi-circle extending out from the family. There was an opening at the far side of the circle through which the Irishman led the camel. Residents of the oasis, knowing the disposition of the animal, held their breath to see what would happen when it was hemmed in on all sides. Half of them were ready to spring up and flee if the situation deteriorated!

Finn, as the children had heard so many times, was talking to the beast in a soft voice. One couldn't distinguish what he was saying because the language was unfamiliar, but every so often a rumble would emerge from the animal's throat as if it were answering him. They came to a stop in front of the bride's parents.

"My everything for your daughter," he said clearly in Arabic through the blue covering across his face.

He handed the lead rope to Jugurtha and stepped back. The leader wasted no time in passing the rope to his wife, mindful of the snorting sound beginning to well up in the jamal's throat as the animal observed it was no longer connected to its owner.

"We accept your gift," said Kella calmly, with the hint of a smile at her husband's apprehension. "Would you be so kind as to return it to the herd?"

Normally, one of the daughters, or a servant, would have led the animal to the back of the tent to display its new ownership. Continued snorting and the stamping of a front foot by the enormous camel, however, indicated it would be wise to get the rope right back into the hands of the young man before them.

"As you wish," said Finn, trying to keep a straight face. He took the lead and, bending close to the animal's head, said something unintelligible to it as they turned to leave the circle. Bran's hands flew to her face just in time to cover a giggle. She was the only one in the whole gathering who understood the English words.

"Well done, old friend. It wouldn't be wise to stampede over the bride's parents on my wedding day!"

14

AFTER THE MARRIAGE CELEBRATION, Finn and Tiziri moved into a tent specially set up for them at the edge of the camp. Bran and Pinar were frequent visitors during the following weeks. They were only three years younger than the beautiful bride and had taken to her instantly. In the recesses of Kella's tent, they learned from the sisters all that had happened since Finn and his camel had staggered into the oasis. The stories were told and retold because Bran had an insatiable curiosity about her brother's experiences, and laughter often rang out behind the curtains over the spying and trickery of the three sisters.

Pinar's status was unusual. Technically, she was a captive of the Tuaregs but because of Bran's relationship to Finn, and because almost everyone secretly knew Pinar was Jugurtha's wife's niece, she and the chaperone were treated like guests of honor. Kella went out of her way to make sure Pinar felt welcome in every possible way. Bran, Pinar, and the chaperone slept and ate in Jugurtha and Kella's tent. Pinar and the chaperone—a woman of 30 named Farah—were free to move about the camp as they wished. It turned out Farah was a childless widow who loved children. Within days, she made friends with several young mothers and spent most of her time with them.

Bran and Pinar were inseparable, although the former's status had changed as well. Clearly, the desert people didn't consider her a slave; in fact, it was an unspoken view that she now owned the Pasha's daughter! A subtle transition took place as she dropped the servant role and began treating Pinar as a sister, which the Pasha's daughter found unexpectedly enjoyable. The two gave numerous demonstrations with their bows, amazing everyone, particularly the warriors. Before long, the children were begging for lessons! Finn introduced the girls to camel riding. Although technique was different from horseback riding, the concept of being mounted on a swift and agile animal was the same, and both proved quick learners.

"If the Stable Master could only see us now," said Bran as her brother led them through a high-speed exercise aboard young nagas.

"I think the rabbits would have the upper hand right now." Pinar laughed as her mount swerved unexpectedly and nearly dislodged her.

In this atmosphere a pleasant month passed, but Jugurtha knew he was running out of time to return Pinar.

15

THE PASHA STARED AS a figure in blue was ushered into the big room with its windows overlooking the sea. Sunlight reflecting off the water highlighted large vases of flowers scattered about the area. His advisors, resplendent in colorful robes, were clustered nearby on ornate chairs and the escort captain stood just to his right. Minutes dragged on as the leader redirected his gaze to some papers he'd been studying. Finally he raised his gaze to the dark eyes above the veil.

"Yes?"

"The raiders wish to return your daughter," said the man in a deep, measured voice. "She and her chaperone are unharmed and have been well cared for."

In the silence that followed, every eye in the room was directed at the messenger. Ever since word of the attack had reached him, the Pasha's men had been scouring the desert, reaching farther and farther into the vast wilderness to track down the raiders. The force had been too large to come from one band. Someone, somewhere, would know about the raid, and torture would extract the rest of the information.

"What about her slave?" said the Pasha.

"She will escort her mistress home, but the raiders will not release her."

At this the Pasha raised his eyebrows but said nothing aloud, thinking to himself, "*We'll see about that.*"

"When?"

"Next week. They will be left at the oasis where she raced with the other girls. You will be informed of the day."

"And the gold?" The Pasha's eyes darkened. He was the ruler of Tunis, used to tribute. Never had anyone dared to rob him, much less kidnap his daughter.

"They sent no word of the gold."

"What's to keep me from putting your eyes out and turning you over to the archers?" In his anger, the Pasha couldn't resist the question, although he already knew the answer.

"If I don't returned unharmed, you will never see your daughter again," the man said evenly.

"Get out before I run you through myself!" the Pasha shouted, throwing his papers in the man's face.

16

THE CAPTAIN WAITED AT the oasis with 10 mounted soldiers. It was mid-afternoon on the day designated for Pinar's release, but so far no one had appeared. Time was getting short to return to Tunis before the gates closed and he anxiously scanned the surrounding hills shimmering in the heat.

He had been given the opportunity to redeem himself for the girl's abduction only because it was clear he had been willing to sell his life to save her during the caravan battle. The blow to his head had left him befuddled for days. If he failed again, Kadar and the torture chamber awaited.

With a sigh of relief he saw three figures on horseback appear from the north and descend a rocky hill toward him. Even from a distance, he recognized the gray and white fillies normally ridden by Pinar and Hibah. The third horse must carry the chaperone. As they drew close, the captain rode out to meet them.

"Your mother and father have been worried," he said. "Did the raiders mistreat you?"

"To the contrary," said Pinar, "they treated us very well. Farah made some new friends and Hibah and I learned to ride camels!" She gave a short laugh, "They're quite different than horses, you know. And how are you? When we left, you still didn't know what was going on."

"It took me a long time to recover," he admitted. " But it's late and we need to hurry if we're going to reach the gate before it closes."

"Very well," she said.

They set off at a canter. Bran, riding beside Pinar, felt a weight lift off her shoulders. Her mistress was safe now in the familiar company of the captain and his soldiers. The Irish girl had insisted on going to the oasis, against the arguments of both Jugurtha and Finn. She had told them she owed a great debt to the Pasha's daughter for giving her back a life. She was determined to see the girl safely into the hands of trusted men before escaping to the desert to rejoin her brother.

The plan was for her to bolt from the group as they approached the gate. The captain wouldn't risk leaving Pinar to chase her slave, and Bran had explained patiently that no one could catch the gray. Jugurtha and Finn had reluctantly agreed to the idea. They would wait in the hills just out of sight of the gate.

However, just before the captain and the girls reached the city, a troop of 50 mounted soldiers appeared and surrounded them, led by the Pasha himself.

"I've come to personally escort the three of you on the last mile home!" he announced with a big smile.

With the captain and his men in the middle, the Pasha led the whole group at a full run toward the gate. The late afternoon crowd scattered as the horses thundered down on them and Bran, hemmed in on all sides, had no choice but to enter the city among the other riders. Once inside, the riders slowed and the Pasha moved to ride beside the girls.

"I was informed that the raiders wouldn't release Hibah but I couldn't permit the loss of my daughter's favorite slave, could I?" he said triumphantly.

17

Finn and Jugurtha, lying on the crest of a hill a few hundred yards away, watched in stunned silence. The crowd had surged back after the riders passed, filling the entrance so the great gates were momentarily stopped from closing.

"I've got to get her!" Finn struggled to his feet and started to run down the hill toward the warriors and camels waiting below.

"Stop! The gates will be closed in a minute and you'll just draw attention to yourself!" Jugurtha scrambled after him, full of concern for his son-in-law. "The last thing you want is to tip off the Pasha that we're in the area! We'll rescue her another way!" He'd never seen the younger man so agitated.

"How?" The Irishman stopped alongside his naga and turned to face the Tuareg. "I've not found her only to lose her again."

"You haven't lost her. We know exactly where she is—in the harem with Pinar."

"What if Pinar tells her father about me?"

"She may, but I doubt it. She's not likely to betray the slave who's saved her life several times! The two are like sisters. The Pasha has patrols out looking for us, but he'll be looking in the wrong places."

"Why?" said Finn.

"Because we'll be within the city instead of outside it."

18

THE NEXT MORNING TWO figures in nondescript robes and turbans joined the morning throng at the West Gate. One had a tagelmust adjusted to cover his whole face, barely revealing eyes which were directed at the ground to avoid revealing the unusual brown color with flecks of gold. The other was loosely veiled, showing the dark skin and eyes characteristic of North African people. An hour later, having taken a circuitous route that doubled back on itself many times to expose potential followers, the pair reached a door in a narrow alley. At their knock, a tiny old woman with pure white hair and skin the color of well-used leather opened the door. She stared at the strangers blankly until the darker one pulled his veil down.

"Jugurtha!" she said, one hand flying to her mouth. "You haven't been in the city for 25 years! You must get inside!" She stood aside for both to enter. "What are you doing here?"

"Amnay, let me present my mother's sister, Lemta. Lemta this is my son-in-law Amnay," the Tuareg said in a formal voice, ignoring the question. He suddenly bent to catch the little woman up in his arms. "I've longed to see you ever since I fled with Kella! You look wonderful, just as they've told me!" He set her gently back down. "As you know, Tiziri is Amnay's wife!"

"Yes," said Lemta. "So this is the great camel rider." She stared up at the brown eyes and blond hair, now free of the head covering. "Ahh, he's very handsome in the European way, even more so than I heard!"

"Lemta sends me messengers with news of Tunis," said Jugurtha. "The messengers carry news of the camp back to her. She probably knows more about you than you can imagine!"

"Surely this is dangerous for you," said Finn as the woman ushered them down the hall to a surprisingly large room looking out on a beautiful garden. "Particularly since my father-in-law continues to raid the caravans."

"Bah, who would suspect an old woman with a cane hobbling around the markets, so poor she rarely buys anything?"

"Unless they understood the quality of her hearing and noticed her proximity to tradesmen exchanging information," said Jugurtha, "or knew of the visitors that come to her door in the dead of night with useful information."

"Jugurtha pays extremely well for useful information," explained his aunt. "The informants are careful to be discreet."

Over bread and goat cheese Jugurtha told Lemta the story of the raid, Bran and Finn's reunion, and her unforeseen return to the harem.

"I've sent my men back to the desert to assemble a fighting force," said the Tuareg. "Before they return, we've got to develop a strategy to free Hibah, and we need to make sure she is not in any danger in the meantime. She and the Pasha's daughter seemed close while in the desert but one never knows what will be revealed to the Pasha now that they are back." The old woman stared into space for several minutes.

"I know an old slave who's a cook for Suliman Reis. Sometimes, she's asked to make special dishes for the Pasha's family. Perhaps she can help."

19

WHEN TOLD THE NEXT afternoon by Lemta that the personal slave to the Pasha's oldest daughter was an Irish girl who was feeling poorly, the old cook brightened.

"I know that the Pasha and First Wife love Irish Bread and Butter Pudding, but I haven't been asked to make it for many months. It's a treat the Reis has sent to them from time to time. Surely, the First wife would share some with a valued personal slave who is feeling poorly," she said.

She and Lemta sat at a wooden table in her kitchen. Their matching white hair was offset by the contrasting color of their skin: pale for the cook, and dark brown for Lemta.

"Do you suppose inquiry could be made at the harem?" asked Lemta in a concerned tone.

"If she's truly Irish, as you say," announced the cook, "there's nothing like Bread and Butter Pudding to cheer up those of us from the emerald isle. Over the years I've even gotten the Reis' household to enjoy it! The master is away right now, but I don't suppose he'd mind if I asked Francois to inquire at the harem."

"Be sure to have your slave ask about the servant girl's health."

"Of course. Poor lass, she can surely use some comfort from home."

Two days later, when Lemta called on the cook she learned the First Wife had been delighted by the inquiry and was most anxious to have some Bread and Butter Pudding. But the huge black eunuch on the other side of the speaking grate had seemed confused by the question about the Irish girl. He said that she'd never been in better health.

20

THERE WAS A SOFT knock at the Stable Master's door in the paddock. The old man woke instantly, reaching for a sword hidden under his pallet. His small window showed stars blazing in the night sky: it was far from dawn. There'd been no disturbance from the stalls and no noise from the horses in the corral outside his window. Whoever had come did not want to be discovered. Assassination was a possibility, though remote. No one in the Pasha's entourage had cause for complaint with the old Tuareg, but one never knew. Standing beside the door, the sword in his right hand, he put his left hand on the wooden bolt but didn't draw it.

"Yes?" he said in a low voice.

"We mean you no harm, Stable Master. We wish to talk," someone said quietly.

"We?" questioned the old man.

"Jugurtha of the Tuareg and his son-in-law," came the answer. For a moment, there was silence as the Stable Master digested the information. Jugurtha was perhaps the most famous of the desert leaders, feared as a raider, respected as a fighter. As a young man, he had often come to the stables while visiting the old Pasha's court. They had raced many horses alongside each other down the beach, although the challenger had never beaten the Stable Master, then in his 40's. Yes, the old Tuareg knew his visitor: Jugurtha's grandfather had been his father's best friend. However, Jugurtha's elopement with Kella had banned him forever from Tunis. He opened the door.

"Something must have happened to bring you into the city," said the Stable Master as the three sat in the darkness of his room a few minutes later. "Something very important."

"Yes, old friend," said the Tuareg leader and commenced to tell him the whole story.

"I know this girl, Hibah," said the trainer when Jugurtha had finished. "She came with the Pasha's daughter to learn riding. At first we thought her bow and arrows were playthings, but one day I saw the arrowheads: razor sharp steel. I began to suspect we'd all been mistaken about the weapons, and an incident in the market proved it."

"We heard about that," said Finn.

"When the girls' riding ability improved, they wanted to start shooting from horseback. That's when Bako began to show up, and I had the chance to learn what he'd been teaching them."

"Bako?" asked Jugurtha.

"He's one of the eunuchs in charge of protecting the harem. He is a skilled archer, captured in battle far from here. It's said he could fire five arrows so fast the eye couldn't see them leave the bow. All would be touching in the bull's-eye 25 yards away." Finn gave a soft whistle.

"That's hard to believe!"

"Your sister's almost as good."

"We've seen her and Pinar shoot at the oasis," said Jugurtha. "It was more of an exhibition, hitting fruit in the air, that sort of thing. But Hibah did hold 15 of my warriors at bay during the raid!"

"Had they attacked, some would have died before they knew what hit them," said the trainer dryly. "How will you rescue her?"

"I've warriors coming," said the desert leader. "We plan to raid the harem late at night."

"You can get all your men safely inside the city?"

"No. But if the beach gate were open …" the statement hung in the air.

Silence stretched on for minutes. Finn gazed at the starlit sky through the window and thought of Tiziri sleeping far away in the desert. She was probably with her sisters and Kella in the big tent. He missed her terribly. When he got home, he would devise a way to sneak her into Tunis so she could experience the wonderful markets he'd seen.

"It was daylight the last time," said the old man finally. "No one suspected the gate had been unlocked. This time, they'll know it was me and I'll pay with my life."

"Not if you return to the desert where you belong, my old friend," said Jugurtha. "Besides, we'll need some of your horses to escape the city quickly and someone will have to care for them when we get home."

21

"You were gone for almost two weeks!" said Francois as he and Cormac strolled back to the galley after supper.

"Yes," said the redhead. "It just happened that an Egyptian ship and a Spanish ship were passing Italy within a few days of each other. Our spies reported both worth taking, so we cut down rations and stayed at sea after relieving the Egyptian captain of his gold."

"And the Spanish? Didn't they resist?"

"They started to, but the sight of Dumaka swinging his chains inspired a quick surrender!"

"What next?"

"I think we'll be in port for a couple of weeks. The Reis wants to make sure his three sailing ships are well provisioned before sending them out into the Atlantic again. Do you think the Spanish goods will be profitable?"

"Indeed, you're making the Reis rich beyond all the other captains!"

"It keeps him in a good mood on the galley," said the Irishman. "Any news about the Pasha's daughter?"

"Oh, yes. She was returned unharmed by the raiders last week, while you were gone."

"Unharmed?" Cormac was curious, since the desert raiders were reported to be ruthless.

"The report is that she was completely unharmed; she even rode in on her own horse. But there seems to be conflicting information about the personal slave who returned with her."

"Conflicting?" asked the Irishman absentmindedly, his thoughts turning to repairs needed on the galley as they passed the stall of a shipwright.

"Well, an odd thing happened a few days after they returned. The cook sent me to the harem to inquire whether the First Wife would like some Bread and Butter Pudding. Years ago, the Pasha had sampled it at dinner with the Reis and, since then, the family has frequently requested the dish. But the real reason for the inquiry was that our cook heard somewhere the daughter's personal slave had returned from the desert sick. She thought Irish food would comfort her and specifically told me to ask about the girl."

"She's probably right, that pudding is wonderful," the redhead answered, still preoccupied.

"But the strange thing is that the big slave behind the door said she was fine. When I persisted, thinking he was mistaken or was thinking of the wrong slave, he became adamant and firmly stated that the girl with the green eyes attending the Pasha's daughter was in perfect health."

There was a moment's silence, then Cormac's head snapped around and he grabbed both Francois' arms in a grip so hard that the Reis' slave flinched.

"What did you say?" he demanded, eyes boring into the Frenchman's.

"He said the slave attending the Mistress was in perfect health." Francois had never seen the Irishman so intense. His blue eyes had turned almost gray and had a dangerous look.

"No, you said 'Irish food, and the slave with the green eyes,'" Cormac spoke the words slowly.

"Uhh, yes. That's what the big man said, 'the girl with the green eyes who attends the Pasha's daughter.' That's exactly what he said. You're hurting my arms."

"I'm sorry," the redhead's face relaxed, he released his grip, and took a step back. "How old is the daughter?"

"I don't know, but the cook will. What's this all about?"

"My sister has green eyes. Let's go find the cook." With that, he started back toward the Reis' house at such a pace his friend had to trot to keep up.

22

THAT EVENING, NO ONE paid attention to two nondescript travelers casually making their way out of the West Gate against the surge of people and animals trying to get in before it closed. Once outside, they mingled with those remaining there who were preparing to spend the night against the city walls. When it was dark, they slipped away from the camp and crept to the low western hills where a shadowy figure rose from behind a boulder to greet them.

"I've camels in the ravine," said Gwasila.

"Good," said Jugurtha. "How many men did you bring?"

"Only 25 on such short notice."

"That'll have to do," said the leader grimly. "Where are they?"

"At a small spring 40 minutes ride from here. Your three daughters are with them."

"What! You brought my daughters?"

"I had no choice. Tiziri somehow got the big jamal to attack anyone approaching the camel herd for mounts, until I agreed to bring her and her sisters. She said she had to see her husband before the attack because the odds were so overwhelming she feared for his life. Tinitran said the same about me, and Tamenzut's beloved Tariq is among our fighters."

"I knew that jamal was going to be trouble," said Jugurtha glumly.

Finn's heart pounded at the prospect of seeing his beautiful wife, his wide grin hidden in the darkness. The great camel had warmed to Tiziri from the moment they were married, seeming to grasp that she had become part of the family. Other than Finn, she was the only person it allowed close without erupting in rage.

As the three approached the spring, brilliant starlight revealed the shadowy figures of men and kneeling camels. Scarcely had they dismounted, when a dark figure rushed forward to grab Finn in a fierce embrace.

"What are you doing here?" he said, trying to sound severe but failing completely.

"I couldn't stay away, my love."

"We can't let you near the fight."

"I know. I just wanted to be close to you."

"We'll find a way to hide you until it's over. Now I have to join your father for the planning."

Gently disengaging himself, he gave a last touch to her fingers and headed for the assembled warriors. The presence of the three young women complicated Jugurtha's plan. He couldn't spare any men from the attack and he didn't dare leave the girls alone in the desert. In the end, he decided to take the three into Tunis the next morning and hide them with Lemta. He and Finn would rejoin the fighters that evening and enter the city through the sea gate, opened by the Stable Master. Since the raid was only to capture a slave, it might not cause too much of a stir, and they could return to Tunis for the girls when the excitement died down.

23

"So at last I actually get to meet the one who was sent to the quarry." The cook studied the man sitting in front of her. "Francois stole food from the kitchen to feed you the first time you passed through. He begged for even more when you unexpectedly returned. We were both astonished at your survival."

"Miracles sometimes happen," said Cormac.

He and the Frenchman had roused the Reis' cook during the night to question her about the strange inquiry she'd sent concerning the slave girl. In the beginning the cook was guarded, but when they explained that MacLir Reis had a sister with green eyes who was about the same age as the Pasha's daughter, she told them of Lemta's visit.

"She seemed very concerned about the slave's condition and asked if I could find out anything," the cook said. "Lemta is a dear friend, so I agreed to help. The Bread and Butter Pudding seemed to be a good excuse to gather information."

"A very good idea," said Cormac. "Do you know where Lemta lives?"

"I do," said the cook.

Thus, a soft knock sounded on Lemta's door as the sun rose. A cloaked figure, with brilliant blue eyes and a great white scar on his forehead, courteously asked permission to enter.

"If the cook told you how to find me, she and Francois must trust you." Lemta said after he revealed his identity.

"We're all slaves and have a mutual trust," said the redhead. "Now, let me tell you why I've come." He started his tale, explaining that the slave girl might be his sister, whereupon the old woman's eyes suddenly widened and one hand flew to her mouth.

"Are there three of you?" she gasped.

"Why yes, how did you know?"

"Your brother was here in this very room not four days ago!"

"Here?" he said in some confusion. "My brother?"

"Yes, he's a famous camel rider known as Amnay. He was a slave who escaped the caravans; he and his great camel nearly died in the deep desert before finding the oasis where my nephew lives. Now he's a free man, counted as a warrior among the Tuareg, and married to my nephew's youngest daughter! He's quite a handsome young man," she added enthusiastically.

Lemta went on to describe how Finn had encountered Bran during the raid on the Pasha's caravan, only to lose her when she was helplessly swept into the city with Pinar's rescuers.

Cormac sat in stunned silence. His brother a Tuareg warrior? And married! Finn and Bran reconnecting after years of slavery! It was almost too much to grasp … he had to make contact with Finn!

"What's their plan for rescuing my sister?"

"I don't know. Jugurtha said he'd sent for warriors, but he didn't tell me more."

"He can't get into the city after dark, I wonder …" the redhead paused. There was a light rap on the door.

"Who could that be?" asked Lemta, thinking to herself that the spies she dealt with always came at night. She disappeared down the narrow hall. Cormac drew his sword and melted back into the shadows along the wall. He heard muffled voices; then a figure rushed into the room and threw back his blue tagelmust to reveal a mass of blonde hair and a strikingly handsome face.

"Finn?" Cormac slipped into the light, hardly daring to believe his eyes.

"My brother," said Finn, stepping forward to embrace him in a great bear hug. "I can't believe it's you!" The two men clung to each other, unbidden tears flowing down their faces. Cormac finally pushed the younger man back to get a better look at him.

"You're a bit taller than I am now," he said with a smile. "And handsome indeed, as Lemta said!"

"You look strong as an ox," said Finn staring at his brother's heavily muscled arms and physique. "And I see someone tried to brain you." He stared at the great white scar.

"Not someone, something!" said his older brother, suddenly realizing that others had entered the room. "Oh, I see you're not alone." He turned his gaze to the three beautiful young women in black robes, whose veils had been lowered upon entering the home. Behind them stood a fierce looking Tuareg warrior clad in blue.

"Ahh, this is my wife Tiziri," said Finn, switching to Arabic. He led her forward and Cormac bowed, took her hand and kissed it as though she were a Queen, his red hair tumbling forward over his shoulders.

"My sisters Tamenzut and Tinitran," she said with a delighted smile, gesturing to the others, "and accomplices in spying on your brother."

"I'll have to hear more about that," said the Irishman, bowing to them. He turned toward Jugurtha. To his utter surprise, the veiled man stepped forward and embraced him, then moved slightly back and gripped his right forearm in greeting.

"A fighting man if I'm not mistaken," he said, noting the sword at the Irishman's waist. "The brother of my son-in-law will always be welcome in my tent. We know of the courage and loyalty that runs in your family."

24

Bran and Pinar returned to their harem routine, once exciting, but now tame compared to the adventures they'd experienced. On their second day home, they resumed practice with Bako because the Pasha now refused to allow them to ride outside the city for hunting. The eunuch wanted to hear everything about the raid and how Bran had protected her mistress. His eyes glowed with pride, and his great voice rumbled with laughter as Pinar recounted the circle of warriors held at bay by the diminutive archer.

"All your training paid off, Hibah. I'm proud of you," he said.

Bran looked down, blushing, but her heart swelled. Such a compliment from a proven warrior was praise indeed! The girls questioned him about what to do if they were again confronted with human targets.

"What you experienced in the attack is not likely to happen again," he explained. "You did well, Hibah, to disable those men rather than kill them. There were too many raiders and you would have been put to death if you had taken lives."

"It was strange," replied Bran. "In the market attack, I acted without hesitation, but in the desert I clearly felt I shouldn't shoot to kill." She made no mention of the little girl who'd appeared with the warning not to kill anyone.

The eunuch nodded and set them to work on shooting at broken pieces of pottery flipped through the air. When they complained about the small size, he explained with a grin that their real life experience now called for greater proficiency!

Learning the extent of the Pasha's outrage at the caravan attack, neither of the girls mentioned Finn to anyone. They feared Bran would be considered an accomplice to the raid and turned over to Kadar despite her position as Pinar's slave. The only person Pinar spoke to about their captivity was her mother.

"The Tuareg treated us so well," she said one evening shortly after they got home. "We learned to ride camels and stayed in the leader's own tent. His wife Kella was so kind to me."

"Kella, did you say 'Kella'?" the First Wife's eyes opened wide and one hand flew up to cover her mouth.

"That was her name. Why?" asked Pinar.

"What did she look like?"

"One of the most beautiful women I've ever seen, except for you that is," said the girl enthusiastically. "Her face was oval, her mouth perfectly formed." Her mother stared at her.

"Did she have a little white scar on one side of her chin?"

"I don't know," said Pinar, turning to Bran. "Was there a scar on her chin?"

"Yes. I noticed it several times. It was very small, shaped in a curve," said the slave. The First Wife put both hands to her mouth and eyes sparkling, gave a delighted giggle.

"It *is* Kella," she whispered.

"Who is she, Mother?" asked Pinar in astonishment.

"She was my very best friend when I was growing up. We did everything together. Her father was the Pasha and my father was a wealthy ship builder. We were the fastest runners of all the girls we played with. When we were six years old, she fell during a race and cut her chin on a small rock. The cut left a scar and, because of it, our mothers never let us race again."

"But why have I never met her if you were best friends?" Pinar wanted to know.

"When we were 15, a handsome young Tuareg warrior appeared at court to learn about trade with the European countries. He and Kella fell deeply in love at first sight. Months later, they wanted to marry but her father forbade it, thinking the Tuareg not worthy. One night, the warrior brought fighters into Tunis and in the morning she managed to slip out of the harem and join him. But someone saw them and sounded the alarm. The Tuareg fought their way out through the Sea Gate by the stables and vanished into the desert. The Pasha was enraged and had his soldiers spent years looking for them, but Jugurtha was always one step ahead and they were never captured."

She stared at Pinar. "A few years later, I married your father, Kella's older brother. The man whose tent you stayed in is your uncle."

25

THE ONLY PLACE THE girls could talk openly was in the pool at night and Abigail was just as astounded as they were about the background of Kella and Jugurtha.

"I can't believe it," said Bran, as all three floated on their backs in the warm water. "My brother is married to your cousin!"

"And my uncle's wife is my mother's best friend!" said Pinar. "We've agreed not to say anything to Father for a while. My grandfather was angry enough to try to stop them from marrying and now Jugurtha has taken my father's gold, adding to the insult."

"If only there were some way to get them together," said Bran. "I'm sure the Pasha loves his sister, and I know your mother has a special place in her heart for Kella. Maybe they could all work things out if they saw each other and remembered how they feel." Pinar stared at the ceiling. "What do you think Finn and Jugurtha are going to do?"

"I don't know, but I think they'll come for me."

"I can't imagine life without you!"

"I think your life's going to change soon," said Bran, glancing at Abigail with a wink and a giggle. "Do you remember the young man who was hanging around the paddock every day of the last two weeks before we left for Ghadames?"

"Sort of," Pinar said, although Bran knew very well she'd noticed him.

"You told me he's the brother of one of your riding friends," Bran said pointedly. "An accomplished rider and hunter himself."

"Well, that's what I think I heard from his sister."

"You know you heard it," Bran corrected her with another laugh. "From the look I've seen in his eyes, I suspect he'll be hanging around tomorrow when we go to see your father about letting us ride on the beach. Why, it wouldn't surprise me if he asked the Pasha to let him ride with you. Why, he might even try to have me follow at a distance instead of beside the filly's hip! The last thing this fellow wants is for me to be closely following you around everywhere."

"Don't be ridiculous," said Pinar ducking under the water. But when they went to visit her father the next day, Bran spotted the very same young man watching them from the crowd at the door.

26

"How are you planning to rescue our sister?" asked Cormac, sipping the strong coffee Lemta had brewed.

"I have 25 men hidden in the desert," said Jugurtha. He proceeded to outline the plan for entering the city through the Sea Gate.

" But, how are you going to get Bran out of the harem? The barred doors are massive and guarded by eunuchs on the inside."

"One of my men, dressed in the white robes of a palace slave, will approach the speaking grate and tell the guard that the Pasha has been taken seriously ill and the physician has requested that the First Wife help attend to him. The eunuch will have to open the door to let her out and when he does, the rest of us, hidden by the side of the entrance, will burst in."

"But how will you know where to find Bran?"

"My wife Kella grew up in the harem; she described where the First Wife's apartment is. While I hold the door with the men, Amnay and Gwasila will slip up to the rooms and get Hibah. It will only take minutes; then we'll go to the paddock and escape on the Pasha's horses." It was the first time Cormac had heard his sibling's Arabic name.

"What about your daughters?"

"Their appearance was unexpected," said Jugurtha. "I'm afraid the heart led, rather than the head. They'll have to stay with Lemta until it's safe for us to return."

"I will keep an eye on them as well," offered the redhead. He turned to Finn.

"When this is over, we'll arrange a meeting to plan our return to Ireland. For nearly two years I've been captaining the Reis' galley and he's been setting aside five percent of the profits for me. It will be paid when he frees me in a couple of months, at which time I'll be assigned a ship as one of his lieutenants. The profits have been vast, so I'll have the riches and a vessel to get us home. Through Lemta we'll arrange for you, Tiziri, and Bran to leave the desert and join me."

"My brother a pirate captain?" Finn said in astonishment.

"A pirate captain who is still a slave, although close to becoming free," said Cormac. "I've managed to avoid the customary practice of taking slaves by showing Suliman Reis the greater profitability of acquiring treasure through pure intimidation. The scars on my back are a constant reminder to avoid sending people to the auction!"

"Aye, those scars match my own," said Amnay.

27

CLOUDS SCUDDED ACROSS THE sliver moon, casting flickering shadows on the plaza between the palace and the harem. Cormac and Francois stood hidden in the shadows of a building edging the area. It was well past midnight, and no one was about save an occasional hooded figure hurrying along the streets on some errand. For no particular reason, the Irishman had decided to wake Francois and bring him along; his knowledge of the city might be of help this night.

"There they are," whispered Cormac.

Shapes appeared, moving along the walls of the palace and flitting across the open space to stand on either side of the massive harem door. Behind them strode a figure in white, affecting a fast walk as though on an important mission. Upon reaching the door, he pounded several times so hard that the sound easily reached the concealed observers. For a moment nothing happened; then a bit of light showed as the panel was slid aside from the barred speaking grate. The figure in white stepped close to the grate to deliver the message. After a brief pause the panel shut.

For a moment all was still as the raiders and the watchers waited for the door to open. Then the night air was rent with an explosion of sound as a great bell on the harem tower began to ring!

"They sounded the alarm," Francois said in a shocked voice as men with torches suddenly appeared in the palace doors and raced toward the harem. Others quickly followed, until a stream of soldiers with flickering lights was pouring across the plaza! There was no time to escape. The Tuareg warriors, now gathered in a group at the great door, took on the assault with flashing swords and war cries.

"I've got to help my brother," said Cormac, pulling his weapon and starting forward.

"No," hissed Francois, grabbing him, "there are too many soldiers! You'll be killed!"

The redhead realized he was right; there were now at least 50 of the Pasha's men attacking the raiders and more on the way every minute. Fortunately, with the building at their backs, the desert men were holding their own, spread in a tight semi-circle and fighting with deadly efficiency as soldiers pressing behind pushed those in front into their blades. But Cormac knew the Tuareg couldn't hold out for long against such odds. All at once he realised what to do. Grasping Francois by both arms, he spoke urgently.

"Go to Lemta's house; you'll find three young Tuareg women there. Tell Lemta what's happened and bring the girls to the wharf near the galley. Stay hidden with them until I come. If I don't show up, return them to the house before dawn. They must not be captured. Do you understand?"

"Yes," said the Frenchman, but his friend was already sprinting down the street. Minutes later, Cormac leaped to the deck of the galley, grabbed the shackle key and rushed to the sleeping Dumaka. At his light touch the man came instantly awake. "Free all the men as quickly as you can, but be quiet," whispered MacLir Reis. "Arm as many as you can with chains. The time has come!"

White teeth flashed in the dark as the giant smiled broadly. Instantly he was freeing the man next to him. With amazing speed, slave after slave was unshackled; in minutes, 280 men surrounded the redhead on the wharf. At least a third of them held six-foot lengths of chain and another 30 were armed with swords left on board by pirates. No emaciated oarsmen were these, but strong robust slaves, thanks to the diet Cormac's success had achieved for them.

"It's time to go home," said the Irishman. "But first we've got some work to do." He gestured to the big man who had sat behind Dumaka on the benches for 15 months.

"Gael, take 10 men with swords and 30 men with chains. At the far end of the wharf are three sailing ships just in from the Atlantic. They belong to the Reis and each will have a skeleton crew aboard. Take control of the nearest one, without alarming the other two, and rig it for departure. Don't kill any of the crew; I need them for bargaining to get us out of Tunis."

"It'll be a pleasure," said the ex-sea captain. He quickly chose a group of men, and led them at a run down the wharf.

"The rest of you, follow me," said Cormac, dashing off at full speed in the opposite direction, Dumaka matching him stride for stride.

28

B RAN BOLTED UPRIGHT ON her pallet at the foot of Pinar's bed. A bell was ringing, and muffled shouting drifted through the windows facing the ocean.

"What's going on?" A drowsy Pinar lifted her head from the pillows.

"It's an alarm. I'll find out what's happening. Stay here!" The slave was on her feet in an instant. Reaching for her bow and quiver, she slipped out of the room as Kelebek rushed in and climbed into bed with her sister, crying that she was scared.

As Bran reached the front door of the apartment, a shadow materialized out of the darkness.

"That's the alarm bell to alert the palace guard that something's wrong at the harem."

The whispered words were in English and Bran knew that Abigail had also been roused by the noise. Ever since fetching Bran from the garden slaves, Abigail had treated her as a little sister. At first it was training the Irish girl in all the little courtesies that made a slave indispensable to her owner; then it was getting to know her as a person. As they exchanged background histories, Bran learned that Abigail had lost both parents to disease and was captured on her way from England to Italy to live with distant relatives. In turn, Abigail was fascinated by tales of Bran's family and never got tired of hearing about her mother. When Hibah returned from the desert, Abraj was as excited as the younger girl about the possibility she might be rescued by her brother.

Both of them slid through the door and shut it quietly. The noise was much louder in the courtyard, and Bran realized a battle was in progress outside the main entrance. Racing down the stairs, they sprinted for the massive wooden door. Here the sounds were clear: clashing of steel, shouts of anger, and screams from the wounded. One of the eunuchs peered through the speaking grate at the melee outside.

"What's happening?" Bran cried, running to him. It was Bako.

"Some men tried to get in by saying they had an urgent message from the physician for the First Wife to come to the Palace. Normally, we'd have hurried to get her, but the First Wife was already with the Pasha at the palace tonight, so we realized it was a trick. Now, the soldiers have them trapped against the door, but those blue-robed men are giving a good account of themselves," he said admiringly.

"Blue-robed?" She shouted above the din.

"Yes." The black man turned, surprised by her reaction.

"That's my brother and his friends! They've come to rescue me! You've got to let me out!"

"Your brother? Out there?" he swung back to look through the grate at uproar outside. "No, Hibah, you'd be killed like the rest of them," he said, "more soldiers are coming. They'll overwhelm your brother's men. I can't let you out."

"Help me with this bench," she cried, rushing to a heavy mahogany bench nearby. "I want to look out."

The black man effortlessly swung the bench against the door and Bran stepped up to stare through the barred opening. An eerie sight met her eyes. Flickering light from dozens of torches revealed a mass of shadowy figures moving erratically in the starlit plaza. Just outside the door, she could make out a semi-circle of turbaned men with their backs to her. They were ducking, feinting, and thrusting swords into the soldiers attacking them. Directly in front of her was a fighter with no turban, long blonde hair spilling down his back.

"It's Finn," she screamed, turning to Bako. "You've got to let me out to help him!"

"I can't do that, Hibah, but I can do this," said the eunuch, grabbing another heavy bench and smashing it against the marble floor. He snatched up one of the thick legs that broke off and slammed it with all his strength against the iron grate covering the speaking hole. The metal bent outward and a second blow sent it spinning to the ground, leaving an opening 10 inches square in the door.

29

T HIS WAS NO MOVING fight from the back of a swift camel. It was hand-to-hand combat, without let-up, against an enemy whose ranks instantly closed when a man went down. Helping the desert warriors was light from torches inside the harem shining through the speaking grate. It illuminated the front line of attackers, but left the Tuareg fighting in the shadows of the wall. The torches streaming out of the palace in the hands of the Pasha's men were at the back of the fray and failed to light the immediate battle area, otherwise Jugurtha's men might have been quickly overrun.

Nevertheless, the situation was desperate and Finn found himself using all the tactics he'd learned from months of training at the oasis. Standing shoulder-to-shoulder with the Tuareg leader, he parried sword after sword swung at him and countered with deadly thrusts of his blade into any abdomen or throat left momentarily exposed. He remembered to stay calm, despite the fury of the battle, and was thus able to create an almost impenetrable defense against the screaming men trying to get at him. A blade grazed him here and there, but did no serious damage. Blood poured from the soldiers' wounds as they fell and those coming behind slipped and stumbled over their fallen comrades, adding to the melee and giving a decided advantage to the desert fighters.

Pressed in as they were, the soldiers in front couldn't maneuver freely and the flashing steel of the warriors began to create a mound of bodies at the edge of their tight semicircle over which the Pasha's men had to scramble to reach them. But gradually the sheer number of soldiers began to take effect, and blue-clad fighters started to fall. Those remaining closed the gap to maintain their perimeter, keeping the great door of the harem centered behind them. Fatigue began to take a toll, and the speed of parry and thrust started to slow. The Arabs on the front line sensed victory and pressed the assault, screaming in triumph.

30

"I'M SORRY I GOT you into this," shouted Finn above the tumult. "I should have come for her on my own."

"No son of mine will ever fight on his own," roared the Jugurtha, his blade nearly severing an assailant's arm with a backhand swing. "I won't allow it!" Even in the heat of action, Finn didn't miss the form of address.

"And no father of mine would die if I could battle my way out of this!"

Finn sidestepped a vicious swing at his head and countered with a thrust into the soldier's throat.

"Watch out," he yelled as two soldiers simultaneously attacked Jugurtha.

The leader blocked the sword directed at his waist, leaving himself exposed to the blade aimed at his neck by the second man. Finn watched in horror as the sword swung down in a deadly arc, accompanied by a shout of success from the soldier. Inches from Jugurtha's neck, the steel was jerked away as the man stumbled backward and fell, the shaft of an arrow protruding from his left eye. In another instant, the second soldier dropped with an arrow through his neck.

"It seems we have help, but don't look back," yelled Jugurtha.

Arrows continued to appear with deadly effect, dropping soldiers one after another, but Jugurtha's warning was timely as the space in front of them continuously filled with new men. Gwasila, fighting on Finn's left, and Tariq to Jugurtha's right, were determined to stand to the end with the Irishman and the father of the women they loved. Every warrior's sword arm was red with blood to the shoulder, and all four at the center of the line had been wounded to some degree.

The Tuareg line was shrinking, and Jugurtha knew the blue-clad fighters wouldn't last much longer. Save the murderous arrows from behind continuing to spread death, more of his men would already have fallen. Sweat stung their eyes, blurring vision, and arms felt dead from the continuous shock of blade against blade. Shadowy bodies thrust forward, once again taking up the shouts of victory as the line of raiders backed against the great door started to break.

Suddenly, the soldiers fell back under the bellowed commands of a man in gold robes shouldering his way through their ranks. He held a glittering sword in one hand and beside him walked an enormous, bearded figure robed in black with a curved scimitar in each hand.

"The Pasha and Kadar," muttered Jugurtha in the silence that suddenly descended. "Kadar will want to keep us alive to torture. Us and anyone connected to us that they capture," he added. "We'll have to kill him, but leave the Pasha to me." An idea had begun to form in his head.

The Pasha and Kadar reached the pile of bodies in front of the warriors. Jugurtha's tagelmust had long since fallen away and when the Pasha saw him, his eyes narrowed and then widened in recognition.

"You!" he said, with a triumphant glint in his eyes. "At last I can pay you back for stealing my sister!" He started forward over the dead bodies and aimed a series of vicious swings at the Tuareg's legs, but Jugurtha deftly blocked every blow without retaliating.

"Wait," the Tuareg cried. "There's another way!" But the Pasha pressed his attack.

Kadar focused on Finn, his swords swirling like scythes in the air. The Irishman would have been cut down were it not for Gwasila leaping in to block one of the scimitars with his own sword. As it was, both were driven back against the harem doors by the ferocity of the attack.

Fighting for his life, Finn was only dimly aware of a great noise filling the square. He didn't dare take his eyes off Kadar as he and Gwasila desperately parried the flashing blades of the giant, but he sensed the soldiers around them turning to look back at the palace. Suddenly, there was no one in front of them except the Pasha and Kadar. The remaining Tuareg fighters moved in to attack the two, but stopped at a shout from their leader.

"Don't harm the Pasha, he's my wife's brother!"

Outnumbered for the moment, the leader of Tunis lowered his sword and stared at the desert commander in confusion.

The tumult in the plaza was now so great that all heads turned to see what was happening. Finn was stunned to see a great crowd of shadowy figures rushing out from a side street to engage the soldiers from behind in a tidal wave of ferocity and war cries. As chaos filled the square, Finn saw what looked like disembodied ropes swirling in the air. He realized the ropes were being swung by the horde of men charging into the plaza, shouting at the top of their lungs. The odd thing was that any soldier brushed by a rope fell instantly under the feet of the oncoming men.

"What's happening?" Finn stared at Jugurtha.

"I don't know," said his father-in-law.

31

Behind the door, Bran was suddenly joined on the bench by Pinar, bow and arrows in hand.

"What's going on, Hibah?"

"Jugurtha and Finn tried to trick Bako into letting them in so they could rescue me, but it didn't work and he sounded the alarm. The soldiers have had them and their men pinned against the door and would have killed them all except for my arrows."

"That's my father and Kadar," interrupted Pinar, "but they're surrounded by Jugurtha's men!"

"I know. Someone is attacking your father's soldiers from behind and they've turned around to defend themselves."

"What are we going to do?" Pinar stared transfixed by the dim melee in the plaza.

"I don't know, but I've got to have Bako open the door." Bran jumped off the bench.

As Pinar peered through the hole in the door, she saw the little group right outside standing and staring at the battle raging in the middle of the plaza. Suddenly her father shook his head as he rejected the truce implied when Jugurtha commanded his men to spare him. Raising his sword, he took a step toward the unsuspecting Tuareg leader who was still fixated on the plaza.

"Jugurtha, watch out!" She screamed.

The warrior turned just in time to lunge back from the deadly blow directed at his head, but slipped on a pool of blood and went down. The Pasha swung his sword again at the fallen man, but it never connected as an arrow suddenly drove the blade from his hand with a loud "tang!"

"Father," shouted Pinar through the opening, as she notched another arrow. "That's my uncle! Don't hurt him!"

Her astounded father, hands vibrating from the impact of the arrow against his sword, looked at the door and then at Jugurtha, who had scrambled to his feet, weapon in hand. The two stared at each other.

Kadar used the moment to renew his attack on Finn and Gwasila, swinging his scimitars with blinding speed. Both barely managed to block the blows before they jumped out of range. Their companions closed in, and the huge Arab was forced to lower his swords.

"Keep an eye on him," yelled Gwasila, turning to gape in astonishment at the plaza.

In the dim light, he could barely make out a massive figure making its way toward them through the packed throng of soldiers. He was swinging something with each arm, emitting blood curdling war cries. Anyone within eight feet of him was cut down in a burst of blood and shrieks of anguish. Panic preceded him, as those in his path realized what was coming and fought to get out of the way, sometimes using their swords against fellow soldiers in their desperation. In the light of flickering torches, the man was an apparition of doom, spreading destruction against any who stood in his way.

As he drew closer, the few remaining torches finally revealed a huge black man whirling long, heavy chains with each arm. Like scythes, the lethal metal mowed down everyone within reach. To the giant's left, just beyond the reach of the chain, strode a powerfully built man with flaming red hair highlighted by the remaining torches. Splattered with blood, he wielded a sword with deadly efficiency against any soldier unfortunate enough to step in his path. Behind the pair, a horde of men followed, shouting like demons and attacking the mass of soldiers in the plaza with swords and chains of their own.

Just as zebra scatter at the charge of a lion, the Pasha's men broke and fled from the deadly pair, leaving an open path to Jugurtha and his men. Kadar, nearly as big as the man with the chains, whirled about to see what the others were looking at. His little black eyes glittered as he took in the scene and something snapped in his brain. With an unearthly scream, he burst through the circle and rushed at the two men, both scimitars raised high in the air and angled to bite deep into the black man's neck from either side

Without breaking stride, the oncoming giant swung the chain in his right hand and broke both sword blades in half. The chain in his left hand simultaneously traversed a lower arc and smashed into the side of Kadar's head with an explosion of blood and bone. The Arab's body toppled and pitched forward onto the plaza tiles.

"No pirate in his right mind would ever raise both swords over his head to attack," said Dumaka calmly as he stepped over the corpse.

In the silence that suddenly fell over the plaza, the two men stopped in front of the little group at the harem door.

32

"I'M SORRY WE COULDN'T get here sooner," Cormac said, gesturing at the fallen Tuareg combatants. "When I saw the soldiers pouring out of the palace, I raced to get reinforcements, but I wasn't sure if you could last until I got back."

"We're forever indebted," said the Tuareg leader. "Without you, none of us would have survived. As it is, I suspect your sister and my niece saved my life even before you arrived, so I'm thrice obligated!" He smiled and turned toward the great door just as it opened and Bran burst out, closely followed by Pinar and Abigail. Pinar ran to her father and Bran to Finn.

"I thought they were going to kill you," cried the Irish girl.

"We guessed those might be your arrows," Finn said, picking his sister up in a great bear hug. "But we never heard the door open."

"I fired through the speaking grate. Bako broke it open and we stood on a bench to shoot through the hole, because he wouldn't let us out."

"You might want to thank the brother who helped you save us," Finn whispered in her ear as he gently set her down. Bran stared at him in disbelief for a moment before turning to look across the mound of soldiers' bodies at the muscular swordsman with the bloodstained blouse who stood beaming at her. His great white scar had been etched in her memory for years.

"Cormac!" she cried, bursting into tears. In another instant she was in his arms, being whirled around as the others looked on with wide grins.

"I knew it was you in the cart that day," she sobbed against his neck.

"I thought I heard someone call my name," he said, remembering the crowded scene at the gate so long ago.

"I was with a group of riders, but the horses were moving too fast to stop."

"I wondered," said her brother, still holding her tight. "I saw them go by, but couldn't understand who would know me in Tunis."

33

PINAR RAN TO HER father and grabbed his hands.

"I couldn't let you hurt my uncle, no matter how mad you are at him. He has taken very good care of Kella, and their daughters have become my close friends," she said. "One of them is married to Hibah's brother. He's the tall warrior standing there with the long yellow hair. He was a caravan slave, but escaped and found Jugurtha's camp. He saved my uncle's life in a lion attack and was granted his freedom. His Tuareg name is 'Amnay' and there is no better rider and trainer of camels in the desert."

All the anger suddenly drained out of the Pasha and he could only nod as he listened to his daughter and realized what a beautiful young woman she had become; in fact, her fierce passion and strength reminded him of his sister Kella.

"See the man with the red hair?" Pinar went on. "That's Hibah's other brother ... the slave I asked you to find years ago."

The Pasha stared intently at Cormac, who was still hugging Bran.

"That's Hibah's brother?" He replied. "That's MacLir Reis, one of the most feared pirates in the Mediterranean. There isn't a merchant captain who dares to resist the galley he commands with Suleyman Reis. Once he and his friend with the chains are identified, the target vessel simply lowers sails and waits for the pirates to board. At least twice he has saved the life of Suleyman Reis."

He led Pinar over to Cormac and gave a slight bow of the head.

"As a young man, I only had limited success with my galley against my father's enemies. Often I barely escaped with my life, but I went out time and again because of my love of the ocean. Had I the likes of you and your friend at my side, many attacks against Tunis would have been avoided."

He turned to Dumaka. "You have delivered justice to Kadar. His history of sadistic cruelty was a problem I should have addressed long ago."

Overcome with emotion, he now turned to face Jugurtha.

"It seems our families have become reacquainted, and our favored slave Hibah has become a sister-in-law to one of my nieces! Had I but known that, it should have resulted in her freedom without all this." He waved his hand at the bodies strewn all over the plaza. He paused to control his emotions. "It would please me very much to bring my wife and daughters to visit you and Kella. With your permission of course."

The Tuareg leader stared in astonishment before answering.

"For years Kella has longed to see her brother and her best childhood friend," he said. "Strange are the circumstances that brought us together this night, but my family and I would gladly welcome you in our tent."

The Pasha accepted the invitation with another bow of his head. The gesture hid not only his smile, but the suspicious hint of moisture in his eyes.

34

At that very moment there was a loud exclamation and Bako burst from behind the harem door. As the others watched in amazement, he strode forward to stare at the large man standing beside Cormac.

"Dumaka?" The word rumbled from deep in his chest. There was a moment of silence, then the oarsman dropped the chains from his bloodstained hands and peered intently at the eunuch.

"Bako? Is it you?" Dumaka's voice broke with emotion. "Is this possible? I was only a youth when you disappeared while hunting. We thought you had been killed by a lion. The men searched for days but could find no trace of your body. Your children and I grew up mourning your death." The two massive men embraced, tears flowing.

"No lion and no death. Slavers ambushed me and brought me across the desert to this place," said Bako. "Eventually, because of my size, I was put in the harem to protect the Pasha's wives. But tell me of my children."

"When we have time I'll tell you everything, but they were well when I last saw them. Years after you disappeared, slave raiders attacked the village and several of us fought them for long enough to allow the others to escape, including your children and their families."

"Families?"

"Yes! You have eight grandchildren now--fine boys and girls who often pestered me for stories about their famous grandfather and his feats with the bow."

"Bako is my uncle and a renowned archer," Dumaka explained to the astounded onlookers.

"He's responsible for these dead men," Bran interrupted, pointing at the bodies pierced with arrows. "He taught Pinar and me to shoot."

During the exchange, Finn had been studying Dumaka. Something finally clicked in his memory.

"You!" he said. "You told me about lions and creatures of the plains, herds of cattle, and men with spears who stand on one leg. I was the camel handler who brought you extra water during nights on the caravan. You swore you'd be free someday. You inspired me to never lose my own dream of freedom. When things got so bad that I could have given up, I always thought of you!"

The black face split wide in a grin and a deep laugh rolled forth. "How you've changed! You were so thin and scrawny; I thought the first sandstorm would blow you across the desert! But you had a way with the camels. Even I could see it."

"A sandstorm did blow me away," Finn exclaimed. "To freedom!"

35

"WHERE'S BRAN," SAID CORMAC, noticing that his sister had disappeared. The words were hardly out of his mouth when his sister emerged from the harem, followed by a crowd of raggedly dressed older women and children being shepherded by Abigail. Bran ran to Cormac.

"These are the kitchen and garden slaves that I worked with, we've got to take them!" She said.

"How did you get them away from the overseers?" asked Bako.

"None of them bothered me in the gardens, where they have seen me practice, but the two in the kitchen put a knife to this little one's throat," said Bran, one arm around a scrawny six-year-old and the other holding her bow. "That was a mistake. They'll never torture anyone again."

"There's room on the ship, but I think we should ... er ... consult the Pasha," said the redhead, turning toward the Arab leader.

"The first wife and I worried about those two in the kitchen," said the Pasha. "They were forbidden to torture women or children but we heard they did anyway. Despite the rumors, we could never find any evidence."

"That's because they secretly disposed of the bodies," said Bran grimly. There was a moment of silence as the Pasha processed this information.

"This is quite a crowd of my workers you want to take with you," he said finally.

"Father, Hibah was never rewarded for saving my life," said Pinar. "Perhaps these slaves should be our gift to her, including Abigail who has been a true friend to us both. Mother loves Abigail, but I think she will understand. Hibah was a gift to me. Let their freedom, and hers, be our gift for all she has done."

Although surrounded by Cormac's men, the Pasha hesitated, uncertain how to handle the situation. He was averse to losing the valued Bako, along with a number of slaves, including one of his wife's personal attendants. Seeing the dilemma, Jugurtha stepped forward.

"The Stable Master has also decided to return to the desert with us, along with a few of his favorite horses," he said, noting the look of shock in the Pasha's eyes. "I've been thinking that my share of the gold from … our recent raid … would be more than sufficient to replace these workers and the horses. With it you will also be able to find a gifted and younger horse trainer. It would please me to return the gold to you as soon as I get home. Furthermore, it seems unseemly to me that the caravans of honored family members should ever be exposed to a raid."

Finn, watching this exchange, and knowing Jugurtha as well as he did, could have sworn he saw a twinkle in his father-in-law's eyes as this last promise was delivered.

Despite the defeat of his men in the plaza, the proposal offered the Pasha a resolution. Recovering a large portion of his gold would not only save his dignity in the eyes of his people, but compensate him for the loss of his workers. The pledge of future protection for his personal caravans was of enormous value. He gravely accepted, pleased in many ways about how things had turned out for him and his family.

"It's time to leave," said Jugurtha, stepping forward to grasp the forearm of his brother-in-law. "Kella and I look forward to a visit from your family. Perhaps you could join us for the annual race of the best desert horses?" Since his escape from Tunis, Jugurtha had always hosted the event in a place unknown to the Pasha and he knew the ruler of Tunis sorely missed the great occasion. Jugurtha noted the flash of pleasure in the Pasha's eyes as the invitation was accepted.

Jugurtha and Cormac had quietly agreed to meet three days later at an isolated bay far along the southeast coastline, where the Tuareg leader would provide camels, horses and provisions for Bako and Dumaka to return home across the desert.

When Cormac privately explained that Francois was bringing the Tuareg's three daughters to the vessel, Gwasila and Tariq moved forward to stand beside him and Finn. Their animals would be led by others to the rendezvous point: they would travel on the ship with their beloved women.

Turning to Abigail standing close beside her, Bran said, "Did you hear? You're coming too. You have a home and a family now: with us in Baltimore. Mother will love you like one of her own children!"

As tears of gratitude filled her eyes, all the English girl could do was nod her head in acceptance.

"Hibah, do you have to go?" Pinar threw her arms around Bran. "What will I do without you?" Both of them began to cry.

"Look for that young man, but don't let him know how well you can shoot," said Bran with a sob. "Or how well you can ride! You might scare him off." She pulled herself gently away. "It's time for me to go home and see my mother."

"I know," said the Pasha's daughter. "I'll never forget you, sister of my heart."

36

THE REDHEAD, HIS SIBLINGS, and the two desert fighters raced ahead through the darkened streets, leaving the oarsmen, Dumaka, and Bako to escort the newly freed women and children more slowly. Once away from the plaza, the city was quiet and they arrived at the docks to find that Gael's men in their eagerness had overcome the crews of all three ships and were busy loading food and supplies from the first two into the third. The pirates, bound and gagged, were neatly laid out side-by-side along the wharf.

There was a quiet but joyous reunion as Francois emerged from hiding with the three girls and Lemta (who had insisted on coming in case anything went awry). When the former harem slaves arrived from the plaza, all were quickly helped aboard. The oarsmen scattered to locations on deck and in the rigging, preparing for departure. Hawsers holding the ship to the wharf were loosened and the crew stood ready for Cormac's command to sail. The redhead and Francois stood on the dock.

"Do you want to come with us?" asked the Irishman. "I can give you a new life, in return for all you've done for me." The question hung in the air.

"I've been with the Reis since I was five years old," said the Frenchman after a pause. "He treats me very well and I have no family left in France. This is the only life I know."

"Very well," said Cormac. "Please give this message to your Master …"

A voice from the dark interrupted him.

"Give it to him yourself," said Suleyman Reis, striding from the shadows, leading his gray stallion. He handed the reins to Francois and faced Cormac.

"You've taken the name 'MacLir Reis.' Are you going to turn your back on all you've accomplished?"

Without answering, Cormac turned and beckoned to Finn and Bran, standing at the head of the gangplank. A minute later the blond warrior and the beautiful girl with green eyes stood on either side of him in the light of the great wharf torches.

"My brother and sister," he said, by way of introduction. "When you sacked Baltimore, the three of us were among those captured. At the auction, my little sister was so scared I tried to stop your men from taking her. That's when you condemned me to the quarry: no one wanted to buy a troublemaker. Instead of rebelling, I served you well at the quarry; I served you well as an oarsman; and I served you well as captain of the galley. Twice I saved your life.

"After escaping from the caravans, my brother saved the life of the Tuareg leader who had become his owner. For that, he was freed and treated as the leader's son.

"Our sister was taken to the harem and became the personal slave to the Pasha's oldest daughter. On more than one occasion, my sister saved the life of her mistress, and was called by her 'my heart's sister' less than an hour ago.

"The oarsmen now aboard this ship have served both you and me during the many months I've stood at your side, enabling us to more than double your riches. You've treated them well and they've worked hard, not the least Dumaka, who's feared by every ship master on the Mediterranean.

"You promised me freedom two years ago if I survived. I have survived, and the share of plunder you've been setting aside for me should be enough to pay for this vessel and to replace all the oarsmen. My siblings and I, and every other person on this ship, were beyond ransom, but our freedom has been fought for, earned, and paid with blood. I can now leave knowing you have been treated fairly."

Minutes dragged by as the Dutchman stared at Cormac.

"I've never known a man like you," he said at last. "And it seems your brother and sister are cut from the same mold. If you ever change your mind, I will welcome one, or all of you as full partners in any endeavor I undertake." He turned away from the stunned trio and mounted his stallion. "Please untie my men before you sail."

Suleyman Reis rode slowly away, Francois walking at the stallion's side.

37

THE SUN WAS WELL past its zenith three days later when the two-masted ship rounded a headland and entered a large cove surrounded by grassy hills. Horses and camels grazing on the slopes, and smoke rising from fires on the beach, indicated Jugurtha had already arrived. As Gael dropped anchor in the clear water 200-yards off shore, a great shout rose from warriors gathered around the fires. In short order, boats were lowered from the ship and headed toward the beach, the first carrying Tiziri and her sisters.

"I know one father who won't relax until he sees his daughters in the flesh," the blond had said to his brother with a laugh.

Soon, all but a few men left to tend the ship had been ferried ashore. Cormac arrived in the last boat with Gael, Bran, Abigail, Dumaka, and Bako. Bran, who had hardly left Cormac's side since departing Tunis, had come to realize that Dumaka also shadowed her brother. He was never more than a step or two away from the redhead.

They waded onto the beach to find an enormous feast prepared by the Tuareg warriors. It seemed a village not far away had sold them many goats and sheep ... now roasting over numerous fires. Scarcely had Bran reached dry ground than a slender form in blue approached.

"I see you prefer a ship to my beautiful gray filly!" said a familiar voice behind the tagelmust.

"Stable Master! I didn't know you were coming!" She threw her arms around him.

"Oh, a beautiful girl must save her embraces for the right young man," he said, but held her gently for a moment anyway. "I couldn't let Jugurtha continue to only ride camels and neglect the equine side of his desert heritage. These camel riders have a lot to learn about horses!"

"But what about the Pasha's herd?"

"Well, I've brought my favorite horses to care for, but the fact is that I've been in the city far too long. It is past time for somebody else to oversee his stables, and let me return home," he said, gesturing to the spectacular view of the dunes rising behind him to meet an azure sky.

Much later, Jugurtha, Cormac, Bran, Abigail, Dumaka and Bako sat beside a fire watching flames flicker along a piece of driftwood. Scattered across the beach were the sleeping bodies of former kitchen and garden slaves, galley slaves, and Tuareg warriors. The night sky was filled with millions of stars and the murmur of low waves rolling onto the beach filled the background.

Earlier in the evening, Gwasila had finally asked Jugurtha for Trinitran's hand in marriage and the Tuareg leader had gruffly given his consent, his wide smile hidden behind his veil. Around one side of a nearby fire, the three sisters were excitedly planning a double wedding, while across the flames the husbands-to-be and Finn rehashed the battle in the plaza.

Upon hearing of the Reis' offer to the siblings, Jugurtha's eyes had gleamed.

"Suleyman Reis is a rich man. The Pasha is a rich man," he said. "Events have changed our relationships, so we are no longer in a position to plunder their riches. However, there might be a better way."

The others stared at him in confusion.

"If you were in business with the Reis, your fierce reputation would insure that your vessels wouldn't be attacked. You could invest in ships to bring him the latest fashions, artwork, and silks from Europe. This would not only provide him with the goods he now raids from merchant vessels, but also greatly enhance his status in Tunis by elevating him from mere pirate to businessman."

Cormac nodded in agreement.

"At the same time," the desert leader went on, "and on the same ships, you could bring me a few of those swift English horses I've been hearing so much about. If the Stable Master finds them to be as fast as reported, I'll challenge the Pasha and the Reis to a series of races. Faced with a possible threat to the supremacy of Arabian horses, they and their friends will wager heavily on their own animals."

Snorts of laughter from around the fire greeted this proposal because everyone present know of the Arabs' love for betting on horse races. But the desert warrior wasn't finished.

"Bring me the right horses, at any price, and I'll put aside 10% of the winnings for you."

38

GOODBYES HAD BEEN HARD, reflected Cormac, standing beside the helmsman a week after they parted with Jugurtha. A strong breeze carried them nor'east and sunlight glinted off the swells. Two gulls rode the wind to starboard, tracking their progress. The ex-galley slaves had taken great pride in the ship and he watched three teams swabbing and polishing decks and woodwork.

His eyes grew moist as he thought about Dumaka and the experiences they'd shared after the giant joined him at the oar. They'd been inseparable for two years, first by chains, then by choice, and their parting had been difficult despite the knowledge that each was going home at last. They knew they'd never see one another again.

Huge Bako had held Bran like a little girl, her arms around his neck, stroking her head and murmuring how proud he was of her and his wishes for her future, while the Stable Master clung to them both. All three were crying unabashedly when she was finally set down.

Finn and Tiziri had sat with Jugurtha, explaining gently that they wouldn't be returning with him to the desert. Both were concerned that he and Kella wouldn't understand.

"I knew it soon after you came ashore," the Tuareg had said, eyes softening with love as he reached for his daughter's hand. "One couldn't listen to your description of three days at sea without realizing how excited you are to explore the outside world with Amnay. Your mother and I only desire that your life be happy and fulfilled, wherever the path may take you." He paused. "My one regret is that somehow we'll have to care for the old jamal by ourselves!"

He'd then produced two sizeable leather pouches of gold from beneath his robes and handed them to Finn.

"One is your share from the raid, and the other a personal gift from me to your brother. He gave his riches for the ship and his fellow oarsmen; he'll need this for a new start in life. As for the Pasha, a very generous share of his gold will be returned as promised." The Irishman, having traded his tagelmust for a headband, had leaned forward and gripped his father-in-law's forearm.

"We'll be back, Father. Lemta will send word. Cormac and I have decided to act on your suggestion and negotiate a partnership with Suleyman Reis to supply Tunis with European goods. As you advised, such an agreement will protect us from pirates and create good business." He'd paused for a moment and then grinned. "Cormac mentioned the horses. We'll find some fast ones for the Stable Master to work with."

The redhead smiled as the wind blew through his long hair. On the foredeck, two dark heads flanked a golden one as Tiziri, Bran, and Abigail, surrounded by a cluster of children, watched dolphins riding the bow wave. The three young women had become fast friends in their short time together and when they were anywhere near Cormac, he found himself unable to take his eyes off the pretty English girl. She was so distracting that he completely failed to observe Bran and Tiziri watching this with great amusement.

Gael and many of the men who had lost families had already told him they didn't want to be dropped off on the European coastlines, preferring to sail with him as crew. Others had promised to do their best to return the children and women to their homes when dropped off in the countries from which they'd been taken. He'd calculated that there'd be more than enough sailors left to man this ship and possibly another.

In awe at the overwhelming changes in their circumstances, his mind turned to the words spoken by Mrs. Doyle to the Baltimore women years before on the trip to Tunis. He'd shared with Finn and Bran the mysterious commands he'd received at the quarry and aboard the galley. They, in turn, had described the man in the white robe and the little girl with flowers. None of them had an explanation for the encounters. Was it possible Mrs. Doyle had spoken the truth?

"For He will command His angels concerning you, to guard you in all your ways …"

Perhaps they needed to talk to a priest about this. All at once, despite the ocean breeze, the unmistakable scent of gardenias filled the air around him.

THE END

Epilogue

GLANCING AT THE HARBOR, a striking woman with long black hair noticed a twin-masted ship easing through the breakwater under the noonday sun. She didn't recognize it, but there were so many vessels anchoring in the harbor these days she gave it no thought. She leaned over the fence and scattered corn to three large geese, a catch in her throat as she remembered the screeches from her young daughter ages ago when similar birds had chased her about, nipping at her legs.

For six long years, she'd prayed every day for the safety and return of her children. No matter how hard the priest tried to convince her otherwise, she still blamed herself for going to her sister's farm that night. If she'd stayed, her husband might not have been killed and they could have gone into slavery together, perhaps to be sold as a family.

She was still beautiful, despite lines on her forehead and a deep sadness in her eyes. Through the years, a few men had tried to court her, only to be quickly turned away. She had refused to move to the farm, choosing to live in the small stone house in the village, supplying vegetables, eggs, and geese to the market. She'd taken in little Shamus Fitzgerald, orphaned in the raid and found wandering in the hills days later. He was now a strapping 12-year-old working for the boatmaker down at the dock.

Opening the garden gate, she stepped in to inspect her crop, careful to close it behind her against the approach of daring rabbits. A few pesky weeds poked up among the immaculate rows and, muttering objections, she went down on her knees to pull them. She was still weeding 30 minutes later, when the garden gate squeaked open behind her …

REQUEST FOR REVIEWS

I hope you enjoyed this book. Would you do me a favor?
Like all authors, I rely on online reviews to encourage future sales. Your opinion is invaluable. Would you take a few moments to share your assessment of my book wherever you purchased it or on your favorite on-line review site? Your opinion will help the book marketplace become more transparent and useful to all.

Thank you very much!
David Sage

AUTHOR BIO

For 40 years, David Sage has captivated audiences with original stories told in the oral tradition. Each story is created extemporaneously, drawn from his knowledge and a wide range of experiences gained in traveling the world. His vivid imagination often takes an historical event as a launching point for a fictional adventure.

Known as "Mr. Sage" by thousands of kids around the USA, he spins tales to preschoolers through retirees. He has also developed a successful school curriculum, using his stories, to stimulate imagination and creative writing. In 2011, he began to convert his narratives into books and his recently completed series, *The Heirs of the Medallion*, has entranced readers around the country.

Mr. Sage makes his home in Story, Wyoming, not far from the ranch where he grew up.